The Troubadour's Romance

ROBYN CARR

LITTLE, BROWN AND COMPANY

Boston   Toronto

FIRST EDITION

Library of Congress Cataloging in Publication Data

Carr, Robyn.
 The troubadour's romance.

 I. Title.
 PS3553.A76334T7   1985   813'.54   85-211
 ISBN 0-316-12976-3

Designed by Patricia Girvin Dunbar

Published simultaneously in Canada
by Little, Brown & Company (Canada) Limited

PRINTED IN THE UNITED STATES OF AMERICA

This work is dedicated to Ivy Eleanor Crandall, my beloved grandmother, who gave me the gift of a happy childhood and continues to give to so many children.

The Troubadour's Romance

THE BOWERS THAT VÉRONIQUE OCCUPIED WERE RICH by the English standard, but now more than at any other time she longed for the comfort of France. She had accustomed herself to the drabness of English castles, the absence of the finer silks and fragrances, and even to the cold, damp weather. But there was still no feeling of home.

It was growing late in the year and she hungered for spring; it was chill and heartless and she feared she would never know warm tenderness again in her life. Just three days past childbearing and barely moving out of her bed, she yearned for an embrace of goodness or the light of pride in a husband's eyes. But all of that was hopeless and there was naught to pray for but mercy.

In this vulnerable state and residing much alone with her thoughts, Véronique could not reach for her baby daughter without going over in her mind each detail that had brought her to the present. And she began instinctively to give consideration to how she could save this baby girl from the same fate.

She had grown up without a mother; her father had been a devoted knight who worshiped Queen Eleanor in the fashion she most adored — chastely and from afar. He would have at any moment laid down his very life that her shoe would not be muddied. To preserve this dedication that Eleanor was intent on, she allowed the motherless child, Véronique, to live in her household.

Véronique did not presume that she was as a daughter to the queen; rather, she was a very special servant and ward of Her Majesty. Just as her father, Sir Flavian, had done, Véronique learned to partake in the lamenting love verse flavored with the chivalry of Arthur's court and the honorable pursuit of unrequited love. Véronique became, in time, not just a waiting woman for the queen; she rose in her own right to the status of court poetess. She was beautiful, untainted, and glowing with sublime rapture.

As a child she had resided near Eleanor during her marriage to Louis le Jeune, and later had journeyed with Eleanor to England, when she married for the second time. Her new husband, King Henry, was crowned in 1154. In the twelve years since, she had only seen her beloved Poitiers four times, for although Eleanor traveled to France often, Véronique did not accompany her every time. The home of her birth was near Narbonne, and she had seen that fair place even less.

She had either attended or been close at hand for the queen's childbearing, yet she bore her own child with little assist. The labor had been tedious and drawing, for Véronique was nearly thirty years old. Had Sir Flavian lived beyond the Welsh campaign of the year before, she might have borne this bastard daughter in a farmer's sty in France. When Sir Flavian left to fight the Welsh for Henry, he fell to one knee before his queen, praised her beauty with his usual reverence and supplication, and beseeched her to "look to Véronique and hers should my life's blood be shed upon Your Majesty's husband's cloak of honor."

Eleanor smiled in kind supremacy and murmured, "When have I not, sir knight? You of all would know that while I cannot reward your fealty with earthly pleasure, I can yield that loyalty of service which you entrust solely to me. Go with cause and without fear. I treasure Véronique as richly as you."

The mature virgin, bidden to her queen, took the news of her father's death as fearlessly as he had died, for her place with the queen had been promised. It was to be a nun's life without the costume, since Véronique's place was to beautify Eleanor's surroundings and lament of love unattainable and pure. The theme of the poems, the discussion, and even the acting done about Eleanor was constant arousal, with consummation the ultimate flaw, as if the seduction was the joy and the actual union of lovers a disappointment. Marriage was not denied Véronique; it was simply never mentioned. It was assumed she was content with the role of seeker of pure love, and furthermore, no suitors met with the queen's satisfaction. Marriage would mean leaving the queen, and that would cost her dearly.

It came as small wonder then that Eleanor considered the betrayal deep and personal when Véronique yielded to a lover's caress. No touch had tempted her until his, no lips had brushed her silken cheek until she'd felt his breath, hot and flaming, close to her ear. 'Twas in the troubadour fashion that he had courted her; he was first inspired as they looked across the room at each other, then he sang of her throughout the ladies' bowers — while all thought that the object of his madness was Eleanor. Then his fingers, roughened from working the sword and lance, had stroked her flesh, melting her resolve for purity. Ice met fire and theirs was an instant flood of passion.

The splendor of his fealty and lust held her strong for his return from a mission for Henry. Upon his homecoming he would speak, nay, *plead* for her release from the queen, and she would bask in his ardor all her life. It was Véronique's private fear that when Eleanor became aware of their love, she would be jealous and cruel. The queen's sensuality and lusty looks were as hungry as Henry's, and ofttimes when she looked at Véronique's suitor, her gaze warmed and held promise. Although Eleanor would be faithful to the king, her love of being worshiped as the perfect woman was boundless, and many times she was angry when one of her troubadours found satisfaction with a woman who was free to return his love.

Véronique's brave and handsome lover did not return to her. Time melted away, and she came to fear him dead and herself bearing fruit from their coupling; yet she shed no tear and held her eyes level and soft as she amused and served her queen. She dared not ask after her suitor, for the troubadour fashion was to maintain complete anonymity among lovers. And she heard no word of him until the first flutterings of her child whispered within her womb. A returning knight spoke of Véronique's lover briefly, and he aroused much laughter as he described the man's pursuit of a wealthy widow residing in the south of England. He had been approved by her, it was said, and could not be rousted from that demesne without owning it through her hand. He quite delayed the troops with his folly, until they left him to seek his lady.

In that very moment, Véronique knew the bitterness of the lie she had been living. The many years of love's whisperings were nonsense to her, for she was sullied and spoiled not only for a man, but for her station beside Eleanor. In her thoughts she instantly abandoned the languishing drivel of the troubadours and was hard put to discover what she could salvage of her life. She begged forgiveness from a priest and then sought out Eleanor, confessing her deed.

Eleanor slapped her and raged at the indecency and dishonor. This was as Véronique had expected. As she had also foreseen, the queen then softened, asking solicitously for the name of the child's father, but Véronique refused to identify her lover.

"Tell me then," the queen demanded, "that the king is not the father of your babe."

Véronique let her eyes drop and could not face her. The king's passions were lusty and hard to resist. He kept Eleanor often with child and scattered his seed elsewhere with little discretion. Even Véronique, sheltered as she was by the queen's watchful eye, had been bothered by Henry on many occasions. She did not feel at risk in his presence, being neither tempted by nor submissive to his desires. There was no longing within her for the energetic king. Yet Eleanor had begun to sense she was losing him, for his affairs were more frequent than in the early years of their marriage. So long as Henry kept himself strictly to bedmates who would not threaten her position, she was stoically tolerant.

Eleanor had cause to be fearful. Her marriage to Louis had been annulled after a decade and a half on the grounds of consanguinity. Those same ancestral lines could be found within her marriage to Henry, should he too seek annulment. Véronique knew all of this well and took it close to heart as she sought shelter and sustenance at this time, when a woman in her plight could expect to be granted none. Véronique held onto Eleanor's small seed of doubt, knowing the queen would not turn away her husband's child, although she might shun the mother.

"Name him or free Henry from your accusation," Eleanor demanded once more.

"Would you spare me no dignity, Madame?" she had murmured, her moist green eyes twinkling. "Would you have me list those men who did not use me and grant you the identity by default? I beg mercy . . . that he is not here beside me proves there is no man. What matter? I am alone. The child is mine . . . alone."

"Sir Flavian chafes even as we speak," Eleanor snarled. "His beloved remains writhe in pain in his grave."

Véronique raised her eyes and looked beseechingly at her queen. There was a new strength there, born of worldly suffering and a scarred heart. "Nay, Madame, he rests at peace even now, for you gave your oath to me and mine."

Véronique was dismissed from her usual entertainment of the ladies and troubadours. Chambers were vacated for her solitary existence and she ventured out but rarely. Eleanor visited on occasion, her mood sometimes black and mean, no doubt wondering which man who praised her had lain with her handmaiden. Other times she proved tractable and could even be considered kind. It wasn't as though Eleanor was ignorant of the plight of women, whose lives were bent on the whims of men. For herself, when Louis had rejected her, she quickly had to marry Henry lest she be kidnapped and forced into marriage at the point of a dagger. There was naught to stay such an act, and Eleanor was too ambitious to marry a lesser man.

Véronique's door to her chamber was watched: no men lingered without to betray an interest in the beautiful woman's condition, leaving the queen at a further loss. Once, when the queen was in a more compassionate mood, she reached out a hand to caress Véronique's long, red-gold hair and gently asked, "Do you mourn, dear sweet? Did love touch you but once and leave you filled with life but empty of hope?"

"Oh, yea, Madame," she replied. " 'Twas the cruelest thing

that when I would give, I was robbed. I once thought love a heaven of bliss impossible to find, then thought next that I held it at my breast, then what I held was a dagger that ripped my heart from me and left me naught. Now I say truly, I do not know love, nor have I ever. Yet a child is to be born. I grieve for all women and their babes."

"But my sweet Véronique, do you see the cost of love? 'Tis why men of greater heart sing of *amor de lonh*," Eleanor whispered in her beloved Provençal tongue. Then she laughed softly and added, "Love from afar does little to sate the hunger, but neither does it fill your belly thusly. Have you come to know which is worse? To hunger for love . . . or to be fed and, indeed, full upon it?"

"Nay, Madame," Véronique replied softly. "For I am full upon it — it grows and moves within me — yet . . . I hunger still. And, I fear, I always shall."

It was greatly to Véronique's advantage that the queen could not forfeit her own oath and beg the attentions of her knights. Nor could Eleanor afford to display her affections openly, since adultery for a queen was high treason and punishable by death. But she was intensely romantic, albeit vicariously. She and her courtiers speculated endlessly on the truest form of love. It was as much an occupation of hers as any other thing she did.

So while this handmaiden of the queen was not coddled, neither was she turned away and sheared. Her rooms were well tended and richly appointed. A midwife was called and servants were installed. The birthing was long and tiring, but Véronique delivered a daughter marked by the same reddish-gold locks and white skin as her own.

And now, on the third day of the child's life, Eleanor was going to grace this bower with her presence. Véronique was both joyful and frightened.

Eleanor had lived two score and four years, yet she was stately and beautiful and adored by men across the land. Her spine was straight and her posture mighty. If her present condition was any clue, old age would never trespass where her strong will reigned. As Véronique watched her approach the bed, her eyes lit up with admiration, as always when in the presence of Her Majesty.

Eleanor drew back the bed curtains and looked down at the suckling infant. "She nurses well?"

"Aye, Madame. She is slight but strong."

"What will you do with her now, Véronique?"

"I am at your mercy, Your Majesty. I beg counsel."

"Let me raise the child," Eleanor said suddenly.

Véronique looked sharply at the woman. "But Madame, you have so many . . ."

"Not at my bosom, *ma chère*. There is naught I can do for you, but this one can reside within my protection, unsullied by her dire beginnings. There are those who would keep her close to me and do my bidding. You must tell me: is she French or English?"

Véronique paused briefly before answering, then finally, knowing it would do little good to lie, gave the truth. "She is half of this English kingdom, Madame."

"Will you name him that he might meet his due?" she asked.

"Nay, Madame, I cannot. 'Tis my due that must be met."

"You will not cease in this self-abuse? Where is your pride? You have this royal support in bringing the cur to heel, yet you deny yourself and throw your pitiful state on my mercy."

Tears glistened in Véronique's eyes and she looked with envy to Eleanor. She had wished many times that she could possess that fire and zeal, that ambition and instinct for survival. But time upon time she came up against her shy and lonely feelings and a weakness of spirit.

"Madame," she said tearfully, "of pride I am stripped bare by my deed. And, God forgive me, I would have your mercy before I would take his forced love. 'Tis my shame that I cannot have him if he would not willingly come to me."

In this Eleanor saw a paradox, for it was pride itself that forbade Véronique from asking the queen to force the man into wedlock. Eleanor had a high degree of respect for any woman with a proud and strong disposition. Despite the circumstances, Eleanor's romantic heart swelled. "And do you love him still?" she asked.

"I cannot do otherwise," Véronique murmured. "Though he slays me with his absence and does not look to carry this burden with me, no hand but his ever touched me. And in that touch, though fleeting, there was sinful joy. Yea, Madame, I go alone for want of him."

"Then you are paupered, for all I can give you now is shelter and civil retirement. You may nurse the child for a few months that she might remember a mother's tenderness, then I will have her placed in a noble English home close to me. Betimes I will carry her with my court that she might learn gentle manners, and your dowry will become hers. Fontevrault will be your home. The good sisters are charitable and generous; they will be more so with a word from me. I think mayhap you will in time join the sisters, for this life of the unmarried mother does not suit anything I have known of you."

Eleanor paused, sensing some relief coming into Véronique's expression. She sighed and continued.

"I grieve that you have brought me to this, Véronique. Through all the years of pleasure you have given me, I did not think you would leave me in disgrace."

"I beg pardon, Your Majesty. In time we may yet heal, though I shall not be near you. And though she will have no memory of my touch or voice, I pray some gentle words and moments will give her a stronger beginning than was mine. My mother died birthing me, and I knew no touch save the wolf who left me this prize."

"Surely there was a servant who . . ."

Véronique shrugged. "The senechal's wife nursed many children, and my father tossed one more upon the teetering pile. Nay, there was no loving touch. Mayhap that is the reason I fell prey to it. I would this maid knows more of love than I. Then when love's first touch comes, it will not burn, but rather, glow."

Eleanor's eyes held pity for the first time. "Have you named her?"

"I would leave that to you, Madame, for I yielded her the moment you entered this room."

Eleanor's smile was gentler than it had been in some time. "You yielded all, demoiselle. Give her something more than your brief touch. Give her the name she will carry."

"Félise," Véronique breathed, tears coming to her eyes. She knew in this instant that Eleanor had given her the single thread of hope that she might see her daughter again one day. She would now have a name to seek. "And the name of her grandfather yet she will bear. Félise de Raissa."

The queen gave Véronique's hand a soft squeeze and rose to leave her. Once she was gone, Véronique rested back in the pillows and took pleasure in the child's feeding, stroking the babe's tiny head and smiling a contented smile.

"I do not leave you lightly, fair Félise, but, because you are all that I love, I give you over to the strongest to raise. Be not timid as your mother, nor shrinking and mild. And though I give no name for your sire, you are not without a proud and strong father. Yea, I love him even so. In time he will know full well that his seed brought life, for he will venture to these castle walls again, and you will be ever near the queen. Many years cannot fade but that he asks whose child you might be.

"I am better placed in a convent, *ma petite*," she whispered. "I was never skilled in wifely matters, nor in occupations of men. In all these years beside my queen, I have served with and for women only. But I will not take the veil, my darling child, until I have seen that you prosper." She kissed the tiny reddish head. "We shall be one in spirit, until then."

Chapter One

THE SOUND OF CLATTERING HOOVES AND THE LOUD bellowing of an angered citizen disrupted the quiet afternoon. Félise had let her eyes drift slightly closed as her maid, Daria, brushed her hair. The long, fiery tresses reached nearly to her knees, and when she was seated, they were wont to drag in the rushes. Upon the sound of the street noise, Félise bolted to her feet and dashed to the second-floor window.

This London was alive with happenings, so varied were the sounds, sights, and smells. She had come with her family to wait upon King Henry's pleasure over the Christmas festival and perhaps even visit with the queen. Félise, at the age of eight and ten, had been mostly in the keep of her adoptive parents, traveling abroad only a little, and on this visit to London her spirits were wildly stimulated.

She leaned dangerously out the window to see what was causing the commotion and found a group of a dozen knights crowded together, their destriers' thick flanks brushing up against the walls of the buildings and one another in the narrow street, and the smashed cart full of breads that a merchant had been pulling. The cause of the chaos was obvious. The group of horsed men could not pass the merchant without doing at least a small amount of damage. Some clumsy beast did worse than jar the squat merchant; by the looks of the scene, the wheel was off the cart and the breads were well scattered, and nearly turned back into dough by the monstrous hooves.

His bald head red with fury, fists clenched and voice strangled with rage, the little man bounced on his toes as he berated the knights. "Bumble-headed fools! Clumsy idiots! Look beneath the feet of your donkeys to my baked goods!"

Some men within the group chuckled at the sight of the distraught man, while others sought to placate him. "The wheel can easily be returned to the cart," one knight said. "Minus a few loaves that can be replaced," attempted another.

"You foolhardy jackass," the man stormed at the knight. " 'Twas for Windsor I carried these breads and cakes. These streets are for people, not armies."

Félise giggled brightly from her window. Every hour that passed she found some new amusement or delight in this city. Ofttimes an event below her very bedchamber could intrigue her, for many were the people passing there, from merchants and soldiers to harlots and jugglers. People were always hawking wares, predictions, entertainments, or savory foods. Or beyond, when she ventured out, there was some new corner of the city that held an exciting pastime, entertainment, or fair.

Daria grabbed her mistress from behind, hooking her lean fingers into Félise's gown. "Get thee within," she demanded hotly. "Come now, before you cause a stir among them."

That worry was far from Félise's thoughts. She was out of the reach of these men and watched them in childlike wonder. She knew each of Lord Scelfton's men-at-arms, many of whom were with them in London, and every squire and servant at Twyford keep. These were all new faces; she had never seen the gathering of so many varied groups of knights before. She reached a hand behind her inside the window and motioned Daria to be still.

Even though Félise had just celebrated her eighteenth birthday and by custom was tardy in marrying, she was much the child in her own home and gave no consideration to how these restless knights might view her. She wore a thick velvet gown of deep rose that was lined about the low neckline with miniver. Her sleeves, snugly fitted to her arms, gave her a slender appearance, though full breasts rose provocatively from a pinched bodice. She leaned fully out the window, her elbows resting on the sill. Her hair fell down over her shoulders, its great length of shimmering golden fire cascading out the window.

Félise had never been given cause to be either overly modest or vain about her fair looks. Her mother, although not her natural mother, was humble and gentle and did not boast of her own beauty or Félise's. The sons of the Scelfton household did not dote upon her at all, for they were all older and much about men's diversions. While Félise was not of the same blood as they, she was raised as their sister and therefore no dallying between them would have been allowed. And finally, her adoptive father, Lord Scelfton, took such parental guardianship of her that no knight or yeoman in his demesne would dare look at her with lust, or his neck might be stretched from the nearest oak. She was raised as free as a peacock. Free to roam, ride, play, and tempt fate. There was naught to stay her. She neither revered nor feared men.

Two knights dismounted and began to struggle with the wheel of the cart, its bearer continuing to curse them. There was a shuffling about as the leader of their group, well ahead of the riders, tried to squeeze his horse closer to the trouble. This was difficult for — the round little man was right — the streets were not wide enough for armies.

"Demoiselle," one of the young knights called to her. She looked down and waved, a smile on her lips. He edged his horse nearer, an awkward chore that caused her to laugh the more. "Dare I hope you are prisoner here and in need of rescue?"

She laughed gaily at his play. Her father had hosted tourneys among his neighbors, and the courtly sport of knights and lords among the ladies was not alien to her. "Never that, sir knight, unless you would consider my father's close guard a prison, for he would smite a fair space between your ears should you help me from this perch."

"Ah, but does no one threaten you? I would take him to task, kill him, and lay him at your feet, and your father would gift me with your hand."

She laughed again, giving her head a toss that sent ripples

through her hair and lit her turquoise eyes with a wicked light. She knew these games well and played them easily. To her credit, she was bright and full of wit, finding good sport in every circumstance. She feigned thoughtfulness. "Three older brothers oft plague me. They are knights of Henry and far too strong for me to best. Would you hold them at a distance, kind sir, that I might flee with you?"

The young man, pretty of looks and large of build in his own right, gulped hard as laughter rose among his fellows. "What cruel jibes you hurl, madam, to taunt me with a father and three brothers that would keep me from you." He turned toward his group. "Who has a gift I might give the lady to show my earnest?"

Félise clapped her hands together in delight. One of the knights helping the merchant tossed a glazed loaf to a horsed knight who tossed it to her suitor. He looked up at her, smiling, pressed his lips fondly to the bread, then tossed it to her. She caught it easily and some of the men cheered.

"What, sir knight? Am I to treasure this meager loaf as your honest proposal? Would you have me hold it close to my bosom and cherish it, or am I to devour it quickly? I am accustomed to richer gifts."

"But I am a poor knight," he argued. "Richer for having looked on your beauty."

"Bed the wench another time," a voice cracked above the chatter. "The day is late and we are without means to find a meal and rest until this man's loss is satisfied."

Félise's countenance jerked from the playful young knight to the leader of their troop. He sat taller in his saddle than the others and there was a stern set to his mouth. He seemed more impatient by this trifling than angry, but it was clear he was done with foolery and ready to move past the insulted merchant.

"Sir Royce," the young knight beseeched, "I can neither move my mount toward the trouble to give assist, nor get us to yon inn with haste. In this brief time I am blinded by beauty and cannot move."

There were chuckles again from the group as Sir Royce lifted his eyes to look at Félise. She could see they were a deep and hardened brown even from her distance. His brown brows were bushy and thick and drawn together as he studied her at his leisure. Her playfulness seemed to wane as she stared at him. His shoulders were broad, his face was square, and the hands that held the reins were large and tan. Thick brown hair fell over his brow. Slowly he formed a smile that seemed almost sarcastic, and Félise pulled ever so slightly back into her room.

"Maiden, will you come without and cure this man's blindness with your kiss, or shall we heft him through your window?"

Félise felt now the object of rather than a participant in the joviality. A blush began to creep onto her cheeks. There was something vaguely different about this man's teasing. Unlike his companion, he was a man fully grown and knowledgeable of women. There seemed at least a grain of seriousness in his voice, and her stomach jumped.

"Mayhap you have need of a more determined lover," Sir Royce shouted. "This lad is pretty, but he knows little of women's pleasures. I would not be the rogue to deny you assist."

There was the sound of one low whistle at his blatant proposition. Félise looked to her young suitor to see his reaction to the insult. She found that his eyes were not angry but indeed full of mirth. But the game had lost its flavor for her. She felt slightly vulnerable for the first time, yet all that Sir Royce could touch her with were his eyes.

"The hint of youth beckons me where too many nights of sleeping with the horses would only cool my passion," she flung back at him. She raised a finely arched brow and forced a half-smile that might equal his in sarcasm. "Perhaps you are too old and battle-worn to interest me."

The laughter of the knights at seeing their leader so chastened by the maid was like thunder in the street below. All joined in the mirth, including Sir Royce. He threw back his head in good cheer and seemed pleased by her flippant wit.

"Saucy wench," he shouted, when the laughter had calmed, "come hither that I might show you how old lips do tempt." He threw his arms wide. "I swear, I will hold myself from your richer treasures until you beg me for more."

Félise was about to retort with another careless remark, but her mother's voice from the doorway below caught her tongue before it would be loosed. "Sir knight, do you have some case with my daughter, or do you simply enjoy this banter?"

Félise withdrew the more, wondering if she would be chastised for this play or if these knights might be taken to task. "My lady." Sir Royce half-bowed from his saddle. "The demoiselle distracts my men. Come see how tempting a parcel we sight from the window. I think it most unfair to censure these men; we are where we should be but the maiden is out of place, I think."

"I need not look again to judge her allure, sir. You bear the arms of our king — are you not by oath prepared to protect virtue?"

Félise quickly pulled herself within her room, facing Daria, who was shaking her head with disapproval. She listened intently to the voices outside while looking at her maid's thin, pinched face, careful not to be seen by the men again.

"Indeed, my lady," the knight returned casually. "But your young temptress makes a mockery of my oath. I am not one to take honor too much to heart when faced with witch's locks and a full bosom."

Félise was certain she heard smothered coughs follow the knight's brazen remark. There was a moment of silence, during which the color rose high on her cheeks.

"Sir knight," Lady Edrea questioned calmly, "does your lady wait in yon keep while you dally with my daughter?"

"Never that, madam," he replied. "I am untethered and bent on the business of the king." He chuckled. "I confess it is my preference."

"Then unless you would see your preference quickly changed, I beg you make haste from my house. Your words are too intimate for a maiden's ears, and I would fear to tell Lord Scelfton that promises and oaths were spoken to my daughter this day."

Now the laughter was loud, for the proud lady had put the knight on his heels. His playful courtship could well be taken seriously by Félise's father. It was a good threat and nicely leveled. Félise straightened proudly, her smile superior, though no one could see but Daria.

"We will make haste from here, madam," came Sir Royce's

commanding retort. "And I trust your young temptress is already busied with her threads, as young virgins should be. And madam," he continued, "I give you this advice freely: the lass is in need of counsel. London is for well-guarded and discreet ladies or for harlots. There is no ground between."

Félise felt her cheeks begin to burn with anger and shame, and Daria reached out and pinched her, nodding her head once in emphasis. Félise winced at her maid's reprimand as she heard her mother's voice return softly and with dignity to the warriors who towered over her. "Your advice is well taken, sir. Your travels will not be distracted again on this path, and for any future glance upon my daughter's fairness, either you or your men should plead honorably to Harlan, Lord Scelfton of Twyford, and no other."

"Then we part friends, my lady," Royce replied. "Whichever of you louts upset this cart, draw a coin for this man. We have no more time for folly, even so pleasurable a folly as this."

Félise could hear but did not dare watch the chaos that followed as the men tried to push the cart out of the way to get by. Within moments, the door to her chamber opened and her mother entered, a look of quiet disapproval on her face and her hands clenched together before her. Félise bit her lip rather self-consciously.

"Félise," she sighed.

"Madam, I meant no harm, truly. And were it not for that beast who leads them, 'twas all in good fun."

Edrea shook her head slowly. "His point is well taken. You were raised within the halls that housed a hundred honorable men. You do not know the dangers that could prevail when strangers look upon your fair face."

"But madam, until he turned the game, 'twas only jesting we did." She shivered slightly. "He is vulgar and slow-witted."

Edrea frowned. "Neither that, dear. He is a man quick in knowing what he wants. Such a man will wed you and not some stripling youth that plays at courtship." As she moved toward Félise, her eyes softened and she reached out a hand to stroke her daughter's glorious hair. "I may have done you ill. You have been too safe to be wise. Do you think all men as well mannered as your brothers? Félise, you must abandon these childish notions and have a care." Edrea's eyes dropped to her daughter's full, swelling breasts. She sighed heavily. "We will discuss a husband for you instantly. It cannot wait another day."

"But Mother, I —"

Edrea held up her hand, and her soft eyes took on that steely quality that meant no argument would be considered. "It is decided. I will not consider further delay."

The living arrangements for Harlan Scelfton and his family were comprised of the larger portion of an inn, comfortable enough for the family, servants, knights, and squires who traveled with him. Although his service to Henry had been long and devoted, it still came as a surprise when the king requested his presence in the city during the Christmas celebrations. Edrea and Félise were alive with excitement at the prospect of trading with the merchants and visiting court, his sons were enthusiastic over the opportunity to greet old acquaintances, but Harlan braced himself for what the king would require of him.

When Félise noticed his frown of concern and his distracted manner, she inquired of him, "My lord, is there some trouble that brings us here?"

Answering with as much honesty as he could, he said, "I can't say trouble, lass, but I know Henry calls me because he has need of something."

Félise simply shrugged and gave him her prettiest smile. "Could the king ask anything of you that you'd not willingly give?" she asked, knowing well his loyalty.

Harlan couldn't suppress his own smile. She had ever the talent of simplifying things to a better level of understanding. Since she had come to him at the tender age of seven, she had soothed his family's hurts and softened the roughness in their lives. He adored her. "Nay, love. I will better show my honor at being asked."

When the time for the audience came, Harlan was asked to present his lady, Edrea, also. Félise excitedly helped her mother prepare herself, fluttering about her rooms in search of wraps, jewels, ribbons, or any extra bauble that would enhance her appearance. While her parents were away, Félise could barely remain still, she was so eager to hear every detail of the palace; the royal couple, only briefly united for a family holiday; and all the pomp and politics surrounding them.

Félise had some vague memory of such things, for her life had been near the queen. As near as she could surmise, her mother had been an unmarried servant to the queen who, when Félise was born, had either died or been sent far away, never to return. Eleanor, in a rare mood of compassion, had taken custody and placed her as an infant with a noble family in Poitou, where she kept her court. Then Eleanor had failed in a plot to overthrow her husband and had been captured. She had been held prisoner ever since.

Félise had then been shipped in a rather haphazard way back toward England. No monies were to be spent on this ward of the imprisoned queen, and the noble family that had fawned over her while Eleanor was her sworn protector quickly lost interest. She was a mere child and in possession of a trunk of clothes, a ragged doll fashioned years earlier by some French hand, and a mass of tangled red curls. She was unceremoniously dumped on Henry's stoop at Westminster, and someone had to do something with her. A kindly bishop knew a family in the south that grieved the death of their own daughter, and he took great liberty in sending this waif to Twyford to see if the lord and lady would give her a home.

Félise had many times considered how sad her circumstance might have been but for Lord Scelfton and Lady Edrea. They did far more than feed and house her: they bathed her in love, and her life was rich with possessions and devotion. She thought of herself as their own. Lord Harlan could extend his property with his sons' able warring skills and hard labor, so he generously fixed this child with a dowry, fine clothes, and a sound education. And Lady Edrea, who found tenderness lacking in her life with three stout boys to raise, relished having a daughter to pamper. There was no deficiency of love in their household.

Félise virtually ran circles around her parents when they returned from Windsor. The day had been long for her, alone with the servants. "What did they wear, madam? What did the king ask? Was Duke Richard present? Did the queen seem sad or ill? Was she friendly with the king? Did you hear minstrels or see jugglers?" Finally her mother laughed lightly, drawing off her mantle.

"Félise, I beg you let us in the door."

"Oh, madam, were there ladies-in-waiting there? Was the king with a mistress?" Excitement flooded her so that she barely noticed her father's dour mood. Lord Scelfton's eyes were downcast as he brushed past his wife and daughter to enter the hall. "Oh, madam," Félise suddenly gasped. "Has my lord been called to arms?"

"Nay, my love," she said softly. "But he is displeased. Come and help me soothe him."

Harlan was already draining a large draught of ale when joined by the women. Félise began to feel the tension in the room, for although Edrea was more controlled, it was discernible that she likewise felt some discomfort.

Harlan slammed the empty tankard down onto the table. "In one breath we are thanked and called fit guardians, and in the other denied the privilege of completing the chore. By damn, the insult is too great. I have served well these many years."

"My lord, no insult was meant. 'Tis just that Eleanor be given her due now, for without her generosity in the past, we'd not have had these many pleasurable years," Edrea returned.

"And now they would be revoked," he blustered.

"Nor that, Harlan. Her request is simple and decent, and I pray you remember, she has suffered a great deal. Indeed, though she seems well seated at Henry's side, it is only for a moment. And then her prison is again her home. Have patience."

"Madam, you've taken leave of your own good wits. The woman is treasonous and sought to rob Henry of his kingdom. How can I pity her prison when I fought against her sons for my king? And for your part, *you* sent a missive to her that —"

"My lord," she said loudly and with stern conviction to halt his tirade, "let us use measured care with this news. We are without choice, and whether my action was right or wrong, I would have the matter quietly behind us. Now, need you be drunk of ale to speak with our daughter, or will you lower the cup and your voice?"

Harlan slowly let his hand leave the tankard on the table and strode to the blazing hearth. He turned once to beckon Félise, who stood astounded at her parents' harsh words. He pointed to the bench near the fire, indicating that she should sit there. Edrea followed and sat beside her. It was many long moments before he turned toward them.

"The queen requests your presence at court for a few days," he said, anger still rumbling in his voice.

Félise's eyes widened and her mouth gaped. She could not fathom the reason for all their anger and agitation over something that sounded like a gift of great merriment. "She would have *me* at court?" she asked quietly.

Edrea took her daughter's hand and scowled at her husband. "Lord Scelfton only uses his words generously when he is angered. In making simple explanations he is like a strangled bird. Now, listen to me carefully that you might understand this simple request, for it is meant to be entirely in your best interests."

Harlan growled something low and uncomplimentary and returned to his tankard to fill it. Edrea responded to his action by briefly narrowing her eyes and setting her mouth in a disapproving line. Then she turned back to Félise.

"Your natural mother was a woman of some importance to the queen, although I can't say the reason or what has become of her. As the matter rests, the queen generously allowed for your upbringing in Poitou, close enough for her to see that you were cared for. When she was imprisoned, there was naught she could do to ensure your safety, and you were sent to England. When we heard of your plight and took you in, the priest who brought you explained your circumstances. Truly, had Eleanor not revolted and attempted so much against Henry, you would likely have been raised in the palace with many eager to attend you, for it is greatly possible that was the queen's plan.

"The missive your father speaks of was mine, written by my own hand. I sent word to the queen in her prison in Winchester that you were in our safe custody, in case she ever thought of your welfare. I do not pardon her action against her husband, but I had pity for her despair. I never gained reply, but then, could she have been denied correspondence?

"But at this time the royal family is gathering, a rare thing in their troubled midst. And Eleanor has been granted some few luxuries. It appears she is without means but has given thought to you these many years and would see that you are well cared for. She kindly grants your mother's dower lands, said to be modest, to be added to Lord Scelfton's dower gifts. This small parcel is in Duke Richard's Aquitaine. Certainly her years of solitude have lent her a softer nature." Edrea looked at her grumbling husband. "I suppose she has many regrets and sorrows."

"Many," Harlan said without gentleness.

Félise looked at her mother in some confusion. "Why is my lord angry?" she asked quietly.

"He despises interference in his household and is worried that the queen will use you against our will."

"Would she?" Félise asked. "Surely she could not."

"I think not," Edrea said with a smile. "I suppose she will influence your hand in marriage, since you are of that age and it is our chief occupation. That could only better the prospect. She is without the means to abduct you against your will."

"The tale is that Félise's mother was a prisoner of Eleanor and —" Harlan began, showing still greater agitation.

"The tale, kind sir, does not include imprisonment. It is said that the lady-in-waiting who bore our Félise was nobly bred and lived a chaste life beside the queen until she was despoiled by some errant knight and killed herself in shame."

Félise quickly grasped her mother's wrist. "There are tales about my mother?"

Edrea smiled with some tolerance. "Your beginning was prior to the time of Eleanor's court in Poitou, where troubadours sang of pure and devoted love; indeed, there was some romantic conjecture about your birth." She shrugged. "As there has been verse of Rosamond and others. I promise you it has not followed your upbringing with us. For all the world cares, you are Félise

Scelfton. Romantic speculation was the great pursuit of the time
. . . before our queen was locked away."

Félise swallowed hard, contemplating this. "Yet I go to Windsor. And what tales will I find there? Will they call me bastard
and shun me?"

Edrea's eyes grew serious. "Nay, darling. They have need of
rich beauty such as yours. And your father is a jealous man who
holds his own tight within his fist. He babbles when a firm mind
would gain him more."

"How long must I stay there?" she asked.

"But a few days, and then we will return to Twyford."

"But I've never been away from you," Félise argued.

"Nor shall you be," Edrea smiled. "We will keep this residence, but the king has kindly included us in the dinners that you
will attend. So you see, there is no worry, but a grand time to be
long remembered."

Félise looked toward Harlan in wait of some encouragement
from him. He was a tall man whose tawny hair held more gray
than gold, and his thick jowls were tensed. But finally he seemed
to relax his features, whether involuntarily or by effort was uncertain. "Aye, a time to be remembered," he grunted. "She is
right," he relented. "I am a jealous father and would not have
you flaunted about the court."

"I suppose it gives no comfort that you despise the queen,"
Félise attempted somewhat lamely.

He looked away from her again, his jaw twitching slightly.
"Aye. Though it's more distrust than hate. But you will go. This
one time only." He forced a smile that was far from sincere.
"You may begin to gather your gowns now, for on the morrow
we will take you there."

Félise looked to her mother and Edrea gave a smile and a nod.
She tried to rise slowly and even give a measure of reluctance to
her step, but it was impossible. She nearly skipped. Although this
tale of her mother had made her slightly anxious, she couldn't
deny a surge of excitement at spending a few days at court.

When she was out of the room and gaining the stairs, Harlan
turned to Edrea with a look of worried disapproval. "You have
allayed all her fears when she should be put on her guard."

"I cannot agree," the lady returned. "There is nothing she can do to guard herself now."

"She is being used as a pawn to divide a kingdom to Henry's advantage," he blustered, his voice held carefully low.

"The pawn may achieve the treasure if you are right. Let us see, Harlan."

He shook his head. "Listen to me, for you have refused to understand the folly of this. The queen's motives be damned. Whether she is moved by compassion or selfishness means nothing to me. Henry would not gift her this without his own ends. Eleanor is here for one purpose only: Henry uses her to aid him in his alliance with his sons. He acknowledges some old dowry of lands in Aquitaine for Félise and asks that we include her dower lands in England. With a purse so rich, some English lord of Henry's can acquire much and make his oath to the king first and hold property under Richard. It is as common a ploy as sending a spy into Richard's camp. And our daughter, madam, provides the means. If it did not suit Henry, he would deny the original dowry and leave our daughter alone."

"And why do you fear?" she asked him. "The land in France is not such a prize. I hear 'tis a small demesne that's been managed these many years by a seneschal. The king would not even disclose the location or family name. I say you smell trouble where there is none. Who pleads for the hand of a maid with an unknown dowry?"

"If the importance to the king becomes known, many will, my lady. And their characters may not be good. Indeed, some may be commissioned by Richard. Or John. I want my daughter neatly settled, not abducted for her wealth and made a prisoner of some oafish knight."

Lady Edrea rose slowly, brushing down her heavy velvet gown and raising her chin proudly. "Then make your presence felt, my lord, so that her protection is a known fact. And let us get this matter done to our satisfaction. Your king is no fool, or you would not have battled for him these many years. And while you lay indignities to Eleanor by the score, she is wise in the plights of women and land and will see some purpose served by our daughter's marriage."

· 25 ·

"I cannot abide these manipulations," he growled.

"Nay, Harlan. You cannot abide your lack of control where it has never before been questioned." She approached him gently, running a hand along his arm. He looked down at her and she smiled tenderly. His grouchy features smoothed, for he could never deny her sweetness. This woman had held ever strong through the years of labor she endured for love of him. When faced with her firm strength, he could feel as vulnerable as a lad. Her show of meek femininity could make him feel powerful and stalwart.

He turned her in his arms and put his hands to her still-slim waist. "You turn my most anguished thoughts to sweeter things, my lady. Even now." He gently kissed her lips, and there, after knowing her so well for over thirty years, he felt the same lilting in his chest from her response. "I would have Félise know a marriage like ours. What chance, when her lands add more flavor than her simple womanhood?"

Edrea laughed at her worried spouse and planted kisses on his face. "Harlan, you boast such wisdom in fighting and farming and breeding of war horses, yet you know nothing of your own daughter." She looped her arms around his neck. "What knight of ambition, his arms hewn of the hardest rock, would not crumble to sand when met with her sorceress eyes? What lord of this kingdom would turn away from her winsome smile or mark in cruelty her velvet skin? Aye, her lands become a prize, but no prize greater than her beauty and charm."

She kissed his lips long and lovingly, feeling the same surge of passion she knew when first they met. When they parted, she knew that his mind was almost turned to other things. "My lord, allay your fears. Félise will turn the most brutal beast into a lad to do her bidding. Now come, we cannot change a royal command, but we can fill the night without worry."

He took her hand, pressing it to his lips. "I hope you are right, lady," he said. "But meanwhile, madam, you may lead me from worry."

"With pleasure, my lord," she murmured, allowing him to escort her to the stairs.

Chapter Two

ALTHOUGH THE AIR WAS COLD, THERE WAS AN ABUN-
dance of sunshine on the day Félise ventured forth to
Windsor. On five steeds they rode, Félise beside her father while behind them were her brothers, Evan, Maelwine, and
Dalton. Since it was her first journey to a royal event, she did not
know that her retinue was unusual nor that it was meant to impress a particular point upon the people at court.

Félise was gowned in rich green velvet embroidered with
golden threads and cloaked by an ermine-lined hooded mantle.
Beside her, her father was garbed in his own rich velvet in the
Twyford colors of silver and blue in his chausses, tunic, and
mantle. The brothers were in full armor and carried the Scelfton
blazon, boasting their family arms and, if that were not im-
pressive enough, their grand size.

The horses were taken at the gate, and once inside, the family
was escorted to the king's presence chamber. They stood at their
leisure for only a few moments before Henry arrived to bid them
welcome. Harlan raised his daughter's hand high on his own and
led her toward the king. Just behind this presentation, the Scelfton men moved protectively near, their expressions solemn and
foreboding. Henry took his seat and smiled very tolerantly at this
display.

"A handsome family, my lord," he said quietly.

"Thank you, my liege," Harlan replied.

Henry looked past Félise to the sons. "You would be confident of arms with these," he said. Félise thought perhaps she noted a hint of envy in the man's eyes. It was a well-known fact that Henry battled with his sons, and it was ever the question as to who might win. In the Scelfton household there was no envy or competition. The wealth was firmly divided, with Evan earning his right to Twyford by being firstborn.

The door at the side of the presence chamber opened and Eleanor entered, four ladies in tow. Though Félise could not remember the queen's features from her youth, there was no question who she was. She wore a rich gown lined about the neck and wrists with fur, and her hair was covered by an elaborate wimple. If her state was impoverished, her clothing did not show it. And if she was old, it was not obvious in her face or gait. She was proudly erect, her skin still smooth and velvety, and her demeanor spoke of power, not submission. Eleanor's reputation was not the best, yet in this figure it was difficult to surmise cruelty, for the queen's smile was gentle and her eyes alert and compassionate.

She bowed first to her husband and Félise wondered what passed between them. Was there yet love, after Eleanor had battled him and he had imprisoned her for so many years? Was this submission true, or did the queen bide her time and play her game before Henry while she plotted in her mind? It was romantic intrigue indeed, for Henry responded with what appeared to be an amiable nod and Eleanor took her seat, leaving the guests to wonder what odd alliance these two had.

The four ladies stood about the room. There were a few fettered knights, a few servants and courtiers, but even though more than a dozen people other than the Scelftons were there, this was in all a private audience. Eleanor leaned forward in her seat. "Take away your cloak, child, and let me look at you," she instructed softly.

Félise self-consciously pushed her hood away and unhooked the fastening at her throat. Harlan helped her from behind and slowly drew the cloak away from her shoulders. One of the women from Eleanor's group came forward to take the cloak from Harlan; she seemed transfixed by Félise's appearance.

Félise did not pose, but simply stood erect and tried to keep her fluttering stomach calm. She had appraised her own choice of gown and coiffure before leaving the inn and decided it would do, but she had not learned vanity and so did not consider herself above the fairness of any other well-dressed woman. But the appearance she gave was exquisite to those in the room. Her lustrous hair was bound in a thick braid that had been wrapped about her head. The gown she wore gave depth to her large eyes and brought out more of their green than blue, and her cheeks and lips appeared to have been ever so lightly brushed by a peach. She was taller than many women — taller than Lady Edrea and the woman who took her cloak. Her slender form and narrow waist only emphasized her full bosom and long, graceful fingers. She was quickly recognized as beautiful and lithesome.

It seemed to her that long moments had passed while she was being scrutinized by all eyes. Her father tried to ease her discomfort and draw the attention away from his daughter. "Your Majesty," Harlan said quietly.

Eleanor's attention was easily gained. She straightened and smiled at Lord Scelfton. "Quite right, my lord," she said with a little laugh. "We mustn't make Lady Félise fear us by our rude stares. My dear, your loveliness is uncommon. You'll forgive us?"

It was then that Félise noticed that the woman who held her cloak stared up at her with a mesmerized expression. When Félise met her eyes, the woman lowered her gaze and returned to her queen's side, holding the cloak and stroking it almost reverently.

"Your point is well taken," Henry said to Harlan, a slight chuckle in his voice. "Having never met the maid, I could not have known why you would fear to have her out of your protection." He gestured again to the men behind Félise. "Would you have them stay to guard her bower door, or will you trust me to protect this valuable prize?"

"I am at your service, my liege," Harlan said with assurance.

Henry rose and stepped down from his dais. He extended a hand toward Harlan. "I cannot keep her from being ogled by every fuzz-faced lad that catches sight of her, but I will see her virtue untainted for her future husband. You may turn your army to other pursuits."

Harlan bowed. "Yea, my liege."

"Bring your lady tomorrow and we will dine together."

Félise glanced a bit uncertainly at her father, not quite ready for him to leave her, but knowing he must. Félise would stay at Windsor and only be visited by her family. A moment of doubt at this adventure caused her stomach to flutter anew. She had no idea what she was to do next.

Harlan turned her, kissed her cheek, and gave her a comforting pat on the arm. He looked again to his king. "I am at your service, Sire," he said. Then turning, he led the way out of the room, his sons following.

"Show the lady to her room," Eleanor instructed the woman who held Félise's cloak. "See that she is comfortable and that her belongings find her."

The woman, startled out of her reverie, moved toward Félise with a gentle smile. "My lady?" she inquired. And then leading the way, Félise was taken upstairs and through halls and galleries to a bedchamber that was to be hers during her stay.

Although her time with the king and queen had been brief, her maid and her belongings had arrived and Daria was nervously laying things away and setting out the articles Félise used daily. "Come, lady," her escort softly urged. "Will you have a scented bath or a small meal? I could have wine brought or even oils to soften your skin. What is your pleasure?"

Félise looked at the woman closely for the first time. She wore a plain wimple that covered her head and left only the oval shape of her face to view. She was petite of stature and her hands were small. Her glittering green eyes were kindly and crinkled about the corners. Félise thought she was approximately Lady Edrea's age, and uncommonly soft-spoken — her voice barely rose above a whisper. It was possible this woman had resided with Eleanor in her imprisonment, for her clothes were decent but not rich.

"You are so kind to me. What is your name?" she asked.

The woman's eyes grew round for just an instant, then she

smiled easily as she considered the question. "I have lived in a convent for many years and am known among the nuns as Vespera. It is not my given name, but my preference."

"You are not a nun," Félise said, frowning.

"Nay, not now. But I think soon I shall be. I most certainly share all their vows and prayers."

Félise paused for a moment and considered the woman. "I have need of nothing," she finally said.

"I could brush your hair," the woman offered. "Or lay out a gown?"

"Will I be required to change my gown?" she asked. "I fear I do not know what I am to do save sit in this chamber."

"An escort will come to take you to the hall to sup with Her Majesty and the others. Your gown is perfect for the meal; the color becomes your skin. And on the morrow when you are not occupied, you must see the chapel and the gardens. They are not as beautiful as in spring, but are immense and well tended. Do not confine yourself to these rooms, my lady, for who knows when Windsor will be graced with your loveliness again?"

"Am I free to wander about?" she asked.

The woman laughed lightly. "I trust you are safe in Henry's house, lady. If you feel uneasy at the prospect, take your woman with you."

"Thank you, madam. You're very kind."

She nodded humbly and turned to go to the door. Once there, she turned back and looked at Félise again. "You've grown into a beautiful woman," she said, a wistful tone in her voice. "You must make your parents very proud."

Félise cocked her head slightly, wondering at the woman's unusually familiar behavior. "They have not complained overmuch," she said softly, "though I know I am a trial."

Vespera smiled then — a gentle and beguiling smile that gave her youth and beauty of her own. "Nay," she whispered. "They would not complain. You are a treasure."

And then turning again, the woman quit the room with quiet grace.

* * *

The great hall held the evening feast and many nobles were present. Henry was flanked by his queen and sons Richard and John, and about them were a dozen long tables for other guests. Félise was seated near enough to the king and queen that they might easily watch her, but too far for conversation. However esteemed their positions, they were in fact the only people within the room she had met.

There were eight seated at the table she occupied, and she longed for the presence of her parents. Beside her sat a dowager baroness whose company was welcome, for she proved friendly, but Félise had nothing in common with the elderly widow from the north. On her right came a tardy knight, just gaining his marked seat after the meal had been laid out. As he groped for his place, his eyes fell on her and instantly lit up in appreciation.

He bowed to her. "My lady, I fear to test my good fortune," he began. "Sir Wharton is my name."

"A pleasure, sir," she said very quietly, turning her eyes quickly back to her plate. Internally she scoffed at herself. She was quick-witted and outspoken enough when lolling in her window or at a gathering in her parents' home, but here, void of escort, she could barely find the confidence to meet the man's eyes.

He took his seat quickly, his manner showing he was pleased. "I am to be your dinner companion, fairest lady. Might I lay some name to you?"

"Forgive me," she said, looking at him again. "I am Félise Scelfton."

"And your family? Could we perchance be of some earlier acquaintance?"

"I can't say, sir. My father is Harlan, Lord Scelfton; Twyford is our home."

He raised his goblet slowly to his lips and drank while watching her. When he lowered his hand to the table, there was a smile on his lips. "I know the old lord," he confirmed. "And I've ridden with your brother, Maelwine, on more than one occasion."

Félise's countenance lightened instantly. Even though she didn't know Sir Wharton personally, she immediately felt safer in his company if he was a family friend. The tightness of her stomach relaxed as he entertained her with stories of his travels and discussed at length the rich land of his father. His family resided north of London, while Félise's Twyford was south, but it happened that over the years their families had been in the same company on several occasions.

As she became more comfortable and the dinner went on with laughter and much revelry, she began to notice Sir Wharton's dark handsomeness and chivalrous nature. "Maelwine kept your existence a secret from me out of kindness. Had I known of you earlier, I would have been mad with longing and not fit for fighting," he said.

She laughed at the prospect. "Indeed, Maelwine did you no kindness. In all his brotherly affection, he does not take much notice of me, but rather boasts the beauty of the women he meets upon his travels."

"Ah, then he has not graced your father's walls with his presence in some years and remembers you only as a child."

"Neither that, Sir Wharton. Maelwine and the others brought me here," she informed him.

Wharton looked around the room. "Do they keep watch, or are you in need of protection lest you be snatched away by some lusty knight?"

"I need no protection, sir," she said, looking sidelong at the king and queen. "Do you make your service available?" she asked, raising one brow.

"At your call, my lady," he said, inclining his head toward her and taking her hand in both of his.

Félise laughed softly, enjoying this much more than she thought she would. "It occurs to me, sir knight, that the wolf offers to stand guard over the hen."

He smiled then in warm communication, his eyes beginning to smoulder like hot coals, but Félise's attention was drawn past him to a familiar face. Over Sir Wharton's shoulder and across two tables she saw two men staring at her. They were standing, for the meal was coming to a finish and people were beginning to mill around the room. Had they been seated, she would not have seen either of them.

Her smile vanished and she felt her tension returning, for it was in fact Sir Royce, the man who had played so brazenly beneath her window. She couldn't place the other man as one of his group, but then she could remember few of them distinctly. While his companion looked at her tenderly, Royce seemed to scowl. His eyes were narrow and there was no trace of a smile.

Wharton followed her eyes and found them placed to Sir Royce. "Do you know that man, demoiselle?" he asked her.

"Nay," she said quickly. "That is, we have never been introduced, though I know who he is, in a manner."

"Ah, your father has warned you to be wary of him?"

Her eyes were quickly diverted to Wharton. "Nay," she replied, looking at him curiously. She had almost instinctively been frightened of Royce, but she couldn't name the reason. His eyes, perhaps — so cool and unforgiving. Or his roguish spirit or even his size, greater than that of many men. "Need I be?" she asked.

"Aye, fair Félise," Wharton said, his own expression hardening considerably as if he was himself guarded where this Sir Royce was concerned. "Royce is not to be trusted."

"But is he not a knight of Henry?" she asked.

"Not all knights of Henry are honorable men, madam. Forsooth, when the king has need of fighting skills, he oft commands a troop of heathens and barbarians; those same ones will betimes affect a gentler pose for the king's court, but their manner changes not — only their clothes. Royce is treacherous."

Félise had no great urgings toward justice for Royce, but she was bright enough to know Wharton had really said little beyond admitting a personal dislike for the other knight. "What crimes would you lay to him?" she asked, begging some clarification.

Wharton thought for a moment and then brushed aside the question with an excuse of sorts. "Nay, lady, I will not dishonor myself by repeating loose slander. If he could be held accountable for crimes, he would not linger here over the king's own roast of boar, so leave it understood that his reputation has not reached the justice of his fellows. I once called myself a friend to the Leighton family and soon learned that they scorn friendship in favor of thievery and murder. Yet it cannot be proved, or they'd have all been hanged. Use caution where he is concerned. He may have sworn his oath, but he gives short shrift to chivalry."

Félise swallowed hard. She could not deny a strong tendency to believe Wharton, for in her brief association with Royce she pondered his behavior among women. "I will take care," she whispered, looking over and noting that the men were no longer in view. She smiled at her companion. "Rest assured, I could not care for better company, and you are to be toasted for your honorable nature."

Royce brooded over the last bit of ale before him while Sir Boltof spoke. "Is it clear by her company that the pleas have begun?"

"You are certain she is the one?" Royce asked.

"Aye, Royce, the word has traveled quickly from bower to camp. She is endowed by the queen and the Scelfton house. The extent of the lands is not fully known, but the talk is that her purse will bring a fine wedding gift to the chosen groom. You are close to the king's ear, Royce. What say you?"

Royce continued to stare into his cup, grumbling something inaudible. He began to feel uneasy about the wench, and he wasn't sure if it was because of her saucy behavior at her window a few days before or the fact that she seemed to be enjoying herself with Sir Wharton.

"Do you wait for an offer from me?" Boltof asked. Royce looked at him in surprise. "I am a reasonable man and we are to be brothers in due time. I would manage a settlement from the maid's dower purse if you would urge the king on my behalf."

"I want none of her purse. What of the maid, Boltof?" Royce asked, his manner coltish and impatient. "Do you think to make her acquaintance and assure yourself she is not a shrew before you wed her here and now?"

"Of beauty there is none lacking, and the money would better than cure some old debts. I have little need to judge her character when her assets are so appealing. I'll play my court upon your word and even split the sum with you."

Royce drank the remainder of the ale from his cup and looked at Boltof. They had been friends for a long time, but he sometimes questioned Boltof's common sense. "I've seen the wench before, Boltof. She is the one I told you of, seeking the favors of an entire troop of men from her bedroom window. It could be her fairness and hefty purse are worth only a lifetime of misery."

Boltof smiled first and then laughed loudly. He slammed his own mug on the table and pressed his face near to speak confidentially to Royce. "All the better. I'll see her flayed as an adulteress, and no one will question my authority over her lands."

Royce frowned at the idea while from his other side Celeste rubbed her arm against his as she drew near. "What is this conference with my brother, Royce?" she asked. "Do you make battle plans when the eve is meant for merriment?"

Royce turned to the woman and tried to smile. "He leads me on a chase after more riches, as is always Boltof's wont, madam. I beg him cease for a brief time of leisure, but he builds more plans in his mind."

Boltof leaned toward them and now the three heads were close together. "Henry would hear Royce's plea on my behalf for the heiress seated beside Wharton. Her purse is heavy, but I waited to see her to be assured she was not a cow dressed in velvet and gold. And that one," he said, indicating Wharton with his mug, "has already begun paying court to her. Before dawn the line of men will be long and deep. Our family could make good use of the dowry, eh, Celeste?"

This talk caused Royce to sulk for reasons he couldn't name. His manner became all the more surly. "Then seek out the maid, Boltof, and see what manner of woman she is."

"Why won't you help him?" Celeste asked solicitously. "It is not as though Boltof denies you in any way."

"The matter of seeking out Henry for a man well able to speak for himself does not sit well with me. You are sworn to him," he said to Boltof. "Make your plea to the king on your own behalf."

Boltof's eyes darkened and he frowned. "You stand in better stead with the king," he complained. " 'Tis a common fact. I would not have asked for assist, had I known how niggardly you hold your influence."

"My influence is bigger in your mind," Royce returned. "And if I do have the power to persuade the king, 'tis only because I have never tried."

Celeste let her lips come close enough to Royce's ear so that he felt her breath on his cheek. "Have this matter done for Boltof," she pleaded sweetly. "He plagues you and makes you forget that we have plans that need attention."

He turned to her then with the patient smile that had become a habit for him. He judged her soft, pale features yet again, reassuring himself that she was lovely enough. Celeste was older than a maid just venturing toward marriage, and Royce had finally conceded that they should be wed. She had, after all, yielded him more than was decent for him to take. In addition, she sought out no more eager groom, but was patient with his brooding reluctance and had held herself for him for five years.

He had first met Boltof a decade and a half before, when they were lads completing their training for knighthood. Through Boltof he had made the acquaintance of his sister, Celeste, and their stepfather, Lord Orrick, and from that time on, the young woman had had her sights on him for her husband. Royce had not felt any immediate stirring, but as time passed he became fond of Celeste and valued Boltof's friendship. He added to that a deep respect for Lord Orrick. The old lord was in fact the member of their family with whom Royce felt the most kinship.

For a very long time he had felt a strange nagging about Boltof and Celeste, who were plagued by his resistance to joining with them by marriage. He could often shrug off the feelings as usual for a man without family ties, whose love of adventure outpaced his need for a wife. Sometimes a deeper foreboding threatened; Royce had often considered that it would be for the good of all if he left no heirs. In any case, finding a proper dame to wed concerned him least of all, and he had to be hurried to the decision for Celeste by her stepfather and brother. Lord Orrick had just a few months past announced himself. "The marriage of my daughter is of imminent necessity if I am to see her thrive rather than shrivel. You may speak for her, sir knight, or have done with her affections."

Royce begged time to put his house in order before any betrothal contract was drawn, and the Lord, ever gallant in his dealings, allowed for the new year to be reached and the betrothal and wedding done swiftly after.

Still, his decision troubled him. He had no reason to distrust these people who had loyally held his friendship dear. Indeed, he owed them much. Yet comfort with the commitment had never come.

"Say me nay, if you will," Boltof demanded.

Royce tried to calm the restive feelings he had about the entire situation. He didn't like going to Henry on anyone's behalf, and had the request come from anyone but Boltof, he would have swiftly refused. And the wench, although fair of face and endowed handsomely, caused him some suspicious feelings. He sought a middle ground where Boltof might feel the weight of his loyalty and yet give him enough time to evaluate the situation better. "I would not refuse you this, Boltof," he finally said. "I owe much to your family, and if you must believe I have some power with Henry, then we will see the truth to it. But I would have more time to design my words. And you must seek a closer view of the damsel whose hand you would bid for and be sure that this is the course you should take."

Boltof smiled at Royce and nodded his head firmly. He took the reply not as avoidance, but as a firm resolution from Royce's own lips.

"When all these weddings have been done," Boltof said with a smile, "we shall begin seeding an army on our mutual lands, and the whole of our family will know wealth and power. 'Twas a good day that our paths crossed, Royce. I will long be grateful."

Royce looked at Celeste, who smiled prettily and locked her arm within his. The two of them seemed certain that all their plans for betrothals, weddings, and future sons would be settled to their satisfaction. Royce earnestly wished he could feel as sure.

Chapter Three

THE BELLS TO EARLY-MORNING MASS COULD BE heard in the courtyard of the castle, and from the window of her chamber Félise could see Eleanor venture there, with her ladies following at a fair distance. Beyond, subtly but nevertheless apparent, were guards and knights that roamed freely and with watchful eyes. Their purpose was unquestionable. Eleanor was not trusted by her husband for a moment.

Richard, duke of Aquitaine, had long been known for his religious zeal and was likewise enroute to mass, accompanied by clergy wearing ornate and rich robes. From her high perch Félise marveled at his majesty. He was a tall and handsome man, his clothing rich and impeccable. One could see him at the head of a grand army, for he carried himself as if he would be at ease commanding.

Félise turned from the window to make her own way to chapel, her head covered and her beads and crucifix in her hand. By the time she reached the courtyard, most of those attending mass had already gone inside, and she was relieved that she would be kneeling at the rear of the chapel with the backs of these high-powered nobles to her and not their eyes. It had taken no time at all to notice that people stared at her.

It was the beginning of only her second day at Windsor; this eve she would be joined by her parents. The place did not hold the magic and intrigue she thought to find, and, in truth, her thoughts roved in confusion in her mind. With all those friends of her brothers and sons of her father's acquaintances, she had never been properly courted or asked for her hand. If a case had been brought to Lord Scelfton, he hadn't mentioned it. She found herself ill prepared for her mother's oath that marriage for her was urgent.

She judged the backs of the ladies, lords, and knights. Some older gentlemen were thin or slumped; some knights were broad-shouldered, some paunchy and thick. She knew naught of their holdings, possessions, skills, or habits. In truth, she could be given to some Welsh lord or a knight from the northern clans if her father judged his lot to be worthy and the king and queen found it favorable. And how could that be determined? Surely not by the same standards by which Félise would choose. Harlan would not consider the handsomeness of the man or the gentleness of his nature. Eleanor might be moved by his artful verse and not his honorable nature. Would Henry care more for a man strong of arms than for a man youthful enough to be a good father to sons?

My lady mother is more wise than I allowed, she thought forlornly. The droning Latin of the bishop faded from her ears. She recited the mass out of habit, not thinking about her prayers but occupied with other thoughts: I have watched my friends marry and given no thought to my own wedding. They have delivered their children while I have dallied with my stitchery or my mare, and in all this time, I have never considered the men who might ask for me. I play maiden's games with knights as if I were kept safe in some tower, far from being touched, yet before this week is out, some man will own me. Why have I slept through these years in which I might have at least looked and offered my parents some hint of my preference?

It was no fault of her family, for they had often mentioned her dowry, her prospects, and made some introductions. For herself, although she had taken pains with pleasing her mother as she was taught the management of a household, she had *played* at womanhood and measured herself by the rod that a child uses. She had ignored the fact that she would one day marry and bear a child, and now that day was upon her.

The hour passed slowly, Félise rising and falling to her knees, praying over her beads and keeping her head bowed. It was easier, somehow, to steal this time from mass for brooding than to find solace in her rooms, where Daria would question her. When the bishop was finished, she fled the chapel quickly. Her place near the rear made her flight easier, and she managed the whole mass without being spoken to by anyone.

The lady Vespera had been accurate when describing the gardens. They were well pruned, and the promise of beauty come spring was evident, despite the barren and brown landscape that Félise found. There were paths and benches, all leading to a central courtyard where people would gather for community. Félise walked lazily about the area, hardly looking at the planters, trees, or statues, but concentrating on her foolhardy dismissal of adult concerns. Finally, unresolved, she began her way back to her rooms.

The halls were cold and dank, giving promise to the thought of a blazing hearth. There was no merriment for her now, and she wished to be in the inn with her parents and brothers, or better still, home in the Twyford keep where the servants were her friends and the villeins her playmates. She swept her hood off her head and let it fall around her shoulders. As she walked down the long, dark corridor toward the back stairs to her rooms, she considered her good fortune in knowing the way, for this great palace was a maze of halls and galleries and rooms. She paused suddenly, listening.

"Aye, demoiselle, you are followed."

She turned abruptly and saw Sir Royce poised just a few paces behind her, leaning casually against the wall. He was free of his warring accoutrements now, wearing chausses and tunic in his colors of red and gold. On his left breast he wore his family blazon and on his finger a rich ruby in the crest.

Her eyes flashed in anger, though perhaps fear would have been more appropriate. "Why do you follow me, sir?"

He moved toward her at a leisurely pace and seemed unperturbed by her discomfort. "More out of curiosity than anything, maid Félise. I wondered at your roamings through the grounds and halls. Do you court danger, or has some lover failed to keep his apppointment?"

"I would bid no man keep an appointment alone with me," she quickly replied, aghast at his blatant accusation.

"Ah, the danger, then," he replied with a smile. He reached a finger toward her collar where her hair, shimmering golden in the torchlit hall, had collected and bunched, the bulk of it buried beneath her mantle. A deft finger pulled a long lock of it forward, and he tested its smoothness between his thumb and forefinger. Félise stood numbed by his familiarity, experiencing his action as if she were an observer rather than a participant. Finally realizing he did this freely without her protest, she snatched her hair away from him.

"I was told I was safe in Henry's house," she flung at him. "I trust I would not have been bidden to walk these halls freely had anyone known you were about."

His laughter, deep and low, sent a chill up her back, and the hairs at the base of her neck stood up. "Demoiselle, you have been crudely misinformed. Did Sir Wharton perhaps bid you roam?"

"Nay," she answered, growing more uncomfortable with his presence every moment.

"Good," Royce replied. "He would likely hide himself in some dark corner and pounce upon you. His treatment of women is not gentle, it is said."

Félise tried to summon courage and stood as erect as possible, but in her hands her beads trembled. " 'Tis you, sir knight, lurking in the dark hall ... and Sir Wharton warned me of *your* treatment of women."

Again the tall knight laughed, a soft and rather seductive rumbling. His teeth were bright in this dim space, and his hair seemed to be threaded with gold. The cool and distant brown eyes had warmed and darkened. He studied her face, his smile fading even as his eyes smouldered, and Félise could not decide whether it was fear she felt or a surge of desire.

Wharton was handsome, a thing she could not lay to Royce. His roughened looks were further marred by a scar across one brow and a nose bent twice in its arch. She wondered at his strange appeal, for his face suggested something rugged and dangerous. He seemed more barbarous than the average English knight, resembling her idea of a Viking or German warrior. His build was generous, the strength in his shoulders and upper arms frightening, and in his smile there was a hint of devilish glee, and her knees began to weaken.

"Wharton knows nothing of my treatment of women," he said softly. "I treat very few."

Félise's eyes widened at the crude remark, yet in her only experience with the man, this was typical. He played no courtly games, did not give her compliments where they might find a willing target, and his only verbal expressions were tinged with vulgarity. Her mouth moved well ahead of her mind. "You are not chivalrous, but roguish when you speak."

"And you would have charm, my lady?" he asked, his eyes swiftly sweeping her well-covered form, amusement marking his features. "Wharton does cosset the maids well. I admit, I am not skilled in this, yet I know my mind. I know what I want. And I know how to give back full score what I am given."

"Charm would yield more than rude remarks," she returned easily. "Why are you curious of me? Do you feel anger, still, from my foolery with your knights?"

"Nay." He shrugged. "The men enjoy the harlot's game from time to time."

"Jesu, you spare no dignity with your insults, sir. I but entered the chase from safe distance."

" 'Tis your great inheritance and the bait you set for suitors that draw my interest, Lady Félise. How many have spoken without benefit of an introduction?"

"I know nothing of what —"

"The trap of your land in France, your dower purse in England . . . the prize of your great wealth has spread amongst the circles of men with debts to pay. How will you choose? More important, who will approve your choice? Is it the king?"

"Sir Royce, I fear you are mistaken," she attempted, shaken by his remarks.

"How can I be? This I have heard from many sources, that

you are here by royal command and your purpose is to achieve a marriage to make the king a good political alliance."

"Nay," she said, shaking her head. "Lest you fall victim to wagging tongues, 'tis a simple misunderstanding. My mother, close to the queen before Eleanor's removal to Old Sarum Castle, leaves a modest dowry of lands that have been managed by a castellan in France. The dowry my father provides is likewise modest. It comes to not more than is adequate, neither plot being large enough to make much matter or yield much revenue. I am here only for a brace of days to enjoy the court because of this old friendship." Félise knew that he would not discern the difference between the natural mother she could not remember and Lady Edrea. They could be one and the same, from her telling.

"This is a hoax?" he asked, frowning.

"I think that the story, while truthful enough, has grown large in the minds of ambitious men. As to choice, I trust my father will judge my betrothed, not the king."

She turned sharply then, intending to flee from his presence, but he snatched her arm and drew her back to him.

"Don't fly, *chérie*," he said, holding her much too closely. She looked up into his eyes, first frightened by his strength and nearness and also confused by his strange pursuit. He seemed to scorn her, as if she were the last woman on earth he would be bothered with, yet he had followed her and now held her so that she could not move.

"You hurt me," she attempted softly, but in his eyes she could see he did not hear. He looked at her in a strange, besotted way, perhaps not seeing her at all. She was frozen by the hypnotic stare, her legs growing weak and her heart beginning to beat frantically. Above their heads a torch flickered in a draft common to the dark passageways, but neither noticed. Nor did any sudden breeze lessen the unusual heat that Félise felt flood through her. His head slowly bent as his eyes gradually closed and she felt his breath trespass warmly upon her startled mouth, and then the touch of his flesh, soft and delicate, brushed her lips.

The hold on her arms slackened and all sense of time and space was gone. Her beads dropped from her hand, and she found herself held firmly against his hard, muscular chest, with no memory of how or when she had moved. And as though entranced, her own arms rose to embrace his shoulders. His mouth demanded more than a mere caress and moved over her lips in search of a greater passion. She felt the power of his kiss part her lips, and a surging warmth roamed deep in the softness of her mouth.

Félise was lost. She searched her memory for some experience of a lover's kiss and found none. She tried in vain to recall a dream in which she could summon no will to resist. There was nothing in all her life to prepare her for this man's touch or the feelings that possessed her when his lips commanded hers. A river of emotion — weakness, fear, elation, response — assailed her from every facet of her being. She was warm to flushing, then chilled through her bones. She began to tremble and a small whimper of despair left her, for she was in no measure in control of her own mind or body.

He released her mouth and a hungry feeling enveloped her, though she could in no way say what she craved. While he looked into her eyes with glowing desire, she had only a startled expression for him, failing to understand any of what had just passed between them.

He suddenly stiffened, and though he held her possessively, he turned and looked behind him, around the dark gallery. His eyes narrowed and he frowned. As she looked up at him she was reminded of a cat that, sensing trouble, sharpens all its senses. "What is it?" she whispered.

He looked back at her. "I felt someone watch, but there is no one." The spell was broken. His embrace slackened and his voice was low and mocking when he spoke, his expression changed and completely unreadable. "No matter what you were told, maiden, you would be safer alone in the wood than in these halls. Bolt your door and venture beyond with only the greatest of care."

He took her arm and, turning her, led her through the hall toward the back stairs and her rooms. He required no direction to lead her, making it clear he had known where she was housed. When she was before her bower door, he turned abruptly, presenting his back almost angrily, and left her to stare at his departure in confusion. She had the vaguest feeling she had been violated quite beyond all propriety, yet the hunger persisted and she fought herself from calling him back.

Within moments he had vanished, and she simply sought the solace of her chamber, entering and throwing the bolt behind her. Daria rose from her chair beside the fire where she sat mending and stopped short when she saw the expression on Félise's face.

Sir Royce had left no mark and she was not in any way disheveled. But for a stray lock of hair that fell over her breast and curled beneath her waist, she looked as she had when she left her rooms for mass. Yet in her moist eyes there was a startled knowledge, and on her parted lips, brightened from the power of his kiss, there was the shock of awareness of something wonderfully fearful. She was as speechless as she was breathless and could barely recognize Daria, though she looked fully at her.

"Holy Mother of God," Félise whispered, her voice inaudible as her lips moved over the words that were both exclamation and prayer. Daria took two steps toward her and her world suddenly seemed to come crashing down around her. Her breath caught in her throat in a jagged sob. Tears wet her eyes and flowed down her cheeks, and her hands began to tremble. "Daria," she sobbed, alarmingly overrun by emotion. "I . . . I . . . lost my prayer beads . . ."

A squire delivered Félise again to the dining hall, but this time she was greeted affectionately by Lady Edrea. Lord Scelfton likewise kissed his daughter's cheeks, but his mood was no lighter than it had been the evening before she left his care.

"I'm so very glad you're with me," she told her mother more than once, clinging possessively to Lady Edrea's hand. She was still aware of the looks that were cast her way, but during her meal she conversed only with her parents and those who shared their table. The others were thankfully either women well beyond her in years or already married. No potential suitors shared their table.

Lord Scelfton greeted one dinner companion with special fondness. An aging baron, a man of perhaps sixty years and deformed from some old warring injury, approached them and bowed, giving his name as Aswin, Lord Orrick. Harlan came forward of his wife and daughter and took his hand in friendship, startling the man with recognition. They then embraced each other in reunion.

Aswin dragged one leg when he walked, and when seated it remained straight and stiff. In addition, one of his arms was held tightly at his side, the fingers bent and gnarled and appearing useless. It seemed his entire left side was crippled.

Edrea made his acquaintance warmly, for she was never a woman to be put off by an affliction. Félise was somewhat withdrawn at first, but as the evening progressed and she listened to her father and Aswin laughingly exchange tales of old knights long since retired from battle, she found Aswin amusing, warm, and delightful company.

"Aye, Harlan, so long ago we rode upon the Welsh. I fail to remember it as clearly as you do. In my memory, we were sadly overtaken by barbarous lords and fled spears and arrows lest we have our faces shaved without our request." Aswin laughed good-naturedly. "In your recollection, 'twas quite the other way — we were heroes of the day. Forsooth, I drink to *your* memory."

Through the laughter, Harlan exclaimed, " 'Twas your head that took a rock hurled by one of those bastards, and you could not count your fingers for a fortnight."

They drank and toasted each remembered tale, laughing at both victory and folly. It was a long time before their attentions included the ladies. "Edrea," Aswin confided, "I would have you know he spoke of you when we were on the campaign together, for long before your wedding he labored poorly when you were apart. I wearied with this besotted groom's musings, but now that we've finally met, I see the reason for his trials."

"He said you had a smooth tongue, my lord," Edrea laughed lightly. "And it is a practiced verse you sing."

"Ah, you do me wrong. I have long since given up singing of

love and the verse is gone from my heart. I am widowed," he said, slamming his fist on the table. "Would Harlan approve me as a husband for your young goddess?"

Félise knew they spoke in jest, and she found herself laughing, enjoying her father's outrageous behavior. It was not often that Harlan acted in so frivolous and jolly a manner.

"You old bull," Harlan scoffed at Aswin. "I know your surly ways and wouldn't let you near any woman of my household."

"Let us hear from the lady," Aswin demanded.

Félise inclined her head. "You make me swoon with your quicksilver voice, my lord, but I am a poor lass without my father's blessing."

Aswin leaned his face closer to Félise. "Then let us flee him, damsel, and take ourselves away from his brutish wit."

He made a play as if he would rise, but the leg was stiff and uncooperative and he dropped himself back to his bench, much to the amusement of his dinner companions. " 'Tis useless, maid. I am too late to chase the wenches and must ever endure my loneliness with the company of my horses." He clicked his tongue, raised one eyebrow, and, smiling, lowered his voice as if he were imparting a secret. "I have taught them to come when I whistle."

"Oh-ho," Harlan shouted. " 'Twould take you a year of new moons to have this maid answer your whistle. She is disinclined to answer any command."

"How did you gain your injury, my lord?" Eldrea politely inquired. "I think I did not hear my lord mention the circumstances."

" 'Twas for the most part a foolish accident, lady, a result of foolery amongst the men I rode with years ago. We were bored on our campaign in the south and, on the excuse of practicing arms, began a jesting tournament. There was much of jesting," he said as he shrugged. "For myself, I was commonly the one responsible for pranks and tricks, but this once the trick was on me. Someone loosed the saddle straps and I might have only fallen and bruised my pride, but my horse was frightened and ran out of control, dumping me on sharp rocks. The clumsy mule took his rest atop me. My hip, knee, shoulder, and head were smashed."

"I'm so grieved to hear it, my lord. And there is no improvement?"

"Nay, but that my disposition is improved. Lady Dulcine was responsible for that. My fellows left me on her stoop, and she a recent widow. They returned to the king, while the good woman nursed me for over a year. When I finally gained enough health to ride — and it took months to relearn that once well-honed skill — I returned to King Henry, only to find that my troop had not imparted my injury, but spun a tale of my courtship of the widow." He laughed lightly. "There seemed naught to do but return and in truth court Dulcine. She proved a tolerable woman . . . and there was naught to keep me from her."

Edrea smiled at the romantic tale. "Then I would say you gained from your woes . . . in good measure."

The baron's eyes grew somewhat wistful and he seemed focused for a moment on Félise, contemplating her rare beauty. "I gained in some measure," he murmured. "But I lost treasures untold." He shook himself and forced a lighter mood. "I will not make my injury greater in my mind. Yea, I have gained through my trials. When I hear some ungrateful young whelp moan at his light purse or rugged campaign, I set his attitude right with a simple story to show him his good fortune. I find I have more joy in my life even with my lameness than many a cocky young swain finds in perfect health."

"I know nothing of your lameness," Harlan professed. "It happens your wit was not bruised. You lay me low even now with your tongue."

"I but remind you of true events," Aswin argued happily. "Someone must, when you are wont to spin tales of glory." He nodded once. "Tell me of this young woman's plight. Why is she yet unmarried?"

"That will be taken care of with haste," Harlan informed him. "An old family demesne in Aquitaine dangles before the eyes of these roving studs, and I have gifted her dower lands in England. Henry presses for her company at court to appease some whim of Eleanor's, and already the young men pant at my doorstep begging an introduction." He shrugged. " 'Tis just a matter of days before we settle on a husband for her."

Aswin whistled low. "So it is she," he said knowingly. "You are right, Harlan, the word is well out. Even my son speaks of her."

"Your son?" Harlan asked, suddenly interested. Even Félise's ears perked up, for she genuinely liked this gentleman. "I wasn't aware —"

"My stepson, if you please. Dulcine gave over to my care her two children, Boltof, a knight of Henry, and Celeste. You might do well to consider Boltof, my lord. He is strong and able."

"And I will," Harlan said, happier about his daughter's situation than he had been since it all began. " 'Twould balm my hurts to have a man who is closer to the family than those strangers seeking riches alone. I would rest easier, finding someone I could trust."

"The tale is that the king will influence your choice of husband," Aswin remarked.

"He will influence us away from alliances with the duke." Harlan shrugged. "How can I blame him for that? Has he not already battled with his wife and his own sons to keep his crown? And with all the trouble in their family, those Englishmen who would not give Richard aid are not easy to discover. Henry has but a few he can trust. Those knights of Henry who sympathize with the duke are cautious."

"Where are the fathers and sons who serve each other's purpose?" Aswin mused. Then his attention was drawn away to a young man standing alongside their table. He returned his amused gaze to Harlan, murmuring, "A young stag in rut seeks a kindness from us."

Harlan returned the smile knowingly and rose, Aswin rising with more difficulty. The young man approached with a gleeful light in his eyes. He bowed before the elder lords and ladies.

"I would present my son, Sir Boltof," Aswin said. "Lord Scelfton and Lady Edrea." Then he sighed heavily. "The woman whose acquaintance you have anticipated, Lady Félise."

Boltof postured over her hand for a long moment, seemingly finding the proper words difficult. Aswin finally urged the younger man onto the bench that he might be eased by conversation. Félise looked at him with a puzzled frown. She thought she had seen him before, but he was difficult to place.

"Have we been introduced before, sir?" she asked.

"Nay, lady, I would have remembered."

"But your face is familiar to me."

"I have watched you from afar, in this very hall."

"That must be when I saw you," she said, but she was unsure, for many stared at her but she was usually unable to meet their eyes.

Boltof made every attempt at impressing her, telling her about his many travels, the home he shared with Aswin, his prowess in battle, and his frequency at court. Félise was entertained, but more so by Aswin. And since her encounter earlier in the day with Sir Royce, she had been feeling even more strange about this entire marriage problem.

" 'Twas in Anjou with Royce that I . . ."

"Royce," she breathed unconsciously, startled by the mention of his name. "You ride with Royce?"

Boltof stiffened slightly. "He is a good friend, but we each command our own arms, madam. I am not a vassal of his."

"Nay, I did not mean . . . that is, I have twice met this Sir Royce and I may have seen you with him." She immediately flushed, thinking Boltof might have been in Royce's company the afternoon she had so brazenly leaned out of her window and toyed with the knights. "But then, perhaps not . . ."

"I couldn't say when, lady, but I've been about these last two days, and mayhap we passed in the courtyard or halls."

"I suppose we have . . ."

"So you've made the acquaintance of my future son, Sir Royce," Aswin broke in, leaving Félise startled once again. "Aye, the lad will wed my Celeste early in the new year. Harlan, you know Sir Royce Leighton, do you not?"

"Nay," he frowned. "The name —"

"For his father, long dead. He is the son and namesake of

Royce Leighton of Segeland. You would remember. The old Leighton had a dreary reputation."

Harlan frowned. "There is sour talk of Segeland —"

"Babble," Aswin blustered. "Royce is as fine a man as I've ever known. But truth, many men prefer rumors, especially those of the darkest nature, to knowing the real man. I will vouch for Royce. He is an honorable man and a fine knight."

"His family was none too fine. There were many ill-concealed battles," Harlan continued.

"Years ago," Aswin allowed. "But all that is buried, for Royce is the only one left. Aye, there were family battles that rival the king's own, but they are laid away with Royce in possession of Segeland Castle and the town. He has courted Celeste for many years, and 'tis my hope the wedding will be soon — before she is past childbearing. His work for Henry has left Segeland to crumbling, for he spends little of his time there. Indeed," Aswin laughed, "I can't doubt the lad's intentions for Celeste, he is more in my home than his."

Félise began to feel warm and flushed listening to this talk. She observed the narrowing of her father's eyes when Royce's family was discussed. Yet, Lord Orrick defended him, perhaps because of Royce's claim on his daughter or his friendship with Aswin's son. But it was always the same: no one laid criminal charges to him, but there was some strange suspicion surrounding him. And other peculiar feelings arose in her upon hearing of his betrothal. Would a man soon to be wed kiss another woman with such passion? A chill possessed her suddenly and she trembled.

Félise leaned close to her mother. "Madam, will you be allowed to visit me in my chamber?"

Edrea frowned slightly. "I think I would not be forbidden. Are you ill?"

"Nay, but I am weary and would go there for quiet. Madam, will you come?"

Edrea studied her daughter closely, failing to find the reason for her sudden withdrawal. Then she turned to her husband and whispered to him. He gave a nod and Edrea stood, drawing her daughter up with her. "I beg your indulgence, my lords, but I would see to my daughter's retiring. Good eventide."

"Good eventide, madam," Aswin quickly replied. "I look forward to our next meeting."

When Edrea had drawn Félise well away from the hall and into the seclusion of the stairs, she took Félise's hand in hers as they walked. "What troubles you, dear heart?"

" 'Tis naught, madam. I am weary."

"Nay, you of all can endure a long day. That is not the problem."

"It is this hellish business of marriage," Félise boldly exclaimed, forgetting herself completely. "Beg pardon, madam, but this odd dowry prize frightens me. There is not a man at court who hasn't heard of some lands in Richard's Aquitaine and lands in my father's demesne. Those knaves who would not have plied me with a kind word would today cloak me in silver for my merest smile. I don't know what to do."

Edrea smiled tolerantly as they walked. "You might enjoy it," she replied.

"But madam, the courtly gentleman of the day might be a beast of the morrow, once my dowry is promised."

"I think not, Félise. You can judge a man's character better than that. And I beg you remember: this is the first time you have been in the company of so many men. You were too protected in your father's house."

"Mother, I want to go home," she said, a small whimpering sound coming from her.

Edrea halted and turned her daughter to face her. "Félise, have done with this childish display. You are a woman now and your time has come. I cannot take you home, nor can your father. If you are frightened, pray for courage; if you are confused, pray for sight. If you find all of this unpleasant, think on this: your father and I can protect you for only a short time longer. After you are given in marriage, you must rely on your husband for protection and guidance or, lacking that, upon yourself. You must find some strength within yourself. You might ask it of God."

"Oh, madam, do not berate me," she pleaded. "I would not have you ashamed of me, 'tis only that I can't abide these fears I have. I have no strength at all. And how am I to expect any help from God?"

Edrea looked at the glowing beauty before her, remembering with some pain that she had contributed nothing to the lass's fairness. She reached out a hand and stroked the child's soft cheek. She couldn't even be in the company of Félise without thinking on the strange luck the girl had enjoyed all her life — from ward of the queen to daughter in a loving family to a sought-after bride. Any other orphaned girl-child might have been left to starve alone, yet this one grew up in riches and grace. This dowry, however burdensome at this moment, was yet another incredible piece of good fortune. There was no doubt every man who saw her would have asked after her even without the dowry, but this only served to bring the strongest and most noble to the forefront of her consideration.

Edrea worried only slightly about who might be thrust on Félise and thereby forced into their family. It was indeed possible that many adjustments for all of them lay in the future. But a few things were certain if a man were approved by either King Henry or Lord Scelfton: the man would be strong and well fixed in his own right; he would be loyal to the crown; he must be youthful enough to protect his bride from those who would usurp him. Edrea was certain that one day this would all seem a blessed predicament.

"I should think you would be confident of God's help," she murmured. "He has surely seen to you all these years."

Edrea entered Félise's chamber with her and Félise sat down before her dressing table. Daria rose to the task of taking down her mistress's hair and unfastening her gown while Edrea stood behind her and watched. As Daria intently focused her attention on the long, wound braid, Félise stretched a trembling hand toward her table. She fingered her prayer beads weakly.

"Daria? You found my beads?" she asked hopefully.

Daria gave an uninterested glance toward the beads. "Nay, mum. But they're found. You might've left them right there all the time."

Félise knew better. "You were here, in this chamber, all the day?"

"An' where would I go?" the maid complained. "Aye, I've been nowhere else."

"Who was here while I was gone?"

Daria sighed impatiently. "No one. Nary a soul. An' I could've used someone to talk with. These castle servants think themselves too important to bother with us country folk."

"But someone was here," Félise insisted, her stomach tightening as she had a mental picture of Sir Royce sneaking into her rooms. "Someone returned my prayer beads."

Edrea stepped closer and began to unfasten the back of Félise's gown, although she was getting in Daria's way. "You are more distracted than I've ever seen you, Félise. Surely you forgot them and they were here all along."

"Nay, Mother. I lost them in the gallery and —"

"Come, darling. Let's get you to bed. You've let this visit to Windsor cause you unnatural worry. Forget the beads and have a good rest."

Félise looked behind her, first at Daria, who was grimacing in impatience, and then at Edrea, who wore a worried frown. "Aye, madam. I will go to bed," she finally said.

Chapter Four

THE QUEEN'S TIRE-WOMAN, VESPERA, VISITED FÉ-
lise's chamber every afternoon on brief errands. She
brought herbs for the wine on one occasion, combs
from Her Majesty on another, and a gift of oils for the bath on
yet another. Félise found herself looking forward to the short
conversations, for Vespera's gentleness and comforting tones put
her at ease. Yet this woman was never in evidence when there
were many people around.

Four days had been spent at Windsor. Félise found herself approached by many men, but Sir Boltof and Sir Wharton were the
two most determined. On an afternoon when she relented and
allowed Vespera to comb her hair, she spoke of them.

"Sir Wharton is handsome and the wealth he boasts is great,"
she said blandly. "Sir Boltof is eager and not as rich, I think, but
I have made the acquaintance of his father and he is much to my
liking."

"And of the men themselves, my lady," Vespera softly inquired. "Who wins your preference?"

Félise sighed. "It matters very little," she murmured.

Vespera laughed softly. "Surely one has found a place within
your heart."

"Nay, there is no one," she said, her voice drawing out. "Sir
Boltof, I suppose. It would please my father."

"Your happiness will please Lord Scelfton, maid Félise," Ves-

· 56 ·

pera whispered, drawing the comb through the long tresses, admiring the shining silkiness.

"Lord Scelfton and Lord Orrick were friends in years gone by and have only recently renewed their friendship. Indeed, Lord Orrick is a fine man, a joy to be near. His son would please me for that reason. I would not be so lonely away from my parents."

Vespera's hand froze. Her eyes, usually so composed, betrayed sudden emotion.

"Lord Orrick," Vespera breathed.

"Aye, do you know of him?"

Gradually Vespera began to move the comb again. "He has a young son?" she asked.

"Sir Boltof," Félise said absently. "He is a civil host whene'er we meet, and his future is as promising as any knight of Henry, I suppose. But it is the old lord I find pleasureable. Yea, I would not be so grieved to marry close to a family my father approves. At least I am assured Sir Boltof would not keep me from my mother, but would relish the visiting."

Félise drew her gown up to her knees and picked at the hem, judging the fraying it had suffered. She had not noticed that Vespera's hand began to move the comb in nervous jerks. Félise dropped the hem and sat erect, sighing. "We would have many children, I suppose, and they would enjoy two very fine grandfathers."

The comb clattered to the floor. Félise turned to look at Vespera, whose countenance was completely discomposed. "I beg-pardon, my lady, I . . . I did not mean to . . ." She stopped suddenly, retrieving the comb. "I beg pardon," she said again, bobbing in a fluttering way.

" 'Tis only a comb," Félise replied, taking it from Vespera.

"Milady," the woman said. "You will speak for this Sir Boltof?"

Félise turned away from the maid again, looking at nothing in particular. "If I say naught, Lord Scelfton will choose for me. There are at least some things I know about Boltof." She shrugged. "Left alone, Lord Scelfton may choose him out of fondness for his father. My brother, Maelwine, may be moved to speak for Wharton; Wharton tells me they are old friends. It will be one of them, I suppose. My father promises there will be an answer before I leave Windsor three days hence."

"And this Wharton —"

"Sir Wharton," Félise remembered aloud. "There is nothing lacking in handsomeness, but he makes me ill at ease on some accounts."

"How so, lady?" she asked.

Félise wore a puzzled frown. "He is courteous and good-natured," she said. "Too much so, I think. 'Tis not a hardship to have a handsome knight boast of my beauty. But ofttimes he is a braggart, speaking out of turn about his strength and family wealth. And when he speaks of my family and the dower purse I hold, his eyes gleam with envy." She sighed heavily. "Forsooth, I trust Wharton would wed my mare if she held my purse. He plays so mightily for attention, when I've not granted him the merest kiss, that I must believe my dowry is more important to him than any other thing I possess. It does not bode well of love between us." She sighed pensively. "I do not loathe him, please understand. I have the feeling he lies to me."

Félise turned to look at Vespera and noticed that the woman stood idly gazing off into space, seemingly entranced. She thought perhaps none of her words regarding Wharton was heard and Vespera had only asked about him out of politeness.

Vespera turned suddenly and walked toward the door. Reaching that portal, she looked back at Félise. "Excuse me, my lady, but I must be about my other duties."

"You've only just arrived," Félise protested.

"Her Majesty asked me to see to your comfort, but she will miss me if I'm away too long. Pardon."

"Will you come back?" she asked, realizing she not only enjoyed the company of this woman, but was lonely in the long hours awaiting the next meal.

Vespera smiled and nodded, quickly leaving the room.

Félise had nothing to occupy her when her presence was not desired in the chambers of the queen or in the hall. After her unexpected meeting with Sir Royce, she had given up any idea of walking about the castle or grounds and took Daria with her to morning mass, much to the maid's dislike. Now she roamed around her room, thinking the same thoughts that had occupied her for several days: choosing the most appealing groom.

When she paused beside the window and looked below, her confusion mounted. She could see the walkway to the chapel; Vespera paced before the doors, her motions greatly agitated. This quiet woman usually moved with the self-effacement of nuns, her hands gently folded, head slightly bent, and steps short and small. But as she moved before the chapel doors, she took wide, eager steps, hands fluttering before her and head up. Félise found not only her behavior odd, but also the fact that she would excuse herself on the queen's business and go elsewhere.

Within a few moments a priest came out of the church and Vespera genuflected before him, crossing herself. She rose quickly and seemed to be speaking rapidly, something else Félise had never seen her do. Félise remembered that she had never seen Vespera at mass with the others and wondered why this woman who by her admission lived among nuns did not rise for the morning communion. Then the priest and Vespera slowly walked together into the chapel, and once they were out of sight, Félise only wondered for another moment at the unusual events before her mind was taken with other things — the style of gown she would wear that eve and the arrangement of her hair.

Royce made his way from his lodgings to Windsor with measured slowness. He stopped to purchase a gift from a merchant for Celeste, selecting some scented soaps that he thought would please her. He carried the parcel as he rode and at one point raised it to his nose. The rose, lilac, and lily scents combined to produce an odd floral bouquet, and his thoughts were bent not on Celeste, but on a maid with lively eyes the color of the sea meeting the sky and golden hair streaked with fire. As he lowered the soaps, he found that he had ridden past her family's place of residence and was looking at the very window from which he had first viewed her.

He looked at that window as if she once again leaned out, her hair streaming down well below the sill and her hands clapping in glee as she laughed with the knights. He frowned sullenly, for he was well aware of what had happened to him.

Celeste should not be criticized for her plain looks. She was a gentle lady. And she appeared to remain as true and steadfast as any wife should be. Over several years, while he plied his attentions on her, she had ignored his sad reputation and that of his family, never questioned him about his occupation or travels, and waited eagerly for each of his visits. She mourned his departure and, as far as he knew, had kept herself from other men since the first time his lips had touched hers. He had no reason to doubt that she was an honorable woman.

But this Félise had pounced upon London in all her tempestuous beauty and hexed him twice, for he had tasted those sweet lips and felt her body next to his. For all Celeste's attributes, he could not put the temptress from his mind. To his further insult, she was handsomely endowed and sought after by Boltof.

It was to this end he was driven, for after many days of watching the young swains trample each other for just a look at her, she was due to depart the court with her family, and Royce would be forced to speak to the king on behalf of his friend. The chore in itself was distasteful. In his many dealings with Henry he had asked no favor. He found the monarch more generous than he ever expected, for Henry relied much on him, and he hated to taint their relationship with solicitation.

And Henry might willingly oblige him. He could not bear to meet Félise on every occasion he was near Lord Orrick's home. He wondered how he would again enjoy the warm affections of Celeste, when every fiber of his being cried out to be satisfied by Félise. He was obsessed by want of her, and for that he felt a surge of anger. No woman had lingered long in his mind, not even the one he was to marry.

There was good reason that Royce ignored women and in the main found Celeste the only one worthy of marriage. There had been a long legacy of family conflict and affliction behind him. His father had battled with his uncle; his brother had fought their father and himself. His own mother was another man's wife, stolen by his father and held prisoner at Segeland. She had hated the very sight of Royce and claimed the rose-colored blemish that had marked his back since birth was the touch of the devil, a reminder of his father's misdeed.

Royce, the youngest of three boys, had left his father's home when he was twelve to live with his grandfather. His mother was likely driven insane by her captivity. His father had kept more than one mistress, and his two elder brothers had died under mysterious circumstances. The Leighton family had long warred with every relative and neighbor within range of their army. For many years no member of the Leighton family had been entirely trusted.

Royce had decided early in his life that he would never bequeath the ills of his ancestors and Segeland. When the time for marrying to satisfy custom was upon him, Celeste was close at hand. This woman, plain and demure, cost him neither sleep nor conflict of emotion. And, brutish as it was, he had lain with her already on several occasions and she had not come with child. There was hope she was barren. While Celeste worried with disappointing him, he was tremendously relieved by the prospect of begetting no heirs. He would be pleased to have Boltof's children inherit Segeland and so put an end to the gruesome history it had so far possessed.

The only man ever to trust him without question was Henry. He had served as the king's vassal and knight for years numbering over a dozen and the two men were loyal to each other. With the dwindling of his family and the lengthening of his service to the crown, Royce had gathered more credibility with a few fellows, among them Lord Orrick and Boltof.

When he had felt that sense of family within Lord Orrick's house he had coveted it, and now within months he would be part of that household. It chafed him and frightened him to think of the conflict that would arise if Félise, too, were part of that family. It was like the repeat of the nightmare surrounding his own birth, and he feared the legacy of his family trials rising anew, beginning with the desire he had for a woman who did not belong to him.

When he asked for a portion of Henry's time, he was immediately obliged, as he knew he would be. Henry would see him at his convenience. His horse was taken at the gate and he was directed to the king's bedchamber. Henry further complimented their friendship by being completely at his leisure. By the looks of the room, the king had just finished a midday repast and reclined in simple chausses and tunic, drinking from a goblet of wine.

Royce bowed to his king, but Henry scoffed at the formality. "Sit, Royce, and take up a cup. Get your business done and we can tell our usual lies." He guffawed at his own wit, pointing to the chair near him. "Bring this man drink," he shouted to a page.

Royce sat, feeling the heavy weight of this burden and resenting the chore ahead. He broached the subject quickly, not waiting for his libation. "I have requested audience, Sire, to discuss the marriage of a maid in your court, Lady Félise Scelfton."

Henry's eyebrows were raised instantly, his mouth formed a round O, and he leaned forward in his chair. "I could not have hoped for so much, Royce. Speak."

"It appears her dower lands would serve you well, and since she is a comely maid, she and her future husband must be matched with caution and consideration."

Henry sat back, smiling. "I have taken many liberties with her family for that reason. With lands in France, I must supervise her hand. You would understand, Royce."

"Of a certain, my liege. Her family does not resist your authority over her marriage?"

"Harlan Scelfton does not like my interference, but if in the end I can please myself, his lordship, the lady, and a man of my bidding, I will have done a good piece of work. At this moment, I see the prospects for that well upon me. Go on, Royce, speak your piece."

"Sir Boltof is of strong arms and good family. He is my friend and seeks the hand of Lady Félise. I would approve the match and seek your approval, Sire."

Henry's jovial expression fled and his eyes darkened. "Boltof?" he questioned. He shrugged. "I find no fault with the man, but he is not the one who comes to mind."

"Another bidding for her hand is Wharton. He is strong, true, but ambitious to a fault. He is the second son of a strong lord and his inheritance is weak. I worry that he would go with Philip or Richard or any promise of power and wealth. I think it would be a mistake to aid him in any way."

"Yet I would put Wharton above Boltof," the king replied.

"Sire?" Royce questioned.

"Wharton at least does me the honor of coming on his own behalf. Boltof sends you."

Royce lowered his eyes. "Sir Boltof believes I have some special influence with you, Your Majesty. I warned him that it grew larger in his head."

Henry leaned near. "He senses our alliance true, and knowing your way among men, you have not boasted. Indeed, you could triple your wealth by building on your royal friendship. Even my son the duke, God save him, sees in you a promising ally for his future demesne, for your loyalty cannot be bought. You will aid the crown and abide by a royal order to your death. But if Boltof wanted to earn the same trust, he would come on his own. What of you, Royce?"

Royce shrugged, finding it difficult to look at Henry. "I did not want to do this, but better Boltof than Wharton."

"Do we do Wharton wrong?" Henry asked. "There was talk of a friendship between Wharton and your brother, and later a battle that ended Sir Aylworth Leighton's life." Henry eyed Royce's deepening scowl with great interest. "It left Segeland to you."

"It is only talk, Sire."

"But you distrust Wharton . . ."

"I distrusted all members of my own family. Are you aware that I was raised to my knighthood by my grandfather? Aye, and there was bad blood between my parents and me. I had barely come to know Aylworth when he died. He was ten years my senior and held Segeland, and I am told he did little better than my father with the land. It is a fact that I did not want it. Even now, it would pain me little to have it gone."

"Sir Wharton was his companion," the king went on.

"For a brief space of time we at least had a common goal, for I met Aylworth and Wharton on a Welsh campaign years ago. Boltof rode with me, Wharton with my brother. In the end, having quelled the uprising, there was booty from the hall and town. Wharton and Aylworth argued over their shares, each accusing the other." He shrugged and looked away. "I cannot defend either knight. They were both greedy and neither seemed above theft . . . or other crimes. But Aylworth was killed . . . while he slept."

"And you suspect Wharton?"

"I knew no other with a stake in what Aylworth held. Yet I stood accused as well. It was bandied about that I rose to Segeland with his death. By what noble gesture might I prove that a lie? I did not love my brother, but neither did I want the land.

"But this I will say, Sire. Boltof defended me, and for his loyalty I owe him. Whether we agree on this matter or not, I have no reason to trust Wharton and every reason to consider Boltof a trustworthy knight."

"Do you and Wharton quarrel still?" Henry asked, raising a dubious brow and perring closely at Royce.

"Nay, Sire. The matter was buried with Aylworth more than four years ago. Sir Wharton and I do not speak or share a cup. But neither do we war. Truly, I would not close my eyes if Wharton were near."

"It is possible you and Wharton do each other wrong. You say you were all on the campaign together?" Royce nodded. "And for a time you were friends?"

"I could not admit to a fondness, Sire. I had only just encountered my brother, for the first time since leaving Segeland. I did not consider that I could become his friend and vassal. I was prepared to go on my way after the campaign, as was he."

"I know Wharton's family and the man, and have not thought more ill of him than you. But I will say no more on that. Mayhap the two of you will one day settle the matter." He was quiet a moment more, pondering this old feud. Then he proceeded with the matter at hand. "Royce, tell me how you view the Lady Félise. Do you find her a worthy bride?"

"What needs be considered, Sire? She is comely and rich. She needs to have a husband loyal to the crown and a good manager of lands. His arms must be strong and his loyalty firm. Many would meet the requirements."

"You speak naught of her allure," Henry said coyly.

"There is no need. Those who desire the lady number from each page besotted by her fairness to doddering old lords in want of enough money to pay their debts. Who would know to which of her attributes they were drawn? Beauty or wealth or your pleasure? Methinks if you have the authority, you would do well to choose a knight or lord close to your own interests."

Henry sat back in his chair and took a long pull on his wine. The page approached with a cup for Sir Royce and he drank of it leisurely, counting his business done. He forced future problems from his mind, believing he had paid loyalty to both Boltof and Henry. For Henry, Boltof was not a bad choice. For the latter, the request had been made. He did not look at his king to see if he had struck fertile ground with his words.

"You are right, Royce. I must approve a noble I trust, one who can bear my scrutiny. Your friend will be disappointed in your influence with me. I cannot approve Sir Boltof."

"But Sire, I —"

"It is you I would have marry the demoiselle."

Royce's eyes rounded in shock, his back straightened almost as if he would defend himself. "I? Sire, I —"

Henry frowned but said nothing, and Royce stopped his argument instantly.

"Why, Your Majesty?" he said.

"For the very reasons you have named. You are loyal and strong of arms, and the woman is a gift of beauty and wealth. I thought you would be pleased."

"Sire, I am bidden to Lady Celeste, stepdaughter of Lord Orrick and Boltof's sister."

"Scelfton's daughter will serve you better. If Lady Celeste is desirable, it will not be long before another is found to replace you."

"Her family, Sire," Royce said, each word drawing pain. "Lord Orrick trusts me to make right my affections for his daughter. Boltof seeks brotherhood with me. And further, Lord Scelfton would more readily approve any other — we've had no dealings, yet Lord Scelfton's sons were in the past set upon by my brother. I beg pardon, Sire, but you would do ill with this choice. It would please no one."

"Nay, Royce, it is by far the best choice. But 'twill be a burdensome one for a time. And what I have to say on the matter will make it more so. I have told Lord Scelfton that I have a preference for Félise's hand and I will give him the news just before he is due to take her home. This I will do; I will name you."

Royce felt his chest tighten. "Sire, Lord Scelfton will be displeased. He approves Boltof."

"In the past I have ignored the rumblings that shook the very earth on which I stood, only to regret my patience." The king paused. "This time the marriage will be done and consummated before I name you to Scelfton. I will do you one service: I will tell my lord of Twyford that you wed his daughter by my order. It will not lessen his anger, but neither will he attack or reprove you."

"Surely the woman can return to Twyford for —"

"I won't allow any failure. I trust Scelfton's arms to be strong, but mayhap no stronger than some knight of Aquitaine or even Wharton. You will be aided in abducting the woman from the very chamber I allow her and taking her away from here before she is missed. I will vouch for her safety in your hands and try to give her parents some ease. Then you may appease yourself and seek forgiveness from the Scelfton house, Orrick and his, and any other who might take offense. This is my order, Sir Royce, and any man who would chastise you for following the command of your king was never in truth your friend."

Royce remembered with chilling clarity the wild-eyed look of his mother when they chanced to see each other. He felt a rising panic at the thought of stealing his bride, forsaking his friends, and future years of ill will with the mighty family of Twyford.

"Will you do my bidding, Royce?" Henry asked him.

" 'Tis a bad omen to go against Wharton," he said solemnly.

"Do you fear the knight, Royce?"

"Nay, Sire. But it was a simpler matter to avoid him than to fight him. Neither of us can prove the other guilty."

"Will you take the lady, Royce, as I ask?" the king demanded.

The ticklish memory of her inexperienced response, the softness of her lips on his, and the wild beating of her heart against his chest caused him to quiver slightly. She was frightened of him, this he knew. But something within her had reached out to him in their brief embrace, and suddenly he knew that he was better placed fighting all hell to keep her than trying futilely to keep himself from her.

He wanted her more desperately than he had ever wanted anything in his life. And by a word, she was his.

"Yea, Sire."

Chapter Five

"MADAM," FÉLISE SAID WITH ALL THE SINCERITY SHE could muster, "I would not have you shamed by my behavior, nor would I disgrace my lord father with childish arguments. But nothing in my life has prepared me for this dreadful event. I don't know the man, his circumstance, or what my life will be."

Edrea let a small laugh escape her, in spite of herself. The women sat in a small half-circle in Félise's chamber working needles into rough cloth. Daria applied her needlework to mending, Vespera's needle busily plucked at a veil, and the noblewomen worked tapestry designs with colored threads. Lady Edrea had begged the company of her daughter on her last day at Windsor because the maid seemed distraught and nervous. On the morrow they would have meetings with the king, and when all were satisfied, a betrothal would be announced.

"Few of us know what our life will be, Félise," Edrea said with patience.

"You know, madam," she argued. "You will go home to Twyford and things will be much as they were."

Vespera reached across to Lady Edrea's lap and, with a quiet laugh of her own, touched the woman's hand. "Your daughter forgets that you were once a young bride taken from your father's home to wed a knight you scarcely knew."

"But you knew Father," Félise protested, a pout in her voice and on her lips.

"Aye, for two years," Edrea replied, lifting her chin a notch. "But in that two years I saw him four times. He was my father's choice."

"I would relish two years," Félise retorted, stabbing her needle through the cloth.

"I was four and ten," Edrea exclaimed. "And upon my first introduction to Harlan, he was brutish and clumsy. He frightened me." Her voice grew wistful then, and there was a faint smile on her lips. "But I think I loved him even then." Edrea worked her needle skillfully and did not look at her daughter when she spoke. "Harlan was a rugged young man who had ridden with armies for years, and he paid no attention to ladies of proper retirement. He found it hard to play the groom and harder still to coddle me when I wept for my mother. But in time and with the arrival of our sons, we became more important to each other, and by the time I weaned my firstborn, I could not imagine life without him."

"I may not be so lucky as to find a man as wonderful as Father awaiting me before the priest," Félise grumbled.

"Or rather," Edrea said tolerantly, "you may find a man as indisposed to marriage as you. If you find yourself thus, poor Félise, you might try a soft course with him and see what your labors yield. Answer his clumsy touch with warmth, the rule of his house with quiet obedience, and his oafish step with a pleasant smile. If you snarl at your new husband, you will find more of his back turned against you than his helping hand reaching out to you. But if you strive to do him honor and show him your gentle strength, you will gain not only his respect, but his love."

Félise let her cloth fall abruptly to her lap and looked at her mother with glistening eyes and a quivering chin. She held her mouth in a grim line to try to forestall an outburst. "Madame, I don't know how that is done," she said sullenly.

"It's of no matter *how*, Félise," Edrea said firmly. "If it is your goal, you will find the way."

Félise looked around the small group for solace, seeing all eyes on her. Edrea looked at her with stern dignity, showing with her eyes that she could not and would not coddle her any further. Whether or not Félise was ready, Edrea would cut her loose and let her make her way into wifehood. Vespera had a rather pained look, as though she pitied the girl, but nodded ever so slightly at Lady Edrea's words. And Daria's expression caused Félise to flinch slightly. The maid, unmarried herself and approaching thirty, had a gleefully wicked smile of superiority, as if seeing her mistress's comeuppance felt rather good.

Félise's eyes cleared and her voice became rather small. "There's nothing I can do, is there?" she asked.

"Yea, daughter," Edrea said. "You can bear this with grace and dignity. You are a rich woman . . . and very soon a powerful man will wed you. Your influence and your husband's will not be small in this kingdom of Henry's. You must draw on all you have learned to be certain your monies and powers are well used." Edrea took a deep breath. "Dress so that we might meet your father in the hall. And leave your fretting in this circle of women."

Félise slowly rose and turned away from the women, Daria close behind her to help her dress. Edrea's hands rested in her lap and she turned watering eyes toward the hearth. She felt a gentle hand touch her arm and she turned to look into Vespera's sympathetic eyes.

"It was easier, I think, to hold her on my knees when she was bruised from a fall or hurt because her brothers scorned her," Edrea whispered. She squeezed Vespera's hand. "I pray I have not spoiled the child from being a good wife."

Vespera shook her head and looked down.

"God willing, I will attend her with her firstborn and this fear will be well behind us. I can't know until then whether I have taught her anything at all."

"Lady, you have been a wonderful mother to her. She should thank you." Then very quietly Vespera added, "I thank you."

Edrea smiled warmly. "With so many who love her, how can anything go wrong? Surely the saints protect her."

"The saints and all heaven," Vespera confirmed. She stood and Edrea rose as well. The women walked to the door together arm in arm. Once there, Vespera turned and embraced Lady Edrea as a sister would. "It is hard to leave you," Vespera confided.

"Perhaps it is only for a time. Perhaps we will meet again."
Vespera shook her head. "But you will most certainly be in my prayers." And then as quietly as she had come, she quit the room, leaving Edrea to return to her sewing until Félise was ready to descend into the hall.

To all those in attendance at the dinner, it appeared as though the negotiations for the marriage were well under way, for Harlan led his family to a trestle table seating twelve at the benches. Even though Henry had not officially decreed a betrothal contract, the families of Félise and Boltof gave their approval by their close and happy association. All of Lord Orrick's family was in company; Sir Royce and Celeste, Sir Boltof and Harlan's entire family plus three men-at-arms. Boltof stood to greet Félise and took custody of her, and the meal proceeded with pages and squires carving meat and carrying in food and replacing empty trays with full. There was much merriment among the reunited families, with the exception of Sir Royce and Lady Félise.

Jugglers were performing in the hall for the royal family and the others. Poets and singers and dancers livened the spirits of the court. But Royce's mood was surly and short. He contributed nothing to the conversation and seemed to want to make himself small. Félise often caught him staring at her with a perturbed expression on his face, and thus attempted to avoid meeting his eyes.

For herself, it was a simple matter of being uncomfortable in his company. Memories of their last meeting plagued her the more, now that she had made the acquaintance of Celeste and found her to be agreeable and sweet. In addition, there lingered the tension of thinking herself approved by all present as a bride for Sir Boltof. Her feelings toward Boltof were very vague, and she felt no excitement about a future with him at her side. And marriage with Boltof meant she would encounter Royce on occasion.

Why does he brood? she thought to herself. I threaten no measure of his property, unless he fears I would be unfit for Sir Boltof and seeks to protect him. He has a worthy woman who dotes on him, yet he seems indisposed to her company.

"Royce," Harlan inquired loudly, "where are your men this eve?"

"They have been given duties, my lord," he answered.

"Poor souls," Aswin interrupted. "Have they not been bidden to seek their pleasures in London since your coming? Wherever I inquire, your men are at work."

"They've had their leisure, but each at his own turn. It has taken me ten years to gather the group and to keep them well honed in each duty; some must work while others play."

"A worthy notion," Harlan approved. "You would run no risk of mishap. But ten years? A long time indeed to gather your men-at-arms. What of the Segeland armies?"

Royce shifted uncomfortably. "None of the men who served my family rides with me now. These men have no memory of Segeland's woes."

Harlan leaned closer to Royce. "But they have heard rumors, no doubt."

"Of those, my lord, there are plenty."

Harlan withdrew, frowning slightly, and the conversation went on as before. Boltof was not getting the attention he desired from Félise and drank liberally, jesting in easy camaraderie with her brothers as if he were already a member of the family. Lady Edrea and Celeste found many civil topics for discussion and seemed to enjoy each other well enough.

Félise, quiet and sullen, watched the actions of those around her and listened carefully to their conversations. The men spoke of fighting and horses and the women of housekeeping matters and children. She tried to imagine herself in Boltof's embrace, but the image was difficult for her. Boltof had a certain boyish charm and hard-earned muscles on his short frame. His hair was a wavy mass of dull blond and his skin was fair like his sister's. She wondered if in time, with effort, she would come to treasure the light in his small eyes or crave a touch from his large, square hands. She thought it possible they would have handsome children, but wondered lazily if they would have passion.

She let her thoughts wander to Sir Royce, whose lusty demands were already known to her. Her visions came with more difficulty here, for harder still was the thought of Celeste bending within Royce's iron-hewn arms. Had she yielded to his powerful kiss? Celeste was comely, but far from robust. In Félise's imaginings, Celeste would be crushed by Royce's meagerest caress.

The hour grew later and the queen had left the hall when Sir Boltof asked if he might escort Félise to her rooms. The courtship had drawn itself out to the farthest limits it could go without a sanction for the wedding. He was clearly making his claim known among their families, and Félise felt herself trapped. However she viewed the alliance, it appeared to be well out of her hands. Lady Edrea seemed ready to make some protest, but Lord Scelfton cut her off and gave his loud assent. "Aye, take the lass to her rooms and return quickly. You are on your honor, Sir Boltof."

Boltof had her arm and was leading her away almost before she could bid her parents and their company a decent good night. He had been into his cups, leaving his gait somewhat uneven, and was riding high on what he sensed was approval from her father.

"Sir Boltof," she begged, "please slow your pace and loosen your grip. I go willingly enough; I am not a prisoner."

He slowed abruptly and freed her arm. His manner was instantly humbled. "It is your willingness I want more than anything, Lady Félise. With a word from you, we can post the banns for our marriage."

She almost laughed, for his words were slurred by too much wine. "You needn't fear I would rebuff my father's choice for me," she told him calmly, laying a hand on his arm.

"I would have it be your choice as well, my lady."

Félise smiled tolerantly. "Our acquaintance has been brief and —"

"I knew I loved you instantly," he proclaimed.

"Sir Boltof, you demand much if you would have me pledge my love after but one eve of company. Yet I would not dismiss you. Is that not enough?"

"You might show more warmth, lady, to one who pledges so much so soon."

A slight chuckle rose to her lips. "The better portion of a skin of wine is pledging this night, kind sir. Let us see what the morrow brings." She turned as if she would venture again in the direction of her rooms and found herself quickly pulled into his clumsy embrace.

"But . . . I want you. . . ," he whispered urgently.

Félise believed that for all purposes this match was approved. The king would not likely argue the marriage if Harlan could boast Boltof's loyalty and family. She felt his warm, wine-soaked breath on her face and instinctively turned away, while trying desperately to follow her mother's advice. She had no desire to feel his kiss and could not muster the strength to answer him in warmth. There was no instinctive knowledge to help her guide his errant step with grace or disengage herself without hurting his pride.

"Please, Sir Boltof, would you dishonor me here and now?"

"In a short time you will be my wife," he promised, trying to reach around her waist to pull her nearer.

"The lady protests," she heard a familiar voice interrupt.

Boltof whirled to face the man and Félise was freed in the process. She quickly moved back a pace and saw Sir Wharton and Sir Boltof face each other. Wharton smiled at her, somewhat superior in his sobriety, and gave a slight bow.

"Has a betrothal been announced, demoiselle, or should you like this knave removed?"

"Lord Scelfton himself gave me permission to escort the lady to her rooms. Get thee gone, Wharton."

"Name your reason for this liberty," Wharton demanded. "It was not a simple stroll I came upon here. I bid for the lady's hand as well."

Félise stepped backward another pace and looked at the two men in confused wonder. The gallery through which they passed was wide and torches lit the space, but no others traveled there. She saw Wharton's hand go to the hilt of his sword and she gasped, fearing she would see blood spilled over this episode.

The two men faced off as if ready for a fight, Wharton's tall, dark, and slender frame contrasting with Boltof's stocky, fair appearance.

"Will you speak, demoiselle, or do you yield to the winner?" Wharton demanded loudly.

Félise felt her anger rise along with her fear. She wanted to shout at them that neither of them had the right to put her at the helm of this trouble, but she trembled too severely to speak. She covered her mouth with her hand and turned, fleeing down the gallery toward the hall that led to her rooms. Behind her she heard the thud of a fist finding its mark, but she had no idea which man had fallen and which would be on her heels. Then another blow and groan from the victim eased her mind, and she went unhindered while they took out their anger on each other.

Holding her skirt in her hands, she rounded the corner and moved down the dark hall. She brushed against someone and gasped as her arm was taken.

"Quickly, demoiselle, this way," Royce commanded. He turned her about and led her swiftly through the hall toward an open chamber filled with light. "Whichever of them is still standing in a moment will be right behind you. I have no desire to have to kill either of them." He pulled her in and closed the door quietly behind them, leaning against it.

"What are you doing here?" she demanded.

"I begged Lord Scelfton to allow me to follow, lest Boltof fall asleep in the hall before you were safely to your rooms. The knight grew drunk on your beauty."

"He gave more attention to his cup than to my face, Sir Royce." She took a breath and fanned her face with her hand. "Am I in danger again? Would I be better fixed in the dark hall to await either jackal?"

Royce smiled in amusement, keeping his hands behind his back against the closed door. "I will not accost you, madam, if that is what you fear. I am here by your father's trust, and I have need of alliances such as his. In a moment I will take you to your chamber. Then I shall carry Boltof back to the hall."

"You are certain Boltof will fall? Would you in like help Wharton?"

"Wharton is skilled and Boltof is drunk. Both of them are fools."

Though momentarily taken aback by this offense, Félise's relief at being temporarily safe from their battle overwhelmed any anger. "I couldn't agree with you more," she sighed.

Royce chuckled. "They both beg your good favors, lady. One of them may be your husband soon. You have a sorry lot if you think them fools." She dropped her gaze to her feet, for again she agreed. She felt a finger under her chin and she raised her gaze to meet his. There was a softness in his eyes she had not seen before. "You want none of this, do you, *chérie?*"

"I wish it were all behind me," she said faintly.

"Unfortunately, there is much ahead of you before your woes are over. The man has neither been named nor promised and already there is the threat of bloodshed. Aye, it will be months before you can call the matter done. You could beg a quick wedding and at least put the waiting to an end . . . much like a quick execution."

Her eyes glistened slightly. The prospect of a marriage, a strange new home, and a whole new way of life was not a thing Félise could easily accept, whether the process was quick or drawn out. Her voice trembled slightly when she spoke. "Please, is it safe for us to leave now?"

He looked down at her almost sympathetically, taking her arm to lead the way. His voice was firm but gentle, like an older brother's. "Lady Félise, it occurs to me that you reside in some danger this last night in Windsor. Bolt your door and keep yourself alert to every sound and movement. Until you are safely wed, guard yourself."

"Surely no one would . . ."

He looked deeply into her eyes and she saw his earnest. "Yea, demoiselle. You are too much a prize for your own good. Trust only those you are certain would do you no harm."

She gave a nod and Royce cautiously opened the door. He looked up and down the dark hall and then led her swiftly up the stairs and to her chamber. Once there, he opened the door himself and gave her a little push. "Till we meet again, my lady," he murmured.

She opened her mouth to thank him, but he left her quickly and was out of sight before she could find the words. She shook her head slightly, thinking that each time she met him he came in a different guise. One moment he frightened her, the next he teased or tormented. He could show his scorn or some display of passionate desire. He was her antagonist, then her protector. She shivered as she contemplated whether on their next meeting he would wear yet another new cloak.

In the dark of night when nothing stirred, Félise heard her name urgently whispered. Her slumber was deep and she thought herself in a dream until she let her eyes open and saw Vespera's face above her. "Lady Félise," the woman urged. "Wake yourself. Quickly now."

Félise was slow to rouse. Vespera wore a heavy cloak and Daria was up, stoking the fire and hurrying about the room. She sat up in confusion, pulling the pelts closer to her to ward off the cold. "What is it? Is it still night?"

"Just before midnight, my lady. We have to take you away to safety. Please hurry and dress yourself."

"Safety? But —"

"Even now Sir Wharton gathers a troop of men to steal you away from Windsor. We must hurry."

Félise threw back the covers and stood shivering at the side of the bed. "But *why?*"

Daria was flying about the room at a speed Félise had never before witnessed. Vespera drew a gown hastily from Félise's trunk and struggled to hold it for Félise. "His desire for you is uncommon. While your father and the king wait for a meeting to discuss your marriage, Wharton fears the choice has been made in Sir Boltof's favor."

"They fought earlier this night," Félise mused, her voice muffled in the folds of her dress. She turned her back for Vespera's aid in the fastenings.

"Aye, they fought, and Wharton was much the winner. He left the hall to gather his men together. I think his purpose clear."

The confusion of this abrupt waking was only slowly clearing. Félise spun around to face Vespera. "But you need only send for my father," she declared. "There is no need to flee . . . my father and brothers will . . ."

Vespera put her hands on the girl's shoulders and firmly turned her about again. "There is little time, *ma chère,*" she whispered. "If Sir Wharton cannot steal you while you sleep in your chamber, he will no doubt accost your family on the road to Twyford. All he need do is force his whim, and you are his bride or no man's. Please."

Félise pulled her hair over her shoulder and out of the way, a nagging fear prickling along her spine. She trusted Vespera, but the event seemed out of place and peculiar. She was cautious, but she did not think herself unsafe inside her bolted room. Her screams from within her sealed chamber would do more good than her muffled cries if she were caught unprotected in the hall outside.

"Where do we go?" she asked the tire-woman.

"The castle guard will take us to an inn outside the town and later provide escort to your home."

Daria was frantically throwing articles of grooming and clothing into the coffer and had herself donned a dress, shoes, and cloak. "Does Daria come with me?"

"Of course. We could not leave her to face the villain."

"This is not right," Félise thought aloud. "Would you take me to my father's house?" she asked.

Vespera shook her head. "Lady, if Boltof could but rise, he would likewise do this thing. And the first hiding place sought would be your father's house. Let us use the guard and not threaten your family."

"Nay," Félise said firmly. "I will go with you only if you promise to deliver me to my father. He would not deny protection and I am confident of his ability. I will not flee to another strange place."

Vespera looked at her closely and then finally nodded her head in assent. Félise was quicker with her dressing then, and once her cloak was fastened and her coffer sealed, Vespera went to the door. Two men stood without and the tire-woman indicated the bulging trunk. One of them hefted the baggage while the other led the way down the corridor.

In the courtyard there were saddled horses standing ready and two more men already astride. Their escort lifted the women, one by one, into their saddles and then led the way. Vespera rode without aid, but the reins of Félise's mount were controlled by her escort. Again she felt a gnawing fear; she had not heard Vespera instruct the men to take her to Lord Scelfton's house.

The night was dark with clouds covering the moon and the air was wet and cold. The fur-lined cloak was little protection against winter's harsh breath. The little entourage moved slowly through the streets, a cart holding Félise's trunk squeaking behind them. She looked around at her company without knowing which worry to grasp. Should she fear these men who accompanied her or a possible attack from Wharton?

There was no possible way, in the dark of night, for Félise to know whether they traveled toward or away from her parents. It crossed her mind to attempt to escape this escort, but she had no sense of direction. Then as they turned a corner, they halted before another group of knights and Félise's breath caught. There was no scuffling or show of arms, so this meeting had been planned. One rider dismounted and came toward her.

Sir Royce looked up at her. "My lady," he greeted.

"Sir Royce? Are you to escort me to my father's house?" she asked hopefully, wanting to find relief in his presence.

"I am to escort you, demoiselle, but I fear we cannot join your family tonight. I must take you away from here as quickly as possible."

"I wouldn't be in danger with Lord Scelfton," she said, trying to coax him.

"Of course you would not," he replied easily. "Forsooth, the grand old lord would protect you to his own life's end. But, fair Félise, I fear he would hold you from me, and you belong to me now."

Her eyes grew wide and startled for an instant, and then she knew, beyond any doubt, that Royce had successfully dragged her out of her bed and into the cold night to claim her. He would do the very thing Vespera warned her Wharton would try. Her hand found its way from under her cloak and hit his cheek with a resounding slap. Before she could think, she was jerked out of her saddle and stood on the ground before him. His hands were clamped tightly on her upper arms and he looked down into her startled eyes with fury blazing in his own.

"I will warn you but once, Félise: *never* strike me again." Then he turned to his fellows. "The lady is cold and chooses to warm my lap as we ride. Let's waste as little time as possible."

With the towering strength of a dozen knights all around her, Félise did not struggle against Royce, but she did not aid him in any way in settling herself in his saddle. When they were both astride, he pulled his mantle around her.

Rage burned within her and all sense of fear was gone. She couldn't believe the number of people he had betrayed with his action — Celeste and Lord Orrick, not to mention Boltof, a man he called friend. And her family would be horrified and hard to stay when they learned of this insult.

"You think to rape me and gain my father's blessing?" she caustically flung at him. "Ha! You'll rot in hell before you see the day."

"Nay, madam, that is not my plan. Your father's blessing will be swift on the morrow, for this match is ordered by the king. We will see a priest, whether by dagger point or willingly."

She sat silent and stunned in front of him. "By order of the king?" she heard herself ask.

"Aye."

"Then you . . . you did not bid for marriage . . . and you . . ."

"Let us just say that the event was no more in my plans than yours. It is out of our hands."

"How do I know you speak the truth?" she quizzed.

He let out a long, deep sigh. "Madam, I was betrothed before tonight. You can be damned sure I would be warm in my bed and not galloping through the sleet and cold but for the order of the king. You can save us both further misery by staying quiet."

She leaned back somewhat in the saddle, quite believing him and almost pitying him. She felt the sting of tears burn her eyes, for it was one set of problems to have men fighting over her and quite another type to be forced on a man who wanted none of her. She remembered their last conversation before he installed her in her rooms, and a tear dropped from her cheek onto the large, tanned hands that held the reins.

"Like a quick execution," she murmured.

"Aye," he grunted. "But for whom?"

Chapter Six

THEY ENDURED THE TRAVELING IN SILENCE, FÉLISE drifting periodically into sleep and jolting awake as if a nightmare had seized her. Four hours were spent in the wet and biting chill slowly and quietly moving farther out into the country.

When she did not sleep, she considered the man positioned close behind her. He did not slacken his support nor selfishly hoard the warmth of his mantle, but freely shared what little comfort there was to be had. She could not see him, but it took no effort to remember his face, the implacable soldier's expression and brooding eyes. She had seldom seen him smile, those times when he taunted her being the only occasions. The hands that held the reins were thick and strong. She tried to imagine being fondled by them, but the vision came hard.

A thousand questions plagued her, but she asked not a one. Her spirit was as damp as the air. The proud Félise, she thought with scorn. Holding myself beyond men, desiring none, poised and aloof as they bid for me and fight over me. What better justice than that the game be decided by the highest judge, the king? No more were the courtly games and eager proposals.

Before dawn they approached the gates of a country manor just north of London. In the dark of the predawn hours it was difficult to make out much of the exterior of the manse, but a few stout knocks on the gatekeeper's door announcing Royce and his bride saw the place quickly lit. The gates were opened and a torch-bearing servant guided the entire group to the house. Again they waited, the heavy silence bearing down on Félise. She wondered if this place was to be her home.

When Royce dismounted and went to the great double doors, she decided he must be a stranger here. He spoke for a few moments with the tenant, an elderly man with tousled hair and hastily donned chausses and tunic. Then he returned to his mount to help her down and lead her into the house. "Stable these beasts," he told his men. "There is feed and water for them, and if they're to bear us away from here, you must care for them well."

By the time Félise had entered the modest hall, an elderly woman was just descending the stairs. Félise thought the couple were perhaps caretakers. The woman's gentle smile and soft eyes spoke of kindness; her gray hair and squat, plentiful figure gave her a grandmotherly comfort. The man, tall and thin with a short, sculptured beard of silver, laughed pleasantly as they entered. They were not offended by the interruption of their rest, nor by the intrusion of so many wet and cold people.

"Sir Royce," the man said with a smile, extending his hand in friendship. "Your pardon, sir. We did not expect you before dawn. I know these roads; you made quick work of them."

"I beg your pardon, Master Chaney. You are good to allow us your house."

Chaney gave a short bow and, upon rising, drew the plump woman to his side. "Mistress Chaney," he said, presenting her. She, too, nodded amiably. "Isabel, my lord," she encouraged.

To the introductions, Royce raised Félise's hand. "Lady Félise Scelfton, my bride."

Félise instantly saw pity in the eyes of the woman, accompanied by a slight shaking of her head. She reached forward to take Félise's hands in both of hers. "Dear sweet," she cooed in a pleasing tone. "I trust you will find that lacking which you would have enjoyed in your father's home, but we will do as well by you as can be allowed with so little time for preparations. There is food. Are you hungry?"

Félise simply shook her head. She looked at Royce. "They know our circumstances?" she asked.

He stiffened slightly beside her. "They are loyal vassals of Henry," he said simply. Then, with the frown she had accustomed herself to seeing, he added, "As we all are."

Vespera, Daria, and two of the men who had ridden with them arrived, and the eight of them stood crowded in the narrow entrance to the manor house. To Félise's amazement, Vespera came forward of the group and embraced Isabel as if they were longtime friends. A few whispers were exchanged between them, and then, looking over her shoulder at Félise, Vespera quietly remarked, "I am bidden to my lady until . . . until she requires me no more."

Félise lifted her chin a notch and glowered at the woman. She could not fathom the reason for Vespera's betrayal. Had Royce bought her loyalty, or did she hope to profit from Henry by aiding this match? Isabel noticed Félise's glare and laid her hand on Vespera's arm. "Do not fear, Isabel," Vespera said. "Your generous hospitality will lessen the rub. All will be well."

Vespera turned to Félise. "Will you take your rest, my lady?" she inquired. "There is a chamber for you."

"What of the priest?" she asked haughtily.

"That will be arranged," Isabel promised. "Come, I can light you to your chamber."

The three women followed Isabel up the stairs to a room that had been set aside. Obviously the preparations for this night had been made in advance, for a fire blazed in the hearth and two pallets for Daria and Vespera were arranged at the foot of a more commanding bed. It was a simple room, but comfortable. The bed itself was rich, rising above the floor. There was a table before the hearth, a wooden chest, and a commode. Heavy woolen curtains of a rich rose hue covered the shuttered windows.

"Isabel makes her chamber available to you, Lady Félise," Vespera said. "I know you'll want to thank her."

Félise shook her head in a distracted manner. "Do you forget why I am here, madam?" she asked. "I am a prisoner, a bride against my father's will."

"Pray soften your tongue, Lady Félise," Vespera said, an unusual impatience in her voice. "That this was no fault of yours is true enough, but you would do well to remember that neither are the rest of us to blame."

" 'Tis a lie," Félise countered hotly. "You certainly betrayed our friendship . . . and the friendship of my mother."

"Nay, milady," she argued, her green eyes sparkling as bright as emeralds. "I was bidden by your mother as well as the queen to remain close at your side for as long as possible. And I would have gladly brought you the news that the king sanctioned your betrothal to Sir Royce, but would you have come? With each knave smitten came the threat of your lost virtue and perhaps worse; there was no time for a pretty courtship. You must take caution that you do not place yourself above the needs of kings and their ambitions." She gestured toward the chamber door with one hand, her mouth rigid with barely suppressed intolerance. "Now that fine lord follows his orders as best he might, but he is met with no warmth from you."

Félise felt her eyes begin to tear. That Royce had treated her mostly with contempt since their first meeting was a matter of fact. Even when he led her away from the fight between Wharton and Boltof, he'd called them fools for fighting over her. She pitied her own dire straits at least as fully as his.

"How would you have me address him? He makes no secret of the fact that he was bidden elsewhere until . . . He wants no more of me than I of him. It was he who dragged *me* through the cold and rain to a midnight hiding place. Where is *his* warmth?"

Vespera eyed her with obvious disappointment, shaking her head. "You remember the journey poorly, lady. 'Twas nearly a score of people who rode through chill fog and wet . . . and all bent on protecting your safety and dower purse."

"Vespera," Isabel quietly pleaded, "be gentle. The lass is frightened." She laughed uncomfortably. "The habits of these highborn nobles, to steal their women and assault their neighbors, makes me wonder why they are known as gentlemen. Put her to bed and berate her on the morrow."

Félise stomped childishly toward the hearth to warm her

hands, turning her back on the women. Daria stood in limbo, awaiting orders of some kind while Isabel and Vespera stared at her. She heard Vespera's quiet goodnight and the closing of the door as Isabel left them. Behind her there was movement as Vespera and Daria drew back the covers on her bed and, before long, the sound of one of Royce's men delivering her coffer.

She let herself become lost in the flickering of the fire. She was but a breath from crying out for her mother, a temptation that only furthered her shame. She did not bear this insult with any measure of womanly grace, yet slowly the reasons for this misadventure attacked her clearly. The memory of Boltof and Wharton eager to draw swords was less than a pretty courtship in her mind. Had the king spoken openly on behalf of Royce and allowed time for family contracts and wedding plans, she might have found herself in greater danger. And what of Royce? Would he have willingly played the suitor once named?

A shiver possessed her as she considered his kiss and the strength of his embrace. Had he known then, she wondered, that he was the chosen one? Had he been sworn to secrecy? Her cheeks flamed as she remembered that she had unwillingly met his ardor with some passion of her own, but he had turned from her abruptly, leaving her aching with both desire and embarrassment. He must have been instructed by the king, tried her lips, and fled in disappointment.

She gave herself a quick lesson lest she be naively confused by the next days and weeks. Her father, however devoted, would not send arms against Royce in defiance of King Henry. Mayhap that was why Lady Edrea bid Vespera to remain near if possible — to lessen the hurt and abandonment Félise felt. And as for Royce, he had made his feelings known. He did not seek this marriage any more than she, yet he did seem to bear the burden more reasonably.

Her conscience cried out to her that she was a mere spoiled babe without the strength of conviction a woman must own. Haughty, spoiled, and selfish. Her life was not her own; her future was ruled by dower lands and political considerations. Edrea, whom she admired more than any other woman, would not bemoan the cursed dowry, but wisely use it for what good it could bring.

There needn't be love to form a marriage, she thought dejectedly. She could be no more sure that Boltof or Wharton would have loved her. She let her hands run down her sides, curving toward her slender waist and trembling slightly as she considered the consummation. She remembered Royce's boldness in the dark gallery. The fear of it bit her deeply.

She mused on a woman's obligation to bear children and see them raised. Edrea had never complained that it was not her wish. She brought forth her sons with love and nurturing that spoke of great joy. Nor did she complain of the trials of raising her fiery-haired daughter, though Félise was sure her trials were many. Quite to the contrary, Edrea lamented that Félise had not been born of her own body.

"Come, my lamb," Vespera said, her patience renewed. She drew Félise away from the hearth. "A dry gown and some rest will help more than you realize."

Once the thick feather quilt had been drawn up to her chin and the candles extinguished, Félise's thoughts were likewise kinder and more tolerant. The embers still glowed in the fire and wind passed through the corridors with a chill whistle, a melody that lulled her. If the time is come, she lay thinking, I would rise to it as a woman and have no more of these childish complaints. I pray God delivers me with some tenderness to my fate.

The Chaney house was a merchant's dwelling; Master Chaney had achieved success rare for one of his class. His wool was known as the finest and softest, drawing a good coin and barter. Nine sons, all married and fathers of their own children, drew the trade further and took the cloth to France. In their elder years the Chaneys were able to enjoy the manor house, humble by the standards of a noble dame, rich by the measure a commoner used.

The house boasted seven rooms and a stable and sat upon an enviable plot of land. Close to the city yet free of its clamor and filth, the house was hugged by full brush and trees. The Chaneys employed four servants, fully owned as many horses, and grew or raised all their food.

When she arose, it was the savory smells filling the house that Félise noticed first. Her chamber was empty. Vespera and Daria had not only left the room, but their pallets were gone as well. She rose and went to the window rather than the door, pulling aside the heavy curtains and opening the shutters. The sun was high, marking noon, and the sky had cleared. The chill persisted, but the damp ground was covered by a thin blanket of snow.

Félise admired the grounds on which the unpretentious house stood. There were no gardens, fountains, or stone-laid paths, but it was obvious by the cleared yard and cleanliness that the place was loved. She hugged herself against the cold and scanned the yard, spotting a line of footprints in the white sheet. Following them, her eyes fell upon Royce. He had walked a great distance from the house to where a dense copse of trees lined the property. He had one foot resting atop a stump in a relaxed stance, looking at nothing in particular.

She could see his breath swirling about his face, yet he wore no heavy wrap. Donned in simple chausses, leather tunic, and soft leather boots, he did not resemble the roguish knight. His lack of chain mail did not diminish his size. Even at a great distance his height and breadth were obvious. She toyed with her hair while she studied him. In the absence of weapons strapped to a heavy belt, he looked more like the carpenters or smiths in her father's towns. A sudden irony occurred to her: he did not fear her flight or an abduction by one of her suitors, for he carried not so much as a knife at his waist.

He began to walk toward the house, his head down and his stride even but slow. The aura of command was missing from his approach. If anything, his movement spoke of melancholy. Her heart sank abruptly. She knew well enough how to scorn the advances of a lusty knight; she had no experience in dealing with a man who did not want her.

She quietly pulled the shutters closed and went to the hearth to blow up the fire and place a new log atop the embers. This was barely done when the door opened. Vespera entered first, followed by others, and a rigorous afternoon ensued.

The celebration of the wedding did not resemble a noblewoman's in any way, for it was to be a quaint affair, much like that of a merchant's daughter. There were no visiting dignitaries or village feasts or gathering of decorations. But the women were as invigorated in their enthusiasm as if this were a match between royal heirs. And further, as though the couple were in love and could bear the waiting no longer.

First there was a tray of food delivered to the bride, then a steaming bath with scented soaps. Daria washed Félise's long hair and combed it before a blazing hearth, and even that sour maid had a manner light and gay. "Milady, will you wear the gown of your father's colors, or choose another? The pity there's no time for a bride's frock, one to set off the shine of your hair . . ."

Félise looked at her suspiciously out of the corner of her eye, wondering at her mood. Daria usually prattled a bevy of complaints at the snarls in Félise's long hair. "It appears that your heart is swollen with some fancy love poem," she said. "Do you forget no one is eager for this marriage . . . least of all the man and woman hereby pledging?"

"Ah, milady, I only know the bride is beautiful and Sir Royce a high and handsome man."

Félise turned to look at her fully. "You think him handsome?" she queried.

Daria rolled her eyes and licked her lips. " 'Twouldn't pain me much to think on the bedding . . ."

Félise, tense enough with these preparations and impatient with Daria as a rule anyway, reached behind her to where Daria stood with the comb and gave her a sharp pinch on the back of her hand, gaining a screech from the maid.

"Well, put it from your mind," Félise said angrily. " 'Tis no concern of yours."

Daria resumed her usual tight, pouting look and combed with her customary neglect for tenderness. Félise was slow to be drawn into a festive mood, but Daria was soon back to chattering

· 89 ·

in lighthearted glee about the handsomeness of Sir Royce and the aura of romance surrounding this secret wedding. Félise frowned darkly, wondering if she would ever in her life look back on this day with any fondness.

Vespera helped choose a gown of the palest green velvet decorated with a silver braid. Félise would have hidden her hair under a wimple, but the choice was taken from her when Vespera insisted that the glorious locks trail loosely down her back as would befit a young virgin. A sheer veil was gathered atop her crown and secured with silver pins. When her dressing was complete, three women stood about looking at her, each holding her breath, exclaiming on her beauty with their glowing eyes.

"A moment," Isabel suddenly said, turning and fleeing from the room. She was back almost as quickly as she left, a folded garment in her hands. "I came by the cloth in a good trade, milady, and fashioned it as a sleeping gown for my youngest daughter. Take it for your own bedding. I can find more of the cloth."

Félise tremulously reached for the garment, not sure if she was moved by this generosity or simply shook whenever the consummation was mentioned. She held the gown by the shoulders and it fell forth in a long, shimmering curtain of white. It was a soft, sheer linen, loosely woven and crafted with expert and loving hands. She raised her eyes to Isabel. "It is too precious," she said. "I could not take it."

"My lady, I would be honored if you would."

"Thank you," she said meekly, a vision of Royce rending it in his haste causing her to shudder.

"I have never seen a more beautiful bride than you," Vespera said. She moved forward and, holding Félise's shoulders, gently kissed her cheek. "With but the faintest smile, perhaps sir knight would be moved to tenderness," she whispered.

Félise attempted a smile, but her insides were knotted and her lips quivered. She looked at the women. "I pray forgiveness," she said meekly. "I know my manner does not show that I am grateful. I know you try to make this pleasant for me."

Isabel laughed softly. "Nary a bold bride," she said with a light touch on Félise's hand. "You will soon find there is little to fear. Even yon knight of Henry has some soft place, and you will soon find it. It is the knight's desire to hide his weakness from the thrusting sword; yet a gentle word will lay bare his soul." She smiled warmly. "Venture into his heart with kindness, Lady Félise. Come. If your knight is not impatient, he is blind."

There was no church for the vows, nor choir of voices, nor communion. Royce and Félise knelt before a staircase in the merchant's house while the priest spoke the words and blessed them. Royce's voice was clear and strong, and while Félise willed hers to be equal to his, a tremulous whisper was her best effort.

They rose before the priest and Royce turned her, looking down into her eyes. She felt the warmth of his gaze, but the stern set to his mouth gave her to believe that though he was impatient for her body, he was no more eager for her companionship than she was for his. Then his lips lowered to hers and the searing hunger of his kiss left her breathless and weak. Her arms rose weakly to his and her cheeks blazed in embarrassment, for his display might better be confined to their private moments. As if the thought struck him at the same time, he broke his kiss quite abruptly, leaving her to look up at him in some confusion. She laughed awkwardly. "Patience, my lord," she whispered.

The only reaction her words elicited was an angry frown. She could not fathom his moods. Something in his lips expressed wanting, yet his eyes were filled with contempt. This marriage obviously threw him into dour spirits.

A dinner was served to those present: the knights who had ridden with them, and the members of the household. It was a hefty fare of roasted meats, thick gravies, and breads. There was light conversation and plenty of wine, but no dancers, singers, or jesters. Félise ate her meal slowly, agonizing with each bite as the hour grew later. When Vespera rose from the end of the long feasting table and drew near her, she knew the time had come. Royce's hand held his knife over his plate and she covered it with hers.

"My lord," she whispered, an urgency to her voice. He bent closer to hear her. "I meant no harm. I do not mean to do you ill." He looked at her in complete confusion. Her voice came in the meekest whisper. "Please do not hate me."

His frown wrinkled deeper. "Hate you, madam?"

She opened her mouth as if to speak, but Vespera touched her shoulder and bid her come. Royce's brow relaxed in understanding and he gave a slight smile. But Félise's eyes showed only fear. She saw little more than a brazen leer. She rose to go to the fateful bedchamber.

Again there was a flurry of brushing, primping, dressing. She was ceremoniously seated in the bed, the covers drawn to her waist. The women then stood about. Royce entered with some of his men a pace behind him and stood just inside the door, looking across the room. He smiled appreciatively.

"I need no further assist," he declared. "You may seek your pleasures in the hall; I shall seek mine here."

Vespera approached him with nervous reluctance. "But Sir Royce, the king —"

"You may examine the bedding on the morrow, woman," he said. Though he smiled rather roguishly, there was a strength of conviction in his voice that would brook no argument. "I am not a prancing stag inclined to mount my doe for your amusement. If you know the lass is pure, you will have little reason to doubt she's been bedded."

Vespera stared for a moment, wondering first whether he should be allowed to consummate the marriage privately, then whether she dared leave Félise alone with him. "The custom —" she began.

"There has been nothing of custom thus far," he said flatly. "There were no violets and green herbs for my lady to walk upon, nor jugglers nor minstrels nor acrobats. Our contracts were not drawn, nor were there documents from her father or the king." He paused and glared down on the nervous Vespera, eyes glittering with impatience. "I'll bed the lass in private . . . or not at all."

She looked around and noted that his men had already accepted his dismissal and, however disappointed they were that they would have no chance for jesting and crude remarks, would not press him further. Vespera quickly withdrew, Daria and Isabel fast behind her.

Royce closed the door and barred it, making it clear he would allow no intrusion. He blew out two candles and leisurely approached the frightened creature in the bed. He had not considered what his break from ritual might cause her to think.

"Do you mean to harm me, monseigneur?" she asked.

"Nay, maid. You are a virgin?"

"You need not doubt my chastity, my lord. There has been no one to tread where you will."

"You are afraid?"

She swallowed hard. "I am not a brave woman, but I do not fear you," she attempted.

He smiled down at her, an almost gentle expression on his face. "We'll have it done, Félise. I am not the heathen you judge me to be."

She would have opened her mouth to deny it, but he turned from her and extinguished the other candles. He removed himself to a distant corner of the room to disrobe and returned to the bed, slipping in and drawing the covers over them both. His hands instantly grasped the shoulders of her gown to draw it down over her breasts. She gasped at the quickness of his work and heard his amused chuckle. "You would find it burdensome, *chérie*," he said, swiftly pulling her into his embrace.

In naught but darkness, the fire providing only the meekest glow on the other side of the room, she was left to know him only as a warm shadow. They met skin against skin, his chest crushing her breasts, his hands roving up and down her back, pressing her so close that she feared she would not be able to draw her next breath. His lips instantly took hers. She was awed by the heat of his body, the strength and size of his hands, and her surprising lack of fear. It was perhaps the movements of his hands and body that lulled her; he seemed to expect nothing of experience from her, but went about his business with great confidence. There was an odd quickness within her that prompted her stomach to nip at her heart.

"Fair Félise," he muttered hoarsely, kissing her ear, neck,

shoulder. "You play the woman's game well . . . men are driven to battle to have you. Come, vixen, if you yield, show me . . ." He took her hand and led it to his chest, showing her how to stroke him with the same familiarity he used on her. She clenched her eyes tightly shut, and though no one could see, her cheeks flamed. She shyly touched him as he would have her do, gasping in spite of herself when her hand found the swollen member that would end her maidenhood.

His breathing quickened and he pressed her down into the bed, kissing her now with renewed passion. He tugged at the gown to have it gone. His lips and hands boldly caressed her body; no part of her was to be left untouched. She gritted her teeth in apprehension and wondered how she would have endured this mating with spectators.

Slowly, from a deep place within her, she felt a new warmth. She trembled as a strange yearning possessed her; she leaned into his touch rather than steeling herself against it. She met his mouth with hers and held him closer, confused by her bizarre change of feelings but helpless to stop them. The heat of his skin against hers no longer felt alien. To the contrary, she thought she might suffer cold devastation if he released her.

He murmured her name, his voice thick and heavy in her ear, and she gave herself over to the rising passion. She yielded to him completely, feeling his hands demandingly grasp her hips. She craved more of him, hungry for his thrusts. Then the pain, blinding in its suddenness, caused her to arch in unconcealed anguish. "Easy, my love," he consoled, his breath rasping with his efforts.

Félise fell back into the bed, unmindful of his restrained movements. As the pain ebbed, she was aware of him again, cautiously commanding her body. But the irrepressible hunger was gone and she simply moaned her distress, humiliated by her earlier abandon.

When he had exhausted himself, he gently kissed her cheek. "You need not fear more pain, Félise."

He rolled away from her and lay on his back. Within moments his breathing fell even and calm and she considered his presence beside her. What demon did he command, she wondered, to possess her so completely, then turn away from her so easily? Was a man's life little changed by the heated coupling, while a woman's whole world was traded for a new one?

It seemed hours that she lay quietly thinking on this. The fire burned low, leaving only a few orange coals to glitter in the dark. Her voice was the quietest murmur. "Do you sleep, messire?"

There was no response for a long moment, then he stirred slightly. "Nay."

She sighed heavily, feeling tears begin to threaten. "I am sorry you were forced to wed me, my lord, but —"

"We share a bed, Félise. Can you not use my *name?*" he asked testily.

She choked on a sob at the sound of his impatient voice. "Royce . . ." she sighed, a tear sliding down her temple into her hair.

"So on this day we were both forced. I will hold no grudge against you; 'twas little of your making."

Her heart ached with the desire to feel the gentleness of his arms about her again, if not to hear a kind tone in his voice. She had transcended passion and craved a softer touch, an earnest word. "Will we leave here soon?" she asked.

"Aye. To Segeland. 'Tis a sorry keep." He sighed as if greatly disgruntled by her questions. "It needs a woman's hand."

"I will try to please you, Royce," she said, humbling herself and seeking some favor in his eyes.

He turned his face toward her. "You have not disappointed me thus far, madam. But then, I knew you were not shy."

Her cheeks grew hot with shame, but she spoke anyway. "Will you hold me as a cherished wife, or spurn me with chastisement because of the king's choice?"

"Do not needle me, Félise. The hour is too late for senseless bickering."

She bit her lip for a moment, but proceeded bravely. "Did you love the lady Celeste very much?" she asked.

"Do you wish to please me, Félise?" he asked shortly.

"If it is possible," she murmured.

"Then go to sleep. That would please me."

She sank back into the pillows slowly, carefully turning onto her side away from him. Her tears wet the linen, but she was mournfully silent. The hearth was cold and dark before she found sleep.

Chapter Seven

ROYCE COULD NOT SLEEP. THE WARMTH OF FÉLISE beside him caused such a burden of conflicting feelings that he was plagued most of the night.

She had not fought his advances, which made him most grateful. Facing her scorn would have destroyed his pride and he would have been hard put to finish the deed. It was a curse he lived with; he was most shy of the mark on his back. When he was a small boy and his mother had ridiculed him because of it and his brothers had laughed at him, he had developed a genuine belief that he was repulsive. While most highborn knights and lords sought the services of helpmates in bathing and dressing, Royce demanded his privacy.

He had wanted her again within moments, but he steeled himself against his baser urgings. She might be considered beyond the age of marrying, but Royce was over three decades and found her youth almost alarming. He had not known many young women, his tastes running more toward women of experience who would not force any commitment . . . or Celeste. And though he wished to hold her, when she turned away from him and softly wept, he gave her exactly what he thought she required of him: distance.

It seemed an eternity before he suspected she slept. When she was still and her breathing even, he let himself stroke the soft mound of her curving hip. He gently moved close to her, round-ing her turned back and resting his face in the sweet fragrance of her witch's locks.

Her softness beneath him had ripped him open with the sharpness of a knife, and his soul lay bare before him. She could not possibly have known the many things he had to reckon with because of her. That he had just had his first virgin was the most startling of these. There was little doubt now that Celeste had played him false. Oh, that humble dame had moaned her misery and there had been blood, but there was considerable difference between sound and physical evidence and what a man feels. He was aware of his terse response when Félise asked if he had loved Celeste a great deal. He made a mental promise to share the truth about that with her one day.

Although he felt he had no right to be angry with Celeste — for he had played his affections on her for years without giving her the security of marriage — he did quite easily let go of his guilt at having abandoned her for Félise. He lived easier with that decision now.

But as he lay beside his wife, the overwhelming concern that robbed him of sleep was whether she would continue to hate and fear him. If a child, marked by the Leighton curse, came to her, would she thrust it away in contempt? When she saw the ruinous Segeland, would she rot in misery? He had touched her warm skin and known every turn and curve of her body, but he knew her not at all. His experience of her went only as far as her flirtations at court, her anxious appraisal of him, and the sharp crack of her hand against his cheek when he'd told her they were to be wed.

And I, he thought, who would like to hold her fiercely, closing my hands around her that she cannot flee and no other can ever touch her, tremble in the fear that she will turn into a thistle in my grasp.

His mother had been a beautiful and sensual creature, but her disposition was that of an asp. He conceded that his mother had good reason for her madness, but he took a startling new look at his father. Had that old dragon felt love so penetrating and passion so blinding that he could do nothing but cleave the woman to him, whether she shared the passion or not? Royce wondered at his ability to do things any differently. He could not imagine letting Félise go, and at the merest thought of another man even looking at her, his blood began to boil. Yet ogle her they would, for her beauty was uncommon. And he considered himself large and strong, but far from handsome.

He sighed heavily and, kissing her gently on the cheek, rose from her side. He dressed in the dark, assured himself that she was covered against the chill, and went to the stable. He hung a lantern and began to curry the horses, first his steed and then some of the others. He had wiled away a few hours when the sun came up, but so heavy were his thoughts that he hardly noticed the time. What bridegroom, he thought ruefully, looks for the peace of labor on his wedding night? One fearful of his bride's gaze on his naked flesh, terrified at seeing disgust etched in her beautiful eyes.

When he heard the reigning cock of the yard give his rising crow, he ventured from the stable and up the stairs to the house. He would not leave her embarrassed before her morning maids by his absence. But upon entering the room, he found her gone. The coverlet was pulled back from the bed and her gown lay in a heap in the center. He winced slightly at what Vespera would consider proper evidence of the consummation; it appeared more as some human sacrifice to him. He had passed no other early risers in the house and could not guess where she might have gone.

He went to the window and threw open the shutters, scanning the grounds with an almost frantic feeling rising in his chest. But he quickly spied her. Some distance from the house, her fur-lined cloak held tightly about her, she occupied the same stump he had visited the day before, sitting there alone and gazing into the dense trees. With a great feeling of relief, he closed the shutters and hastened out of the room.

"Félise?" he gently queried when he was close behind her.

She jumped, startled by his voice, and rose and turned quickly to face him. She looked at him for only a moment and, when she saw the perplexed look on his face, gave a small sob and was in his arms. He hardly knew how to react to her, nor could he fathom the reason for her upset. But tears stained her cheeks and she clung to him.

"Quiet now, lady," he said gently. "Here now, what grieves you so this early morning?" He held her away from him and lifted her chin. "I know it is not always a pleasant thing for a maid, but surely I did not hurt you so badly as all that."

Crimson began to mark her cheeks, although she quickly shook her head to reassure him. "I thought you had gone," she said, her voice quivering.

"Gone?" he questioned. "Where?"

She meant to answer, but her chin only quivered pitifully and great tears filled her eyes. He chuckled in spite of himself, rather taken with her childlike misery at the prospect of his leaving.

"I couldn't sleep," he laughed. "Some vixen of my wedding night plagued even my dreams and I was faced with two choices: to wake you and demand more of the same, or leave to seek out the coolness of a winter moon."

She looked up at him, her tears abating some small bit, and tried to brave a smile.

"Now," he said. "Where did you think I would go?"

Félise shrugged and looked down. "I . . . I thought you'd left and would simply have your men deliver me to my — your home."

"God's blood, madam, you truly think me a beast. I know I lack much of the cocky courtier, Félise, but you do me wrong. I have not been so cruel."

She shook her head, still looking down. Again he lifted her chin, forcing her to look at him.

"If I give you my word that you will have fair notice of my travels, will you rest easier?" She nodded, her expression easing almost immediately. "Now what other things must I promise to give you peace of mind?"

"Naught, my lord. But . . ." She nearly lost her nerve, but he would not release her chin and nodded sternly for her to continue. "It is only . . . my lord, you *frown* so."

Royce threw back his head in spontaneous, genuine laughter.

He could barely control his mirth and received only an embarrassed flush from her. "I swear, Félise, it is more the surly set of my jaw and this unsightly scar that make me seem so, not my poor humor."

"You frighten a maid with your black looks," she said quietly, trying to defend herself.

He chuckled still, fixing his features in a determined scowl, showing her just how grim and foolish he could be. She laughed lightly, her red-rimmed eyes taking on some of their usual liveliness. "There, I thought I could chase a smile out of you. You should smile as often as you can, Félise," he said, stroking her hair with his hand. "Though I concede that you probably have great cause for your tears. Not many maids are ordered by a king to take a brutish and ugly master to their beds."

She let her hand rise and lie firmly on his chest. She wished to reassure him, but the words came hard. "I did not know the trouble my dowry would cause, my lord — Royce. My mother wished it to be good fortune for my future . . . to bring only the best nobles to my attention. I do not complain."

"Nonetheless, you were ordered — a stolen bride. I admit it is a difficult burden . . . when you wanted someone else."

It was in her mind to tell him she wanted no man, but for some reason it was not her wants or lack of them that came to mind, but his. "Celeste is a lovely woman. I understand that you would be very disappointed."

He could hardly prevent the drawing together of his brows and the hard line his lips made. The thought of Celeste so early this morning would get no gentler reaction from him. Deep in the night while lying beside his bride, he had been given to wondering how different his life would have been spent beside that slim-flanked dame. And she had very nearly had him; he had never thought beyond marriage to her.

"Félise, ours is not the first marriage of necessity, nor will it be the last. I have little doubt there will be difficult times for us. But I am a man to honor whatever vows I make, no matter the circumstances. Of that you can be sure."

She felt her stomach plummet suddenly. But she immediately

tried to bear the weight of this admission more lightly and make the same commitment to him. Although it was hard for her, she reminded herself that if he was a good husband and treated her with some kindness, she could ask for little more. "I will likewise abide by my vows, Royce," she said softly, hoping she would not cry.

" 'Tis good," he said with a nod of his head. "If you are troubled, Félise, it is my desire that you bring your miseries to the fore rather than fleeing into the wood in the early dawn. I think the worst I could deal you would be safer than your wandering about alone."

She nodded. "You are not angry?" she asked rather timidly.

He smiled quite easily, and she decided that whether or not she was loved, his smile gave her some reassurance. "Only a little, madam. As if it were not enough that I had to worry about those who might, in their addled ways, try to steal you away against the king's intention, I now must worry that you will fly. You have lightened my load with your word."

"My lord, I do not seek to be a greater burden than you already bear. I will not try to escape you. As with you, Henry's command is my father's choice for me and I will abide his decision. If you wake some morning and find me gone, it will not be of my doing." She paused and looked up at him earnestly. She believed he was suspicious of her still — the same suspicion he had had when she'd played with his men from her window and when he'd found her alone in the gallery. The hardest challenge, she believed, would be in showing him her loyalty. "Do you believe me?" she asked.

"Never lie to me, Félise, and I will have no choice but to take every word from your lips as truth. Yea, I believe you. Now, I am for trying to save this day without black looks or tears. What of you?"

She nodded bravely and he turned her, tucking her hand in the crook of his arm and leading her back to the house. They strolled as lovers would, appearing to any onlooker to be comfortable with each other. "Perhaps one day, Félise, you will forgive Henry for giving such serious thought to your rich lands."

A smile tugged at the corners of her mouth and her eyes were aglow, but she would not look up at him and give all her secrets away on this, their very first day. "Perhaps," she said. "If I ever accustom myself to your grim countenance."

In a dim gallery in Windsor, two knights met and, upon seeing each other, paused at a fair distance. It was obvious the meeting was a strained one, and they regarded each other with high suspicion. Boltof was the one to take a further step and relax his expression.

"I thought we should talk, Wharton. We have both been slighted."

Wharton moved closer. "I would have expected you to support him. Have you not called yourself friend?"

Boltof laughed wickedly, his eyes glittering with a strange light. "My bite is the deeper, rest assured. I made myself a friend to Royce when his power with the king became obvious. Henry values the bastard, though I can't say why. And Celeste required little urging to lie with him . . . but what more can I say of my sister? She does not draw many looks from the men, and her estate is not large enough to trap them." He shrugged. "Truth be known, she craves any man. But I am the fool, for he betrayed me . . . as is the way of all Leighton men, is it not?"

Wharton gave a solemn nod, for he had likewise made himself a friend to a Leighton and lived to rue the day.

"Whether you call him betraying or not, I heard the banns posted by Henry's own voice. It is a matter of fact that he sanctioned the marriage —"

"Royce forced him," Boltof nearly shouted, forgetting to keep his anger in check. "I sent him to Henry on my own . . ."

Wharton's smile slowly spread, hearing Boltof's admission. He was possessed by a superior feeling, though he too was not above using the influence of a friend to attain his wants. And he had wanted the woman and her land. She would have made a comely prize in his bed; he had ached for her from the first time he saw her. And her land in France under Richard would have pleased his father, perhaps changing their relationship for the better.

"Yea, I sent Royce to the king for me," Boltof said. "I offered him half the booty for his mighty influence. But he went to Henry for himself. My stake in this is not small, Wharton. He betrayed me and disgraced my sister, for she will bring nothing to our family now. And the insult to my father is beyond your imagination."

"I see little you can do about it," Wharton said unsympathetically. "Perhaps you can buy Celeste a decent marriage if you're clever. Or send her to a convent."

"It matters little to me that the king approves the marriage between Leighton and Scelfton. Indeed, the Scelfton house is in much turmoil over this. My father spent the evening hours with Lord Scelfton and they laid every curse to Royce while killing the better part of a keg. They would not chastise any honorable knight who changes their position."

"But will the Scelfton house move against Royce?" Wharton asked.

Boltof looked away for a moment. "They will not move against Henry."

"That is what I thought. Nor will I."

Boltof's mouth curved into a sinister leer. Wharton might pretend loyalty to the king, but he was known as one who would carry any banner under which there lay a pot of money. "Even if Henry does not know?"

"What do your propose, Boltof? Whatever, it comes from a black heart."

"The best you can do, Wharton, is to lie in the brush and await Royce's back, for he'll not let you within eyesight of his bride. I, too, have heard of your friendships with the Leightons. But I . . ." He paused, smiling more. "If I act the part of a forgiving friend, seeking only compensation for my spoiled sister and the brotherhood of knights, I can get within his house. Forsooth, within his trust."

Wharton's eyes darkened and he turned abruptly to spit on the floor. "Then do your worst, Boltof. Why do you trouble me with your plans?"

"Because I lack the strength of arms to see it through or a

comrade to cover my back. On my own I can offer Royce a fair match, but his men are more skilled than mine and they guard him well. Aye, getting into his house is no problem, but I am without the means to go further." He shrugged. "I have no desire to anger the king, but I don't think it will be too difficult, if we're careful, to wrest Félise away from the rogue. The Leightons are all mad, you know. Her family would regard her rescue as an act of charity."

"Do you mean to bring some accusation against Royce that will free the woman and the lands from his control?"

"It should not be hard. Few need to be convinced of the horror that Segeland is. Since the days of William the Conqueror, the family has stood apart from the crown and levied war on its neighbors. Until Royce," he added. "A plot here and there would see it done." He leaned closer. "What part of the prize do you claim for your assist?"

"You are certain you can get inside his house?"

Boltof nodded sharply, confident of Royce's trust and his own ability to deceive.

"And the woman will not fight your rescue?"

"I think not," he said with a shrug. "She is fond of her father's favor, and Harlan prefers any but Royce. And Royce is an ugly bastard. If Félise does not perish on first sight of Segeland, she will be driven mad by her new husband's rights in bed. The devil himself has marked the man."

Wharton thought for a moment of the plan, failing to give any thought to this so-called devil's mark. He assumed Boltof referred to the poor reputation that followed the family; he knew of no other deformity. "I would have the woman and Aquitaine," he finally said.

Boltof smiled with confidence. "So be it. Though you may get her with Royce's brat in her. I will take what is left — and I must trust you to divide the prize if you are to be victor over the woman and her dowry."

Wharton's eyes began to gleam in anticipation. He thought of her lively eyes and full breasts, and wild nights of passion. He was good with the women; they had swooned for him before. It would not take him long, he perceived, to tickle the same response from her. And the land in France would put him in a clever position with the crown. Henry could not live forever. Richard would be king.

"You will be satisfied with her English soil, that which Harlan supplies as his part of the dowry?"

"Aye, the English land Harlan has made his dower gift . . . and Segeland."

"Segeland?" Wharton repeated, confused.

"You don't think we'll get her while Royce is alive, do you?"

"But I thought a rumor of crime —"

"Aye, rumors and death. He is more clever than his father and brothers were. If he has breath in his body, he will find a way to convince the king he is not guilty. When all concerned know that is he guilty, he will die."

"I don't know, Boltof," Wharton began. But he had already licked his lips in contemplation of his booty. "You are certain this will work?"

"There are many possible ways, Wharton. I know more of Royce than you. And what I don't know, Celeste will supply."

"She will help you?"

"I have long known the path to that passionate heart. Yea, she will help me . . . but I doubt if she'll know it."

"When do you go?" Wharton asked, becoming eager.

"I think patience is the best weapon of the day. I will let Royce enjoy his victory for the moment before I seek to make amends. And as for you, you would do well to scatter about your good intentions. Let the king and those around you believe that you are content to move on to other conquests and have already forgotten the proposition. There are others here that let their scorn show . . . and they were not so near the victory as you and I."

"When do we begin, Boltof? I don't think it wise to wait," he said, for in his mind he was thinking more of getting the woman in his possession before she was burdened with some Leighton offspring.

"Don't be a fool, Wharton. We are thought to be enemies. It

wouldn't do for all who see us to take us for friends. Then when something happens to Royce and you are found with the woman, there will be too much guessing. In fact," he said slyly, "I shall be certain to warn Sir Royce of your ill-concealed disappointment."

Wharton looked at Boltof carefully. He had never much liked the knight, but he had not given him credit for being so clever. "I warrant you've not slept a night since she was taken. Such a plan takes time to prepare."

"It is not an easy thing for me to fall second," Boltof said, his eyes hard and angry. "Especially to someone like Royce. It bites me deep that one so deformed and of such knavish family lines should win such favor, while I . . . I have an old man who will possess my estate until he dies and a spinster sister who will do no better than the veil, for which I will be forced to provide a dowry for her keeping." He laughed cynically. "If I were to leave it up to them, I would be lucky to inherit my own demesne when I am a grandfather. It does not please me that my portions are cut so much to my disadvantage. It is time to change that."

"I wish you luck, Boltof. And I give you fair warning: you may be able to betray Royce easily, but I am a long time in plans of my own, and if you work against me, you will die."

"There is no need to worry, Wharton," he said easily. "There are plenty of women about. But there is not a surplus of gold and land. My mother beggared my estate with her late marriage to the old cripple. If he does not ease his grip on my life soon, he may go the way of Royce."

There was a simple comfort at Chaney House that Félise had felt nowhere else and would not likely feel again. Since it had neither the trappings of a castle or hall nor the squalor of a peasant hut, it was a most unusual place. Master Chaney and his wife, seemingly much in love after decades together, brought forth a modest hospitality that had none of the flair of noble houses, yet was clearly the best of everything they had. It was cozy for Félise; she found herself appreciating the solace of their home more each hour.

Vespera's association with the Chaneys became clear. They had taken their cloth to the convent at Fontevrault, and Vespera, not being a nun, was bidden by the sisters to make the modest purchases. They had shared a mercantile friendship, and it was Vespera who had suggested their home, inconspicuous yet sturdy, as a place where the young couple might safely make and consummate their vows. Vespera was quick to inform Félise that Master Chaney had refused compensation for the lodging and wished only to serve the crown and the two young people. Again Félise was witness to Royce's need to be upstanding and fair, as in his offer of coin for food and lodging. And with Vespera's prodding reminders, she was finding good reason to be grateful for the efforts of all these people.

Félise spent three quiet days and evenings with the women and Royce at the Chaney house. If life were to continue just as it was, she would have no cause to grieve. The conflicting messages she received from her husband did not lead her to assume anything of love passed between them, but neither did she feel as threatened as she had earlier.

Royce did not spend a great deal of time with her, leaving her mostly with her women through the day and sharing the morning and evening meals with her, in the company of all the others. He truly lacked the silver-tongued talents like those Wharton possessed, but at least his mood did not seem dark and grim. He left her alone until late at night and was up and dressed early each morning, so she assumed that he tolerated her very kindly. Indeed, she could not complain of his treatment, but she had no indication that he craved her company.

Until late in the night, when he reached for her in the darkness. It was this that left her confused and uncertain. He could keep his cool distance and betray no inner longing, but he loved her with an abandon and rigor that left her breathless. He would even begin their night together by sending her to bed before he was ready to retire, and then she would hear him come into the chamber and his weight would press down the bed. Long moments passed while he lay still at her side, and it seemed the instant she was convinced there was no gathering storm, she would feel his hands on her and open her eyes to see his face above hers.

After only three days she had come to welcome these late-night interludes, for by day she would watch him from afar, judge his brooding eyes, and wonder what inner truths were hidden behind the concealing darkness of those fiercely drawn brows. Yet when that same gaze hovered over her in their bedchamber, his eyes glittered like smouldering embers and revealed his desires to her. Then she felt she knew all of him and that he, in his passion, allowed her to trespass briefly into his soul.

It was at supper on their third evening together that he spoke of his plans. "I will have to leave you tonight, Félise, and ride to Windsor. The contracts are ready for me to carry with us to Segeland."

"Tonight?"

"It would be most unwise to travel to the palace by day and give away the location of our residence. There are those who strongly feel the insult of our sly marriage."

"But 'tis done," she argued. "What is done cannot be denied. I can belong to no other now."

"Don't delude yourself, *chérie*. There are some who do not care that my mark is on you and I have the king's favor." His eyes took on that grim darkness again, seeming to conceal some inner anger she could not fathom. "You seem not to understand your allure."

"The transfer of lands is written into our marriage contract by the king himself," she said, missing his meaning entirely.

He laughed somewhat brutishly, but there was at least a twinkle in his eyes. He leaned close to her so that others would not overhear. "It is not the land they crave, my love, but that part of you which only I have known."

Félise was still tender enough of this new experience to be embarrassed when she thought of their more intimate moments; she was not at all sure her behavior was pleasing to him. Each morning when she arose, finding herself alone, she'd wonder if he thought she was indelicate, shameless. She could not think otherwise; she had known Celeste and could not imagine that shy creature moaning and clawing and clasping Royce tightly. He drew from her this new being that had no control once kindled by his touch. She was too young and unpracticed to imagine that he would find this pleasing.

"It must pain you mightily that because of me you are forced to travel by night," she said.

"It is no great delight," he replied somewhat shortly. "But then, to protect my interests and live up to my contract, it is what must be done." He took a bite of food from his plate, and without looking at her he added, "Your father will be there."

"My father?" She watched him as he chewed and nodded rather solemnly. "You must dread this meeting," she said.

He turned his gaze to her, waiting. She simply met his eyes, little knowing what he required.

"I had not planned to ask this of you, Félise, but since you do not make the offer . . . you might ease your father's mind some small bit by writing a message that you are well and not abused in your new marriage." She felt instantly foolish for not thinking of this herself, and in her slight stupor, she was momentarily silent. "Unless," he added, solemnly, "You cannot honestly do so."

She mentally shook herself. "Of course I can. It is the least I can do."

He not only did not speak to her again during the remainder of the meal, his attitude was once again cool and removed. She could only think that he was worried about his visit to Windsor and the confrontation with Lord Scelfton, and more than a little put out by her failure to offer him support.

The moment she finished her meal, she hastened to her chamber and requested parchment and a quill from Isabel. It was delivered to her quickly and she set down her words with great care and deep thought:

My dearest mother and father —
That you have labored with worry is in the main my fault because of my many complaints. I no longer begrudge my dowry,

marriage, and, least of all, Sir Royce. Indeed, I have come to
favor my position and only regret that I was not as wise as the
king, for I did not see all that my lord could offer. He treats me
well and I could wish for nothing more in a husband. In time,
I hope, he will thank His Majesty for this fond meddling. Until
we share company again, I am

> *Your most devoted daughter,*
> *Félise*

She rolled the page and put a loose ribbon around it, purposely not waxing or folding it. Should Royce choose to examine her words, which she fully expected him to do, let him see that she did not resist marriage to him. How could she? She did not know much of love, but she knew that it felt divine to bask in the mysterious warm glow of his smouldering eyes and that to be enveloped in his strength brought her greater ease and peace of mind than the hundred or so men-at-arms lining her father's great wall. He was obstinate, secretive, and determined, all the things she loved and feared. His stern and scarred face intrigued more than repelled her. She was beginning to find greater allure in the fact that he could not be called a pretty or boyishly clever young man. His experience titillated her; his manliness, nowhere soft or delicate, excited her. And this, to Félise, was the nearest thing to love she had ever known.

She was thinking of Edrea's words as she lay in her lonely bed. To guide his errant step with a gentle smile, to meet him in warmth and kindness: these were the things she would try to do for him. And in time, perhaps he would forget Celeste and begin to care for her.

She half-expected him to visit their common room only for a change of clothing and to collect her message, but instead he darkened the room and joined her in the bed. Again he lay quietly beside her, as if he barely noticed her. And then she felt his wandering hand, his hesitant lips, and finally he made his intentions clear and she yielded to him all the tender feelings she held tightly in her heart — hidden feelings that she had never shared nor even fully acknowledged. She clung fiercely to the private joy she knew when nothing threatened them and they were alone.

When she rose in the morning, both Royce and the rolled and tied missive were gone.

Chapter Eight

ROYCE TRAVELED BY NIGHT TO WINDSOR, LINGERED there through the day, and returned to the Chaney house under the stars. He arrived before dawn, waking Master Chaney for the second time. He spent the remainder of the darkness in the large dining hall where those who had returned with him found pallets on the floor.

Beside his wife, sharing her warmth and enjoying the feel of her silken flesh, was where he wished to be, but he did not venture there again. Instead he brooded, heavy with the many worries and angry feelings he had brought back from Windsor. Henry could not be faulted for the turn of events, nor could Scelfton. Still, Royce had been insulted. He thought perhaps it was his ancestors he hated most at this moment.

Lord Scelfton had read the missive from his daughter and raised his fierce scowl to Royce. Royce had no idea what his wife had written. He had made himself a promise not to trespass there. Even now, he found it difficult to imagine she cried for her father's rescue. But something in that message had alerted Lord Scelfton to her dissatisfaction. "If I find my daughter in less than the best humor, Leighton, I shall find the way to see you fall," he had blustered.

"If she is discontented," Royce returned with a strong voice, "it is because she is wed without choice and hidden from her family. She suffers not from the harshness of my hand or my purse. I yield her all the customary benefices due a wife in good standing, and on this I make my oath. I am not so rich as you, but neither am I jealous of my money. All I can afford in mercy and coin is hers for the asking." He had bowed shortly, disgruntled that his intention should be questioned, and forced himself to remember that the old lord had little reason to trust him. And of course no one could know how he valued the woman.

The meeting proceeded smoothly then, thanks to Henry's soft touch. Somehow the king managed to give great patience to Harlan's surly mood. He laughed more than once about the discomfort of having two such trusted vassals at odds; how plentiful his kingdom might be should two strong and loyal friends find a common bond. But Lord Scelfton had refused to sign the dower contracts in the end unless Henry would allow some of Twyford's own men-at-arms to aid in carrying the couple to Segeland.

"I have no desire to decry my oath or my allegiance," Harlan argued. "But I will not see my only daughter endangered in the process. I will see her to safety before I promise to accept any man as her husband."

Whether speaking from assurance that Royce would do right by his prize or failure to find a better way, no one could be sure. But Henry agreed to this. "Sign the contracts of marriage and dowry, Harlan," the king said in good humor. "I am confident that Sir Royce, henceforth Lord Leighton, is the best man. And you may send a few escorts to assure yourself."

Thus it was that Royce returned to the Chaney house with not just any of Harlan's loyal vassals, but all three of his sons. He could hardly justify taking his bride again on this night while her hefty brothers tossed upon their pallets just below, however he hungered for her sweet flesh. And hunger he did, thinking peace from this wanting would never come. A stray scent of her, a red-gold thread of her hair laced onto his tunic, the memory of her velvety skin — any thought of her filled him with desire. And that desire blended with pride and fear. It pained him that he felt undeserving of her wealth and beauty.

The feelings assailed him again when she descended into the

hall in the morning. She wore her gown of deep green velvet lined with fur, and her hair was pulled away from her face to trail down her back in a sober braid. She had taken up a custom of dressing in a more casual manner while staying here, leaving off adornment and not fussing over veils, wimples, or elaborate styles. Her simplicity was somehow more appealing than a labored and fancy effect.

As she entered the hall, her eyes lit up to see him and she approached with a smile for him, taking no notice of the others in the room. "Have you only just returned, my lord?" she questioned happily.

"Only a few hours ago," he said, rising from his place at the table.

"A few hours? But —" She stopped herself. "How did you find my father?" she asked solicitously. "Was he agreeable?"

Royce gave his head a short nod, hoping he was keeping his sour mood in check. "In the end he proved so, madam, although he made some further requirements of us."

"How so?" she asked.

"We are to be escorted to Segeland," he responded, knowing full well that however much he tried to control his tone, the aggravation in his voice could be heard. He was ashamed of Segeland; he found it foul enough a prospect to present to Félise, and was less than happy to have a description carried back to Lord Scelfton. He did not know what to expect once the brothers reported where Félise was bound to live. He thought he might be willing to kill anyone who would try to take her away.

He inclined his head toward the three broad-shouldered knights in the hall and Félise followed his gaze. Her eyes widened in surprise.

"Maelwine? Evan? Dalton?" She seemed perplexed by their presence. Félise frowned as each head nodded. These young men had alternately teased and protected her, but on this meeting they were quiet and solemn. She turned her questioning gaze to Royce, whose own dark countenance rested on the Scelfton knights.

Suddenly the dawning came. Only her brothers could see the

angry flare in her bright eyes. "Why are you here?" she asked hotly.

Evan was the one to step forward of his brothers. "To assure our father that you are well and your residence will protect you against aggressors. On the journey to Segeland, Félise, you should have ample protection."

"Does our father mistrust my own hand? I sent him word that I was safe and well and that Royce does honorably by me. What insult is this?"

"I perceive no insult, sister. Your dowry is rich and you are still considered a prize by some knaves who would not be discouraged by the protection of Royce."

"No insult," Royce scoffed, the irritation strong in his voice. "I am approved by His Majesty, but you will follow me home to judge my wealth and protection."

"Nay, Royce, not to judge you but to see to our sister's —"

Félise gave her head a shake, as if in denial. "When will I be done with this wretched purse?" she demanded irately. "Holy Mother of God, I am ogled and pawed and snatched in the dark of night, bedded by the order of the king, and when I perceive the folly done and my life to be my own, though obliged to my lord, my *father* sends his troops." Her voice had risen in anger, a voice that her brothers had heard a time or two, but that no other in the Chaney house knew her to have. Even Vespera ventured down a step or two from the upper level to listen, though she kept carefully out of sight.

Evan's brows drew together. "Whatever piques your temper, Félise, before our father releases lands and monies from his own stores for this marriage, he will be assured it can be well used. We are bidden to carry the word back to him that all is well."

She turned to Royce, finding good reason for his mood, although she didn't know half the reason, for she'd never seen Segeland. "You did not approve their interference?" she asked.

"I had little choice, madam. They were bound by Lord Scelfton and by the king."

She turned her back on her brothers and stepped closer to Royce. Her eyes still blazed with anger and humiliation. Having accepted her lot, she was still being treated as an immature child to be alternately protected and forced, whichever served the immediate need. "Did they keep you from your rightful place of rest?" she asked, keeping her voice low.

Royce lifted an amused brow. He wondered for a moment if the source of her temper lay in sleeping without him for two nights. It did not pain him at all to think that even if she despised him in other things, she might crave his presence in her bed. He smiled his pleasure down on her, though the scrutiny of the Scelftons did not ease him into a romantic mood. "I admit I was more reluctant to join you there," he whispered, indicating the brothers with his eyes. "But they made no special request of me." He shrugged. "I am honored, *chérie*. I did not know I pleased you so well."

In spite of herself her cheeks warmed, the way they always did when facing him in the cool light of morning and hearing one of his roguish remarks about their intimacies. It briefly occurred to her to chastise him for the crudity of his wit, but it was more than that. She was angry with them all — her brothers and her husband — for their impersonal treatment, as if she were but a bag of gold being transported across the country. And of course there was the anxiety that her desires would hold no importance and these brothers would take her home. It was one thing to worry that someone like Wharton would try to wrest her away; it was quite another to think that her family would find some reason to usurp Royce and see him replaced. And, although she had been given no choice, the prospect of another in his place was unthinkable.

"Do they journey with us to Segeland?" she asked. "Soon?"

"We will leave when you have readied your things."

She turned again to her brothers. She tried to keep her hostility covered, wishing to be away from all of them. "You may carry word to Father that I am well. You need not venture so far as —"

A pained look came over Evan, but he cut her off, speaking in spite of his discomfort. "It will not do, Félise. There are rumors . . ."

"Rumors?" She laughed ruefully. "Of a certain, Evan. But do you neglect all your duties for rumors?"

She was not aware that Royce had turned his back on the conversation, but Evan saw. "The story is that his own mother was taken to Segeland in chains."

It came as a surprise, there was no denying that. Félise turned toward Royce but found he would not even look upon the conversation. She made a quick decision not to question this, nor to argue further with her brothers. Somewhere, perhaps beside the softness of a low fire deep in the night when Royce opened his arms and heart to her, she would gently inquire. Not in any fear for herself, but in consideration for what he might have been through. His back bore witness to his anger and shame, and her heart went out to him.

"Then I will see my things readied and we may get quickly to Segeland. You may assure yourselves that I am neither abused nor held against my will."

She walked toward Royce and went around him to look at his face. "I did not complain to my father, messire."

"I did not accuse you," he said.

"Nay, but it almost seems as though —"

"Their presence will be useful on the journey. We'll travel by day with the added arms."

"Is it a long journey, Royce?"

"A few days, no more."

"Very well," she said resolutely. "Let us get the riding done and see to Segeland. I did hear you say it required a good hand, did I not?"

Royce felt the tugging of a prideful smile as he looked down at her. "A woman's hand," he corrected.

She nodded and turned away from him, her skirts swirling, and fled up the stairs. She passed Vespera, that wise dame keeping a serious expression until Félise passed, then allowing a slow smile to spread across her face. Vespera turned and went up the stairs again, feeling her presence was required by Félise and not by the men.

The three men standing at the hearth and judging the back of their sister's husband shared few common characteristics beyond their looks. Evan was the most like his father. Maelwine, closest to Félise in age, was also most kindred to her in spirit. And Dalton, who was ambitious and enjoyed his labors, found this retreat from his own duties to be bothersome. But all of them seriously considered their father's word to be law.

It was Evan who attempted to speak to Royce. "Sir Royce, I judge this inconvenience to be great in your mind, but if you mean to do well by our sister, I see no reason we should not travel in a lighter spirit. We are, after all, bent upon one purpose."

Royce turned to look at them, a nerve twitching in his jaw. He eyed them coldly for a moment and then, taking large steps, left the hall, his action giving the lie to their idea of common purpose.

When the door had closed, Dalton let loose a long, low whistle. Maelwine sat heavily on a stool, and Evan reached for three empty tankards on the table, filling them with cool ale. "He takes this interference badly," Evan said.

Malewine laughed shortly. "You, who have lived so many years with Lord Scelfton, should not wonder at a man who despises any outsider impinging on his authority."

"We are not outsiders," Dalton asserted. "Félise is of our name."

Maelwine looked between his brothers, taking a cup from Evan. "You are blind or fools. She has made her choice. She takes a new name."

"You think she wants him, then?" Evan asked.

"There is no question. The lass has chosen. He plays the game to her satisfaction."

"And if we find him to be unworthy and the keep unsafe?" Evan asked.

" 'Twill be a bed of thorns, Evan," Maelwine answered. "She will not willingly come away with us. Her eyes speak for her; she has cast her lot with him."

Evan sat heavily and took a long pull on his drink. "I see no love pass between Royce and our sister."

"Mark me, Evan," Maelwine said with a sly smile. "We'll see little of love while we hover over the groom with swords drawn. And unless I am wrong about Félise, she may well drive us away at dagger point to have her husband in her bed again. Let us give the man time. She is not a complete fool. Something of worth must lie hidden there."

"She has changed," Evan argued. "Perhaps he abuses her and she is too proud to tell us."

Maelwine laughed loudly at that. He slapped his brother on the shoulder. "Yea, she has changed, but I don't think it is wrought of abuse. We'll watch closely, but I venture we will only see the little one has become a woman . . . and she has found her man."

Four days and nights were spent on the road to Segeland. On the first night, when there was no adequate lodging on the road, they made a camp within the shelter of their wagons. On the second night there was a humble stable for the women, and the men found pallets on the cold ground outside. The third night saw a merchant dispossessed that nobility might sleep more comfortably, and on the final night of the journey there was an adequate travel house in Coventry. Twenty horsed men could have done the trip in two days, but carts, women, and baggage took longer.

Félise tried to keep her spirits light and travel well, but it was an internal battle that would challenge the most courageous person. Royce was distant and glum, riding well ahead of her most of the time. Her brothers, much of the same mood, rode behind her. There was cursing and tension between the Twyford knights and the Segeland troop. The loyalties of each were firmly tied, and Félise had ceased to know with whom she should be bound. She traveled within the group on a spotted palfrey, trying not to think in terms of opposing forces. Vespera rode beside her.

"Do you plan to return to Eleanor or Fontevrault after we have reached Segeland?" Félise asked her.

Vespera looked straight ahead. "I need not," she said quietly. "Neither am I required to stay with you. But, if what Sir Royce says is true, you may have need of an extra hand with the poor place. I am willing."

"I have little understanding of your interest in this," Félise said with candor. "I knew you to be a castle servant bidden to the queen and knew your place was to take my cloak and bring me kindly messages, but after that . . ."

Vespera laughed softly. "I have been bidden to Her Majesty for almost five decades — since I was a child myself," she said, her eyes wistful. "I was released to Fontevrault just before she was taken prisoner by Henry. I cannot accompany her into confinement now."

"But do you stay with me for her?" she asked.

"In a manner. I can reassure her that you are well. And in a manner 'tis for Lady Edrea, for she trusts me. But in the main, 'tis for you. I have said I served the queen for many years. You were born in her house."

Félise was suddenly interested. She had continually put the past far to the rear of her thoughts, for it had little to do with the present. "You knew my mother?" she asked.

Vespera sighed. "Truth, I knew the woman who gave you birth only slightly. I knew she reigned as the most beautiful in Eleanor's court and sang of love and longing in the troubadour fashion. She was a gifted poetess. And I knew she loved a knight of Eleanor's company who left her for another. . . . I knew she loved you. I'm afraid that is very little to know."

"Her name? Do you know her name?"

"She has been gone a very long time, lady. How many years are you?"

"Eight and ten. Too old, some say, to marry."

Vespera laughed again and Félise began to remember that musical ripple as a comfort, before the madness of weddings and beddings had begun. "I think not too old, dear Félise. I think perhaps the time was exactly right. What do you think?"

"I think, madam, that too many are hurt by this."

"But still we move to Segeland, and as I watch you, I see that even though you worry, you venture on. Surely if you wished it otherwise, your brothers would take you home."

"In defiance of the king?" she asked.

"In defiance of God, should you reject the choice made for you."

"You forget, Vespera. It is possible that I already carry my lord's child. 'Tis done."

"Only if you wish it so," Vespera quietly added.

Félise was silent for a moment, thinking heavily on these words. Harlan would give succor not only to her but to any offspring of this hastily consummated union. Edrea would in like rear any child as lovingly as she had her own. It was not as though she was without people who cared for her. But whether the one she wanted cared . . . it was too soon to know. "Until this order from the king, he had an obligation to another," she said quietly, the sting of tears creeping into her eyes.

"We will reach Segeland soon, Félise. Will the weight of jealousy bear down on you and keep you from making a home for Royce?" Vespera asked.

" 'Tis not jealousy," she said softly, turning toward the woman with tear-filled eyes. "Or perhaps it is. I know that Celeste has for many years managed Lord Orrick's home, and my lord has made it clear he regrets that he cannot have her."

Vespera sighed. "Then you shall find a way to change his mind."

"I don't know if that is possible," Félise said dejectedly. "And if it is possible, I do not know the way."

Vespera looked at her sharply, that boldness creeping again into her eyes. "You are clever enough, my lady. I have little knowledge of these worldly things, but Lady Edrea became dear to me . . . and I know she did not fail you. And I know nothing of men, having never been a wife or mistress of a hall, but I, too, judged the fair Celeste when she was in the company of Royce. I did not see him cast any smitten look her way."

"When were you in their company?" she asked.

"I am seldom noticed." Vespera shrugged. "The way of the sisters is to move softly and silently, and I think it has become my way by their example. But I frequented the halls in service to Her Majesty and was oft in the great hall when many others dined. I am not very noticeable . . . but I am careful to take notice."

"Then you have seen the others — Wharton and Boltof?"

"Yea. I saw them."

"And yet you asked me how I found them?"

Vespera looked pointedly at her. "I looked at their eyes as well, my lady. And I saw what you saw. Neither was the worthy knight in my mind."

Félise was instantly distracted by conflicting thoughts. She had been ready to take either man, had her father approved. But now that Royce had made his mark on her, she had trouble imagining the meagerest smile from the cast-off knights.

"And Royce?" she asked Vespera.

The woman looked her way, pausing as if to think her words through. She looked straight ahead again, concentrating for a moment, then looked back at Félise. "I think your lady mother's advice was strong; seek him with all good purpose and find out for yourself what worth lies there. My impression of him means nothing. Ah, it seems you may begin at once," she said with a smile. Both women noticed that Royce had delayed his steed by the side of the road, seeming to wait for most of the train to pass.

Félise's mare was small beside Royce's destrier and the squeaking of the wheels of the cart made conversation much more of a chore for him than it had been for Vespera, who at least rode level with her. Royce became frustrated with the distance between them and the nearness of other riders.

"There has been little enough time to sort through the things I have meant to tell you on this journey," he finally said, his voice somewhat strained. "When we stop for the night, I'll ask you to take a few moments for a private conversation."

Félise was amazed at the formality. She laughed aloud. "I think it can be managed," she mirthfully returned.

He seemed to find no humor, but it didn't matter. She was plagued by a coarse wit, her mother had said. Truly, for her own husband, whether or not he relished the fact, to have lain with her and now to plead softly for a moment of time seemed a bit ridiculous. Although he rode on with the same dour spirit, Félise caught herself laughing once or twice at the preposterous situation. She hoped he'd found the need for some tryst, and her glee alternated with determination to get rid of her burdensome brothers as soon as possible, that Royce might again find his rightful bed.

I am a whore, she thought disdainfully. But thank the Virgin, I am at least a married one.

If Royce felt a growing need for her body, he did not betray it. He rose from his meal at the travel house and announced that he wished to speak with his wife and asked, somewhat caustically, if he would be allowed a private conference. The Scelfton men seemed perplexed by the inquiry and only Maelwine responded. "None among us wishes to keep you from your bride, Sir Royce. I thought that was to be understood."

"You have said so," Royce replied unhappily. "But I do not see your closeness wane." He turned to Félise. "Madam?"

It was wretched, having the family she loved and the man she wanted at such odds. She could not stare venomously at her brothers, for she understood them and their purpose. Neither could she be angry with Royce's hostile nature, for he was entitled to be aggravated with them. She simply put her hand in his and let him lead her out into the cold evening air.

"Segeland lies one half day's travel down this road, madam. There was no way I could prepare the hall for your arrival."

"You have said it was neglected, my lord. I do not fault you for this. Your time has been better spent."

"It is worse than neglected. I have not spent a fortnight in that hall in over a score of years. Many believe it is haunted by the angriest ghosts."

She laughed lightly, hoping to put him at some ease.

"I believe it is haunted by evil," he said pointedly. "I have long felt the weight of a curse on the Leightons — one I would see end, though I will not deny that I've felt the burden myself."

Her smile vanished and she looked at him closely.

"You must at least know your ghosts, Félise. The rumor is

true: my mother was not a willing bride but a captive; she was the wife of some Welsh lord. My father desired her and took her to Segeland in ropes. That he married her within the church is of little import since she had a living husband at the time, which to my way of knowing makes me a bastard."

" 'Tis naught of your concern," she said lightly, trying to smooth the hurt. "You are the heir; it is your home now."

"The hall is rubble and the town dies more with each moon. The people have been angry and ill since I was a boy, and from my grandfather's story, long before then. My father, it is said, murdered his eldest son, though it could have been an accident. My other brother's death was no accident. He will killed while he slept after a bitter quarrel with his friend, Sir Wharton."

Her mouth formed a large O at the news. "Wharton killed your brother?"

"I would be remiss if I did not tell you that Wharton denies any knowledge of Aylworth's death and in like accuses me." He laughed ruefully. "He charges that I was eager to inherit the fair Segeland and killed my brother to have it. Certainly Wharton never saw the place or he would know the lunacy of his words. I will tell you only once: I did not kill my brother. Nor would I ever kill a man who is sleeping and therefore defenseless. You may choose your own belief about it."

"I believe you, Royce," she said quietly.

He seemed to pay little regard to her good faith. He went on with his story of hauntings. "My mother, God rest her, took her own life when she could bear her imprisonment no longer. You will not find this to be a pretty place."

"Is that why you have stayed so long away?" she asked innocently.

"I cannot bear the place . . . but I see the time has come to do what I can to secure family lands. I have tried to escape the name and its curse, yet it will follow."

"There is no curse but fear," she said softly.

"You have not seen the place."

"Will you be disappointed if I am not afraid?" she asked him. "Why do you tell me these things? To drive me farther from my purpose?"

"The purpose of your heart and the king's order are different matters, lady. You must know what you face."

"Why not lighten your watch, Sir Royce? You warn me so often and so heartily that I am left only to think you would prefer one such as Wharton to be successful and steal me. Is this why you resent my brothers? They help to keep me at your side."

"I would only have to seek Wharton and fight him. Nay, I do not hope that he takes you. I only mean for you to know the truth."

She studied his profile, for he spoke without looking into her eyes. The line of his jaw was stern again. She touched it gingerly. "How did you come by the scar, my lord?"

He turned to her, his frown intense. "Do not ask about my scars, Félise. They are hard earned. And raw."

She sighed heavily. How much softness to his anger could she muster, she asked herself. "Was Segeland good enough for Celeste?" she asked. Again his eyes were piercing as if hatred lingered there. But she was persistent. "Was it?" she asked.

"That was a different matter. I would not have taken her there without first making some provisions for her. This marriage was hasty and there was no time."

"Do you mean to treat me as badly as your mother was treated?" she asked, noticing that he winced at the question. She considered that answer enough. "If not, then we shall call the matter done and make the best of our sorry lot." An edge of anger and jealousy crept into her voice. "If Celeste was another matter, I shall try not to let my envy show."

"I mean to take only supervision of your dowry. 'Tis yours, for your children."

She could barely stand his distance, especially at this point in their discussion. She reached a cold hand to his chin and turned his face. "I bid you remember, Sir Royce, that I came to you a pure bride. If the children are mine, so are they thine. I have asked little enough of you."

"I only seek fairness," he said shortly. "I would not turn away from any child."

"Yet my illness sets you on edge," she retorted.

"Illness? Are you not well?"

"I must not be," she said, her voice piqued. She was highly exasperated by his skittish mood and averted face. "But when I came by the plague cannot be further from my knowledge, yet you treat me as though I am dangerous . . . I seldom see your eyes, much less hear your voice."

"Perhaps your protection is too stout," he grumbled.

She looked at the side of his face and shook her head in denial. "Then, sir knight, I gave you more credence than you were due." He looked at her sharply and she shrugged as though she had not spoken. "If Segeland needs some caring for, we shall be busy. I humbly thank you for your frankness. 'Tis a better thing that I know what worries plague you."

He looked at her in some wonder.

"There is something more, monseigneur?" He shook his head. "The night is cold and I shiver," she invited, hoping he would draw her near. Instead, he turned her and led her back into the room with the fire, their conversation done.

Chapter Nine

FÉLISE'S FIRST GLIMPSE OF THE KEEP AND TOWN FROM a distance was so like the picture she'd made in her mind that she doubted her own mortal and therefore limited senses and wondered if she'd dreamt the place. They rose atop a hill, the site obviously chosen for its natural protection. The wall surrounded a modest town. The fields outside were barren in late winter. There were no grazing animals; the wood was a good and safe distance from the hall.

As they came closer, she could clearly see the condition of ill repair. The place appeared to be abandoned but for one or two villagers who cautiously peered out of their simple houses as the riders passed toward the hall. Some Leighton ancestor with visions of power had provided a strong wall and sturdy keep, but little had been done to maintain the place. Her first curiosity rose: since the fundamental necessities were here, why had no one taken the town and hall? They were not defended. Did Royce wish some neighboring noble to usurp him? Did curses and ghosts keep the brigands away?

The keep was raised out of the local stone and looked to be over one hundred years old, perhaps even constructed by some landed Norman centuries ago. It was as solid a structure as a rich man could build in a score of years — yet the village road had not been cleared, filled, or widened in as many years. Smoke from the roofs of the thatched houses indicated residents, but there was no sign of stock, children, or guards.

Félise heard her brothers muttering behind her, quite possibly all asking the same questions as she. They gained the hall; within, the conditions were the same. It was in want of cleaning and staff and apparently housed only sad memories. There was no fire in the hearth, something that even the poorest halls could offer to travelers.

Félise was rather taken with the place, as if it was a simple matter to look past the dust and vermin to see a shining home. The main hall was large and a few trestle tables and benches were scattered about. The cold, dirty hearth would bank a fire that could warm one hundred men-at-arms. The stairway to the second level was wide and solid stone, and the ceiling was high. There were no windows here, which would keep the place warm in winter, cool in summer, and safe in all seasons. She anticipated the second level, hoping to find the same good sense in the construction.

"I have sent Sir Hewe to find the bailiff," Royce informed her.

"There is a bailiff here?" she asked. "What does he do?"

"He is one of the few vassals of my father and brother worth retaining," Royce said somewhat defensively. "He sees mostly to the welfare of the town, his function in the main being to keep some records."

Félise frowned her confusion but did not question Royce further. The answers, she told herself, would come in time. Many curiosities assailed her. Why had these villeins chosen their meager shacks over the warmth of the hall, especially if the lord of all this had abandoned it? Why was there a bailiff to keep records when clearly there were only modest — if any — revenues from this sorry place? Why had Royce's warnings been so vehement, as if the place were a scandalous shack, when in fact it was a worthy if neglected keep?

She had recognized Sir Hewe on the first morning of their travels as the one among Royce's men who had flirted with her in London. He was a friendly and kind young man, though his frivolous behavior had vanished with the marriage. They had nodded at each other once in recognition and from that point on had not so much as allowed their eyes to meet. Félise wondered if Hewe feared Royce.

The bailiff's name was Colbert and he was sturdy, gray haired, and over fifty years. When he entered the hall he gave Royce a short bow, shook his hand, and maintained a serious expression, conveying no special happiness or relief at the reunion. Félise watched them and listened to their brief conversation.

"How many tenants this winter?"

"One hundred or so. Only two deaths during this cold, Sir Royce."

"And stock?"

"Less than the previous year."

"Revenues?"

"Barely anything, sir. But the tithe is met."

"Planting?"

Colbert shrugged. "They save their seed, but 'tis poor. Last harvest saw little."

Félise approached them, gathering that Royce was not going to introduce her properly. When Royce became aware of her, he presented Colbert. "My lady Félise, my wife," he said. "Colbert has been the bailiff here since I was born. He was a young man then."

"Bailiff?" Félise said, smiling at the man, but noticing it did not seem to warm him. "From your conversation, it sounds as though you act more the castellan here. Tell me, Master Colbert, why do the people not use this vacant hall in the cold months?"

"There are many worries to keep them from the hall, lady," he answered easily. "They keep to their huts lest the master return and demand his home, and they fear the place brings bad luck. The priest who visits our town tells them not to conspire with the devil even if Satan provides the warmth of a stone hall."

Félise did not see the darkening of Royce's expression with these words, but rather she laughed softly at Colbert. "Then does no one see to Sir Royce's house? It is badly in need of repair and cleaning."

"I did not require it of them," Royce said. "I did not plan to use the hall as a residence. It has been vacant for some years and was neglected for many years before that."

She looked around, more interested in what would have to be done to make the place habitable than in its ominous reputation. "How long has it been empty?" she asked.

"Since my brother's death . . . just a few years."

"Hmmm. Well, are there those who would be willing to work here?" she asked Colbert. "Some extra labor would do to see the place decent, but we will need a few to remain, lest it go to ruin again. My lord, are there quarters within the hall for one or two families to remain in service to the manor?"

"I would leave that to you, madam, when you've surveyed the place."

"You intend to *live* here?" Colbert asked.

"Of course," Félise replied. "Why do you think we are here?"

"As usual . . . ah . . . I supposed that Sir Royce came to judge the revenues and tithes and . . . pardon, lady. It has been empty a long time. I don't know who to name willing," Colbert said. "They are simple people and frightened of ghosts."

"But there are no ghosts," she said simply. Whatever the malady that plagued all these people, including her husband, Félise was not concerned about malevolent spirits or other imaginings. This was another asset to living with Edrea, who was all good sense and seldom carried away by any superstition.

But she noticed that Royce seemed to look away, his jaw tensed, and Colbert looked down at her with a certain tolerance she read to mean he doubted her bravery more than the presence of evil in the hall. A chuckle escaped her. "May God forgive you both for forgetting His mercy. Go to your people, Colbert, and find me a few stout men and two strong women, and remind them that the living are by far stronger than the dead. And if we are to live here permanently, there is work to be done. Royce?"

His voice came as a strained whisper, as if for her ears alone. "I beg you understand, lady, that it is not so much the spirits of those who died here that frighten these peasants, but more the memory of rule. My grandfather, my uncle, my father, my brother — all were cruel lords. I venture they expect the same from me."

"Then we shall show them otherwise," she returned, an almost cheerful note to her voice. "Will you send Master Colbert to find us a few workers?"

He nodded, but his eyes were glassy and distant. Félise was left to stare at her husband, who seemed almost paralyzed. He was not taking charge of the situation for them. The entry and main hall were slowly filling up with the people who had traveled there with them, but Royce gazed about as if he did not see them. She couldn't help but wonder if his vision of returning here with Celeste after the hall had been cleaned and readied caused him some melancholy.

"Is there a store of provender for these travelers, Royce?" she asked.

"Some," he said distractedly. "I'm certain it is modest: a keg or two of ale, wine, perhaps a bag of grain. We will have to hunt. There would be nothing to butcher for a meal this eventide."

"We were foolish not to carry food from Coventry. Might we send a wagon there now?"

"For the morning?" he asked.

Félise sighed heavily. She would not be put off by his musings over his lost bride. If what he needed was time to adjust to coming here with her, she would at least show her worth.

"Aye, since supplies cannot be brought here any sooner, we should send someone right away. Let us see to the storerooms and chambers. We can't do much before sunset, but dry wood for the fire can be found, small game killed and cleaned and put to roast, and Daria and Vespera can judge the supplies and perhaps add to our meal with bread. Surely there is a laying hen or two in the village."

Royce nodded and began slowly to come to terms with the work ahead. He turned to an older knight he called Sir Trumble and asked him to gather four men for a short hunt, four to take a cart to Coventry, and four to aid him in the stable. When Félise was satisfied that he was busy, she began her own assessment.

Maelwine and Vespera went with Félise, while Dalton and

Evan set out looking for a store of dry firewood to warm the hall, and Daria was instructed to rummage through the kitchens for usable items. It was almost an adventure for Félise, who found there was a great deal more to Segeland than was apparent at first glance. More than a few kegs of good winter ale were found in a storeroom dug under the kitchens. There was decent Gascony wine, a meager amount of bagged meal, a fine collection of dried herbs and spices, and even some trunks of linens that badly needed washing but were otherwise in good condition.

Her original opinion held true as she wandered through the large rooms. When bright fires warmed each hearth, when pots of brewis simmered in great kettles, when tapestry hangings decorated the walls and rushes and rugs lay scattered about the hard floors, this would be a good home. Workers would be needed to make repairs on the road, they would need better than the small game from a short hunt, and there were many places that could use a skilled craftsman to repair walls, doors, and furniture.

Félise did not see what was lacking. She saw what was there. Segeland was large. Strong. The earth on which it stood was fertile. Stuffed in the corners of empty rooms and closets there were broken chairs, benches, and cookware. The draperies were of a good imported cloth, thick and well sewn. She moved faster and chattered more with every new discovery. "These dishes will do, but I fear our lack of mugs . . . a good spring breeze will take the smell out of these quilts . . . there is ale and wine enough for the longest winter . . . the supply of meal is more than adequate until Coventry's stores can be investigated . . . a good hand on this trestle table will give it another score of years . . . oil on these stools will soften the wood and give it a shine . . ."

Vespera followed quietly, nodding with every exclamation. Maelwine followed but grumbled, perhaps more because he wanted to judge the place, not renovate it to her satisfaction. On the second level she was stopped short for a moment. Her breath caught in her throat at what she saw. Twin chambers stood at the top of the high and dangerous staircase. One, the door creaking open loudly, as if in pain, was a lord's chamber, judging by the design of the high bed and chests and table desk. The other, barred heavily from the outside, must have been the lady's chamber. There, Félise suspected, Royce's mother had been held captive.

There was a third door inside, joining the chambers. Here too there were bars and bolts on the lord's side. From within she could see that the rooms were large and equal, but for the doors that gave the lord of the manor the advantage of keeping a prisoner. The window from the lady's chamber was closed with stone and there were brackets on the wall, attached to the stone, that may once have held chains.

Félise walked toward the place where the window was walled up, wondering if this measure had been meant to prevent escape or keep the pitiful woman from jumping to her death. She faced the stone and stared at it as if she would look through it.

"If the bricks are knocked out and a garden fashioned in the inner bailey, it could be viewed from here," she said, a note of sadness in her voice.

"By God, Félise, don't you see what this place is?" Maelwine asked with impatience.

She turned to him. "I see," she said.

"This place, this room and all of the hall, are not worthy of the beasts, much less you."

"Maelwine, it must be made worthy. None of us, not even Royce, had a hand in this travesty."

"I would have you stay in the stable under my guard before I would leave you in this prison."

"Maelwine," she sighed, shaking her head. "This was a bitter place, as Royce explained. It need not remain so."

"How will our father accept the news that you reside in a hall haunted by the evil of generations of Leightons? Good God, the townspeople are so afraid they cannot be induced to work here, and the lord of the manor walks through the rooms as if asleep, indeed in the midst of a nightmare. 'Tis clear his protection is not equal to your status."

Status, she thought wearily. She found herself wishing again for her mother. All the men in her life, from her father and brothers to the king to her husband and the suitors at court, made these dreary assumptions about her status. She was too good to sleep in this dilapidated mansion, but not too good to be ordered wed to a stranger — one that she had even feared. She didn't understand where her true value lay. She wished Maelwine had stayed away and Edrea had been allowed to accompany her. At least her mother's simple wisdom in these matters would be more useful to her now than her brother's criticism.

Through Maelwine's discontented lecture, Félise simply looked at him, not reacting in any way. When he was done she spoke very calmly. "We'll decide upon the sleeping rooms when my lord's preference is known," she said simply, walking past her brother and out of the room.

There was no question but that it would be weeks or months before Segeland and its town would appear equal to a noble demesne. By the time the sun was setting, there were a few rabbits on spits over a fire in the main room, and enough bowls and platters had been scoured to serve the food upon. The grain was stale and provided only flat bread, some eggs were stewing and the drippings from the meat would provide a thick, seasoned gravy. No candles could be found, but torches aplenty lit the large room. Spirits were not low but quiet, since the day had been full for everyone.

Félise didn't know how many of those dining there saw great promise in the hall. Everyone gathered, whether sitting at the long trestle table or on the floor, would be thenceforth in residence, with the exception of the Scelfton men. Twenty or so men-at-arms, plus fourteen pages subject to the knights, two serving women — Daria and Vespera — and the lord and lady would call this home. It was frankly a modest group for a keep of this size, but in her mind she envisioned their growing numbers.

Royce dined beside her, his mood only slightly better. He had spoken little, mainly answering her questions and making no further comment. She had barely seen him about the hall, as his occupation had been to see that the stables were fit for the destriers that would bear his knights. But at least he did not seem beset by some strange confusion. It was not unreasonable, in her mind, that he would be of saddened spirit in this environment.

Still, she continually thought of their days at the Chaney

house. She almost laughed as she remembered wondering if she would ever consider that a tender memory. He had been mostly gentle and kind to her before the Scelfton knights appeared. His mood had been even and he was good-tempered. The nights had been filled with passion, and while it had been new to her, she had reveled in it. What she hoped for Segeland was that it would become a decent home made rich by the robust nature of its tenants and nights like those at the Chaney house. It did not seem impossible. Possible, she thought, if Royce could resign himself to life with her here.

She allowed Daria her freedom in the hall, but bade Vespera to stay near and dine at their table. Thus the woman sat beside Félise and regularly interrupted her meal to make a suggestion or ask a question. They were nearly finished eating when Master Colbert came to the hall with a small group of villagers in tow. He stood just inside the door, twisting his hat in his hands, his companions standing without and in wait.

Félise followed Royce as he rose to see to the bailiff. "I have found two men who will work and whose wives will help in the hall, and four young men . . . the young do not remember Lord Leighton well enough to . . . that is . . ."

"I understand," Royce grumbled. "Bring them in."

Félise strained to look around her large husband and judge these people who would work with her. They kept their eyes mostly downcast as they entered, staying just inside the door and reluctant to come further. Master Colbert recited their names but she could not attach them to individuals. Townsend, Braserus, Mackery, Jeremy, Richter, and Thomas. She nodded with each name, trying to give a comforting smile, but the people were obviously jittery. Royce likewise nodded, but he was a long time silent.

"It will be good to have you in service," he finally said, not much enthusiasm in his voice.

Félise was troubled not only by the people here, but by her husband who seemed to be endorsing this gloom. She took a deep breath and bolstered herself.

"You have lodgings with your families?" she asked.

Nearly all eyes rose to meet hers as the people nodded.

"And you are willing to work in this hall?" Again they nodded. "Then you shall be bidden here during the light hours and you may return to your families for sleep. When such a time comes that you do not think ill of this hall, there will be a place for you through the day and night. And you will be paid for your work. Does this agreement suit you?"

There were nods all around and two smiles from the youngest of the meager group.

"Thank you, Master Colbert. I shall see you again at cockcrow," she said.

When they returned to their dinner, hardly cooled during the brief introductions, Royce turned to her to compliment her. "It would appear you have more experience in this than I would have allowed. I believe you gave them peace of mind."

"My lord, I have no experience whatever in the problems of this hall. I swear by the Virgin, I have never encountered such fear and worry."

"You have not known the place for as long as I . . . nor so long as they."

"You were here as a child?" she asked. He nodded quite gravely. "But not in residence for a very long time?" she asked.

Royce unhurriedly chewed on a mouthful of food, then took a deep breath. "It was in fact my mother's father who saw to my rearing and training. He was allowed a brief visit here to judge his daughter's health. He liked none of what he saw, but the thing that plagued him most was my treatment. He was a fine old gentleman who knew that the worst had already been done and could see no usefulness in any further waste of life. It was apparent I was born of my father and his captive wife . . . but my grandfather thought that to leave me here might be dangerous. He took me away."

"Your father mistreated you?" she asked, trying to keep her questions gentle.

"Nay, but he favored my older brother, Aylworth, and my mother could not look on me. Every year I spent here, I was hiding from one of them, lest some angry hand smite me just for the color of my eyes or set of my jaw." He looked pointedly into her eyes. "This ugly scar, lady, comes from the back of my mother's hand. My father would have gowned my mother richly, and he did give her jewels and furs and many valuable gifts, but none of this soothed her injury. He had taken her from another man; a man who never tried to rescue her. Her hatred burned deep and, in the end, burned me. 'Twas a rich ring my father purchased that caused the mark you look on now."

Félise wished to keep pity from her eyes, but the image of a small boy being struck by his mother caused her agony. She let her hand touch his, and he flinched slightly.

"Riches mean little when love is lacking," she said softly. "When did your mother die?" she asked.

"Not long after my grandfather took me away from here."

"She valued life little," Félise said solemnly.

"She could not tolerate the fact that a man she did not want could take her so easily. Forsooth, he took her, wed her outside the church laws, and got her with child. She had nothing to say of it."

"Did she not try to tolerate him, Royce? Was he so cruel —"

"Félise, *I* do not know. How would I?"

"I'm sorry. I would not cause you pain with bad memories; it's just that it is difficult to understand people who would not try to rise above their misfortune. When I face difficulties —"

"Wherein lies the difference, madam?" he asked, his tone harsh, as if he was offended. "You, of all, would understand the misery of being forced against your will. And if finding that was not insult enough, imagine loving another and being denied him. Surely you would understand my mother's heart better than I." He stopped himself and seemed to struggle with the words. "It is of no matter," he finally said. "You will be neither chained nor abused. If you can find naught but misery here, 'twill be a hell of your own making and one I cannot set right."

He turned back to his dinner, and she watched his internal struggle as it played on his face. His brows drew together and his jaw was tense as he ground the food. Again she believed that his greatest agony lay in having a bride he wished none of thrust upon him. He had been forced, and if that was not a tragedy great enough, he loved and wanted another.

She, too, looked down at her plate. The food itself was poor enough to spoil her appetite, but his hostile words only made the meal that much less desirable. She struggled with tears that threatened to fall. She began to think Royce would repeat his mother's despair, never even looking to see if some gift lay hidden within this indignity.

Félise was not so filled with vanity that she could easily place herself above Lady Celeste, but she wondered how that frail dame had managed to become so treasured in Royce's mind. She was troubled with it, feeling certain that she was nothing like Celeste in any way . . . highly doubting she could be, even if that was her husband's desire.

Need I imitate the lady's pale beauty? she asked herself. Or show him that I am stronger and therefore more worthy? Or mayhap I should remain still while the memory of the other woman fades?

She found little enthusiasm for conversation with any of the others, whose plates were emptying all around her. The long day was quickly coming to an end.

"My lord," she beckoned quietly, not looking at him as she spoke, "we have not yet laid down our pallets. I would leave the matter of rooms to you, though I have looked through the chambers and there is adequate space for all."

He seemed to grow stiff at her side, troubled by the matter.

"The lord's chamber is in civil repair, messire," she said softly. "You will find it comfortable enough. It is perhaps the best room in the hall."

"You have seen the lady's chamber as well?" he asked.

Félise noticed that Maelwine had looked up from his plate and was staring at Royce.

"I have seen it. Work needs be done there, as everywhere else."

"I will not ask that you take the room," Royce said evenly.

"What would you have me do, Royce?" she asked.

He sighed deeply. "There is space enough within the keep; perhaps another room can be found for you."

Félise felt her heart skip a beat. He did not offer to share his room. She had feared, the day through, that he would set her further from him with every passing moment.

"I am aware that the room is the largest available to you, but it is filled with the ghosts of a grim past, and I see no need for you to take it simply because it was designed for the lady of the hall. I, too, saw the condition of the room." He looked at her as if he would look through her. "Name the chamber of your choice and I will lay a fire in that hearth for your comfort."

Félise quieted her trembling insides as best she could, searching for some inner wisdom. Her fondest hope had been that he would offer his room to share, his bed as hers. That he did not was one disappointment. She felt, from his words and actions, that it would be a long time before he would accept her as his wife and lady, but she would not let him set her far away. On some future day, should he prove tractable and willing, she intended to be near. If it was not possible for him to put aside his misery tonight, then she would at least show him that the ghosts of painful memories need not haunt them further.

"The lady's chamber is more than adequate. I will make a few alterations to improve it, with your permission."

"You prefer it over another room?" he asked, his expression strained as if the notion hurt him.

" 'Tis the lady's chamber and shares a common door to the lord's chamber," she said. "That is where I should be." It occurred to her to mention that he could use that door, but she lacked the courage.

Maelwine's fist hit the table in unconcealed rage. "I won't allow my sister in that room until the bars, bolts, and brackets for chains are disposed of."

Royce looked at him sharply, his palms pressed to the table and his thighs straining as if he would rise. Félise put her hand on his arm and spoke quickly to Maelwine. "Then pray hurry to your task of remedy, brother mine, for I am weary and would sooner find sleep than worry over some old furnishings that have no importance to me. If you wish the bars and bolts removed, then you may see to it. And I beg you remember, Royce did not install those implements to use against me." She settled her voice to a gentler tone. "Many changes need to be made, Maelwine. Do not delay us with harsh words and insults."

Royce relaxed his body, though he was still staring at Maelwine. "The lady has chosen her room. Any improvement you deem necessary, you may attend to."

Félise sighed in relief and turned to Vespera. "Will you help me in the chamber, madam? It has been such a long day."

The women escaped up the stairs, Félise fighting back the tears and going quickly, sure in her mind that Maelwine and perhaps her other brothers would be along to take the locks from the doors before she could even collect herself. She entered the room and stood within, breathing deeply, trying to smooth her hurt feelings.

"Félise, you are not afraid of this room?" Vespera asked.

"Nay," she said almost angrily. "Why would I fear this room? 'Tis not a person, but a thing. There is naught here to harm me. It is the room allowed the mistress of this hall, joined to the master's room, and whether he wills it or not, I *am* the lady here now. That he wants none of me is clear, but I will not be placed far down the hall where some lesser servant of his will must reside. I am his wife; I will take the chamber."

"It only *seemed* he did not wish it so," Vespera quietly tried to correct.

"Nay, he does not wish it so," she said, her voice catching. "Many things plague Royce, not the least of which is his marriage with me." Large tears rolled helplessly down her cheeks as she looked beseechingly into Vespera's sympathetic eyes. "He cares naught for dower riches, which should be clear to all of us after seeing his home. The only reason I am here is that he has a fierce loyalty to Henry's order. Would that the king had ordered him to love me as well."

Vespera slowly stroked her arm. "Mayhap that will come with time."

"That challenge is the worst of all," Félise said as she wept. "And one I know not how to meet. But if yon lord of this wretched castle means to show me as weak, he shall fail, for I will work. And if he would reject me for my fear of ghosts, I shall end that tonight, by burying his mother's memory as I live peacefully in her room. And if he chooses his grief and misery over a blessed union that would yield him peace, I cannot change him. But I *will not* help him to cling to his despair."

Her anger vented, she collapsed into Vespera's arms and the woman gently held her, rubbing her back and caressing her hair. "Oh, my darling," she soothed. "I am so very proud of you. 'Twas my prayer every day and every night of my life that you would grow strong and with courage and wisdom. You are the only possible woman to rule this hall. There, sweet . . ."

Félise slowly withdrew from Vespera's arms and looked at her. "Beg pardon, madam," she sniffled. "What did you say?"

Vespera smiled. "I said you are the only woman worthy of making this a home for Royce. No other could possibly do what you can do."

"Before that," she asked. "What did you say before?"

"I said I have prayed for you . . . for your courage and wisdom in this troublesome circumstance. And you see? Our prayers were answered. You shall win this battle, Lady Félise. And I am proud of you."

Félise cocked her head, for that was not what she thought she had heard.

"Dry your eyes," Vespera said, running a gentle finger along Félise's cheek. "I'm certain Sir Maelwine will not let you sleep before the doors are repaired to his liking." She whispered, as if there was some great secret. "Do not let your noble brother see that you weep. He will surely think the worst."

Félise nodded, silently agreeing that this extra protection by her brothers was causing her more trouble than help. She lifted her hem to wipe her eyes, and the two women began unrolling pallets to sleep upon.

Chapter Ten

WITHIN JUST A FEW DAYS, THE WORK INSIDE THE hall had progressed in a manner that pleased everyone. Even Félise, in her most optimistic thoughts, could not have hoped for so much. Each of Royce's men-at-arms seemed to have some special skill in either carpentry, masonry, or another craft that was put to quick use. Money and hard work were needed to make it a rich-looking hall, but it emerged as safe and adequate in little time.

The men Royce had gathered over a period of many years had not served any other Leightons before, and while they were not protected from the gossip about the family, they found no fault with Royce. They, like Félise, seemed to brush aside the old worries of a family curse and worked diligently to make Segeland an acceptable place. That faithful troop took the edge off the bitterness that seemed to hover over the hall and town. Whenever some unkind comment was made about the previous lords, a knight would simply respond, "That was before Sir Royce." Seeing her husband through the eyes of his loyal vassals gave her hope. They had been with him a long time, and none doubted his goodness and strength.

Daria's first assignment to the kitchens had evolved quickly into her management of same. She was heady with the power of commanding the two village women and experimenting with the food brought from the forest and Coventry. Her duties to Félise lapsed immediately, and Félise did not miss the maid's attentions in her bedchamber.

Vespera, on the other hand, quickly assumed the chamber duties for Félise. She began brushing her long hair, preparing her baths, arranging and keeping her clothing and other personal items, and staying close not only as a servant but as a companion. All three women thrived on the change.

Early one morning, while Vespera was laboriously braiding and winding Félise's hair, Félise clicked off a long litany of chores she would attend to. "While this hall could occupy me for long weeks to come, I see that it is time I took a closer look at the town and people. I don't know what Royce has done there."

"He seems to be concerned mainly with the perimeters of the property, the wall, and the stables," Vespera said. "I see him ride out often, but he spends little time here."

Félise thought for a moment. "Perhaps he will accustom himself to this place soon. I worry that he is not best suited to deal with the villeins. He seems to encourage their preoccupation with worries."

"He is worried himself, lady," Vespera said quietly. " 'Tis hard to show a bright countenance when that is not what one feels."

"Indeed," Félise sighed. "His choice of mood is not mine to tamper with, but whatever energy I put into this house, it is only as sound as the people of the town. If their poverty and ills and fears need tending to, we must not await Royce's whim. His dark mood could outlast his people's needs."

They finished a morning meal in the hall and, judging everyone to be hard at work and needing no advice, direction, or supervision, Félise and Vespera walked from the hall to the village. Again Félise found the people to be mostly out of sight. Although it was still too cold for planting and there seemed to be no animals to tend, she wondered why all the activity in and around the hall had not induced these people to open their doors and let themselves be seen. They walked down the road, past the huts, to the end of the town where the gate stood open so that the knights, hunters, and laborers could come and go freely. Still, no one came outside to speak with them.

The house that stood closest to the wall and gate was of the best quality in the town. Here, the door opened and Colbert came outside. "Good morningtide, lady. May I give you some assist?"

Félise was relieved to see him, since all the closed doors had given her a dreary feeling. "Indeed, Master Colbert. I have come from the hall to see these people Lord Leighton will work to protect. Why do they hide from us?"

"Beg pardon, lady, but they are by nature a suspicious lot."

"They are slow to understand that we wish them no ill. I would, in fact, look to their gravest needs. Would you help me, or must I rap on each door?"

He frowned his displeasure. "Mayhap it would be better to give them time to open their doors and —"

"Even you are slow to accept my good intentions toward this place." She smiled at him, trying to dissolve the memory of abuse with a display of kindness. "How can I convince you, sir?"

He sighed, but his stony old face, wrinkled into a grim expression, eased but little. "I am loath to worry you with mean tales, but nearly every person here has seen one of our number either whipped or hung or beaten for the slightest offense. And in the short time since the last Leighton to rule here died, they have had other fears. They have been warned of eternal damnation simply for living here. They have long expected the return of an evil lord."

Félise felt her hackles rising, though she tried to keep her temper. That Royce came from brutal beginnings was understood, but she was losing patience with that old excuse. He had not, in his lifetime, done anything to these people that she was aware of. To make sure, she inquired of Colbert, "Has any among these people suffered punishment by Royce? Has he taken this hall and vented his wrath on this town?"

"Nay, madam, but —"

"Then let us discover these people, Colbert. They need not hover in fear within their homes. We need their help to make this a decent place. And they need the protection and sustenance of a good master."

He shrugged as if beaten and walked ahead of her to the next house. He rapped on the door, but there was no response. He called out to the tenant, announcing himself, and the door cautiously creaked open. A man of perhaps thirty years stood in the frame of the door and appeared already frightened. Colbert introduced him as William, and the man bowed to Félise.

"Do you have a family, William?" Félise asked pleasantly.

"Aye, there are seven here. My wife and five children."

"Five," she exclaimed. "A worthy number."

" 'Twere six. One died last winter."

"Illness?" she asked.

"Um, 'twas hunger, lady," he replied shyly.

Félise straightened as if slapped. "A child starved here, in this house?" she asked indignantly.

"Aye, lady."

"William, are the children hungry now?" she questioned.

"There be little, lady. I farm and hunt, but I save the seed for planting and the game's deep in the wood."

Félise looked past William and tried to see into his small, one-room house. She saw a woman kneeling at the hearth, a child at her breast, and several small ones about the dark room. She felt a prickling anger rise at the sight of their poverty. She could think of no excuse for them to be left in this desperate condition, least of all her husband's melancholy attitude toward this place.

"Do you have provender now that you save for the spring planting?" she asked. The man nodded lamely, reluctantly, as if he wished not to answer lest she take possession of what little he had. "Bid your wife make bread and porridge, and I will see that you have seed aplenty for the planting. And William, we must plan a larger plot for wheat and rye and some fruit trees. This town will grow over the next years and we must be ready to provide. Tonight, before the sun is set, one of Royce's men will bring you meat. I can't have your family thin if you're to work for our harvest."

William looked at her strangely and Félise felt he did not believe her.

"William, henceforth when your family hungers, come to the hall and you will be provided for. We must be as one or none of us shall thrive here."

"The hall, lady?" he asked, somewhat shaken by her suggestion.

"I have been told it was a fearful place in years past, but you have nothing to fear from Lord Leighton. If you choose to starve rather than seek aid from your master, you do us grave dishonor. I would have you take my words close to your heart."

He simply stared at her, and she made a silent promise to herself to have something delivered to the man's house before midday to press her intention closer to his stomach. This condition was deplorable.

"Good morningtide, William," she said, turning from his door.

As they began to walk the short way to the next house, Colbert's sarcasm cut through Félise's already-thin cover of control. "Do you mean to fatten the whole village, my lady?"

She stopped abruptly, enraged by the comment. "Will it disappoint you to learn that I will not fatten them to feed them to the wolves?" she responded, her temper flaring. "Aye, I will feed them all, if that is what is necessary to keep them alive the remainder of the year."

"You will find their manner difficult to understand, lady. They are very slow to learn and may prefer hunger over visiting the hall. They have not had a master to trust in many years."

"Do you conspire with these old tales to see the children starve?" she stormed.

"Nay," he said, defending himself. "It is simply that the grief and fear here are —"

"You cling to that old misery more mightily than any," she raged. "You, who see to the records of this town in Royce's behalf, are as slow to aid us as any oafish mule, with your love of harsh memories. The next house, Colbert. And if you would see a better day come to this burg, you might give your allegiance to my good intention rather than defending this old foolishness."

Her lips were pursed in anger and she waited while Colbert repeated the whole process of announcing himself before the door was opened to him. Again Félise found fear and poverty. She repeated her wish to provide, failing to grasp the cause of the anguish here. By the fourth house, again filled with thin and nervous peasants, she turned to Vespera. "The Leightons must indeed have been a vicious lot to have damaged these people to this extent. I cannot in my darkest nightmare imagine what terrible things must have happened here to yield this horror."

They had visited over a dozen small huts when a door was opened by a thin, elderly woman who Colbert introduced as Ulna, a widow. Félise spoke to her briefly and found her manner slightly less intractable. "How long have you been widowed, Ulna?" Félise asked.

"Been on eight years, lady," she replied. "I have two sons still alive, one in this village, one gone."

Félise looked past her, into her house. "Ulna, you have a loom?"

She became slightly nervous. "Aye, but there's little enough thread."

"But if we can find a source of wool, you can teach some of the others to weave. Ulna, how wonderful! I will see to it as soon as possible. There are many needs in the hall for cloth." She noticed the widow's eyes widen slightly. "I will pay you for your labors, of course."

Ulna smiled shyly, shrugging off any remaining fear. " 'Twould be a pleasure to do your weaving, lady."

"Tell me, Ulna, does your son provide for you? Does he hunt and give you an allotment of meat and grain from his labors?"

"He has four children, but he does what he can for me. He's not much with farming . . . never had the clever hand with crops that he's got with wood . . . but we can't eat carvings, and he's a good man. He tries."

"Carving?" Félise mused. "His services could be of use in the hall —"

"In the hall, lady?"

"Ulna," Félise nearly scolded, but a light laugh and pleasant smile accompanied her admonishment. "I thought you had greater understanding. You have no need to fear the hall; it has already grown into a pleasant place. You are welcome there and I will share with you from my own table if there is need. I will have this town at my table if that is what is required to end the misery here."

Ulna looked questioningly at Colbert as if to ask if this were true. The bailiff might not be filled with trust, but he supported Félise as best he could. "The lady speaks true. She makes her offer of charity to every house and wills this to be a stronger town with full bellies. This bodes well for the spring, Ulna."

The widow looked back at Félise and they exchanged smiles. For the first time that morning, Félise began to feel that there was some hope among these people. "And the master?" Ulna asked with some hesitation.

Félise nodded with assurance. "He troubles with the dark past as much as any of these people, but he is a strong and good lord. He would approve."

Their attention was drawn to the sound of horses, and three riders came through the open gate. Colbert immediately stiffened and his sullen expression returned. Ulna lowered her gaze and quietly withdrew into her house, closing and bolting the door. Félise simply stared curiously at this visiting retinue.

The man leading the group rode a fine destrier and was gowned in rich purple robes. Behind him were two knights, their costumes and horses indicating their equal wealth, their arms glittering with a powerful shine. Félise first imagined this was a wealthy noble neighbor with two men-at-arms.

They rode straight toward the threesome in the middle of the road, and when they were upon them, the fancy lord dismounted. As he approached on foot, Félise noted the clerical garb under his mantle and she genuflected, crossing herself, as did Vespera. But the cleric did not bless her.

"I have not seen you here before," he said suspiciously. "Where have you come from?"

Colbert opened his mouth, but Félise instantly, from some buried instinct, cut him off with her words. "I am lately from London, Father." She touched Colbert's arm and indicated she would speak for herself.

"You may address me as 'lord' or 'monseigneur,' wench. Why are you here?"

"I have lately acquired this hall, monseigneur," she said coyly.

The man laughed loudly, a cruel sound that rang through the streets. Félise turned and looked at Vespera, finding the woman frowning blackly at the priest. "You will find it a hateful place. I trust you will not be here long."

"I plan to be here a very long time," she said evenly. "Why are you here? Do you bring the faith to these people?"

He laughed again and the knights still on horseback joined him. "I am Monseigneur Trothmore of Coventry. I bring the faith and collect the tithe."

"There is no tithe here," she said.

"The church demands a portion for the promise of deliverance," he ordered coolly.

"There is no tithe, Father," she said, pointedly refusing to use the title he demanded. "These poor people starve for want of a meal and have nothing to share with the church."

"On whose authority do you reject the prayers of one ordained by God?" he blustered, his cheeks growing pink with rage.

"On my own," she quietly replied. One of her many questions had been quickly answered by the presence of this man. Her experience with villages had been modest, but there were some things common to all English hamlets. Her father had once reckoned with an evil priest at Twyford, risking the threat of excommunication by driving away an ambitious cleric who would bleed the people of what little they had by selling blessings. "By the look of your rich robes, Father, you do not give the full portion of the tithe to the church and could find a way to take less."

She turned to Colbert. "Fetch my husband or any Scelfton knight, Colbert. And instruct him to bring arms."

"You would raise arms to an emissary of God?" Colbert questioned nervously.

She began to understand the collective fear. There was a good possibility that Royce did not know the poverty of this town could be attributed largely to the selfishness of this one man.

"Go quickly, Colbert. Do as I say."

"Hold your pace," the priest demanded hotly. "You, wench,

would do well to ask these people their preference. They may not choose your civic guard, which would earn them an eternal hell."

"This is hell. Don't you recognize your own creation?"

"You court danger, woman," he warned. "If the church abandons you, there will be little to rule here."

"Go quickly, Colbert, lest this *humble* disciple do worse than threaten to have his gold." Colbert turned, somewhat reluctantly at first, but finally moving at a brisk pace. Vespera leaned near and whispered in her ear. "Take care, lady. The man wears the cleric robes, but his manner gives the lie to his friendship with God." Félise nodded gravely, more than aware of the danger in this action she took.

"You would do well to ask these wretches if they want Satan's rule here, or if they are better parted with a hen or a pig to buy heaven for their dead," he boldly challenged.

The sound of a door opening caught the attention of all present in the street. Ulna stood in the doorway of her hut and looked at the priest, her eyes holding the daggers of a suddenly dawning truth. The priest turned to the widow. "Tell this mistress of yours that you would prefer to part with a bolt of cloth than to suffer eternal fire," he demanded.

Ulna held her grim expression and Félise waited patiently. "My lady speaks true," Ulna finally said. "The hell of this village is made of your greed . . . and she will pay me that I may eat, while you would take my last piece of bread." She paused and looked to Félise for support, the latter smiling proudly, and added, "There is no tithe here, nor can I buy another prayer for my dead husband."

"There will be a curse on this town," the cleric threatened. "And unless you reverse this blasphemy, I will petition for your excommunication."

"The curse has long since died from this town, Friar," Félise said, indicating by the title she used that he was not even a priest in her eyes. "And when you petition, be certain to address King Henry, for it is by his order that I reside in Segeland. He shall be most interested in the power you have attained here."

The priest blustered and stuttered, laying many curses to her and finally settling on one. "You wear the witch's locks of Satan in that red hair, and 'tis clear to any who would look that you are the heathen disguised, bringing eternal doom to this poor lot."

Félise laughed wickedly. "Good sir, do you mean to say that the color of my hair brings more evil than your claim to their very bread? By the Virgin, you must think them all fools."

She heard the opening of another door, then another. She did not turn to see who watched them, and her mounting rage would not allow her silence. "I have offered them food from my table, and you come to take away portions of their humble provender. They bury their children in want, and you, wearing your rich gown, come to claim whatever they have, leaving them to die in fear and shame. Be gone from here and let not your shadow darken my gate again. God in His power is merciful and wishes no man to starve his family to attain a blessing."

The priest grew taller in his anger and his cheeks were aflame with barely concealed hatred. He turned to his knights. "Smite her where she stands. She defies God and my obligation."

Félise gasped as the horsed men drew their swords from the sheaths at their belts. For an instant she believed they would dare to kill for a piglet or a bag of grain. She willed herself courage. "So, 'tis not enough to frighten these poor into submission, you will kill to get your due? I see," she shouted, loudly enough to open every door along the street. "You hereby prove your close acquaintance with the devil, though I did not know until today that Lucifer would sink so low as to disguise himself in the robes of a priest."

The knights froze and the priest stood his ground, but not without a hint of panic in his voice. "Strike her down. Strike down the bitch."

Just then the sound of a horse pounding down the road could be heard. Félise did not dare turn to look, but instead watched the priest's knights closely lest she be forced to dive away from a broadsword. She noticed the priest looked past her to judge the approaching steed, his eyes widening. Maelwine was beside her in moments, staying astride and ready to fight.

"Félise?" he questioned.

"Sir Maelwine, you look on the reason for the hunger in this burg. This rich priest comes here to sell blessings and extract a tithe from these starving people. I have ordered him to leave, and he has threatened my life."

More horses were approaching and a slow and victorious smile spread across Félise's lips. Her hatred of this man and what he had done with his power bit her so deeply she almost wished to see his blood wet the earth.

"From whence do you come?" Maelwine demanded, his voice ringing above the sound of the approaching horses.

"From Coventry," the priest returned.

"Then get thee to Coventry, and we shall see that another priest visits here. And should you venture this way again, be it known you are not welcome. God's mercy on you, if it is not too late."

Other knights had arrived in the street, and the priest quickly nodded toward his guards to sheathe their swords. The priest mounted and they quickly turned their horses and rode away from the town.

Félise looked toward Ulna. "Who else plagues this town?" she asked as gently as she could.

"There have not been thieves in a long while, my lady. There is nothing left to steal."

Félise gave her head a sharp nod. "We shall henceforth close the gate and man the wall, for as we prosper, so will the brigands notice this hamlet again. And these knights of Royce will let no traveling band stake its claim here."

Ulna nodded and smiled. Félise noticed, for the first time since her arrival, that some of the doors were opened more than a crack and people were looking out onto the street.

"Maelwine," she said loudly. "These people are hungry and have need of our charity. Please see that each family gets a share of what has come from Coventry. I trust it will give them more peace than the priest could."

She turned toward the hall, though her assessment of the people had not been completed. Vespera tried to keep pace, but Félise's outrage was so great that her steps were long and quick.

"Madam, Royce did not come."

"I will go to him."

"Madam, he could not have known —"

"What manner of lord would allow this to happen? What manner of bailiff would fail to report this to his master? If he has known of this treatment and failed to correct it, I have given him more credit than he is due. Curse," she muttered. "Curse, indeed."

Royce had ridden hard the day long, avoiding the town and hall. He deposited at the back of the hall the game he'd killed on his ride and instructed Daria to see it cleaned and roasted, then took his horse to the stables to tend him. He encountered Sir Trumble there and gathered the gossip of the day, the most exciting of which was that his tender bride had, in a flaming wrath, banished a priest from the town.

"What was she doing in the village?" Royce asked.

"Judging the needs of the people, it is said," Trumble replied.

"She could not leave that to me?" he asked.

Trumble shrugged, looking somewhat pleased. "Whatever, Royce, when she encountered the priest and judged his greed to harm the peasants, she drove him away." Trumble laughed, a low rumbling in his throat. "Be warned, he promised your lady will burn in hell."

"She did this *alone?*"

"Nay, Royce. Her brother and some of your men were called for. But I have little doubt she'd have whipped the friar herself had no guard appeared. I have not seen a woman's anger reach that height since Eleanor was taken to her prison." Then, still laughing, Trumble left Royce in the stable.

Through the maintenance of his destrier and equipment, Royce seethed. She did not ask his advice, rely on his counsel, wait for his command, or defer to his higher authority. She could have made the acquaintance of the priest, judged his behavior, and brought the matter to Royce's attention. But instead, with her mighty brothers in tow, she took control of the hall, town, and people and did her will.

He stripped off his gamberson and used the water in the stable for washing, sorely vexed by this recent custom as well. He hoped to avoid being caught in any state of undress in his own hall lest someone take notice of his mark and ridicule him. He had already decided that when the Scelfton knights finally departed and he felt at last the ruler of his own demesne, he would use his chamber for his baths — and he hoped that the time would come soon. Until they were gone, he feared some word of his deformity would give them the excuse they desired to take their sister away. The cold water and the mean condition of the stable only heightened his ire.

He heard the stable door close and he whirled around to face the intruder. Félise stood several paces away from him, just inside the door. "I have looked for you the day long, messire," she said.

Droplets of water fell from his hair and dripped off his beard onto his bare chest. Donned in only chausses and soft leather boots, he reached for the linen that hung over a stall. "How long have you been there?" he asked almost angrily.

"I've just come. I didn't mean to startle you, but I asked after you and Sir Trumble said you were here."

He grabbed his gamberson and pulled it over his wet body. "And so you find me. What is it you want?"

"I wished to speak to you, Royce, to explain that I have been to the village and —"

"This I have been told. You have been to the village to judge the peasants and have banished a lowly priest."

"He was not lowly, my lord, but very rich. And his visits here are in the main to strip the people of your town of everything they have. By now it is little enough: they starve."

"But you could not bring this to my ears alone, and allow me the common dignity due a lord of lands by letting me decide on the priest? You found the need to act in my stead?"

"Did I offend you, my lord?" she asked defensively, a bright swell of anger appearing in her blue-green eyes.

"What is *my* purpose here, lady, if you are able enough to manage the men, the hall, the peasants, the priests? Mayhap I should ride hither to some other keep and allow you to rule *your* hall."

She stiffened, her mouth rigid with anger. "You have made none of yourself available to the needs of this town and hall. Forsooth, you are gone from dawn till the setting sun . . . and am I to humbly accept this impoverished lot and make no effort to better it?"

He laughed cynically. "Pardon, madam, I thought you dined each night on food got of my bow and spear. I did not know you missed my labors in the washing of linens."

Her breath drew in sharply, his whooshed out as a dragon's would. They stood, several paces separating them, both tall in their anger, each with eyes blazing and fists clenched. With every exchanged remark, their voices became louder and stronger.

"Many in this hall can hunt, but only a few have the courage to face the conditions of the town. If you absent yourself from your obligation to the people, 'tis mine to assume or else watch the pain caused by these haunts you speak of so often."

"You might allow me to lend myself to their ills in all good time, since I know the nature of this old curse and you do not."

"Curse?" she nearly screamed. "The only curse I see is fear and self-pity."

"There is the curse of the pompous rich dame come to right all wrongs and rule as any dowager, complete with her own army of protectors."

"I did not bid my brothers venture here; indeed, they work as hard as any to see this wretched place fit."

"They flaunt their power and wealth and importance of name as much as you, leaving me to wonder what my part in my own keep is to be."

She put out her hands. "The blisters here come of labors and not of the doling out of coin from my riches," she shouted. "And I have yet to hear one word of praise from you, when this hall has gone from a swine bed to a decent abode."

"You never consulted me, or asked for my approval. You have taken all matters of ruling into your own hands."

"You have never offered service or aid, but only criticized my every effort to offer you a good home where before naught but ghosts and evil and filth stood." Her eyes began to cloud with brilliant tears. "Your place is *husband.* Yet you scorn the right."

"Your place is *wife,*" he shouted. "Yet you act more as king."

"Had the priest had a moment more before the knights rode on us, you might have been freed of that great burden," she raged. She turned to flee, but he reached out and grabbed her arm, pulling her back. He embraced her instantly, crushing her to him. In either her rage or softness, he wanted her so badly that his entire body ached.

"What do you mean to say?" he demanded harshly.

She blinked her eyes tightly closed, the tears flowing from under sealed lids. "They drew their swords," she whispered. "Yea, they were eager for blood." Her eyes opened and she looked deeply into his. "But your only concern is *who rules.*"

He looked at the tears that coursed down her cheeks and let his lips gently taste the salt of her passionate wrath. He had imagined her tantrum in the village street accompanied by her ever-protective brothers. He had not considered that she might have raised this issue with a dangerous man ... *alone.* He couldn't imagine losing her. He covered her mouth with his and felt the rising of his own desires. The sweetness of her mouth and the fragrance of her hair drugged him, and he demanded much with his kiss, devouring her.

When he released her mouth, she looked up at him with glittering eyes that had softened to a deep blue. "Would you take me in the stable, monseigneur?" she whispered.

He let his arms slacken and she turned quickly from him, fleeing from the stable. When she'd disappeared completely from his sight, he turned and let his fist fly into the wall, bruising his knuckles and making a hole that would take a skilled craftsman to repair. He took a few deep breaths and ran his hand through his damp, tousled hair.

"What fool," he asked himself aloud, "thrusts from himself the very thing he wants?"

Some nights, deep in the dark when sleep did not come, he

tossed upon his bed in anguish so deep the pain of it was physical. He loved her as he had never loved, yet abhorred the passion lest she see him more clearly and reject him. His confusion and inability to find the answers worked on his mind so frequently that his mood had been sour and mean since the day her brothers journeyed with him to the Chaney house. He could not decide what was expected of him, nor could he think clearly.

Does she do all this in an effort to please me, or trick me into thinking she can be content? Or does she intend to make Segeland a suitable place, only to find some champion to usurp me? he wondered.

He was wretched, and yet he had taken the woman as his bride and brought her home because it had seemed the lesser of evils. Better to try to hold her, he told himself, than to try to live with only a memory of her.

He kicked a pile of hay and sent it flying into the air. "Women," he cursed. "Nothing but deceit that wants to castrate a man." He stomped out of the stable.

Chapter Eleven

A MATTER THAT HAD PLAGUED ROYCE SINCE THE meeting at Windsor was the fact that the king had instructed him to view and appraise the Aquitaine property and report his findings. The area of land, the revenues, number of tenants, site of the keep, and amount of stock and produce had not been assessed since Sir Flavian de Raissa had died and left the lands with a castellan. The scarce information concerning the parcel of land was that the only child, a daughter, had taken the veil and so the land had become Eleanor's to dispose of, since it fell within her dower demesne. In an act of compassion, Eleanor had let the property fall to Félise, who had been orphaned into her care.

This task, Royce believed, could be accomplished at any time. In the ten days since returning to Segeland he had given the matter grave contemplation. He had come to a decision that was hard earned, wrought of many sleepless nights. He invited one of his favorites, Sir Hewe, to visit his chamber after the evening meal.

Hewe anxiously awaited the topic of discussion. Royce did not hedge. "You are one of the youngest of my men-at-arms," Royce said, handing the young man a chalice of Gascony wine. "Yet I would entrust you with a weighty responsibility, if you think yourself capable."

Hewe virtually beamed with pride. He was large, strong, and

in tourneys and battles he had done well. Hewe believed it was only a matter of time before money and lands would begin to fall his way. He had stayed with Royce after his training because the king took obvious notice of Royce and his men. He could not prevent a boyish smile from spreading all over his young face.

Royce chuckled. "Don't drink a toast yet, Sir Hewe. You may never forgive me for this in the end. Hear me out.

"You know as much of this contract with Henry as any of us. I am not a man to protest my king," he stated firmly. Then he threw his arm wide in the direction of the chamber that Félise occupied. "Neither does it sit well with me to keep a woman prisoner against her family's will to have myself a wife, however rich her dowry."

"But the king has instructed — " Hewe began to argue.

"We are *all* aware of His Majesty's instructions, and I will not disobey. If Lord Scelfton or any of his knights reject the orders of the king, I am honor-bound to try to prevent them. But if the lady refuses — now — I will leave her family to defend her against the crown."

Hewe shook his head in confusion. "I don't understand . . ."

"No, I'm sure you don't." Royce laughed uncomfortably. "I have been bidden to Acquitaine, to view the de Raissa land that has fallen as dowry to my wife. I will leave in the early morning, and you will stay here with fifteen of my strongest men. Your authority is endorsed by me and I will inform the others.

"Your obligations are many. You must guard my wife in my absence, sleeping on the floor outside her door if you deem it a worthy notion. Any aggressor attempting to usurp me must be stopped at my gate. And I will not ask the Scelfton men to leave. Since my allegiance is to Henry and yours is to me, you are bound by oath to kill any one of them who defies this order and takes her away.

"And . . . ," he began, frowning down on the young man with what he hoped was a convincing expression of determination. "If I return to find that you've tampered with the woman, your head will ride a pike on my wall."

"My lord, I would not," Hewe said earnestly. But the young

man's eyes revealed what Royce already knew: the lad had been smitten with his wife from their first encounter. Royce judged that was why the young knight kept a safe distance, spending his nights in the hall seated far from her table and his days on the road far away from her.

"You cannot avoid being near her while you protect her," Royce said firmly.

"By my word, my lord," he said.

"Aye, I would not have called you here if I doubted that. I know her fairness; I know well her charms. 'Twill take a strong and noble sort."

Hewe gave a sharp nod of affirmation. In fact, trusting Hewe was only part of the test. Royce could have chosen a seedy old warhorse like Sir Trumble to sleep outside the lady's door. Trumble, in like, was a strong and trustworthy vassal . . . and the women gave him a wide berth because of his age, size, and homely face. Still, he had decided upon Hewe, youthful at two and twenty, strong and virile, handsome. It was also in his mind to know something of his wife, and her loyalty.

"You have a burdensome chore," Royce continued. "Do you think yourself equal to the task?"

Hewe may have had his doubts, but he nodded resolutely just the same.

"Unfortunately, I have not yet mentioned your greatest challenge." Royce sipped from his cup and looked at Hewe over the rim. He saw the young man gulp uncomfortably. He had already given him chores worthy of an army of men. "You must find a way to understand the workings of her mind. She must *not* be taken from me, she must *not* be assaulted or abused. But if it is her desire to leave this place, you must find it in yourself to look the other way as she flees."

Hewe's eyes grew wide and disbelieving. "My God," he muttered under his breath.

"Yea, you must do it. And then, upon my return, you must contend with me."

"But, my lord, how am I to know —"

"You have your eyes cast to lands and vassals of your own, Sir

Hewe. It is a simple matter to mount a trusted steed and draw your sword or brace your lance, to ride toward opposition with but one quest, to win. But it takes a greater wisdom to deal fairly with your troops, coax the villeins to plant and harvest, offer reward and punishment as befits the circumstance. I see no better training than in this thing you do on my behalf."

"Have you told the lady she is free to go?" Hewe asked.

Royce was silent for a moment, restlessly turning away and then turning full circle to face young Hewe again. "Nay, I'll have none of that. If she goes, she and her family must bear the weight of Henry's wrath. I would keep her and her dowry against heaven and hell, but not against her will." He lowered his voice. "Do you begin to understand?"

Hewe looked down for a moment, sighing heavily. Royce contemplated his friend. Hewe would know that his future depended not only upon his strength, but also upon the wisdom of his actions. But Hewe raised his eyes quickly to Royce, speaking firmly. "My word is my life," the young knight said.

Royce rumbled with laughter. "And in this case, your word is most definitely your life."

Hewe rose, downed the last of the wine, and stood before Royce. "As in other contests, Royce, I will give my best."

Royce nodded. "I will rest easier knowing this. I see there is great hope for you, Hewe. If you pray to the Virgin, mayhap the king will one day thrust some damsel into your arms."

Hewe mumbled something low and, by the sound, rueful.

"Beg pardon, Hewe?"

"I said, ah . . . I do well enough with my meager gifts."

"What, ho! The young buck does not wish these plentiful mercies — riches, beauty . . ." Royce chuckled good-naturedly. In looking at young Hewe, this vigorous knight on the brink of his real manhood, he felt a sympathy. Many were the times he wished to return to that part of his life when the future could be planned on a whim.

It was not always a pleasure to be the recipient of generosity such as Henry's. Grave responsibility accompanied the king's goodwill. Life would have held less bliss on cold nights with Celeste, but likewise less torment. And Royce would never have tossed upon his pallet with the fear that she would leave him. He couldn't have made himself care enough. Suddenly he'd found himself with a new entanglement: a distant and flickering image of the kind of life he wanted more than life itself. And an unreasonable fear of reaching for it.

"Never mind, Sir Hewe. Do as I've asked; do it well and you will find a handsome reward for youself. Just don't ask me what that reward is, yet."

When Hewe had gone, Royce filled his cup again, sitting back in his favorite chair. He could view the blazing hearth over his table. For the first time since his meeting at Windsor he felt a certain peace. He wished there was some way to share the feeling, but he knew no one, save some old ghosts in Segeland keep, who would clearly understand.

The demons gave him brief rest. He soothed himself with the knowledge that he had always managed to survive with some measure of dignity. If he returned to find that Félise was gone, no living person would witness the pain it caused him. That his soul would weep would not show on his face. Or in his step. Or voice.

Somehow, some way, he would be the master of his life.

Deep in the darkness, the wine nearly gone, Royce listened to the melodious humming of a woman. His head, which was about to fall onto his chest in drunken slumber, rose slightly the better to hear the music.

He felt himself smile, though his brain was sodden and he could not appreciate half of the beautiful sounds. Yet he imagined her, wondering if he actually heard her sing, or if he was experiencing another rapturous dream in which she seduced him.

It was a song of love lost, he realized, though the words were muffled to his ears. The woman had longed for her man and he had gone off to a distant place and forgotten her. In her loneliness she wept every day and sang to the stars and the moon every night.

"We shall see, fair lady," he mused quietly, his speech slurred with an overindulgence of wine. "Who is the love gone far away? Will it be your husband? Or has some other caught your heart?" But though the question came, he did not worry. He smiled and let the beauty of her voice soothe him, and soon he fell onto his bed and found badly needed sleep.

There were no more bolts or bars, and her chamber was only a room, not a prison. But Félise wondered at the strange invisible wall that had somehow been erected where no barrier had separated Royce from her before.

She had ignored every well-intentioned interference, retreating to the gloom of this haunted room to be alone. Her brothers, she reasoned, might thoroughly wish her well-being as much as they would follow their father's instructions to the letter, but she'd had far enough of their meddling. It was fair of them to ask Royce for permission to dispose of those accoutrements that had made this lady's chamber a cell, but Maelwine demanded roughly rather than making a request. And her brother had shown no sympathy for the small boy who'd watched his mother's madness in this room.

Vespera intended great comfort with her simple wisdom about sweet submission winning the masterful heart in good time, but Félise missed the feeling of his hands on her. And Daria could not be tolerated, with her giggles whenever he so much as glanced her way. So she sat alone, comfortable that the spirits haunting the room were not interested in her. She wore a dressing gown and sang an old troubadour's love song as she worked a braid into her hair.

He was leaving in the morning and had bidden her a sober good-bye in the company of many others. Unless she had misread his eyes, he was relieved by this obligation; his mood was lighter and the tension around his mouth had eased.

In some ways Félise shared this relief. It was time for their parting, time for her to rise to the challenge of healing some of these old wounds. She hoped and prayed that he would consider her loyalty now and then on his journey. Perhaps if he returned to Segeland to find some rough edges about the hall and town smoothed, he would be more inclined to stay. She held onto the single hope that on some future day she would attend to him, and not just to his house, again.

On impulse, thinking perhaps that whispering these tender thoughts might soften his feelings toward her and bring him back more quickly, she rose and tapped at the door that joined their chambers. There was no answer from within and she knew he had long since retired. She had heard him speaking with one of his men, heard him moving around inside. Her hand pushed against the door, which seemed to float open; her bothers had done their job well, for not only was it impossible to lock, it did not even properly close.

From the doorframe she gazed at his sleeping body, sprawled facedown across the bed. An empty chalice lay tipped on the floor and his arm dangled toward it. He had probably taken a full skin of wine, he slept so peacefully. He had never rested so at her side, but always rigidly flat on his back.

In spite of herself she ventured a step closer, then two. She wished herself brazen enough to let her gown drop to the floor and creep onto the bed beside him. The truth was stronger. She became wanton at his touch, but shamed by her own lack of control in the cool light of morning. Someday, she thought, when I know you well, I shall take measured actions to seduce you, sir knight.

As she studied him it became more clear that the wine had brought him sleep, for his shirt lay on a chair by his table and he was still garbed from the waist down in chausses. What problem, she thought, made natural sleep so hard to find that only heavy drink would bring rest? The fire had burned low and there was a chill in the air, but he was yet uncovered. The cold would rouse him, sober him soon enough, and he would rise to cover himself. The candle was burned only halfway down, and she moved toward the bed to blow it out, for only a few had been purchased in Coventry and she wished to conserve it.

Before she could bring herself to darken the room, she simply stood staring down at the broad, muscular expanse of his back. His skin was so pale against the tan of his hands it almost looked as though he wore gloves. She became more courageous, sensing that his sleep was profound from the wine and he would not sense her presence. She reveled in the unhindered chance to view him, perhaps even touch him.

"My brave husband," she whispered to him. "You would defend me against my own family if need be, arm the walls and bastions with many men ... but can you not take me on your mother's bed? Is there still so much pain from the truth of your birth that you fear to hold me close?" She felt a tear creep into her eye, in pity for the lad she imagined reaching for love and failing ever to find it, though not in pity for the man who lay sleeping. If he reached, she would open her arms. Her hand seemed to move on its own and gently caress his broad back.

She paid no mind to the mark. She had first seen it when she'd caught a glimpse of him washing in the stable. A boy from her own village had been born with such a mark on his backside and his mother, a superstitious peasant woman, had shrieked at the sight of it. But Edrea soothed the woman's fears and simply replaced the old superstition with a different, completely invented, new tale. "Why, woman, would you weep when the sign has been given to you and you alone? Do you know nothing of the stars? When a child is born kissed by the rose of heaven, it means health and prosperity." The woman then began a ritual of dropping the poor lad's diaper to brag about the mark. Félise had asked her mother about the superstition, which Edrea had promised the woman was older than creation. "That mark? 'Tis no more a curiosity than the color of his hair or eyes, but if the woman is fond of deeper meaning, why not give her one that will do some good?"

The Scelftons had laughed endlessly over Edrea, the spinner of tales. But their people were optimistic and strong, in that main because of the hopefulness that Edrea — hence all her family — inspired. So Royce's mark had barely moved Félise. She never even considered it to be as interesting as the scar on his face, which was the product of painful memories. She wondered more often at the hidden scars — those that kept Royce so painfully private and distant.

"Someday, God willing, you will forget these orders and contracts and allow me to be in truth your woman. That is all I long for." She let her lips fall gently to his cheek, pulled the quilt over his body, and blew out the candle. She found her bed, and rest came more easily for having touched him in that brief moment.

As she drifted to sleep, it was in her mind to rise before dawn to see him safely on his way. And not the slightest ray of sun or sound from the manor urged her. She sensed it was time to rise and did so, to fulfill a function important to her: to wish her husband good traveling.

Six knights and two squires were mounted in the courtyard outside the hall at dawn. Royce walked among them, checking the supplies each carried. No cart or train of servants was included in this mission, for the travel across the Channel would have to be light. Royce would make a full party of nine, which seemed to Félise a modest number indeed.

She stood outside the door and kept her snood drawn over her head and her cloak closed. She worried with the unpredictable weather, the roughness of the sea, the meager fare they carried. It was a long while before Royce noticed her quiet surveillance.

He moved toward her with a perplexed look on his face. "My lady, you rise early. I purposely bid you farewell at eventide that your rest would not be interrupted by my leave-taking."

She braved a smile for him. "Did you think I would not choose to rise and bid you a safe journey?" she asked him. "Royce, I have been schooled in these wifely duties."

He took her hands and warmed them with his own. "I forget that you know obligation as well as I."

"I worry that you take too few men with you, Royce. What if there is trouble on the road?"

"Between Segeland and Hastings the roads are wide and safe," he said. "I travel through London, where I will gather the papers and maps to find these new lands."

Félise felt her heart jump. Celeste was probably still in London and she couldn't help but wonder if Royce would take time to give her some apology . . . or even to suggest that they somehow manage to go on loving each other in spite of his ill-timed marriage. "Will you visit friends in London?" she asked, looking down at her feet.

"I think my friends are few, madam. Nay, I shall hasten to France and have the matter of these lands settled to my satisfaction. I have asked my men, Sir Hewe in particular, to see to your needs, and I've left money to that end. Hewe manages the sum, but it is yours to use as you see fit. I trust you to make your family welcome for as long as they desire."

"You will be gone a long time?" she asked.

"It shall seem long, whatever happens. I have journeyed to this territory before, and the trip in itself reaches over a fortnight. Do you worry for your safety?"

"Nay, Royce. But I worry for you. The people in Aquitaine may not relish this new lordship. You should have stronger arms."

He chuckled in spite of himself. "That is not my concern. I do not venture there to fight them, but to view what they have. If there is any resistance to my ownership through your hand, I shall return for a larger troop. But I will take your concern for me as a gesture of your goodwill."

"Do carry my goodwill, my lord. I shall pray that no harm falls your way."

She looked up into his brown eyes with tears in her own, and a moment of tenderness passed between them. She judged the feeling to be much the same as on that morning after their bedding, when she thought he was gone and he then came looking for her. And his hands, gently squeezing and releasing hers, caused a shiver of warm delight to pass through her.

"Fare thee well," he said, his voice a soft caress.

"My lord . . . Royce . . . will you not . . ." She stopped, so unsure of herself and him. She couldn't form the words, but her eyes darkened to the dull green of an angry sea, and he seemed to understand her needs. He lowered his mouth to hers and brushed her lips with his. The softness turned to fire and she melted to him, her arms rising naturally and her body quivering to be closer. He clutched her tightly, devouring her with his mouth, betraying his own hunger. His large hand pressed the small of her back against him. She gave a thought to maintaining some dignity in front of his troop, amazed that even here, in the cold morning air, he could so easily reduce her to shameless desire. When he released her mouth she sighed in some disappointment.

"Fare thee well," she whispered to him. "God will watch you."

He gave her cheek a light caress and then turned, mounted, and led his men toward the road. She stood watching for a long time. She tried to command him with her thoughts to turn and raise a parting hand to her, but he kept his vision to the front. When he had finally passed out of sight, she went back into the hall.

She kept her mantle tight around her, but the first chill of morning had left her — or, more likely, had been driven out of her by his searing lips. The hour was so early that she sat on a bench before the blazing hearth alone, this solitude most essential to her thoughts.

He had gone, she firmly set down in her mind. And she would not judge him by anything but the power of his touch, the desire she tasted in his kiss. She would give no consideration to worries that he would see Celeste or any other woman on the road to France, but let the memory of what his body told her keep her warm and vigilant. Whatever plagued him that he could not freely give himself would pass, and she would stand true to the test of time. There was much to do to secure him to her.

Hewe ventured through the hall. He poured a cup of milk and Félise watched his averted eyes and wondered at his shyness. "My lord tells me that I should come to you with my needs, Sir Hewe. He has advised you, has he not?"

"Aye, madam," he said.

"He said there is money for my use."

Hewe looked at her suspiciously. "Aye, there is some money."

"Good," she said, rising and walking toward him. "We shall have need of it. I suspect Royce may be gone as long as two months."

"You have already discovered a use for the money, lady?" he asked.

She laughed uncomfortably. "I saw the use the day I arrived, Sir Hewe. There is much to be done to make this keep worthy of Royce and his heirs. And the town. Mercy, the town. I doubt he could possibly have left enough, but we will see that he returns to an improved estate. Surely that would please him."

Hewe raised an eyebrow in surprise and looked sideways at her.

She turned her eyes back to the fire and heard Hewe's voice quiet behind her. "An improved estate would please him well, lady. He deserves better than this."

Félise did not turn. She sighed heavily, deep in thought. Finally she rose to face Hewe, her voice low but firm.

"Aye, he deserves all our labors and loyalty. I am certain I shall be occupied every moment he is gone. Yet if it earns one small smile of pleasure from him, it will be well worth the effort." She passed Hewe, moving toward the stairs, turning once to look at him with tear-filled eyes. "Have a stout meal, Hewe. I plan to begin at once to attend to matters that will better my husband's home."

Chapter Twelve

TO SEE A LARGE TROOP OF KNIGHTS PASS THROUGH Coventry was not unusual, for the road between Worcester and Leicester was woven through the town. Also, many enroute to York would travel through Coventry, which was of some consequence in its travel houses, merchant goods, and food.

And there was a church, large and rich by the standards of the time. Monseigneur Trothmore, a common son of a merchant craftsman, had risen through the ranks to a position of authority and wealth in this town. He had managed to wield the authority of the church over the local barons and earls, and much conjecture about who ruled the land floated among the common people.

While the men-at-arms sought a stable for their destriers, Sir Boltof and Sir Wharton lingered within the church for an audience with the priest. As they waited, they quietly conferred.

"Since Royce is gone now to France, and the weather is not with us in our travels, 'tis best to await his return and discover what that Aquitaine property holds, rather than rushing into the keep and overthrowing the Scelfton knights," Boltof said.

"But then, the woman resides much alone. Would it not be better for you to venture there now?" Wharton asked.

Boltof smiled wickedly. "What ho! You would allow me a measure of her time alone?"

"That is not what I meant," Wharton corrected.

"Never mind, Wharton. I wait in the event she denies me admittance when her man is gone. And remember, I dare not go there alone, but must take Celeste if I am to succeed."

"What am I to do while you wait? Sit in this fair shire and count the mares until you deem it time?"

"Patience, Wharton. The longer we wait, the more assurance to those who would watch that there is no bad blood over this marriage. And . . . you do want to know what there is in Aquitaine, do you not?" Wharton nodded, but one of the things he seemed to have little of was patience. He had lost many a contest because he had struck too soon. "Perhaps the Scelfton men will soon be called to their duties and the gate will be easier to open. Remember, I know each and every Leighton knight. I have ridden with Royce."

Their attention was drawn by the entrance of Trothmore, and he always made a grand entrance. Never seen in the humble rags of a priest committed to poverty, this self-acclaimed church leader wore robes of rich cloth, jewels, and heavy velvet mantles. His cap, sewn with gems, rose high above his head, and he was tall enough to create a stir when he moved. His position of power was not conferred to him by the church, but came through the attainment of riches. He had managed to impress most of the higher-ranking ecclesiastics so well that they rarely asked how his high title had come about. Very few people knew he was only a priest.

Wharton and Boltof bowed and crossed themselves, both knowing this was all a show, for the priest was less religious than the Templars. He was every bit a baron whose keep was a church.

"Sir knights," he greeted.

"I am Boltof, and this is Wharton. I sent you the missive."

"How did you know of me?" Trothmore asked.

"I have had occasion to pass through Coventry more than once, and acquaintances have spoken of you." He raised an eyebrow. "Was I correct that you would be of service to a humble knight of Henry?"

Trothmore stiffened. "I would aid any who could rid the land of Leightons for all time. And there is only one left."

"Why do the Leightons chafe you so?" Wharton asked.

Trothmore's expression was grim and his anger was barely concealed. "I have served this church for over a score of years, and as long as there are Leightons in Segeland, there is no faith and I cannot wring a tithe from the burg. 'Tis a well-known fact they worship Satan. Now ruling in the stead of the devil is a witch they call lady. That same one called arms against me and will not allow me within the town. The church will shed them, as in generations past, as a bird sheds its fouled feathers."

Boltof struggled to keep his expression serious, but inwardly he smiled. He would take great pleasure in watching Félise, the beautiful witch, standing her ground and refusing to part with any coin to a wicked priest. But for now, the priest was necessary to his plan.

"By the summer, my lord, you shall begin to see some attempt to unseat the Leighton bastards for good and all. Then you shall have your faith and tithe again. Have you written the papers?"

"I have submitted to the Archbishop the complaints against Segeland and her rulers and requested excommunication for all who reside there . . . until such a time as those whose wickedness rules either beg for forgiveness or die."

"It shall shortly come to Henry's attention, Boltof," Wharton said with a note of panic in his voice.

"Be at ease, Wharton. Henry does not know we are here." He turned to Trothmore. "Our efforts will be of little use if you give us away, my lord. I have a pittance to help you seal your lips."

Trothmore's hand was instantly outstretched, and his angry face relaxed into a sly smile. He loved money and riches more than anything. "Why would I speak against you, when you come so far as this to do God's work?"

"All the better, my lord," Boltof replied, placing a small money bag in the man's hand. "There will be more, when the time is right to move against Segeland. Until then, abide by their order and stay away from there. I see no need to keep them on their guard." He laughed loudly, pleased that things were going so well. "Indeed, 'tis much the better they are relaxed and believing themselves safe, for I shall war with them from within their walls, and Sir Wharton here, from without. I doubt anyone could stand firm against such a sound plan."

"I bid you well, then," Trothmore said, turning from the knights to leave. When he had entered his rectory and closed the door behind him, Wharton turned suspicious eyes to Boltof. "How is it you can trust that man?" he asked.

"Come, Wharton," he chuckled, slapping a hand on his shoulder as if they were longtime friends, and leading him out of the church. "Trothmore is easier to trust than any friend, for it is clear his price is silver or gold. He cares nothing for truth, loyalty, or honor, if only he can have riches. So . . . while he can serve our purpose, let us see that he is well paid."

They came down the stairs of the church and into the crowded Coventry street. "You part more easily with your hard-earned money than I would have supposed," Wharton observed.

Boltof laughed good-naturedly. "Surely you know that I only loan the sum to Trothmore. I intend to have it back."

"Boltof," someone shouted. Both men turned abruptly toward the knight who had called out. "Wharton?" he questioned, dismounting quickly on sight of them.

Wharton frowned when he saw Sir Maelwine, nearly panicking at being seen with Boltof. But Boltof was quicker to see the usefulness of this. He walked briskly toward Maelwine, giving a salute and then stretching out his hand. "By God, what a pleasure to see you again, Maelwine," Boltof said cheerfully. "And of course you are well acquainted with Wharton."

Maelwine rather reluctantly shook the other knight's hand. " 'Twas a long time ago that we parted ways and you rode with the elder Leighton."

Wharton was not quick enough to understand the value of this meeting, and Boltof spoke rapidly, energetically, hoping he would soon gather the sense of it. He laughed lightly and easily. "And so we come full circle in our meeting. You, parted from your friend by a Leighton; I, the friend of a Leighton and enemy of Wharton — all united herein. Can it be old battles could be laid away with a tipped mug?"

"I thought you hated each other," Maelwine said.

Wharton snorted, catching on at last. "The defeated have come to a truce," he said derisively. "We share our miseries better than we fought."

All three then laughed, and Wharton suggested a warm Coventry room for good ale and a chance to tell all the old tales. Maelwine nodded exuberantly, for he was worn from all the hard work and traveling to Coventry for supplies that Segeland demanded. He instructed those with him to gather up their goods while he joined his friends.

Before a blazing hearth in a common room, the three men shared a friendly brew. Maelwine was comforted by their presence. He had parted ways with Wharton a long while back and, upon this reunion, realized how he had missed his company. And although Boltof was a fairly new acquaintance, the friendship of their fathers brought them together.

Maelwine believed their questions about Segeland, Royce, and Félise to be born of simple curiosity, and it gave him the opportunity to talk about his tasks through the past weeks. Several toasts and jests later, they emerged from the common room and stood again in the street. "I am for Segeland," Maelwine said, a bit unsteady on his feet after all the rich brew. "But I found Coventry more to my liking this time than at others. I did not ask — where are you bound?"

Wharton nearly gasped, but Boltof, the silver-tongued schemer, won with his words again. "We have traveled together from London, but from here I go to York and Wharton is on to Gloucester."

Maelwine thought for a moment, but his mind was nearly as scrambled as his footwork. "Gloucester? A bit beyond your road, isn't it?"

"But well worth the travel," Wharton laughed, slapping Maelwine on the back. "I would have our next meeting better planned. What say you, Maelwine?"

"Aye," the knight returned. "I shall soon be free of Segeland

and will send word to you. Perhaps we will put together our troops at some future day and ride together again." Maelwine was unaware of how much valuable information he had already given about Segeland, feeling sure that these two men were his comrades.

"Until you leave, assure Lady Félise that we harbor no anger toward any member of her family," Boltof said. "I shall ride upon Segeland when my duties in York are completed and give Royce my renewed pledge of friendship."

"Aye," Maelwine said, accentuating this with a large belch. "Full circle. A better arrangement than before."

"Tell the lady, Maelwine, that I shall visit Segeland to offer my support," Boltof repeated.

"She will be pleased. She will welcome it." He looked around to see if he could spot his riders and wagon, but no one was in sight. "I am bound to find my fellow travelers. Farewell, and safe travels to you both."

Maelwine turned from them and wove his unsteady way down the street. Boltof chuckled and nudged Wharton. "God, what a piece of work we've done this day, Wharton. Maelwine goes hither to announce my entrance to his sister's home." He laughed loudly, throwing his head back, but Wharton did not share his good humor. "Do you think he could have done better with his news of Segeland and Royce if he had a map and calendar with him?"

Wharton was a bit down in his spirits, aggravated more by the nature of the reunion than uplifted by the amount of useful information they had managed to wheedle. "I betrayed him once and regretted it," Wharton grumbled. "Though he allowed my apology, we did not ride together again, and now . . ."

"He will thank you in the end and would better see you with his sister than a devil Leighton."

"Methinks he's accepted Royce well," Wharton said. "He speaks ill of the place, but he had no rough words for the knight."

"He holds his judgment because of Henry and his father. Who could hold loyal to a Leighton?"

"You did," Wharton reminded him.

Boltof grew serious. "And you see how I am rewarded," he said bitterly. "He leaves my sister soiled and my father disappointed, and I am reduced to scrambling for lands through the meager wits of a wicked priest. Yea, my loyalty to Royce got me plenty." He smiled again, but it was not a gay thought that inspired him. "And it is my plan to properly thank him."

The new year, celebrated in March, was less than a month away, and Félise could see the rich promise on the horizon as she viewed the daily improvements in and around Segeland keep. Hewe ofttimes grumbled that she was a spendthrift, and he wished to show his great loyalty by having money left for Royce to count upon his return, but all in all, the young knight could not decry the need or slight the vast difference about the hall and town. And neither could Hewe say that Félise made impetuous purchases. She focused the use of the small sum on food and other necessities.

But Hewe had little knowledge of how further inspired Félise was. She was satisfied that the people ate better and the rudimentary repairs had been made so that the hall was safe and no one suffered grave ills. But what more she sought could not be accomplished with Royce's meager allotment. Félise did not crave rich items she had not yet earned, but even if it took her years to repay, there were certain things needed by spring to give this place a new birth, a prosperous first year.

She labored over letters to her parents. She had spent days thinking about what she would say and the words she would lay down on parchment. In the end she wrote to her father and mother on separate pages, deeming the news to each to be of a different nature. She also considered the time it would take for the missives to reach them at Twyford, south of London. But she never once considered that they would not yield her what she needed. The moment she saw the messages on their way, she would begin to order the work done with the assurance that the workers could be paid.

Late in the evening, after their meal, she approached her

brothers and asked for a private conference in her chamber. None of them had been in the room they abhorred since the night they readied it for her use. Maelwine was the one to nod in approval at the change some modest cleaning and renovation had yielded. She had instructed Hewe to bring a bench and some chairs from other rooms and join them for the ensuing discussion.

"It is time for the three of you to leave," she said simply.

"I thought it better, Félise, to remain until Royce returned from his sojourn," Maelwine argued.

"I have letters for you to carry to Twyford, and thence you may consider your duty to me done."

"But we have sent letters to our father," Dalton said. "It was his instruction that we keep him apprised of your condition."

She pursed her lips and tried to keep any anger from her voice. "Yea, I know this, but never did you ask me to report my condition. Now, by my own hand, I have set down my words and I should like them delivered to our parents." She sighed. "I believe you have all good intention, but I do not wish my husband to return to find you hovering over me like mother hens. There is no further use for you here, and you'll become old and doddering, wasting away in this humble keep. You need to be on the road and about your own duties."

"We have always helped one another," Evan said.

"And so you shall help me, if you will leave me to my home and my husband. Sir Hewe guards the hall well and Sir Trumble does not relax a moment from the wall. There are servants aplenty within the keep, and the villeins no longer fear my presence. Colbert sees to them . . . and unless you wish to make trips to Coventry for trinkets, there is no use for you."

"We keep the place safe," Evan said.

"Nay, she is right," Dalton argued. "She has Royce's guard and they're a sturdy lot. And since Maelwine encountered the two spurned knights in Coventry and assures us they are no threat, our service here is all but done." He turned to Félise. "I will not lie to you, Félise. I do not find this place worthy of you. 'Tis better, but still poor and small."

"It is not your choice, Dalton."

"Nay, but were it my choice, you would reside with our father at Twyford until a better lot could be found. And I am still uncertain of Royce ... I do not rest easy with his treatment of you."

Hewe stiffened, but Félise raised her hand slightly to indicate she would speak on behalf of Royce. "I think your presence and the condition of this hall chafe him more than anything. He did not treat me with such silence at the Chaney house. Indeed, he was kind and dear ... and he will be again when he returns, if his home is well tended and my guards are gone."

Maelwine looked at Hewe. There were still some rough edges to the relationship between the Scelfton men and Royce's, but none of Félise's brothers could argue that the guard left to Félise was inadequate or less than trustworthy. Maelwine felt uneasy criticizing Royce in front of his man, but he was without choice. It almost appeared that Félise approved the young knight as much as Royce did. Indeed, she seemed to prefer his protection to that of her brothers.

"We could stay until a message arrives that Royce is bound for home, Félise," Maelwine offered.

Félise rose, somewhat weary with these hovering stags. "I try to count myself lucky to have you, and though we grew through years of teasing and fighting, you know I hold your kinship dear. Forsooth, you three, as much as Father and Mother, gave me a home and a family when I had none. I trust you wish me only good fortune. But, my dears, you must let me choose my fortune. I am better the wife of Royce in this humble keep than your sister on the road to Twyford. What comforts there will give me peace and joy? I cannot be a child of Twyford again."

Maelwine leaned forward on his chair and looked closely at Félise. His eyes were warm and hers were cool and level. "Tell us truly, Félise: given freedom, is this man and hall your choice?"

"Yea," she breathed, her eyes moistening. "It will one day be a rich place filled with worthy heirs. You will journey here in years to come and find it much to your liking, for I will not rest until my husband's home flourishes."

"You are confident of his love?" Maelwine pressed.

Félise's cheeks pinkened slightly, but she sought a strong voice. "Neither will I rest until that flourishes."

Maelwine showed his approval by rising and nodding resolutely. "I say we let the lass have her day," he said. "You trust this man as your protector?" he asked, indicating Hewe with his eyes.

"He will not betray the Lord of Segeland," Félise said with certainty.

Dalton rose. "Very well, lady of Segeland. I will hold you to your word, that this sorry place will prosper."

Evan followed, but this brother embraced his sister. "Call us back when there is need," he said.

She nodded, feeling tears gather in her eyes. There was little doubt of their love and loyalty, but their oppressive presence did not allow her to complete the chores that lay ahead.

"I see no reason we should delay," Maelwine said. "We can ready our things by morning and get your letters swiftly to Twyford."

" 'Tis will," she said, and smiled. "I will miss you. But we'll say our farewells in the morn. A good night to you all . . . and please, I do thank you, remember that."

When the Scelfton men had left her chamber, she turned to Hewe to find a glad expression on his face. "Well, Sir Hewe, I am much more your burden now, with my brothers gone."

He lifted her hand to his lips and bowed over it. When he straightened, there was a pleased smile on his lips. "Yea, but you have lightened my load immeasurably, lady."

"Oh? Did they cause you some problem, my brothers?"

"Nay," he said. " 'Twas an order that Royce gave me that I found difficult to carry out. But now I see that my worries are few and my work will be simple and complete."

She cocked her head in some confusion. "If I can be of any assistance, Sir Hewe, you have but to ask."

"You have been a pleasure to serve, lady," he said. "And I look forward to my lord's return, that I may serve you both."

It could not be said that great sadness fell over Segeland when the Scelfton knights departed, for most of Royce's men resented their presence simply because they knew their master did. But the mood toward them had softened a small bit since they had first attached themselves to the newly married couple, for all three brothers were never shy toward work. And though they viewed Royce skeptically, they did not openly criticize him. That they disliked the mess they found at Segeland was not very different from how all the men felt.

Félise gave them letters for home, these being carefully sealed to ensure their privacy. She walked with Hewe and her brothers toward the gate, the latter leading their destriers. When they parted, it was with thanks and good wishes. Hewe, feeling a new tenderness toward Félise, shook each man's hand and promised to remain and care for Félise in their stead.

They were far into the distance when the mighty gates were being pushed closed. The rearmost knight turned at the sound and raised a hand to Félise and Hewe. Hewe waved in return and Félise felt lighter of heart.

"They will return one day, Hewe, and I trust you will help me make them welcome."

Hewe presented his arm to the lady to escort her back to the hall. "When Sir Royce is assured that your family wishes him no ill, even he will welcome these brothers of yours and perhaps one day call them brother as fondly as you."

Félise slowed her step. "You have changed toward them," she observed. "And toward me."

"Have I?" he laughed.

"Perhaps all most of us need, Hewe, is time. In time even Royce . . ." Her voice trailed off into nothing and she walked toward her home.

Hewe gave her hand a reassuring pat, not requiring her to finish the sentence to understand what she was feeling. He wondered why he and Royce had thought that to understand the workings of her mind would be so difficult. She had opened her heart with a few simple utterances. She loved her husband deeply, and craved his love in return. Though she still appeared desirable and beautiful to Hewe, in a manner she had freed him from longing with her declaration for her husband. Hewe's love of loyalty was yet greater than any lust, and he found himself hoping for both husband and wife that they could find the way to each other. "Yea, madam, in time even Royce . . . ," he whispered.

"Hewe, will you have my mare saddled and ride with a few men and me to Daventry? I would be home before sunset. We must leave early."

"Daventry? Whatever you need could be brought from Coventry. That town has more to offer and the distance is not so great."

She shook her head. "What I need cannot be got from Coventry. I would find an honest priest to hear my confession and give me counsel. I know the man in Coventry cannot do this. 'Tis my hope that this wretch, Trothmore, does not serve the city of Daventry. But we can't know before the journey."

"I would ride there forthwith and bring the word back to you. You could travel there tomorrow if there is a priest."

Again she shook her head. "I enjoy a good ride, and I must trust my heart to judge a priest. I knew instantly the devil who came here for the tithe was wicked. I must *see* the next priest before I can be sure that he is good." She stopped and looked at Hewe. "Was it for want of an honest man that this town has suffered so long without a church, or were the Leightons before Royce infidels all?"

"I can't say, madam," he responded truly. "During my years with Sir Royce, he has oft visited a church and partaken of confession and communion. He would not wear the cross, but he is a believer. And he did not speak of his family, though we heard the tales."

Félise sighed heavily as they walked. "It is hard to know, Hewe, whether to try to bury deeper the dead or dig them up and look at their secrets."

"I perceive no great secrets lie buried here, lady. You saw the man Trothmore come openly, with no cloak of mystery. And these people do not hide their misery — it is evident in their slight bodies that they are ill from poverty. The bolts on your chamber door told another dire story. If you continue to look, I trust all the questions you ask yourself will find answers simply. Carry on with faith, madam," he urged.

"You are right, of course," she said, knowing full well there were answers to every question right before her, but she was impatient with the waiting. They reached the door to the hall. "My horse, Hewe?"

He dallied a moment. "Let me go to Daventry ahead of you and bring you word about the priest."

"Nay," she said firmly. "This town has been too long without God. I have filled their bellies, but I cannot feed their souls. Hurry now."

She turned and went into the hall and Hewe stared after her until the door was closed. He smiled in equal parts of awe and respect. "Oh, don't be too sure, lady. I think those who know you are nourished in every way, body and soul."

Fighting down the barest touch of jealousy, he went quickly to the stable. And before he had taken many steps, he was whistling happily.

Chapter Thirteen

ROYCE HAD FOUND THE JOURNEY THROUGH ENGLAND and across the Channel to be harsh and exhausting, but as he neared Narbonne, the closest city of any size to the de Raissa demesne, he enjoyed a bright and early taste of spring. He was not lulled into believing that the cold days were over, but he relished a chance to better view this promised land.

He and his men found shelter in Narbonne for two days. They knew only the approximate location of the estate and feared to push the hospitality of the castellan without first testing their acceptance there. But if he found the place decent and the people friendly, he and his men would perhaps spend some days within whatever house this dower land could boast.

Royce knew only a little about fair Aquitaine. This was the dower land of Eleanor, and it was at her behest that the knights and lords managed here, paying tithe, rent, revenue. This was why Henry would not divorce her. King Louis had made a sad mistake when he gave up Eleanor, for all of Aquitaine had been his through her hand, and with the annulment had returned to the queen. Now, even though Eleanor survived in genteel poverty and confinement, the money from this fertile land fell into England through Henry and Eleanor's son, Richard, the duke of Aquitaine.

Royce could not deny the beauty of the rich, rolling hills. He passed vineyards where some of the finest wines were made. Al-

though the new crops had not yet been planted, there were orchards and fields aplenty, and those farmers who had tenant
homes along the road appeared healthy and happy. It was a
vastly different atmosphere from that at Segeland. It was a thriv-
ing and robust land. Even though he had not yet seen the plot
assigned as the de Raissa dowry, Royce already felt two stinging
desires: to improve Segeland to match this, and one day to bring
Félise here to enjoy the tranquil beauty, even if the house on the
land was not great.

He and a few men spent two days surveying the general area,
for all the information that had been handed down was that de
Raissa had left a parcel of orchard, vineyard, and farming land in
the valley between Toulouse and Narbonne. He knew better
than to spend endless days in search, but he wanted to get a feel
for the place before asking those people he encountered if they
knew the precise location.

At the end of the third day of local travel, the knights, growing both weary and impatient, rode upon a large country manor
built of stone and surrounded by a wall. It was well placed in the
center of the valley and could be seen from the farthest knoll as
they approached. As they drew nearer, it became obvious that
this was a rich house indeed, as large as Segeland and far better
kept. Royce paused in his ride and spoke to his men. "This noble
would know most of the smaller tenants. They do not appear to
man their gate in fear of attack and perhaps will send us straight-
away to this dower place."

Royce rode ahead of his men and spoke first to the gatekeeper,
a young man who did not appear by any manner of his dress,
arms, or attitude to be prepared for an invading foe. "I am
Royce, Lord Leighton, of England, and I bear letters from Her
Majesty, Eleanor, and her husband, the king, granting me lordship of a small demesne once belonging to a knight known as Sir
Flavian de Raissa. Can you direct me?"

The young man nodded and repeated Royce's words to a
knight who then ran quickly toward the manor doors.

"Will you come into the courtyard and give your steeds rest,
Lord Leighton, while Sir Jasper is called?"

"Sir Jasper? He is the lord of this?" he asked.

"Nay, 'tis you who brings letters naming you lord," he said with a brief bow. "Sir Jasper has been the seneschal for many years. He has been expecting you."

Royce was jolted by this news. He had expected a five- or six-room stone farmhouse, perhaps rich enough to boast a stable and with fewer than one hundred tenants. This place was more than he had dared hope for — as was the friendly welcome. All of his men looked around in like wonder, one whistling low and long in awe.

He turned back to the lad at the gate. "How did you come to expect me? I sent no word."

"But the message was delivered here, just the same."

Royce was only a bit perplexed, quickly reasoning that either Henry or Eleanor had sent word ahead that he would claim this on behalf of his wife. He entered, beckoning his men to follow, and they waited in the warm sun within the courtyard for a long time before they were greeted by Sir Jasper.

He was a pleasant man of nearly sixty years who hailed these visiting knights with a warmth that startled them all. "It is good to know you. I am told your English land is too plentiful to expect you to make your home here, but when you come to know the land, my lord, I hope you will visit here often."

"How come you by so much information, Sir Jasper?" he asked.

The man laughed happily. "The heir is much in touch with this land and these people. I hope you will continue to entrust it to me."

Royce frowned. "The heir?" he questioned. "How much is there, Sir Jasper?" he asked, almost afraid of this good fortune.

"As far as you can see, and then more. I have lived here all my life and have left only for short trips in the last twenty years. I served here in the stead of Sir Flavian de Raissa when he traveled with Eleanor to England. That was the first time I managed without his presence, and have since."

"This is a rich place," Royce thought aloud, raising a brow.

Again Jasper laughed, seeming to be greatly at ease with the arrival of this new lord. "Indeed, it is a rich land. But come, you must let me make you welcome. Sample our wine. Our baker makes the best breads in the land. You will stay and grow fat and lazy in this hall. And while you drink and eat, I will tell you the workings of this land and show you the ledgers."

The hall was clean and comfortable, and there were chambers prepared for all the men. Their steeds were taken and tended in the stables, and tubs were soon steaming in the rooms. Since they had spent many days in travel, they did not need much coaxing to give up their dirty clothes and accept fresh ones from Sir Jasper's servants. But these overcautious knights would not part with their mail or arms, still feeling somewhat ill at ease. They had not planned an invasion here, but it often happened that a castellan became attached to land he managed over many years and began to think of himself as lord, balking at giving up his power.

Shortly they were all lulled into trusting, for the food was good, the wine was excellent, and this Jasper did not show any fierceness or hostility. Royce leaned back in his chair after a plentiful meal and sipped from his goblet, peering at Jasper over the rim. He was clean, shaven, full, and warm. Yet it was difficult for him, as usual, to accept contentedness without suspicion. "You are not wary that I will take this from you and remove you?"

Jasper's eyes rounded in amusement for a moment and he smiled. "If you think you can find a better castellan, or a more honest servant, I bid you seek him out. But you must remember: for every two grains I harvest, one is saved for seed, and I have guarded this land with a care that my son might have something to guard . . . and his son and his son . . ."

"That was not my intention, but neither was I prepared for a welcome like this. You give it over to me so easily."

"But, my lord, I was made aware of you some time ago. And I have always worked for the owner of this property, given assurance of my place on the land if I served well. So there is no change in my life, only a change in yours." He paused for a thoughtful moment. "Yet I did not think you would travel here before spring."

"Who made you aware? The king?"

"Nay, it was the heir. I have managed these lands for her for twenty years."

"The queen?"

"Nay, Lady Véronique. She comes every year and carries back the tithe and tax."

"Who is this?" Royce asked, suddenly feeling he knew nothing at all about Félise and her dowry. Not only had it never been said that the inheritance was rich, it had never been imparted to him that there was a living landholder to which the land had been entrusted. "I was told only the location of this land and assumed the place was without heir."

"Not so, Royce. I was in residence here when she was born, nearly fifty years ago. I was a child then myself, but I worshiped her father, who ensured my training as a squire and saw me knighted. When he swore his allegiance to Eleanor and left France, taking the child with him, I stayed here in his behalf.

"Lady Véronique was a woman grown when she was orphaned, and this was to be her dowry, but no husband came to view the land. She was in service to the queen until Eleanor's confinement, but she did not return to us. Véronique chose the convent of Fontevrault over her home. Still she comes, every year, and the tithe goes to the church, the tax to Richard, the queen's heir, and the rents are given to the sisters at Fontevrault for her retirement."

"Then who inherits?"

Jasper sighed uncomfortably. "I would have you understand that we love the lady heir, my lord. Besides her gentleness and love, there are practical reasons for the respect she has earned here. What is left after debts is usually mine to use, that this place may never fail or the people and the farms be reduced to poverty.

"The lady said there was a daughter to inherit, and no one here would dishonor her by asking for the details. If Lady Véronique chooses silence about her widowhood, or if the child was born to her outside a proper marriage, it makes no difference here. She gives this to her daughter at marriage and chooses Fontevrault. And I abide by her choice without question."

"I assure you, Jasper, neither would I wish to see this a less than prosperous place."

Jasper instantly relaxed. "Some do not see the frugal way, but rather wring as much from the land as it will yield, until it dies and there is nothing left. But you wish for sons, my lord, and a place to give them."

Royce contemplated this gravely, for he had seen the effects of greedy lordship on his own home. Still, the question of heirs bothered him. And he did not feel the same obligation to respect the privacy of this Véronique. He only felt a riveting curiosity as to how it came to Félise.

"Véronique?" he mumbled, distracted. "Fontevrault?" Jasper went on with his description of how each minor coin was spent to enlarge the orchards, repair the stables, bestow gifts on the villeins at holidays, plant and harvest. He expounded on the benefit of giving the peasants many celebrations and how his generosity with them had in every way made him and the land richer.

But Royce still thought heavily on this woman. "Jasper," he asked quietly, cutting the man off in the middle of one of his elaborate descriptions, "did this Véronique name her daughter to you?"

"Yea, though I have never seen this child. She was named by her mother: Félise de Raissa. Is this not your wife?"

He sat back in his chair, deep concern wrinkling his brow. He listened absently as Jasper continued, describing the beautiful Véronique. "Hair the red of an angry morning sun, eyes that when she was an excited little girl would glow as green jewels of the sea; she is slight and meek, but betimes an idea drives her and she does not rest until she sees it done. Yet her voice is softer than down, her manner as gentle as a newborn lamb. She is more like one of the sisters than the sisters themselves, but she has vowed not to take the veil and confine herself with the nuns until her daughter is cared for. Tell me, Royce, is Félise de Raissa your wife?"

Royce sat up suddenly. "Yea," he answered. "But she has

been known as Félise Scelfton, growing up in that noble English family. And as any blooded daughter. I was never told of this. I don't know how she has come to me."

Jasper smiled a slow, knowing smile. "Perhaps, my lord, neither does she."

As Twyford castle and the town came into view, the Scelfton knights improved their pace. This place more than tripled Segeland in size and had never suffered a moment of neglect. Over one thousand people occupied the castle and town, yielding many hands and heads to the constant upkeep and improvement. Each heir to Twyford for the past five generations had added to the original keep until it flourished as this grand place.

All were smiling as they rode into the town, raising a hand now and then to an acquaintance and dismounting before the main hall. Things they took for granted when in residence here had been sorely missed, and each one smiled with every small service. Their horses were taken by pages, their mail and mantles pulled off just inside a clean and warm hall by servants, their preferred drinks, whether cold or hot, quickly fetched.

Lord Scelfton, hurrying into the hall from somewhere in the rear, was sweating although it was cold. He wore a soiled linen tunic, chausses, and boots and had a large hunting knife at his belt. It was not beneath the lord of all this to be skinning game, cleaning the stable, or perhaps shoeing a horse. Harlan fiercely loved his labors. He greeted each of his sons with a typical grunt and smile, the combination showing his tendency to be harsh but also his obvious pleasure in his family.

Edrea had been called from the uppermost chambers and she, too, wore her working clothes. A tunic she used for cleaning or sewing and working in the kitchens was worn over her gunna, and her hair was pulled back and covered with a tied kerchief. She was not so stingy with her affection and embraced each son fondly.

"Félise is well?" she asked instantly.

"Aye, madam, we bring her letters."

The conversation stopped there for a few moments as they

bustled about the great room. The fire was stoked, the chairs pulled in around the fire for each to have a decent seat and yet be near enough for comfortable exchange. And once all were seated, boots were pulled off and platters of food were brought to the weary travelers. All amenities provided, Harlan broached the subject of Félise again.

"That you are home leaves me to assume that you found Segeland to your liking?"

"In a manner, Father," Evan said.

Edrea sat up straighter in her chair. "Your missives said that you were delayed to help them settle some improvements on the place. Is it a good place?"

Maelwine laughed shortly. " 'Twas a sty that would shame a pig when we arrived. Not a care had been given the place in years, and the people living around the hall were a pitiful, frightened lot. But by the time we were asked to leave, the comforts there were adequate, I suppose."

"*Asked to leave?*" Harlan blustered.

" 'Twas not Royce, Father," Dalton quickly explained. "It was our sister who saw it fit to excuse us."

"Is she all right?" Edrea asked fearfully.

"Don't ask us to know her mind, madam, but perhaps you should read her letters, and then we will tell as best we can about Segeland. She told us that we interfered with her progress with Royce."

Maelwine produced the rolled parchments and handed one to each of his parents. Harlan's was considerably shorter and he had read it over twice, his face growing red, before Edrea had finished hers the first time through. She sighed heavily and let the long document fall into her lap.

None of the brothers had opened the letters to see what their sister had written, but agreed that if Félise had made the situation appear better than it was, they were under obligation to Harlan to tell him the truth of it. Harlan's first statement revealed that Félise had not colored a pretty picture.

"We leave on the morrow to fetch her home, Henry be damned," he stormed.

Edrea reached for her husband's hand but looked at her sons. "The wall is stout now and the guard a safe and loyal troop?" she asked.

"None of us could argue that, Mother. We had some concern about the local priest, for he was driven from the shire when Félise reasoned him to be evil and greedy. But the men Royce left will not let him in again, and I do not expect him to attack the place, but rather petition for their excommunication. That is an ordeal they can protest without physical injury."

"And the people there — they are on the mend?" she asked.

" 'Twill take a goodly sum of months to prove that, madam. We offered to stay on until Royce was returned, but she would have none of it."

Harlan shook his letter in aggravation. "She has asked to borrow against her dowry for seed, building supplies, weaving materials, many necessary things. How can a father leave his child in a village of ruin and a house that is obviously falling down around her? Nay, we'll fetch her home."

"Harlan," Edrea said softly. "Excuse these men to a bath and their comforts, and here," she said, handing him the pages that Félise had written to her, "read this and be still."

Harlan grumbled in agitation, but Edrea pressed the letter on him and he took it. While he read, she spoke softly to her sons. "You would not have left her in danger, I am assured. That her materials are modest is no threat to her safety. We will talk more later, when you are better rested and clean."

Maelwine shrugged almost apologetically. "Mother, there was little we could do to make Segeland a rich home for Félise, but she seems to thrive on their need for her. And no urging would convince her to leave."

"I do not think it is her great loyalty to Henry that keeps her there, but some strange attraction to Royce," Dalton added.

Edrea raised an eyebrow and smiled. "You do not understand this, Dalton?" she asked.

"He was not openly cruel to her, but he is a surly bastard, just the same," Dalton said.

Edrea looked askance at Harlan. "Yea," she said softly. "I expected as much." Then back to her sons: "Go, and let us settle this argument. And thank you for what you've done for us."

When they left, Edrea waited patiently for Harlan to finish reading the letter. Finally he put it aside. "What does this mean?" he asked hotly.

"It is very simple, my lord. Our daughter loves Royce."

Harlan picked up the parchment again, scanning it impatiently. "It says that nowhere. Nowhere. Where do you see that she loves him?"

"In every word, every mark. Listen to me, Harlan, for you're an old fool with love so plentiful all around you that you've scarce had to look for it in your lifetime.

"In her very first line she admits that it is a far better thing that the marriage was decided before anyone knew Segeland, for you would not have approved it. And better done in secret, for even Royce seems wont to cling to these old ghosts of the Leightons, and she says he is not afflicted beyond sore memories. Then she proceeds to list her needs, stating that it is a choice between patience over the years to see the place prosper, or a quick remedy with our help. And the most important thing, I think, is the need for a church there. Harlan, let us send her twice what she asks. Let her help Royce heal the town and keep . . . that her firstborn can be baptized in their home."

Harlan shook his head in confusion. "How you decipher these secrets is beyond me, woman. Is it not an equal possibility that her length of request is meant to warn us of her deprivation? Would it not be better for us to go there and see these conditions for ourselves?"

"Nay, Harlan. We will go there, but at harvest, when her child is born."

"Child?"

Edrea sighed and took up the parchment again, searching with her eyes and then, finding the place, reading it aloud to her husband.

" 'My brothers will explain the banishment of the priest, which I assure you is all to the good, as I watched my father in this practice in Twyford. But the lack of a friar solely hurts me, and one needs to be found and a small place of worship quickly erected for him to say mass, perform rites, and give these people the Word. I would not fain to birth a son to Royce if there is no man of God to bless him. If you would convince my father to advance the sum for building, I invite you to travel here for our harvest celebrations and view the improvements for yourself. By then, with your help, much will be done ... and quite soon, much will be growing here.'

"Harlan, I feel certain that our Félise suspects she is with child and will harvest crops and a babe when the summer is done. Let us grant her this; we have no reason to deny her."

"I am not certain she is well," he argued. "She may suffer miserably but tries to ease us with these courageous words."

"Harlan, she sent her brothers away. Royce cannot rule while they reside so close. And I am confident that Vespera would not allow Félise to be abused. She would send word to us or steal Félise to safety of her own."

"Vespera? That meddlesome woman has — "

"Has worried over Félise for all her life. We must give this a chance, my lord. Vespera gave Félise to us."

"That is what you say, but there is no proof."

"I trust her word ... I trust her prayers. I *know* that this is true." She paused and tears gathered in her eyes. "We have to mind the order of this conspiracy, Harlan. Félise is not ours."

Harlan slumped slightly. He was no longer angry with his wife, but when he had first found out that Edrea had guarded the reason for Vespera's interference with such secrecy, he had been furious. Just prior to the naming of Royce and the disappearance of Félise from Windsor, Vespera had confided in Lady Edrea.

The search for a proper mate, a sound manager for what would show itself to be rich French property, involved more than the Scelftons, Henry, and various suitors. It mattered not at all how rich the husband be, for what Félise brought to the marriage would build a noble household enviable even by Harlan. The only characteristic the man needed to have was unquestionable loyalty. There were a few Henry would approve, but Royce was the highest in his eyes — and also he was unmarried and old enough to have gained fair experience.

Knowing Harlan worried over the Leighton name, Henry had allowed some interference, provided the man's wealth and resources were not judged, for those came with the dower purse. Only his loyalty to the crown and his moral behavior were to be subject to inspection.

"How do we know yet whether he is a good and honest man?" Harlan asked.

"Félise is headstrong. If she feels he is not and she cannot make him so, she will flee from him. Had anyone known the extent of her wealth, the petitions for her would have confused even Henry."

"Even so, madam, she is in *need*. Perhaps this tiring-woman, Vespera, conspires with Royce."

"Nay, Vespera conspires with no man. 'Tis her property given to Félise, and the woman goes back to the sisters. If she is not truthful, why would she give away such wealth? She begs a short space of time to see her natural daughter well fitted for the remainder of her life, and it is a small thing to ask. Harlan, I beg you to see, *Segeland* is in need; — our Félise has what she wants."

Harlan stood and found a tankard. He banged it on the trestle table and quickly a page came with a pitcher to fill it. He downed the ale almost in one swallow and turned pleading eyes to his wife.

"What would have been lost had *we* been allowed to provide a mate for Félise? How are Henry and this queen's poetess better suited to make the match than *I*?"

Edrea simply shook her head, without answer. "The day a ragged little girl came to us through a priest, I knew she was only mine to raise for a short time. Already vast plans were being worked in places I could not see, for she had a history before she came to me and was not born of my body. I yielded myself to this when I took her. I can't take this opportunity away from her now."

"We could see that she is safe," he offered.

Edrea looked down at the letter again. Félise wrote that much more was needed than supplies for all those people who had lost faith and had never known the comfort of a lord's love. Yet they were hungry and cold, she had said, and for this reason Félise believed they would come to understand faith and hope and love much more quickly if they were fed and kept warm against the winter and found, with the passage of time, that there was no reason to fear her.

Félise did not say much about her husband, except that he had gone to view the dower land in Aquitaine and could be gone for two months. But Edrea read her daughter as clearly through the letter as she could have if she had looked into those bright turquoise eyes. Royce too must be among that number who had lost faith and needed time to learn trust and genuine love.

She smiled in firm inner peace, remembering well the childish temper Félise had displayed while at Windsor. The author of these letters hardly resembled the girl of the castle courtships. She had always believed Félise capable of strength, once she saw some true purpose in it. It was more than time to leave Félise to finish the task of becoming a woman.

"No, Harlan," Edrea said as warmly as she could. "Félise has too much work to entertain us, and surely she would worry whether we approved her efforts."

"I do not see the sense in leaving her thus," Harlan grumbled.

"Well, my dear," she said, rising from her seat and going to him, stroking his upper arms with her hands. "Perhaps you shall, in the fall. She sent her brothers away and clearly asks us to send her aid but leave her be. And so we shall."

"Women," he muttered. "Absent of logic, forever playing these tenderhearted games. 'Tis beyond me how you think to do such great things with time and patience and love, when a good arm and whip will get the walls higher, the guards stronger, and the planting done."

She laughed good-naturedly. "Yea, my love . . . I know it is beyond you."

The first of March came along with blistering winds that yielded in a few days to a teasing warmth. Félise knew that the cold would come and go through the month, and with April, the ground would soften and tilling for planting would have to begin.

The people grew stronger on the generosity of Segeland, but the coin Royce had left was nearly exhausted in the process. He had not sent word, but she reasoned he could not part with even one of his men, and messengers willing to travel to Segeland would be few and costly. She knew he must be frugal, and she took it as a good sign.

Hewe worried about their depleted sums, and Sir Trumble complained about his confinement to the keep when he was much better suited to traveling and fighting. She kept her eyes turned hopefully toward spring, although even she was becoming discouraged by the length of winter and the energy it required to keep everyone looking toward a better tomorrow. When she had failed to find a priest in Daventry, she had fought the feeling of failure, telling herself other towns would be visited until a friar or priest could be found.

She rose earlier than the others to give herself time to prepare for the day. The mistress of a large keep spent little time alone, for someone was forever bringing a problem for her to solve or needing advice or counsel. She treasured the early morning before the keep bustled with activity as a time to collect herself. And it was then, at the break of dawn, that she thought of her husband, praying that he would return a more willing spouse than he had left her.

In mid-March, during a particularly bright afternoon, she was called from the hall by a wildly excited Colbert. "A banner and men approach with a long train," he shouted. "Sir Trumble has bolted the gate and mans the walls. Even the yeomen have run to fetch scythes and pitchforks."

She jumped in surprise, her heart pounding fearfully. "Colbert, how many?" she asked urgently.

"Two hundred or more, lady."

She flew to the door and down the road toward the gate, her face white with terror. Maelwine had imparted to her that neither Boltof nor Wharton carried any lingering hostility over the loss of her dower prize, but she trembled at the prospect that some other came in Royce's absence to usurp him.

As she ran, holding her skirts up, she barely thought about

what was going on around her. People were running, men, women, and even the children, gathering in meager stock bought in Coventry and entrusted to them, and wielding mean weapons against attack. It crossed her mind briefly that when she had arrived the people had simply hidden, but now they were driven to protect their homes.

There was a ramp leading to the top of the wall that held no more than two people to view the land. Trumble's men balanced precariously atop ladders to look over the wall, intending to use these modest perches to shoot arrows at the foe. Félise called up to Sir Trumble. "Help me up! I would see this army."

"The way is steep, lady. The rise is shaky."

She looked around, seeing nothing but panic in all quarters, and with a powerful determination, she lifted her skirt and began the climb without assist. Seeing her intention to get up to the top of the wall, Trumble came down a step or two and held out his hand, pulling her up beside him, but not without admonishing her. "You would do better to let me guard your safety, lady, from the ground up."

"And you, sir knight, would do better to — "

She stopped abruptly as she viewed the reason for the alarm. A train of better than twenty wagons was accompanied by over one hundred knights. But what she saw was not an approaching foe. The banner carried ahead of the troops was her father's, and the wagons carried supplies for building, not destroying.

She gave a joyful laugh and her hands came quickly to her face as glad tears filled her eyes. Whatever they sent her from Twyford was many times what was necessary. And she had not been frugal with her requests; she had asked for the loan of everything needed to make Segeland comfortable.

"Oh, Sir Trumble, open the gate. My father sends goods. 'Tis the banner of Twyford . . . surely not come to fight." He looked at her suspiciously and she laughed at his grumpy face. "By God, Trumble, bid them open the gate!"

Trumble did not relax completely until a knight rode through the gate and paused. Félise recognized him, but as far as she could see, not one member of her family ventured here. These were vassals of Twyford; the load had not been given to her brothers. They had paid her the highest tribute in their understanding and respect for her decision.

"I bear letters to Lady Félise Leighton, Baroness of Segeland."

She straightened proudly. She had not thought much about Royce's elevation to full baron until that moment. She moved toward the knight, who, upon seeing her, dismounted and handed her a scroll. She opened it quickly.

> *Lady Félise,*
> *Your debt is happiness. If these carts do not bear the full remedy to your problems, sacrifice these goods to Segeland and journey to Twyford where there is a home and care for you. Our loan is this: we loan you to the lord of Segeland, for only so long as this remains your choice.*

The missive was signed by the lord and lady of Twyford. A tear crept down her cheek. It was unheard of to snatch a woman home to her father, just as it was incredible to gift a daughter with wagonloads of goods.

A breathless Vespera was at her side, looking in wonder at the huge entourage of knights and wagons.

"We cannot remain, lady, but must remove the goods from all but two wagons and depart at once. Lord Harlan cannot be long without these many guards, but the baggage needed protection. My lord bids you keep two wagons, and the others must return to the Twyford towns before the planting."

"Of course," she replied, almost too happy for words. "Please, bring the wagons to the hall and we'll begin at once."

A clamoring through the gate began and the people of Segeland stood around with gaping mouths as the train proceeded toward the hall. Félise passed the letter from her parents to Vespera, who was also moved to tears by the brief message. "They are extraordinary, lady," she said breathlessly.

A gelding bearing a small, bald man and heavily laden with leather saddlebags approached. "The lady of Segeland?" he asked.

She noticed the silver cross that hung around his neck. "Aye, Father," she affirmed.

"I was told you have need of a priest, and I am lately freed of my obligation near Twyford. Lady Edrea of Twyford paid my passage and said you might offer shelter."

"Make your home in the hall, Father, until a better rectory is found for you," she said with a smile.

"Thank you, lady," he said, spurring his horse down the road toward the towering hall.

Félise looked at Vespera with glowing eyes. She could not express what she felt. That her parents could believe in her to this generous extent was beyond her wildest dreams. She opened her mouth several times to speak but, failing to find words, finally collapsed into Vespera's arms and wept joyfully.

"Yea, you are blessed," Vespera murmured.

"I can't say why they give me so much, when I have given them so little. I am not even born of them, but a poor wretch they took in out of charity . . . and yet their charity never ceases." Tears coursed down her cheeks. "I will never find the means to repay all of this."

Vespera patted her affectionately. "That you choose to show charity to those in need is payment, lady. If you can heal the sorrow in this burg alone, there is great purpose in your life. Perhaps this is why you were born."

"Yea, perhaps," she said, sniffing back her tears. Setting the town to rights and improving the hall were things she could do. The pity she couldn't call for some healing balm from Twyford that would entice her husband to love her. But that would come, she promised herself. She would not rest until it did. "I shall try. God willing, we shall see all the sorrows healed."

Chapter Fourteen

It happened that not all that the Scelftons sent to Segeland was appropriate to their needs. Félise deemed it wise to trade some goods for others, rather than bear any insult to her parents with respect to their gifts by returning them. So, when many more bags of seed than they could use arrived, Félise set Hewe to the task of taking a wagonload to Coventry to trade for animal stock. And when bolts of cloth would be better traded for twice as many spindles of thread and yarn and more looms for the village women, she excused Vespera to accompany a small group of travelers to arrange that trade.

So many trips to Coventry had been made that it had been arranged that a local house would receive those from Segeland each time. It was usual that, the journey being short, they stayed only one night. Arriving in the afternoon and settling in the merchant's house, Vespera and Hewe set about their trading, ate a hearty dinner, slept a short night, and rose early, quite pleased with the goods and ready to journey back to Segeland.

Vespera approached her young escort before he had finished his morning meal. "Sir Hewe, I know the urgency that we be upon the road, but would you allow time for one last item?"

"What?" he questioned, his mouth full of bread.

She seated herself across from him and urged him to continue to eat while she explained. "When I was in search of yarns and threads for my lady, I did come across a bolt of fine cloth that I would like to purchase for her. 'Tis a frivolous item, but I can't resist. And with a bit of lace, it will make a fine morning gown for her." Vespera shrugged somewhat shyly. "I have saved a small sum for the purchase, if you would escort me to the merchant."

Hewe put down his knife and frowned as he contemplated this. "I would take you, but there are two conditions. First, the price must already be to your liking, for we have no time to argue with the merchant. And second, you must let me share in the purchase of the gift."

"It is not necessary, sir knight, as I can assure you I have the sum. It does not beggar me."

"You misunderstand me, madam. I do not pity your poor state. It is only that I, too, have seen baubles and laces that would do my lady honor."

Vespera broke into a rare, wide smile. She could not express her personal pride that Félise's behavior elicited love and respect from all who came to know her. She had been aware of Hewe's initial avoidance of Félise, and likewise aware that as he spent time with her, he had begun to hold her in ardent respect.

"As I have said, I found a bolt of rich cloth for a morning gown, and if you will allow, I will purchase that. Then, if it pleases you, I will help you select a perfect lace for the trim, that your gift to her may be as rich."

"We are agreed," he said happily. "I'll have the horses and wagons readied while we make our purchases, and then we'll get quickly back to Segeland."

Vespera waited at the small table in the merchant's dining hall while Hewe alerted those few who had traveled with them to make ready. They quickly sought out the cloth merchant and found that he was also well stocked with beautiful laces and trims and threads. Pleased with the prices the man demanded and the nature of their gifts to Félise, they walked briskly and happily back toward their party of travelers.

Vespera slowed her pace for a moment and then grasped Hewe's arm to stop him in mid-stride. He looked at her quizzically but found that her eyes were locked on two men who stood talking outside the massive Coventry church. He looked at them for a moment, breathing one name. "Boltof?"

She pulled him out of sight of the street, within the doorframe of a baker, and her mouth was set in an angry line. "Do not let them see us, Sir Hewe. It is Boltof and Sir Wharton."

"Wharton? I was told they had buried their differences." He shrugged.

"Aye," she said angrily. "Buried their differences and yet the two of them linger for so long . . . so close to Segeland. It was a long while ago that Sir Maelwine found the two together here, and both, he said, were bound for other places. Something is wrong."

Hewe stiffened at the mere possibility that these two would tarry here to cause some threat to his lord and lady. He unconsciously flexed the muscles in his arms and set his jaw in a grim line, ready for confrontation. "Then I will learn their intention at once."

"Nay," she said in an urgent whisper. "That is useless, for if they're bent on trouble, they will not tell you. Better that we know they meet in Coventry and keep our eyes and ears sharp. If they know we have seen them, they may hatch some plan to misguide our step. If they think themselves safe, they may act with foolish confidence. Let us hie from this place before they know they've been seen."

"Would it not be better to let them know that we see this new friendship blooming so close to Segeland's gate?" he asked.

"Hear me, Hewe. There stand two men who not only wanted Lady Félise and her lands, but petitioned King Henry for her hand. And what do they share? Only their disappointment at having been overturned in favor of Royce. They are up to no good."

Hewe looked around the frame of the baker's door. " 'Tis not my custom to lurk in passageways, spying, when I am set to demand a proper answer for such actions."

Vespera touched his arm. "I know it is not your way, but I am small and weak and have learned much from quiet passages and open ears. And if, in the end, we protect what Royce holds, the method matters least of all.

"They do not know me. I will pass them while they're in conversation if you will quietly go through the baker's shop and leave by a rear door. 'Tis your face they will know."

Hewe thought for a moment but quickly decided she was the wiser, and since they were bent on a single purpose, it was better to see what knowledge leaked out than to risk a confrontation that would only yield a lie.

He nodded to her and she wasted no time in lowering her head, tucking her hands into her mantle, and setting out in the direction of Wharton and Boltof. She did not betray herself by turning to see if Hewe had entered the shop, but rather paused beside the two men and pretended to examine some leather purses displayed on a merchant's cart beside them. With her back turned to the men, she lingered a moment.

"When do you go?" Wharton asked.

"In a few days. When Celeste arrives to meet me."

"You are certain you can gain friendly admittance?"

"Aye. Royce is a highly responsible man. He will wish to make good his roguish behavior. And of course, on the grounds of friendship, he will admit us. I know the man. And we have cleared the way with Félise through Maelwine."

"You will send me word?"

"Aye, stay in Coventry with a few men. I will send a message to you through the priest, Trothmore, when I am admitted to the keep. Or failing that, later, when it is time for some action from you."

There was a long pause before Wharton spoke again. "You are certain that Celeste will help us?"

"She has always done exactly as I've bidden her. 'Twas me who brought Royce to her in the first place. She relies on my help. I tell her what to do and when to do it."

"I hope you are right," Wharton said. Vespera thought she heard a note of distrust or apprehension in Wharton's voice.

"How may I help your selection, madam?" the leather craftsman asked. "A purse for yourself or your husband? A well-crafted sheath for a knife? I have bridles and saddles, but they are too large for the cart, yet I can tell you the way to my shop and my son will help you select what you need."

"Nay, there is nothing. I simply admire your fine talent," she said softly, smiling at the man.

"Surely this pouch caught your eye . . . ," he attempted.

"It is lovely, but I will make no purchase today," she answered.

He gave a grunt and moved away to a more likely customer. Vespera caressed the leather pouch, straining her ears for more of the conversation behind her, but she heard nothing. She cautiously turned and spotted Boltof's bulky frame as he walked alone down the street. She silently cursed the merchant for causing her to miss their last exchange and words of parting, and turned in the opposite direction to see Wharton traveling away.

When she reached Hewe at the wagons, all was ready for their journey. He approached her eagerly.

"They are plotting," she said, a note of agitation in her voice, "but I have no idea what they hope to gain. I know only this: Boltof and Celeste will venture to Segeland and gain entrance under the guise of friendship, and Wharton waits here for some instruction. Perhaps they plan an attack on the keep, I cannot say."

"Then Boltof will be surprised when he is not allowed within."

Vespera thought for a moment, quietly chewing her lip. "If their plan is set awry this time, they will only devise another. The next time we will not have foreknowledge. Nay, Hewe, I think it best to let Boltof within and watch him as a hungry rat watches the scraps from the table. When he moves to threaten, he will be caught."

"Lady Félise must be warned," Hewe said resolutely.

"Warn Royce, when he is returned. And my lady will be cautioned not to trust them, but we will take care not to worry her. Let us guard her even better than we have, and let Royce be the one to tell her the reason."

"I don't know if it is wise to tamper with them if they mean to do her harm," Hewe argued.

"It would be worse if we stopped them now, and months or a year from now were faced with some surprise devilment. Let us take a lesson from the knaves: we will work in secret as they do and we will be ready for them. If they mean to usurp Royce or harm the lady, they have but one chance. Once caught, they will not live to try again."

"It is like a thousand Christmas holidays," Félise exclaimed. "First, all that has been sent from Twyford; now, this. You are so good to me." She embraced Vespera in grateful thanks for the lovely gift and the woman accepted the gesture, returning the affection with a tight squeeze of her own.

But Sir Hewe chafed and turned bright pink up to his brow when Félise encircled him with her arms. He stammered uncomfortably, keeping his arms fixed straight at his side as he suffered through her torturous clinging.

Félise stepped back and looked at the rigid knight, who looked like an oversized boy, frightened to death. She could not suppress a teasing giggle. "Don't worry, Hewe. I swear I will not tell Sir Royce how you shamelessly beg my affection. He should find little cause to run you through — at least not for taking such advantage of me."

Clutching the prized bundle to her breast, she fled up the stairs to her chamber with the thought of immediately laying out the cloth and designing something with her shears. Vespera followed and quietly watched as Félise excitedly considered the many possibilities. "I suppose Royce will be returned soon, and I should like to hurry the new gown," she chattered.

"Have you any word, lady?" Vespera asked.

"Nay, but a messenger is too costly. He warned me it might well take two months. I am certain he will send word if he is delayed." But she frowned slightly, either doubtful of her husband's consideration for her worry or puzzled with the best way to cut the cloth.

"Do you know how to send word to him?"

"Nay. I know the lands in Aquitaine are formerly of the de Raissa family, but not the location. That is what he travels to find." She turned to Vespera. "Something of my mother's kin, but none is living."

Vespera turned her face away, but Félise did not notice. "What of the Leightons? Are any still living?"

"Not to my knowledge," she answered, paying more attention to the cloth than to the question.

"What shall you do if friends or family come to Segeland?"

"I suppose I shall try to make them welcome and comfortable. But who would come here?"

"Did Maelwine not suggest that Boltof would visit?"

Félise turned to Vespera with an incredulous look on her face. "Aye, but I assumed that would be much later. Surely he would not venture here without an invitation from Royce." Vespera shrugged as if she could not answer. "What manner of man would be bold enough to do such a thing?"

"I met Sir Boltof in passing at Windsor," Vespera lied. "I think him bold enough."

Félise sighed at the possibility. "You could be right, but should he arrive unsummoned, poor Sir Hewe will faint for loss of sleep. That trusty knight would strap himself to my skirts and sleep by my door lest any man so much as look my way. He takes his oath to my husband very seriously."

"More's the mercy."

Félise simply ignored Vespera's comment and busied herself with the new fabric, finally deciding on a style that would reveal much of her bosom and had long, flowing sleeves. The color had been chosen to compliment her hair and eyes and was of a shining turquoise hue. She cut out the pieces that very day.

In the following days she stole away to her chamber whenever her usual toils did not occupy her. She sewed the cloth with silver thread, trimmed it with a white and silver lace trim, and tried it on for a proper fit with every new seam. She thought of how Royce might view her in the candlelight or early dawn in the dressing gown. She hoped the style and color would please him, if not seduce him.

On the fifth day that she sewed, again with time she could ill afford to spare, Sir Hewe knocked on her chamber door. She thought perhaps Hewe might never view the finished garment, bold as it was, and so left the piece on her bed as she bade him enter. He would have this one opportunity to see how skillfully she joined the gift of threads and trim to the fabric.

But Hewe entered wearing a troubled look and did not glance about the chamber. "My lady, Sir Boltof and Lady Celeste approach the hall. Sir Trumble has admitted them. They will be here in a moment."

Her eyes widened in disbelief. How could she face either of them? What would she find to say to Celeste, who must surely hate her now? And Boltof— did he mean to court her away from Segeland and her husband? "Hewe, do they say why they've come?"

Hewe shrugged as if he did not know, but answered just the same. "They have brought you a fine wedding gift: a gentle mount of considerable value. Boltof claims his friendship with Royce is too precious a thing to be set asunder by King Henry's order."

Félise rose and found her legs shaky as she stood. "That explains Boltof," she said, her heart beating wildly. "What of Celeste?"

Again Hewe shrugged. "The same, I assume."

"What am I to do with them?"

Hewe shook his head, having no answer at all. "Two chambers can be found for them, if you will it. Or, if it is your preference, I can set them on the road home."

She chewed her lip thoughtfully, holding her hands clasped in front of her. The quaking of her insides would not still. She was terrified of facing them alone, not to mention the disquiet she felt at the thought of Royce returning to find his old lover in residence.

Again, as many times before, she longed for Lady Edrea's wisdom and Lord Scelfton's blustering bullheadedness.

"Nay, Royce would be ashamed of my poor hospitality. This is my husband's home, and friends of his shall be comfortable here, even if I am not." She took a deep breath and tried to stand erect, demanding of herself that she at least appear to be dignified and strong.

She approached Hewe, her worried frown still evident. She dearly hoped that by the time she faced the couple she could present a gracious mien. "Poor Hewe. Your work shall be made difficult once again."

Hewe tried to smile away her discomfort. "I think 'tis better to watch a wolf who is securely penned than to seek his trail in the open country. Come, lady. We will greet them, and Sir Boltof and his sister shall be assured that you are safe from harm while I am here." He presented his arm to lead her below. "And remember, do not pity me. I cherish my labors."

Félise had to fight for self-control. She would have trembled miserably had Hewe not stood straight and determined at her side. Several long moments passed within the entry before Lady Celeste and Sir Boltof dismounted and came forward to greet her. It was Boltof who pressed himself ahead of his sister and spoke.

"Dear Lady Félise," he said, reaching out a hand to her. She allowed him to take her hand, damp though it was, and press a kiss on its back. "We honor you with gifts in celebration of your wedding and, more important, a declaration of friendship. Our households need not be in conflict because of past obligations."

Félise felt her pulse pick up. How often, she wondered, would these two remind her of Royce's past?

"How very kind of you, sir knight. My thanks."

"And Royce? Is he out on some errand?"

"Nay, he is yet in Aquitaine. Did he not tell you?"

"He did not," Boltof said, looking quite surprised.

Félise found it difficult to believe that no one of Lord Orrick's household had had word from Royce. Although her husband made no mention, she had seen him working dutifully on letters and assumed he had at least written apologies to that family, if not visited them while in London.

She raised a questioning eyebrow. "Surely my brother told you?"

"He may have mentioned it, lady, but I gave little heed. When does he return?"

"Soon, I hope. He would certainly hate to miss your visit."

Trying to hide her frown of displeasure, she moved past Boltof and sank into a deep curtsy before Celeste. "My lady," she crooned, smiling as well as she could under the pressure of the moment. "How good of you to come."

Celeste matched the curtsy with one of her own, keeping her eyes shyly downcast. "It is kind of you to receive us," she nearly whispered.

"And why would I not?" Félise said. "My husband's close friendship with your family has been a valuable thing to him and something I am certain he hopes will continue." She paused, waiting for Celeste's eyes to meet hers that she might judge the effect of her words. In the pale blue she saw the pain of lost love and none of the toughness of a woman bent on vengeance. Celeste appeared a hurt little lamb, at least as uncomfortable with the situation as Félise. "Alas," Félise continued quietly. "My husband consoles me that ours is not the first union of necessity, nor shall it be the last. 'Tis our hope that friends and family will work as fervently as we to see our king well pleased."

Celeste only nodded a bit forlornly, trying to smile. Félise looked suspiciously out of the corner of her eye and saw Boltof's frown of displeasure.

"Your journey has been a long one," Félise said. "Sir Hewe, if you will show our guests to their chambers, I will instruct the cooks to prepare a gallant fare for their evening meal."

"Aye, it is a long ride to Segeland," Boltof said, looking around the hall and judging its worth. "And I am tired and hungry." He bowed over the lady's hand. "You will find us better company after a short rest, madam. My thanks."

Boltof took his sister's hand and led her, behind Sir Hewe, up the stairs. Félise watched them each step of the way. Many unusual things confused her. The one thing that she had quickly determined was that they were not here to secure her friendship, however much it looked that way. She did not think she could voice her suspicions to Royce, should he return during their visit. But she heartily hoped for his swift return.

She felt a presence beside her and turned to see Vespera also watching the couple ascend the stairs. Hers was not a perplexed frown, but a black scowl.

"Madam," Félise whispered, "you are most certainly a sooth-sayer. How did you guess they would come?"

Vespera continued to look at the staircase, although the visitors were out of sight. A certain fury flickered across her brow and she did not answer Félise. "They are about trouble," Vespera finally said.

"That is fact," Félise said. "The journey from Lord Orrick's home would take days, especially with a woman of Celeste's delicacy. Yet they are clean and appear rested. They have not traveled far. And Boltof would have me believe they were unaware of Sir Royce's absence. In my heart I know Boltof wished to arrive here while I was much alone. Does some army of knights perhaps wait in yon glen to attack us?"

"We will set Sir Trumble to survey the land, but I trust he will find nothing. Boltof is clever."

"Vespera, does Boltof bring his sister to tempt Sir Royce from me?"

"Nay, I think not. That fair dame could not seduce the saddle off a horse."

"But Royce admits he loved her deeply."

"You mistook him, surely. Nay, whatever Boltof intends here, he does not use Celeste as a temptress."

Félise's whisper was soft and carried the edge of fear. "Vespera, do they mean me harm?" Vespera's eyes met Félise's. "If I am dead, my dower lands belong to Royce. Mayhap my husband would share the wealth with his former betrothed and her brother."

Vespera took a deep breath and looked closely into Félise's eyes, meaning to have her words carried home to the young woman's heart. "If they planned to come here to bring you to doubt your husband, already they have success. Be wary, Félise. Royce is ofttimes a surly man, but he has shown his concern for you and cannot prefer the lady Celeste. Even should such a horror tempt the skittish groom, the men of Twyford would not let him live if harm came to you from any quarter. Rest easy on that and let yourself trust your man. He did not call Boltof to Sege-land."

Félise nodded but continued to fret, for she couldn't fathom the purpose of this visit. Her insides told her it did not bode well for them.

Vespera patted her hand. "We will watch him, lass. He dare not touch a hair on your head. Until Royce returns to us, his loyal vassals will keep guard."

Félise nodded bravely. "I am wishing that Maelwine had but moved the mighty bolts and locks to the *inside* of my chamber doors."

Vespera's eyes wandered about the room, though she looked at nothing in particular. "Your safety will be attended to," she said distractedly. "Be wary, love, but do not be frightened. You have snared the wolf in your own den, and though he does not know it, he is much at our mercy now."

Chapter Fifteen

ROYCE DROVE HIMSELF HARD TOWARD SEGELAND, taking far more risks than he was wise in doing. He had tampered with the absolute trust of his men by pushing them so hard and making such feeble excuses for the speed of their travel.

He left three men to stay in London in wait upon King Henry with many pages of revenue descriptions, maps, and intricate details about the de Raissa lands, not wishing nor seeing reason to stay himself, and took those remaining on a heartlessly bold trek toward his manse. "While the weather is dry and clear, we must make use of it," he had said, although he knew well that any journey at night was less wise than day movement through a rainstorm. He compromised the costly destriers on which they rode by chancing their stepping into a shallow hole or fatally slipping down a concealed crevice.

"I've been too long away, and there is much to be done at Segeland," he said, knowing it was his curiosity about Vespera and whether Félise was still there that drove him. He had thought to stumble upon a traveling tryst, as most knights on sojourn are apt to do, but no village wench, inn maid, or harlot coerced his mood. Not even the bold ones tickled any desire within him.

He had not wanted to return to Segeland with the rush of uncontrollable desire he felt, for he thought it a dangerous notion. He hoped he could restrain his lust and approach her with a husbandly concern. But what if he should find her gone? Or angry, after his long absence? Or her brothers worse in their hovering?

"My lord, a half day's journey on the morrow would see us within the town walls by midday," one of his men declared, the complaining tone clear in his voice.

But returning under the cover of night did not distress Royce, for should Félise be within her chamber asleep, he would not be above creeping past her brothers to wake her. His calculations put him at Segeland just before midnight, when all manor residents would be soundly sleeping. The darkness had suited him well before, and it would serve him now. And with that, he would not have to view much of the keep that depressed his spirit so.

Rousing Sir Trumble's attention to open the gate had proven simple enough, for that trusty soul would let no lesser knight keep this post in the dark hours. And after dismissing his men to the stables, Royce found the hall to be open. There were no bars necessary if Trumble held the wall. He smiled in satisfaction at this, for what he lacked in material things he certainly could equal in the competence and loyalty of his men.

He knelt before the hearth in the main room and placed two dry logs atop the smouldering embers, blowing up the flames. He would at least take the chill off his body before investigating the lady's chamber for whatever deserts lay within.

Pulling his mail and hauberk off and flinging them aside, he noticed the room only when the fire had brightened. It had become a warm and tasteful place, with tapestries hung, candles placed about in metal and wood holders, chairs and tables completely repaired and in some cases rebuilt and polished with oil. In addition to herbed rushes on the ground, there were skins and rugs. Handsomely crafted pitchers and bowls stood in useful decoration on the tables. He smiled in equal parts of pride and relief. These small indications of Félise's continued perseverance pleased him well.

A certain melancholy settled over him, for there had been a time when he had rejected this hall. And later, after Aylworth's death when this belonged to him, he could barely bring himself to visit the place. But now, with Félise working to make it a home any man would be proud of, he was changed.

He nearly laughed at himself, for the decor of the room and the implication of her presence caused his manhood to swell against his chausses. He was aroused before even setting eyes on her.

"Welcome, my lord."

He turned toward the stairway to find Vespera descending, holding a candle to light her way through the dark passages. She wore her drab and modest dressing robe over a nightdress and her hair was conspicuously covered. Royce had never known a woman to dress for bed with veils or wimples. Was her dark nun's costume a ritual, deception, or simply the only garb she owned?

He bowed. "Madam. Does my lady sleep?"

"Aye, my lord. Would you have me wake her?"

"Nay, 'tis you I wanted to see, in any event. And I have no hesitation in waking her myself."

She came down the few remaining steps into the room, a knowing look on her face.

"How did you find Aquitaine?" she asked.

"You've kept it quite well."

Her breath came out in a relieved sigh. "Jasper is a talented castellan. I hope you plan to retain him."

"Is that decision mine, lady?" he asked, pointedly using a worthy title in his conversation with her.

" 'Tis yours through your lady wife," she said gently. Her eyes glowed with an emotion that Royce had never seen before. She seemed pleased. But in looking at the tenderness of her expression, he realized that this was one of the few times he had had a full view of her face. She had concealed herself all this time with a mask of modesty and shyness, either intentionally or by rote. She had kept her eyes cast away from perusal, her face turned from inspection. All had considered her habits nunlike, when possibly she had only been inclined toward mystery. Now, as she let him view her face fully, her eyes open to him, he could see why. If he imagined fiery gold hair beneath her veil, he could see a strong resemblance, especially in the mouth and eyes. This was Félise's natural mother.

"Have you told her?" he asked.

"Nay."

"Why not?"

"I could not find the way. And I cannot see what purpose would be served."

"But yet you have involved yourself in her life far beyond anyone's imaginings, lady. And you've stayed protectively close."

"I had imagined all these years since she was taken from me that I might supervise her in some way. Now I see she is fit, and I may retire to Fontevrault." She paused and looked at him earnestly. "Jasper will not speak of me further if I ask him not to," she added. "It is safe to take Félise to view her grandfather's lands."

Royce couldn't help but ponder the reason for her secretiveness. "But you have allowed me to gain knowledge of this arrangment."

"Messire, it was never my intention to deceive you. Had there been a better way for you to know the truth, I would have told you all. Do you feel tricked? Nay, you are not. It is all very simple and just — you are the only choice for Lady Félise, the only possible man for her. As she is the only woman for you. There are no others, nor could there ever be."

He crossed his arms over his broad chest, peering at her. "How so, lady?"

"The knowledge may little please you," she attempted.

He gave a sharp nod, and, mostly out of habit, his eyes grew fierce in demand for an answer. She did not shrink from his scowl, but smiled easily. "I saw you kiss her." A light flush marked her cheeks, but her embarrassment seemed not to be linked with the confession, but perhaps more with what she had viewed. "The cold gallery grew warm in the moment." She shrugged lightly. " 'Twas not the heat of a man's lust alone that stirred me, but the glow of both man and woman, intent on each other."

Royce thought perhaps he might blush as well, and commanded himself to remain in cool appraisal of this situation. He leaned against the nearest table and looked at her curiously. He remembered the moment, and in his mind the memory of a presence watching them was almost as clear as the softness of his wife's supple form as he held her. "I think it possible, madam, that you felt more of that kiss than I."

"Not so," she said. "I spent my life singing of such passions as I saw that day, and I know it comes but once in each life. I would not have it pass Lady Félise as it has others."

He understood immediately what had moved her. This was her own story of love lost — lost but for the child that came of it.

"And so you witnessed a brief encounter in a gallery and took the reins and made a match. This is your custom?" he asked in a slightly teasing voice.

"Never before and never again, kind sir," she said, an equal mirth in her voice. "But I felt the need to know who this bold knight who fondled the demoiselle might be. Those few I know well enough to trust approved you above all others. I know your road has been one of hardship, but you are not alone in that. Many have grown strong because of their troubles. And I never believed every Leighton must be afflicted," she said, shaking her head. "Not any more than I can be made to believe that a bastard child should be scorned and held away from family love." Her eyes glowed as if from some inner knowledge as she looked at him. "I think you are lucky to have each other; and with each other, you may accomplish many good things."

"What of her family?" he asked.

"Ah, the Scelftons." She smiled. "They have endorsed her every whim. They deserve her continued devotion. That they have not warmed to you yet does not mean they do not accept you. 'Tis a well-known fact that Lord Scelfton chafes at any interference with his family. He'll come around."

"Who among us knows the truth?" he asked.

She let her gaze drop for the first time since they began their quiet talk. "I came quickly to trust Lady Edrea, feeling a debt to her for all she has done for Félise. 'Twas I who asked the king to name you. To work with Henry is better than to work against him, and in this I have been well schooled. But I could not allow this to frighten Lady Edrea. I made my confession to her and explained away as many of her fears as I could. She is a strong woman — so wise and good. I am certain she has confided in her husband by now, but I fear not soon enough, for the Scelfton knights irritated your humor sorely."

"Where do those worthies sleep?" he asked, his voice growing piqued just at the reminder of them.

"At Twyford, my lord. They have long since departed."

"Ah," he said, the scorn heavy in his voice. "When the wolf was gone and the lamb could not be assaulted, they ceased in their ardent protection."

"That was not the way of it," she argued. "But your lady wife may have a better explanation for you than I."

"Just one thing, lady. Will you name her father?"

She shook her head. "If there were any need, I would not withhold that from you. But it serves only my shame to name him. Rest assured he is a noble sire and there is no reason to be wary of future generations. If I named him to you, you would be well pleased with the strength of his blood, but I beg you not to ask it of me. Some pain still comes of my sin."

He shook his head in some delighted confusion. "I don't know, lady, whether to thank you or cast you out. I have never liked being meddled with to this extent, regardless of the intention."

"I need no thanks and it will not be necessary to cast me out. 'Tis time I returned to my home. I will soon leave Segeland, when there is no further need for me here." She turned quietly away, as if to go back to her bed. Then turning back to him, she spoke softly. "I waited for your return, my lord, to be assured that you knew everything due you. I meant you no injury and would only see you prosper . . . and with you, your young wife. Please believe this to be truth."

Royce took two large steps, took the candle from her hand, and held her elbow. He looked down into her eyes, gentleness and understanding in his. "Stay, Lady Véronique," he whispered. "I won't tell her."

She smiled at the sympathy. "I fear I shall never leave if I allow myself to stay now. And this is my place for only a short while longer."

He escorted her up the first step, planning to light her way up the stairs. "It becomes more your place with each day, lady. And should you choose to tell Félise the truth, I think she would be pleased."

Vespera stopped sharply and looked at him with a pained expression. "Ah! But do you not see, Royce? When your heart aches with love, just the fear of having it thrust away is enough to frighten the boldest from spilling their simple truth."

He gently touched her cheekbone with his knuckle. "Surely, dearest lady, we were born under twin stars," he whispered.

"We share many things, Royce." She smiled. "The most important being our love for yon lady. Keep her well, I beg you."

As they gained the top of the stairs, a shadow caused Royce to stiffen. A man stood outside his wife's door. Sir Hewe came out of the darkness and his sleepy face shone in the candlelight.

"You guard her door as she sleeps?" Royce questioned, his hackles rising as he considered the need for this.

Vespera quickly touched his arm. "Did you not order Sir Hewe to keep the lady safe beyond all question?" She looked pointedly at Hewe. "The knight does you honor as your vassal, my lord, for he does not rest even when all seems at ease. But now you are home, Sir Hewe can light me to my chamber and you may rest beside your wife to make sure she is well and safe." She took the candle from Royce's hand and gave it to Hewe. "You will wish to sleep, and Sir Hewe can speak to you on the morrow. That is soon enough to discuss estate affairs, is it not?"

"My lord," Hewe began, seemingly ready to launch into a long discussion, but he stopped abruptly and smiled. "The morrow is soon enough," he finally said. He took Vespera's arm and led her away down the hall, leaving Royce outside Félise's door.

When Félise's chamber door softly opened, the hearth vents high on the wall created a cool breeze and she stirred, sleepily wondering why Vespera shuffled around in the darkness. She murmured softly in her sleep and pulled the quilt more tightly around her.

Perhaps because of her depth of sleep, the touch of a hand on her hair did not startle her. She rolled in half-sleep and looked up at him, breathing his name.

"Royce."

She saw his large physique and tousled hair in profile above her, and at her sleepy sigh, he lowered himself to sit on the bed. A single candle barely lit the room from near the door and his image was dark. But she would have known his touch, scent, and silhouette in the blackest cavern. "I am sorry to disturb you," he whispered.

"I would be disturbed had you failed to come," she said, opening her arms to him.

He grasped her quickly to him, kissing her fiercely, and her mind whirled in joyful pleasure. She held him as tightly, yielding more in her drowsiness than she could have in the cool evening and in full consciousness. She knew she lacked the courage when fully awake to invite him to her this openly, yet she had dreamed of this moment for what seemed like years. Not a day had passed since they left the Chaney house that she hadn't craved his touch, the wonder of his lips on her flesh, the sensation of his naked power pressing her down into the bed.

And strangely, she did not feel ashamed or shy of these passions that filled her, but rather proud of them.

Royce pulled away to shed his clothing, and although his body was shielded by the darkness, she drank in what she could see of him and became only more courageous with these new feelings. She boldly surveyed his body with her eyes and glowed at what she saw. She heard the sound of her own soft laughter as if it came from across the room. Throwing back the coverlet to let him within, she said, "My lord, you come home to me starved. 'Tis well. Come, husband."

"Do not become vain," he gently teased, tempting a round breast with tender fingers. "Perhaps there was nothing better along the road."

She kissed his ear and neck and chest. "Your oafish remarks are ill timed," she whispered.

"Thus far," he murmured, caressing her with playful strokes down the length of her body, "my timing is perfect."

She moaned softly, turning in his arms, hungrier for him than she had ever hungered in her life. It had been fear, she thought as she touched him as bravely as he touched her. It had been the fear that they would never again share this that had plagued her. She had been lulled by the more desirable duties of a wife and then had suffered as they were cruelly revoked, replaced only by distance and labor. Long before he left for France she had wanted his strong arms, powerful fingers, hard and heavy thighs, yet he had placed himself sullenly apart from her. Since her arrival at Segeland, she had felt more like a servant than a wife.

She let her hands roam over his muscular back and caress his mighty arms. She turned her face and kissed the fingers that touched her hair. She stroked his hips and thighs lovingly, all the while kissing and nibbling his shoulder, neck, and ear. Never, she thought desperately, you must *never* shun my bed again.

She opened her body and heart to him, pulling him into her, demanding as she had never dared before, and glowing all over as she heard his sigh of pleasure. She locked slender fingers into the thick hair at the back of his head and rode with him, their ardor mounting in speed and determination.

His sighs were accompanied by the quickening of her gasps as she held him, met him, gave with him, and took from him. And suddenly a wild frenetic bursting shower of fire and ice consumed her.

"Royce!"

She clutched him as if the joy were painful in its crescendo and might never end, until, it ebbing some small bit, she shivered at the wonder of this strange, new sensation.

He murmured thick, barely intelligible words into her hair and neck, holding her damp body tightly. Félise thought of the power she had just experienced and nearly collapsed in delighted confusion. But he was not yet full of her and moved again, a rhythmic pace that slowly built to a demanding thrusting until the explosive pleasure was his, causing him to convulse, shudder, and collapse upon her.

She held him, gently stroking his neck and back as though she tended him in recovery. She had never in all her imaginings contemplated this kind of intimate joy. A whole new world had just been briefly observed. It was as though the curtain had been lifted on the black sky and a universe of stars never seen before had come into her sight. She had wondered before how it was she was lured to his lovemaking, and even why she should crave his touch, finding the pleasant sensations strangley lacking. She chuckled softly as she considered that if this was the benefit of sharing his bed, she would rarely be without a round belly.

"I am not alone in my need," he whispered, his breath playing teasing little games against her ear that caused her to tremble.

"Aye, but you were alone with the knowledge," she said, amazed at the brazen laugh in her voice. She would not have believed such adventure could be found with him.

They lay quietly for a while, simply enjoying the moist warmth of their exhausted bodies pressed closely together. When he would have rolled away from her, she stopped him. "Don't . . ."

Still, he eased his weight and lay on his side beside her, drawing a moan of despair as he left her body. "You will become spoiled," he said.

"I beg it. My labors have earned meaning."

"Who has schooled you in my absence, wench?" he asked. She turned her face toward him, detecting a note of playful cynicism in his voice.

" 'Twas not Colbert," she laughed. "That grand sheriff fears God and the Testament more than a monk would. Could it have been Hewe? Nay, the boy blushes and runs in fear of your sword. Or Trumble? But that honorable old stag needs a full skin of wine to speak without a stutter to the peevish maid Daria."

"Whoever," he said, kissing her ear. "Remind me to thank him."

"Royce," she asked seriously, "will you leave me again?"

"May I return to you thusly?" he countered.

"If I swear that you need not journey far to receive a decent welcome in your home, will you stay?"

"I have no pressing duties."

"Nay, my lord, I mean . . . Royce, I do not relish your anger.

I do not wish to earn your presence with hardship and long partings." She paused and bit her lip. "A husband true — that is my desire."

He lowered his mouth to hers and his kiss was deep and meaningful. "Can you keep the Twyford knights from guarding my door at night?" he asked.

"They are gone, but in their place you will find other distractions."

"Who could draw my attention from your affection, lady? Is the queen in residence?"

Félise drew in her breath and willed herself further bravery. "Nay, messire. 'Tis the lady Celeste."

Royce instantly stiffened, caught completely off guard by the news. Many thoughts assailed him. He had sent a short note apologizing to Celeste, a letter of explanation to her father, and nothing at all to Boltof. He had avoided her very carefully while in London prior to his journey to Aquitaine. And now he returned to this. "*Here?*"

"And Sir Boltof. They have been here for nearly a week."

"And you made them welcome?"

"Aye. I thought you would have it so."

He moaned in equal parts of despair and anger. "What is it they wish of us . . . now?"

"Friendship. That is their spoken purpose, Royce."

"Ah, friendship. And has Boltof been civil?"

"He does not court me," she said. "But I am not at ease."

"Does he threaten you?"

"Nay."

"And Celeste?"

She blinked her eyes fearfully closed. "She is kind."

He sat up abruptly, a loud groan escaping him. He threw his long legs over the side of the bed, sitting upright beside her and jostling her in the process.

"Do you leave me now?" she asked, a tearful whimper in her voice. He turned in wonder at the question. "I would know the truth, messire. I know you grieve for her, and I cannot remove myself and place her in my stead. Not by will nor by authority.

But I would know the truth; can you not share my bed with her close presence in this hall?"

"Félise?" he questioned.

"I prayed you would somehow forget your desire for her, that somehow I could make you forget. If it cannot be so, I would have the truth. I will not stand quietly aside while you struggle with your anguish over losing her."

"My God," he breathed. "You think I *love* her?"

"It is what you let me believe," she quietly confessed.

He began to laugh at the idiocy of what his silence had won him. "Did you pity me that I had to give up so much and settle for so little in a wife?" he asked, his voice choked with laughter.

Félise did not catch the jest. She began to weep. The pressures of having those two within her house had greatly tired her. "I know you had no choice and I will abide by my obligations as well as you."

His mouth found hers and he rolled with her on the bed, clutching her fiercely to him. He let his lips roam the supple mounds and curves of her body and he chuckled softly as she responded to his touch as naturally as before.

"So, woman, you need yet more assurance of my preference? Then let this be a night of tests, that you never doubt me again."

As he touched, teased, played, and possessed, Félise gained a glowing rapture that would light her from within for days and months and years to come. By the time the rooster crowed, she found little room for doubt.

Chapter Sixteen

SEGELAND DID NOT BOAST GARDENS, WINDING PATHS, fountains, or other fancy accoutrements, although there was room for such and one day the place might be so endowed. For the moment it was a purely functional house. Royce lingered in the yard between the keep and the stables, trying to envision a more decorative area for the future, a place that his wife might view from her chamber window once the bricked enclosure was opened again. He would see it done before spring ventured further onto the land.

He heard the doors opening and noticed that the one he had sent for had come. When he had awakened, early this morning, he had found Vespera in the dining hall and asked her to fetch Lady Celeste. Vespera guided the woman, pointed toward Royce, and then gently closed the door. Celeste, cloaked against the morning chill, approached him warily.

Royce walked a few steps toward her, reaching out a hand to her. She pulled her hand from inside her fur-lined cloak and accepted his, although her expression was stern. Royce had not expected delight from her upon their reunion. In truth, he had not expected to see her at all, much less in his own house. He bowed over her hand and kissed it.

"Why do you call me out of my warm bed to come into the cold? Could we not as well meet before the fire in the hall?"

"My apologies, lady. I owe you many. As to the first concern,

I wanted your ear before anyone's and I wished our conference to be private." He cast his eyes about and saw that only a few of the most ambitious pages and castlefolk wandered between keep and stable and town. "There is no closet or corner from which an eavesdropper could listen to us, and any observers from the hall or stable will see that we keep a discreet distance."

Celeste stiffened and pursed her lips, but her expression was of pain, not anger. Her pale blue eyes began to tear and she lifted her chin a notch, speaking with a slightly quavering voice. "Indeed, we must remain discreet, whatever else."

He sighed heavily. "You are so bitter, Celeste."

She cast her eyes downward and Royce felt a sharp pang of sympathy. Bitterness and hatred, both of which he felt he deserved from her, were not easy emotions for Celeste to maintain. But he had hurt her so deeply.

"I would not have expected less, lady. Truly I know better than anyone how badly I spurned you. Yet all I can offer you now is my deepest apology. There is naught else."

When her eyes rose to his, he saw that tears marked her cheeks. "And I am left with nothing at all. Soiled by you, cast off by you."

"The best of plans oft go awry," he said.

"Our plan, my lord, left me soiled for another."

Royce frowned. "I warned you, early, that should I die upon the field, you would be ill-suited as a bride. Yet 'twas a risk you desired to take."

"I think, perhaps, burying you would have left me more dignity than this."

He rubbed the back of his neck as though he worried with finding the right words. "Some things need to be settled between us. First, I am poor at present; though I am rich of dowry and future revenues, the improvements on this place have paupered me. But I am prepared to promise you a small pension to be delivered later . . . perhaps in two years. Should you marry at a future time, the sum will increase your dower purse. Should you seek retirement, it would provide sustenance for your future.

"I would consider it a gift to ease my conscience, for I know your situation is at present dire, and part of that is because of me."

"Oh, Jesu, part? What portion of my plight does not rest on your conscience?"

"I do not wish to quarrel, Celeste. Do not force me to be cruel."

"God above, I would never urge your further cruelty. Rogue that you are, you coaxed a virgin's answer, spoiled me for other men and that — "

"You were not a virgin," he said flatly.

Her eyes focused on his, widening at the remark, and her hand, which had been tucked into her cloak, came out raised as if to strike. He grasped her wrist and held it there.

"I did not seduce you, lady, but 'twas much the other way. And the evidence you would have me take for your maidenhood was a meager trick played by harlots for many years. Yea, I had my doubts even then, but was not a clever stag, for women were not much a pastime of mine. And it did not matter to me; I do not chastise you even now." He took in a breath and seemed to rise taller, with conviction in his voice. "My wife was a virgin. Your seduction was a ploy and a trap."

Celeste began to tremble and weep openly, appearing to be crushed to her very core. "Royce," she sobbed pleadingly, "I *loved* you."

He put his hands on her upper arms. "I believe you," he said as gently as he could. "I will tell you again, I do not chastise you even now. Some youthful mistake; a misguided step? You were not a child when I met you, lady. I don't judge you harshly. I know you cared deeply and wished marriage with me. So strongly, dear lady, that you gambled I would be trapped by your lost virtue." He paused for a moment, lifting her chin and looking deeply into her eyes. "I believe you would have been true as a wife."

"Why do you tell me this? Why do you humiliate me? What is your plan? To swear to my father that I played you false? Is it not enough that we have been as one and you eased your affections on my humble body and now . . . now, I am abandoned to be the ward of a selfish and oafish brother and crippled father?"

"Cease, lady! I did not call you here to listen to your tirade, but to settle my debt to you. I did not beg you to wait upon my desire for marriage; that you did of free will. I accepted the betrothal contract willingly, broke it willingly, and on that account I owe you. As to your oafish brother — yea, you are his responsibility if you cannot find a husband. And your father? Must you count him crippled when he has done as well by you as any whole father? Think, Celeste, on whose shoulders this burden truly lies. 'Tis you who chose all those things that have brought you to this place."

She sniffed loudly, pulling a cloth from inside her mantle to dry her eyes and nose. Her fingers trembled and he took it from her to help, holding it under her nose as a father would for a small child.

"I am to accept some pension and go on my way?" she asked.

"First you must tell me why you are here."

"We are calling as those of good breeding should, to offer congratulations and bring gifts."

He slowly shook his head. "You did not wish to come here. You knew the experience would be shameful for you. Being here at all leaves you little dignity."

"Boltof urged me to rise above my misfortune and — "

"Nay, lady, I do not believe you. Why has Boltof brought you here? The truth now, for you know you lie poorly."

She gave a slight huff, like a child caught in a lie. "It is unfair that you demand so much of me. You are the man who has known me in the closest way, and whatever you think — youthful mistake or misguided virgin — no one has known so much of me. My truths, dreams, hopes, and deepest devotion have been yours. Perhaps there were those suitors who roughly courted me and took before I could give . . ."

Royce arched an eyebrow in stunned but amused silence. *Suitors?* Celeste was not a wanton woman. She was unusually kind and soft-spoken and dedicated. But something he had suspected and paid little heed to was now coming out more clearly. She was not terribly clever. In fact, she was foolish and naïve, although not a tender maiden by any means. From her statement, it was apparent she might have attempted to use her body as a ploy with more than one man to gain marriage. Royce began to count himself lucky that their plans had been foiled. And she went on undaunted, missing his surprised expression.

"But with you 'twas all different. I loved you so much. I lived for your slightest nod, a glance, a touch. I held so true and waited so patiently for you to settle marriage with me, the woman whose bed you willingly shared. I gave my secret dreams to you and let you know me so well that even now, betrayed by you, you can easily read my thoughts and demand truth. Why should I help you? I should hate you."

He took her limp hand in both of his, rubbing it as if to warm it. He saw Celeste as an ally now, for she would foolishly tell him anything he wished to know, if he carefully questioned her. "I concede your disappointment and indeed heartache. But you've little reason for hate. Had Henry not bade me take Lady Félise, we would be wed now, and that is the truth."

"You did not ask for Félise?" she questioned slyly.

"Nay, I sought out Henry for your brother, as the two of you insisted." He peered at her closely. "Do you doubt that Henry prefers me over Boltof?" he asked.

"I suppose . . ."

"An order, Celeste, as I wrote to you and Lord Orrick. To strengthen Henry's position in his government and his family. And I abide by my king's command to my death. Further, 'tis a lesson more for Boltof than you, but one day you must come to realize that plotting so for betterment often ends poorly. Had you not asked this favor of me, I would not be wed to Félise now."

Celeste was clearly frustrated by the confusion of the situation. She was no more skilled in complex conspiracies than she was in romantic games. Royce watched this play on her face as her eyes darted and her mouth twisted. "I should have refused Boltof in the very beginning."

"What does he ask of you, Celeste?"

"Oh, I mean to say the very beginning, when he told me of you and what a good prize you would be as a husband. Not many women, he promised, would be plying their favors to you and with but a bit of coaxing you could be my husband. He admired your strength and your inheritance."

"My inheritance?" he queried. "I had none when I met you."

"But Boltof knew that one day you would have lands and a sound reputation. He boasted your friendship with men in high places and your warring skills. And he was right about you. And he was right to predict that I would love you."

Royce could not prevent a suspicious frown. Something gnawed at his mind. It was not unusual for a knight to seek one of his fellows for his sister, nor odd that Boltof would predict that Royce would better himself by arms and repute. But in Celeste's simple explanation it was almost as if Boltof had had a hand in fate. Had Royce's brother lived, after all, Royce would not be in Segeland now. And Boltof had been in the same camp with Royce and Sir Wharton when Aylworth had been killed.

Had Henry granted Royce's favor, Boltof would have Félise *and* be heir to his own family lands. And Celeste would reside in Segeland with Royce, costing Boltof no coin for her care.

"Things went awry for Boltof when the king would not approve him as Félise's husband," Royce said. But in his mind he could not rest it that easily. Boltof had been tampering with Royce's future, as if playing with some pawn, for years. He set his mind to watch carefully this one he had called his closest friend.

"Aye," Celeste replied. "For now his plight is only the worse. He sees me as a burden, has no rich woman to wed, and Lord Orrick, crippled though he is, will hold our family lands for many years, making Boltof a grandfather before he rules his own demesne."

"And so? What does your brother wish of me? I know the man well, and he often has a plan to include riches. And you have come here without invitation when we are ill fixed to be hosts. Boltof strains the friendship. I would know why."

Celeste looked at him boldly. "Perhaps he wishes a settlement, as you should expect. You shamed our family, cost Boltof dearly, and leave us paupered in money and dreams," she said. "I don't think your offer of a sum for me at some later time will soothe him."

Royce shrugged. "He has little choice. Should I choose, I can rescind even that offer."

"He hopes that I can persuade you to do better by us. It is not too late to . . ."

There was no need for her to finish. Royce knew the rest as he knew Boltof. "It is too late for any of this to be changed. Surely you realize that."

"Why can it not be? You could take the matter into your own hands, have the marriage declared void by some excuse. Tell her that I am with child, that Boltof will provide well for her. Divide the property with my brother and let us — "

"Does he ask you to seduce me?" Royce asked. Celeste dropped her gaze and a light flush marked her cheeks. Royce suddenly knew that Boltof had always been the one to encourage Celeste to risk her virtue to trap a man into wedlock. Likely it had been Boltof who taught her the indelicate trick of timing her seduction with her menses and groaning in pain at the consummation. Boltof, more than Royce, had been fond of wenching and especially drawn to young virgins. Though Royce could not prove such a secret pact between brother and sister, he had begun to know much of these two and their many plans. He simply wouldn't have believed their deceptions could reach these limits.

He shook his head, but pity showed in his eyes. Celeste could not answer him. He felt a stirring anger toward Boltof, but at the same time an anger with himself. He should have been suspicious long ago. But until now, Royce's actions had quite pleased their whims. He bristled at the naïveté he had shown them, thinking the love and friendship true, while they labored for years to use him.

"You must refuse him, Celeste. I will not bend to any seduction. Do not shame yourself further for Boltof. I am wed. Albeit first by order, 'tis now much by my will. You are not with child, and though you've been hurt, it is as much by your own foolishness as by my advantage over you. I will be fair with you, lady, but know this and take it to your brother's ears: I will kill the man that threatens my wife and my home — even if he is Boltof."

She looked at him through glassy eyes, and the pained disappointment that set her mouth was grim. "You love her."

She is mine, he nearly said, but did not voice this. He knew himself to be plagued by her, drugged by her beauty and effervescence. He had dreamt of her on nights away and prayed she would greet his return. He stood amazed, each passing day, at her quiet and dignified determination as she labored to set his sorry home to rights. He sometimes wished to damn her for her high-flown ways, yet he swelled with pride as she showed her constant respect for him by her diligence. Whether beside her in bed or many miles away in France, he knew in his heart that she was true. This puzzled him, for he did not see himself as more handsome than others, nor more desirable because of possessions. Yet she not only accepted this union, but seemed to crave it and hold it dear.

If I have been tricked by her witch's locks and adoring eyes, he thought, then so be it. I will play the willing victim and be her knight.

"Yea, I love her. And I hold our marriage contract above all other oaths."

"I had hoped . . ." she began, but her voice trailed off as she saw the conviction in his eyes. She shook her head as if in denial, and her tears ran unheeded down her cheeks.

"I labor with the right words, Celeste. I cannot explain myself better than this: I saw in you a good woman and useful wife and would have met you to pledge that. I thought myself to care. I would have played the husband true for you, yet our lives did not venture so far. And now all I can tell you is that Félise is my wife and has my oath and honor and love for all time. Yea, I must turn you away, and I will pray that your pain from this circumstance is short. Perhaps you will find happiness with an honorable man who can give you more loyalty than I could. And with this a warning: if you let Boltof use you to snare a husband, you will find your cup empty again and again."

"You kill me with your words. My heart aches."

"Aye," he said softly, trying to remember that Celeste was also Boltof's victim, and probably not the clever conspirator here. "I am sorry."

She tried to shrug, but it was really a gesture of defeat that pricked his conscience. He wished he had seen that Boltof used her. And he deeply regretted stilling his instincts years before, when the desire was lacking and he knew better than to entwine himself with Celeste. But there had been no other to snare him, and she had been available at every turn. Such is the plight of a man who grows older without bonds.

Now his bonds were of the strongest, surest sort. From a king's command to consuming love, his body and heart were completely tethered.

"You should not have loved one so careless as me."

"But *she* has your heart . . ."

"This is a poor place for you. You deserve a quiet resting place to reckon with your hurt. Refuse Boltof's plans and schemes and go home to Lord Orrick, where there is no reminder of the betrayal you feel."

"She risked nothing and has all of you and I . . . I gave all, chanced all, and am turned away in shame . . ."

"I will take you to the hall, lady. You may wish to leave us this very day and . . ."

"She could have had any man — indeed, she toyed with many."

He grabbed her fiercely by the arms and forced his voice quiet when it would boom into her head. "Even you, in your disappointment, will not decry her good name. 'Twas not Félise who tried to trap me with her body, nor did she fling virtue and good sense aside in an effort to gain. I understand that you claim love and devotion as your reasons for your actions, and I have not berated you for your foolishness. You gained nothing and lost all and I pity you. But you *will not* abuse my wife's good reputation in her own house."

He took a deep breath and let his angry stare bore into her. "You are unwise to listen to Boltof. You should not have traveled here to wear your woes on your breast and attempt to haunt me or trap me. 'Tis done. I have no more patience with your broken heart."

He led her, less than gently, toward the manse and walked with her into the largest room, where the hearth now blazed and many gathered to break the fast. Even Boltof was present, and that one's eyes widened as Royce brought Celeste into the room.

Royce faced Boltof, and while he had risen that morning with the notion of treading carefully, he was spent of their plots and notions to better their circumstances.

His voice was a coarse whisper meant for Boltof's ears alone. "I have done your sister poorly on some counts," he fairly growled. "But that *you* would bring her here and leave her no dignity names you a worse protector than I could ever have been."

Boltof smiled easily. "We came in friendship, Royce. We were to be brothers. 'Twas a pledge made as much to me as to Celeste. I did not think you would face your obligations so poorly. Are we to be called friends beyond today? Or do you cast us out?"

Royce's eyes darkened and reflected the anger that was slowly building. He knew he must quit the room quickly before his fist moved well ahead of his mind and laid Boltof low.

"My obligations will be met, whether to your satisfaction I cannot say. As to friendship beyond this day, I would not dare predict." He took a step in the direction of the stairs and looked back at Boltof. "If I listen to another demand from someone who would be a friend — nay, *brother* — I will end the possibility myself."

That said, he mounted the stairs quickly, trying to put enough space between Celeste, Boltof, and himself to ponder the outrage of it all. The worst feeling that rose in him concerned his own naïveté in trusting them so completely, nearly becoming entrapped by both of them.

* * *

Félise had stirred in early morning, still flushed with the memories of the night. But as she stretched out arms to embrace Royce, she again found her empty bed.

She sat up with a start, for this time she had rested with the comfort that his reclusive ways would finally be at an end and they would rise with the sun together. Disappointment overwhelmed her and anger began to stir within her. She instantly set her mind: she would not be his lover in the dark of night, only to be rejected in the light of day. Whatever his dilemma, the struggle that brought him to her only in this secretive manner, only in great need of her body, she would meet the challenge and somehow set it aside.

She slipped into her nightdress and the new morning wrapper she had fashioned, found her soft leather slippers, and made her way directly to his chamber. No help there, she thought, for not only was he not within, nothing had been disturbed.

She went to the window, hoping to spot him enroute to the stables, his favorite place for peaceful toils. What she saw in the yard below caused her heart to lurch.

He stood speaking with a woman. Although she was cloaked and a hood covered her head, Félise knew it must be Celeste. She watched as Royce held a cloth to her nose and wiped tears from her cheeks.

Félise turned away, her eyes wide and the color drained from her face. She was afraid to see more. If Royce embraced Celeste, or kissed her, Félise knew she could not trust herself to pursue him in good faith and with hope.

She went quickly from the chamber and nearly collided with Daria, who was just on her way below to start her day of work. "Daria, please have some boys from the kitchen fetch water for my lord's bath," she instructed.

"My lord?" Daria questioned.

"Royce has returned, late last night, and I would set a steaming tub for him. And," she said as an afterthought, "send a platter of food, that we may break the fast in leisure in his chamber."

Daria giggled, covering her mouth. Félise frowned at her maid's inanity, for it seemed Daria was of a constant romantic bent, yet it was unlikely she had ever been kissed. And Félise was not as intent on romance as she was on winning her husband once and for all.

The full tub steamed, the boys having used the water already boiling in the cookery below, and a bowl of porridge sat on the hearth along with bread and meat for their morning meal. Félise sat in Royce's chair and waited, trying to still her nervous stomach and wondering how she would handle the situation if he did not return to his chamber this morning. Or if he became angry upon finding her within.

She did not have to wonder long, for he soon snatched open his door. Upon seeing her, he curtailed what seemed to be an angry gesture and eyed her and the tub. His expression softened into a gentle smile. "Good morning, my love. What is this?"

"A morning bath and something to break the fast." She rose and went to him, putting the thought of Celeste as far from her mind as possible. "I was disappointed that you were gone when I awoke, but I will not shirk my other wifely duties."

He chuckled and kissed her nose. "Should you choose, you may serve me only as you did last night, and I will hire an army to do the other chores." He smiled roguishly. "You need your rest."

But Félise was serious. "Come, my lord. You must crave a leisurely bath after so many weeks of travel."

"Indeed," he relented. "But you need not assist me. It has also been my custom to enjoy a private bath."

"But since I am here . . ."

"We will share a morsel and then you may occupy yourself with your other chores while I bathe," he said.

"Nay," she returned, shaking her head. She began to unfasten the laces of his gamberson and drew it aside. "You must not be shy of my ministrations, whatever has been your custom."

He frowned in confusion. "But there is no need — "

" 'Tis my need, if you will," she went on, not looking into his eyes but pushing the gamberson over his broad shoulders and then walking around to his back to pull the garment off. "I am the wife who cleans your hall and orders your servants. I am the wife to ease your manhood and give you pleasure. I will be the wife to know all your needs — to aid your bath, fetch your meals, and bear your children. Until then, I cannot claim myself in truth your wife, for you hide yourself from me in the light of day."

Royce winced slightly at her words and then turned around to face her. "Lady, to aid my bath is hardly necessary. To fetch my meals, less so. We have many helpmates to do these things."

"But Royce," she said, her eyes glittering in earnest, "it does not please me that you creep into my bed only in the dark of night and abandon me before the first light of dawn. I would have more of your time to learn your habits, your needs, and your desires — not only those needs met in our common bed."

He put a finger under her chin and lightly kissed her lips. "What if, Félise, when you know me more intimately, you do not like what you find?"

She reached for his other hand, which still hung at his side, and placed it on her stomach. "Some months hence you will be a father. Yet I know only a small part of you. I cannot fight your seclusion, your obligations to Celeste, or your past. But I must ask you to give me a chance to be fully your friend . . . fully your wife. I need a strong father for my son."

"A child?" he questioned.

She nodded. "The Chaney house, I suppose, since there has been no time since. Punish me for my wanton ways, messire, but I have dearly missed your presence. And if I have to fight for you, I will."

Royce's arms came around her waist and his eyes grew dark and warm. He swelled with love and pride. Somewhere in his mind there was a lurking fear, but he quickly decided he must face the truth. There were parts of her that *he* wished to know as well. "You are a seductress, woman." He smiled, kissing her fondly. "Don't you worry what I'll think of this brazen behavior?"

She smiled devilishly. "In time you will beg me to take a moment to warm your water or scrub your back, but there will be too many children clinging to my skirts for me to serve you."

He extracted himself from her and went to the chair, sitting to take off his boots. "You have purchased your own fate, love," he said, his expression serious. "But there is a child growing and in this you are right. We have lost the luxury of playing our marriage as a game and must henceforth rule this house together, as man and wife." His voice lowered to a hoarse whisper. "I warn you, if you find some part of me that does not appeal, it is too late for me to release you."

She laughed softly at his grim countenance. "Royce, you are so able a warrior and so timid a mate. Ah . . . in the dark of night you are the boldest man, but in the light of day you blush as any maid at the thought of my wifely ministrations. Come, husband."

She pulled off the fetching morning gown for greater ease in helping him wash. This left her wearing only the sheer night-dress through which her bountiful beauty could be easily viewed. His eyes instantly devoured every part of her, but his expression did not lighten. He rose, turned his back to her, and slowly pulled his linen shirt over his head.

Félise had the full view of the mark she had seen earlier. It was the size of a man's hand, covering perhaps a quarter of his back, and a dull pink in color. Still, it did not even occur to her that this was his reason for preferring darkness to light.

He turned back toward her and unfastened the cross garters of his hose, all the while eyeing her suspiciously. She only smiled, moving to the tub and taking up the sponge in her hand, waiting for him to get in. He watched her closely as he moved toward the tub and settled himself in the water. He leaned forward that she might scrub his back.

Félise lathered the sponge and, kneeling, got on with her task, humming lightly as she did so. He leaned his elbows on his raised knees and gave her several moments at her work. When she'd rinsed the soap from his back, he reclined in the tub and looked at her with troubled eyes.

"You do not mention it," he said. "Do you mean to be kind to this deformed man?"

"Deformed?" she questioned. " 'Tis a birthmark. I have seen them before."

"Like this?" he asked.

"Nay," she laughed. "One of the village children had such a mark on his backside. My mother said he was kissed by the rose of heaven and promised it brought good fortune. I saw your mark when you were washing in the stables."

"It does not distress you?" She shook her head. "Do you worry that your son might bear such a mark?"

She shrugged. " 'Twould be a helpful reminder that he is your son. Nay, how does it matter?"

"My mother called it the devil's mark. She said I was cursed."

Félise felt a deep sympathy for the boy who had been ignored and hated by his mother. And now she knew why he had resorted to darkness to love her. How senseless, she thought, that something so insignificant could have come between them for so long. Hadn't their problems been great enough without this, too, being a burden for him?

She leaned into the tub, her breasts pressing and swelling on the rim, and gently touched his lips with hers. The water splashed and wet her gown, rendering it useless as any cover of her nakedness.

"She made your boyhood difficult, my lord. But now you are a man and should be able to plainly see, no devil has marked you." She kissed him again, long and deeply. "Indeed, an angel must watch over you. This rose you wear on your back is part of the man I love."

He reached his arms under hers and embraced her, pulling her into his bath, extracting a squeal of surprise and then a giggle from her. "I was to *help* you bathe, not share your tub, messire," she laughed, squeezing the sponge over his head. But she did not try to escape him.

"You were worried about the mark?" she finally asked.

He shrugged, but smiled. The grim line to his mouth had faded. "I thought you would find it repulsive," he admitted.

She put her arms around his neck and looked closely into his eyes. "Your mother's treatment of you cursed you with a useless fear. I wish you to believe that as long as I live, our children will feel their mother's love, no matter the shape of their bodies or minds. Not all trees are straight and tall, their leaves the common green, but all are beautiful and made by God." She smiled warmly. "Now, pray, what other things must you tell me, that I am not sore surprised by some devilish habit I cannot abide?"

He shivered slightly under her and she knew that his bath was at an end and he would pursue other pleasures. Her cheeks grew warm in anticipation and she felt her skin tingle. It was destined to be a long while before they shared their meal. His lips were like hot coals on the delicate rise of her breasts. "There are one or two other things, wench," he said hoarsely. "But I doubt you will be surprised."

Chapter Seventeen

THEIR MARRIAGE BEING NIGH ON THREE MONTHS old, it would seem they could not be allowed all the seclusion of a new bride and groom, even though the entire household must be aware of their greater-than-two-month separation. Before Félise could rise, dry herself, and don her morning gown, the tapping at Royce's door had become insistent.

"A moment," Royce said, sighing in frustration as Félise wiggled from him to gather her gown. She shed the soaked nightgown and pulled on the morning gown in its place. Royce's eyes warmed at the mere sight of her, with the ends of her luxurious hair still dripping from their play. The tapping came again. Royce began to rise from his bath, then on second consideration stayed there. "Who disturbs me so early?" he demanded.

"Sir Hewe, milord," came the reply.

Félise gathered the drawstring under her breasts and gave it a sharp tug. Royce frowned as he looked at her. "I have not seen that wrapper before," he said.

She smiled brightly. "A morning gown, my lord. I made it from a gift of cloth and trim purchased by Vespera and Sir Hewe. Do you like it?"

"I think it meant for a husband's eyes alone," he observed.

"Indeed, it was sewn most hopefully for a husband's seduction," she said brazenly.

"Aye, and you've done well with a bolt of cloth, lady. It will warm Sir Hewe's blood a mite as well."

"I'll leave you to Hewe," she said, her cheeks flushing slightly.

"Nay, love. He brings his report on this estate. 'Tis your home. Stay. If he looks at you more than once, I will kill him."

The tapping came again. "My lord? May we speak?"

"I do not wish to embarrass the young knight," she said, troubled, tugging at her bodice as if to cover more of her swelling breasts.

Royce smiled roguishly. His bold gaze warmed her as he leisurely appraised her beauty. "Consider it a gift to the man. It far outshines his to you. I fear to rise lest I shock him further."

Again Hewe knocked. "Blast you, come in," Royce shouted. Before he even acknowledged the young knight's presence, he turned to Félise. "A goblet, my love, would ease my aches the more," he beckoned.

Félise welcomed the chance to turn from Hewe's first glimpse and pour her husband a drink from a decanter of wine.

Hewe fidgeted slightly before Royce. "I . . . ah . . . if there is a better time."

Royce gave the man a good-natured frown and said, "Truly there are better moments, but if you will excuse my bath, I will hear you."

Hewe pulled a stool from before the hearth and looked cautiously away as Félise handed Royce his wine and then retreated to a place discreetly behind Hewe. Royce chuckled. "Your gift adorns my wife well. My thanks. All my knights should serve my pleasure so well."

Hewe could not suppress a light coloring of his cheeks.

" 'Twas the lady Vespera's idea," he said somewhat shyly.

"Just the same, the two of you did well. Now, what have you to tell me?"

"I had thought . . . that is . . . the lady might prefer some other occupation while we talk."

"Nay, this is her home. Let her remain."

"But Royce, I . . ."

Royce sat up a bit in the tub. "Do you report some misconduct on the part of my wife?"

"Nay, Royce, but I . . . there are those things I did not share with my lady."

Royce sat back, better liking that answer than another Hewe might have given him. "Share them now, then." He noticed that Félise took a step closer to the conversation.

"Your pardon, lady . . . I did not wish to frighten you, though you were always well guarded." Hewe turned his head slightly in Félise's direction but was not bold enough to look at her while she was so scantily dressed. He turned back to Royce. "I know you are aware that Boltof is here, but there is more.

"Sir Maelwine first sighted Sir Boltof in Coventry, and he was there with Sir Wharton. We accepted that strange brotherhood as a truce, for they said they had buried their differences over the lady Félise and the dowry, since you were named. They told Maelwine that they had met in Coventry and were bound for other places. It was then that Boltof assured Maelwine he would come to Segeland to impress you with his loyal friendship, that all might happily abide this order of the king.

"But less than a fortnight past, they were together in Coventry again. While I went with Vespera to purchase the lady's gift, we saw them. I took a rear passage back to where our troop waited while Vespera walked by them, lingering close enough to hear their exchange. They plot some overthrow here, but we know nothing more."

Royce's scowl blackened, though not from surprise. In the course of this very interesting morning he could have guessed as much.

"It was in my mind to turn them away when they came, but the serving woman convinced me it is better to let Boltof in and try to foil his plan, rather then find him lurking about in some thickly wooded copse, in wait." He cleared his throat. "The woman, Vespera, is an accomplished spy. She watches and listens closely, though no one pays her any heed. Sometimes, by God, she is invisible."

Royce gave a sly smile and looked at his wife. Félise wore a confused frown and ventured still closer to the conversation. "Aye," he said to Hewe, "Vespera is adept in this."

"So they are within the hall, Vespera taking on any chore that can place her in hearing of their conversations, while I have guarded my lady all the day and night. From what was said between the two in Coventry, Wharton lingers close at hand with men. It is possible some attack is planned."

Félise came even closer. "That is why Vespera is so often absent. I have had to seek her out to help me in my rooms. Hewe, you should have told me."

"Pardon, lady. 'Twas Vespera who cautioned me to silence. She cannot weave her way close to them when everyone within this hall shows their suspicion in their eyes. What say you, Royce?"

"How does Boltof use Celeste in this?" he asked.

"In truth, I don't know. Even Boltof should know that Celeste is no match for Lady Félise. He cannot mean to tempt you with his sister."

"He suggested this to Lady Celeste," Royce said. "I think I have convinced her this would be foolish and she would only further shame herself." He reached out to Félise, who moved to take his hand, no longer concerned with her immodest gown. Even Hewe kept his eyes discreetly on her face as she took her place in a chair near enough to Royce's tub to bridge the space with her hand holding his. "Although it pains Lady Celeste, she knows I am committed to my wife and have no interest in her affections." His wife squeezed his hand in warm communication. "If Boltof pressures her," he went on, "she will refuse. But that is not our problem. He has another use for her. We need to know what it is."

Sir Hewe gave a snort. "Royce, I do not fear battle, nor am I shy of strength, but this method Vespera insists upon sits ill with me. To allow him into this hall and so close to you when there is every reason to suspect he is about trouble, this burdens me greatly. I would have it out with him."

"Nay," Royce said easily. "Vespera is right: he is better placed within our sight than in Coventry with Wharton, making plans away from our ears. But I will force him to hurry, for I will tell him that his presence strains our friendship. This very eve I will take him aside and strongly urge that he take his sister from here. Yet I do not intend to push him beyond his plan. Let us give him time to work his plots. I will give him one week."

He looked to Félise. "Though we sleep lightly for a week, it may ensure a lifetime of better nights ahead." And then to Hewe, he added, "We'll get the best of him now, and be free of him later."

"I hope you are right, Royce. I have never trusted the man."

Royce frowned at this comment. "You have been with me for a long time, Hewe. Since you were a squire. When did you begin to distrust Boltof?"

Hewe struggled with the answer, for he could scarcely name the time. "Boltof is not strong of arms, and few have been eager to pledge any loyalty to him. In truth, you are the only man of reputation that has given him an oath of friendship, for it is well known that Boltof only befriends those who might better his influence or purse." Hewe's cheeks took on a dark pink stain as he went on, clearly uncomfortable with this honesty. "When he speaks of his friendship with you, he is boasting much as a man does when he is counting his coin. Rather than building his own fortune, he has only deepened his alliance with you."

Royce thought heavily for a moment. "You remember Aylworth? My brother?" he asked Hewe.

The young knight nodded. "I was there," Hewe said quietly.

"Do you think Wharton killed him?" Royce asked with direct boldness.

"Nay, Royce. Wharton is stubborn and greedy, but I have seen him upon the field and in tourneys. He fights fairly. Your brother was killed while he slept. With his own knife."

"And do you suspect me?" he asked.

"I would not have made my oath to you when I was knighted had I thought you that kind of man."

Royce sat up in his tub, leaning his elbows on his raised knees. He looked closely at Hewe. "Who, besides me, would have profited from Aylworth's death?"

"Aylworth, rest him, was not known for kindness to his servants and squires . . ."

"No peasant or sallow youth possessed the strength or courage to do what was done. Another — "

"Wharton claimed the booty — "

"Nay," Royce replied. "The riches Wharton and Aylworth fought over were awarded to Henry, since the dispute could not be settled. And I feared to touch the meagerest sum, lest I stand accused of murder. I was courting Celeste, although there was no marriage contract between us. You know as well as any of my men how I would have avoided laying claims to Segeland and did not desire Aylworth's worldly goods. I ask you again; who would profit?"

Royce leaned back in the tub again, his eyes shrewdly watching Hewe as the man came to a slow understanding. But it was not Hewe who spoke.

"Boltof," Félise whispered. She leaned closer to her husband as if in sudden fear.

Royce's voice was a whisper. "All these years I would not have considered this. Boltof was the one to support me, to defend me. He claimed I was with him the whole of the night on which Aylworth was killed. He swore that between us we killed the better part of a keg, yet that was a lie. I thanked him for his blind loyalty and swore I did not slay my brother.

"Yet who was unaccounted for? 'Twas Boltof no one watched, for he had no reason we knew of to kill the man. Consider his patience: he struck years before a betrothal with Celeste was firm, content to wait upon my responsible nature. Sir Hewe, I think it highly likely that we house the worst kind of killer in Segeland Hall. A cowardly one."

The room was weighted with a heavy silence while they pondered the possibility. The only sound was a splash as Royce moved in his tub.

"What will you do, Royce?" Hewe finally asked.

"I will take my time with a plan, Hewe. It might be a simple matter to banish Boltof, fight him, or trick him into revealing his purpose here. But I would know more. I think this man killed my brother to better his own lot. Celeste is not clever, and she has listened to Boltof even more trustingly than I. He would have me a rich lord and married to his sister, and he has long envied my friendship with the king.

"Yea, I will give careful thought to my plan, for I think I will find sleep difficult until I know the full extent of his treachery. I have been fooled by him for long enough. Who knows we watch him?"

"Only Vespera and Sir Trumble," he replied.

"Good. Better that only a few know, for now. When you encounter Vespera, tell her to come to me by way of my lady's chamber, so that she draws no suspicions. I have need of her."

Hewe nodded and rose to leave them. Royce sat rubbing his chin for several minutes after the door had closed. When he finally looked up, he saw fear etched into bright turquoise eyes. "A linen, love," he quietly asked. "My water cools."

She fetched the linen and held it up for him as he stepped out of the tub. When he had rubbed the wetness off his skin and tucked the towel around his waist, he reached for her and embraced her. She leaned her head against his chest and sighed. "Royce, I am afraid," she whispered.

He lifted her chin with a finger and looked into her eyes. "I love you, Félise. You may trust that I will keep you safe."

"Can you imagine my worst fears? Boltof asked my father for my hand in marriage, and, had I been allowed a choice, I would have spoken for him over Wharton. And now . . ." She stopped herself and shuddered.

He ran his palm over her hair, gathering it in his large hand and squeezing the silky softness with his fingers. " 'Tis much worse than you realize. I went to King Henry to ask for you for Boltof. That was when the king insisted that I take you. I called Boltof friend and he asked this favor of me. I felt I owed him at least that much."

She looked up at him and frowned, but her eyes glowed. "You are a rogue, Royce! You would have sold me to Boltof, and you didn't even know me."

"I knew you well. I warned Boltof that you were the same

vixen to dally with my troop, and he should suspect your virtue."

"Royce! Did you really?"

"Aye. And happily I find the same brazen wench willing to share my bath." He raised a brow. "Shall we finish our 'bath,' my love?"

"Royce, I think I won't sleep until Boltof is gone from here."

"I won't let him hurt you. If we're clever this once, we'll never have to worry about him again."

She looked up at him and smiled. "I trust you," she murmured warmly. Her eyes glittered devilishly. "You have sent Hewe for Vespera. Your 'bath' will have to wait, for that gentle soul has never known a man and you would shock her."

"Never? Surely you don't think Vespera so innocent as that? This one who spies and plots with us?"

"She has lived all her life with nuns," Félise said with a shrug.

"Yet she shows a motherly protection for you," Royce attempted.

"'Tis the difference in our ages and her love for Lady Edrea," Félise reasoned.

"You have been so beset by the troubles of this hall, your surly husband, and threats from old lovers that you haven't had the time to ponder Vespera. Félise, don't you wonder at her protection and devotion?"

"I had not. I thought the queen . . ."

Her voice trailed off as she began to consider the woman. Félise could not name the reason for Vespera's continued presence or for her willingness to take such brazen risks to defend them from the devious plots of Celeste and Boltof. This handmaiden to the queen, who had retired to the nuns at the time of Eleanor's imprisonment yet was not in want of money, stayed curiously close at hand while Félise struggled to establsh her right to her husband and her new home.

She looked suspiciously at Royce. "Do you know more?"

He nodded and there was a smile tugging at the corners of his mouth.

"Will you tell me?"

He sighed and drew her near. "Let us have done with this unpleasant matter of Boltof. We need Vespera's help, and I would not betray her confidence now and send her fleeing away from Segeland. Later, my love. Later."

Vespera sighed and leaned heavily against the cool stone wall in the dark gallery. She appeared brave, yet within she trembled, for although she tried not to let it show, this creeping about to eavesdrop frightened her. Her worries were twofold: that she would be discovered and hurt, or discovered and therefore unable to help Félise and Royce set Boltof's plan awry.

Vespera approached fifty years. She was no longer as agile, as quick. She felt far too old for adventures such as this and had never in her youth had the courage to take so many chances. Were it not for Félise, were it not so critical, she would have melted into the darkest corner and quietly ignored all these conspiracies.

Royce had painstakingly recited his story for her, going over each detail from the day he met Boltof, through his affair with Celeste and the plot of her seduction, and all the circumstances surrounding Aylworth's death. All through this story his young wife had sat possessively at his side. She alternately widened her eyes in surprise, flushed in embarrassment, and pinched her mouth in white-lipped rage. She affectionately placed her hand on his thigh, stroked his arm, or smoothed his tunic over his broad shoulders.

Vespera forced herself to ignore these intimate ministrations and focus on Royce's words. Royce meant for her to know all so that her listening and watching could be more effective. And his information had certainly enlightened her. But the one thing that had struck her hardest when she left his chamber was the knowledge that Royce and Félise truly belonged to each other now. Vespera knew her time in Segeland would be over with Boltof's downfall.

In these short months she enjoyed the pride of watching her daughter succeed where many a weaker maid would have failed. Félise was all that Vespera prayed she would grow to be — strong, beautiful, bright, and wise. When so many ills could have befallen this child, the angels had cared for her and bestowed her with mother's quiet, gentle, and pleasing nature and her sire's strength and determination.

However sad the prospect of saying good-bye, Vespera had done what she had intended to do. The lands in Aquitaine were settled on her heir and she could have a comfortable retirement. Félise had a husband strong and true and would be safe in Royce's care. Vespera was too timid to claim maternity, which would require explaining that when Félise was a mere six months old she had given her into Eleanor's care and became a resident of Fontevrault. Félise had parents in the Scelfton household and might only resent having been abandoned by her natural mother. It was better to be a servant, one who would soon depart with fond farewells and genuine appreciation and affection on both sides of the relationship.

After Boltof, Vespera took a breath and slithered along the walls toward an antechamber through which she would find back stairs. The conversation she had overheard in Lady Celeste's room had finally revealed some of Boltof's plan. But poor Celeste! The woman had such foolhardy delusions. Vespera feared for her.

"He asks us to leave his house by Sunday next," Boltof had whispered. "So it is before Sunday that we must act."

Vespera had delivered linens and was busily pulling them tight on the bed. Knowing they would not speak further with her in the room, Vespera finally fluffed the cover onto the bed and, lowering her gaze, crept quietly out of the room, gently closing the door.

She had dashed around the corner to look up and down the long, dark hallway and then back to the door, pressing her ear against the stout portal.

"I won't do it," Celeste cried. "He has warned me to deny you if you would have me seduce him. He will not come to my chamber at night. He won't."

"He will if you tell him you will betray me," Boltof said. "Claim secrecy for that. Promise to tell him how I plan to steal his bride. Royce will fear this, for his own mother was a stolen bride and he knows well it can be done. Lure him to your chamber when the moon has set and no servants are about to overhear.

"I will excuse myself to Daventry to meet a friend and promise to return for you on Sunday. But I won't go. I will wait in the north glen, where I can't be seen, and I will return to find him in your rooms. 'Twill goad the Lady Félise to have her husband take his lover under her nose."

"Nay, he will deny it," she insisted. "And how will you enter the keep? Sir Trumble will admit no one after the sun has set."

"I might show Trumble my lame horse and plead a spoiled sojourn. He would let me in. And I will send a message to Wharton so that he is ready with men and horses should Royce attack me. You'll see, Celeste. It will work."

"How? How will Félise take you over Royce now? Even if he comes to my chambers, he won't come to my bed. How do you hope to make Félise believe that we are again lovers?"

"Leave that to me, Celeste. You have little reason to doubt me. Had the king not commanded Royce in this marriage, you would be his wife now."

"But it is done," she had retorted.

Boltof's voice had become threatening and deep. "I promised you a hearty groom with an inheritance, and I have not failed you yet. He had his family lands, you had him, and now Henry delays us, but we are not finished. If you can only get him into this room, I will do the rest. You will do as I say."

There was no sound from within the room and Vespera moved silently down the hall toward the back stairs where she could flee unnoticed. She didn't know exactly what Boltof planned, but perhaps the whole of it rested in the message he would send to Wharton. She hoped that would tell more of the story, for however naïve Celeste was, Vespera did not believe Boltof would use arms against Royce to get what he wanted.

She had little doubt that Boltof had killed Royce's brother. Boltof had promised himself a rich brother-in-law and saw his chance in the quarrel between Wharton and Aylworth. He had covered his involvement well in his defense of Royce. Sir Wharton, she surmised, would be very interested to know how Boltof would have sacrificed him. She moved quickly down the stairs, through the cookery, and back to the hall. There she gathered several logs for the hearth and ventured up the front stairs toward Félise's chamber as if delivering firewood. As she paused to knock on the chamber door, Boltof came down the gallery on his way to the stairs.

"My lord?" she questioned shyly, not looking directly at him. "I go to Coventry two days hence to purchase wool for my lady's looms. She bade me ask if there is some trinket the lady Celeste desires. Can I buy something for the lady's journey?"

Boltof thought quietly for a moment. "I will ask the lady," he said, turning to descend the stairs.

Vespera nodded and turned back toward Félise's door.

"You," Boltof beckoned, getting her attention again. "You are the lady's scribe?" he asked coyly.

"Nay, messire," she replied quietly. "I serve her chamber. I cannot read." Then she looked up at him and tried a shy smile. "But I can count sums and never yield the wrong coin in barter."

"Ah," he said. "If I give you coins for a lighter mantle for Lady Celeste's journey, do you think you can buy it without error?"

"Aye, messire. I have done so many times. I often purchase clothing for my lady."

" 'Tis well. And if I allow a small sum for your trouble, could you take a letter to a priest there?"

"Aye, sir. I have seen the church."

"I know the priest; he was a friend of my father's. I will give some thought to a letter for him, since I have made no effort to visit the man. Perhaps I will send him monies for the church. Find me before you leave."

"Aye, sir."

As she turned again to Félise's door, she hid her face that Boltof would not see her sly smile.

Royce lingered over large pieces of cloth on which he had inked a replica of his lands, his house and walls, and the road to

Coventry. He tried to judge where Boltof would hide in wait. In the morning Vespera would leave with three horsed escorts for Coventry, although Royce did not like the idea of her bearing a message to Trothmore meant for Wharton. He thought it too dangerous. But she had approached Boltof and gained his trust before he could stop her. And it seemed that Boltof was not at all suspicious of Vespera.

Vespera leaned over his shoulder. "There is something of Boltof's plan we do not know. He has ridden the perimeters of your land and must know a way to enter without Trumble's knowledge."

"The wall is well repaired," Royce argued.

"Ropes?" she asked.

"He would risk being seen. That cannot be his way."

Vespera sighed in frustration. "I cannot see how he has convinced Celeste that the trap of finding you in her chambers will make you appear her lover. A sleeping herb in your wine? Does he mean to hide within her rooms and strike you down, disrobe you, and put you in her bed?"

"He uses Celeste in some way, but not as a seductress, I assure you. I am as confused as you," Royce said.

"Perhaps he truly plans to abduct Félise, and have Wharton's help waiting outside the gate," Vespera attempted.

"Nay, though she will be well guarded just the same. There are two things we know of Boltof. He is very patient; he is content to plot and wait, using Trothmore to attack one part of my reputation while he and Wharton weaken my hold on Félise and her dowry. Even so serious a thing as excommunication from the church takes many months.

"And Boltof thinks himself clever, but he knows he is limited in warring skills and muscle. The man avoids any direct battle and would not steal away my wife and live with the threat that I would find him . . . and kill him."

He looked into Vespera's worried eyes. "Whatever he plans, madam, he will attempt in the dark of night when no one knows. That is why I am certain he lies to Celeste and hopes to enter Segeland unseen, leaving the same way." A twinkle crept into his eyes. "But I, too, know darkness well. I am almost as skilled in this as you."

"I cannot help you from Coventry, my lord," she said, worried.

"When you leave here to seek Wharton, you are done with Boltof. When you return, you will find him chained, dead, or gone."

"Have a care, Royce," she whispered.

"If there is no opportunity to read his letter to Coventry before you leave Segeland . . ."

"I know what to do, my lord," she replied confidently.

"And I won't rest until I determine how he plans to enter the hall unseen, for I too am certain of his treachery."

A knock at the door interrupted them and Vespera quietly left Royce's room to enter Félise's chamber. She would not allow any intruder to see her in the lord's chamber.

Royce carefully folded the pieces of cloth and placed them in his coffer before allowing anyone to enter.

Sir Hewe opened the door. "Another visitor, Royce. It is the old lord, Orrick. He approaches the gate, alone."

"Orrick? Why the devil . . ."

He could not believe that Lord Orrick would conspire with Boltof. That would come as too much of a shock. From the moment his suspicions had been raised, he had decided that Aswin knew nothing of his stepson's plotting. He couldn't imagine what this visit meant and took himself quickly down the road toward the gate, determined to intercept him.

Lord Orrick was easy to identify, for he rode poorly and without any assist. He held the reins with his one good hand, the other, gnarled, against his side. Both feet were in the stirrups, but Royce knew that one leg was useless. It was madness for him to ride any distance alone, without servants or guards. He was helpless should the horse need a stronger command and completely vulnerable if any brigands attacked him. Royce met him before he was far into the town and approached him, frowning his suspicion and his displeasure.

"Lord Orrick," he said. "Will you dismount?"

The old lord, usually pleasant and even jovial in spite of his handicaps, was glowering blackly. "They are here, are they not?" he growled.

"My lord?"

"Celeste and her brother. They are not at home, nor in London, nor have they left word about their travels." His eyes were narrowed to slits, his gray hair tousled from days of difficult riding, his clothes torn and dirty. He turned from Royce and spit into the dust. "Those two are bent on making trouble."

Royce let his features relax somewhat. "My lord," he breathed, reaching up to his friend to help him dismount. "You should not have come. I have the trouble in hand and watch Boltof carefully." He braced Aswin against his body and carefully lowered him to the ground.

Aswin held his weight on his good side and searched his saddle for the staff he had tucked under the leather straps. Once found, he leaned on that and cursed the horse. "Damned beast has not a breath of compassion for a cripple. I'll turn him into soup!" He looked back at Royce. "I warned them to let the matter be, but I knew as I looked at the boy's sullen mouth that he would not. And though I'd have had it otherwise, since her mother died, Celeste will hear only Boltof. And he seldom wishes her well."

"I thought you supported Boltof."

"I have tried to be a good elder for the boy, but he will take no example from me. He was against Dulcine's marriage to me because it delayed his inheritance from his true father. And since then he has only spoken kindly to me when in the presence of others or if there is something he needs. He is in a hurry for his way."

Royce studied the old lord for a moment. "You did not encourage them to come here?"

"Blood of Christ, never! I was sorry for Celeste, but years ago I knew she was not the woman for you. When you made free with her affections for so long, I did the father's part as I must and pushed you toward marriage. Aye, Royce, I knew you were too involved with my stepdaughter. But truth, it was more that I wished to find a son in you than a husband for Celeste." He spat again, clearing the dust from his throat and the disgust from his words. "I never could reason your attraction to her. Félise is the daughter of one of my closest friends. I would not rise against Harlan for any reason. I only wish the lass well."

"But you endorsed Boltof to Lord Harlan," Royce said.

Aswin shook his head almost sadly. "I had never had such high hopes as those I suddenly enjoyed when I dined with Harlan's family. Do you see this old man's dreams? Those two whelps could bring two fine children into my home. I could have you through Celeste, and the Lady Félise might have turned the worst of Boltof into a proper knight. I had no right, Royce, but still I wished to do honor to Dulcine by helping her children." He shrugged. "My disappointment at losing you equaled Celeste's, I vow. But I would not allow those two to plot against Henry's order. The king is wiser than I allowed."

Royce chuckled. He should have known it was foolish to distrust this man even for a moment. He looked over his shoulder and saw that they were still far from the hall. They had paused beside Ulna's modest house. "Come, Aswin. Let us hide you quickly. The widow Ulna will give you a proper meal."

"Hide me? Take me to yon hall and I'll rid the place of serpents!"

"We have much to discuss before you next meet your stepchildren. It appears that I was alone in trusting them."

"By damn, 'tis a pity. Dulcine was a good and kind woman. But she failed with those two. I hope I am not too late."

"I hope no one has seen you, for your arrival could dampen Boltof's courage. He has a mighty plan afoot here. There is only one way I can catch him: I must let him try to see it through."

"How can I help you?" the old lord asked.

"First, you must get out of sight," he said, smiling. "And next, you must give me a great deal of time to explain."

Chapter Eighteen

VESPERA ROSE EARLY ON THE DAY OF HER TRIP TO Coventry to make preparations. After a light morning meal, she went to Celeste's chamber and knocked on the door. She was not surprised to find Boltof already within, although she had wondered if Celeste would be the one to give her the message to carry. He greeted Vespera warmly, putting his most courtly manners on display for her.

"It is good of you to offer these services, madam." He smiled. "My sister is most appreciative."

Vespera looked at Celeste, who sat meekly on a stool near the bed. It was obvious by her drawn features that she had become exhausted and frightened. She wondered how badly Boltof threatened and abused his sister to force her to follow his instructions.

"Does my lady have a preference for the color of cloak?" she asked.

"Nay," Celeste replied solemnly, barely raising her eyes. "Anything will do."

Vespera looked at Celeste with pity. Her appearance had changed remarkably from what it had been at Windsor, when she had stood erect and proud. Though plain, she had possessed an inner glow when she was full on the devotion of Royce. Now, rejected, she seemed to be dying inside. She had only Boltof now.

"Come, Celeste," Boltof insisted happily. "A deep green, to

darken your eyes and set off the gold of your hair? A royal purple? Blue?"

"It doesn't matter."

"Well, you see the lady's skin is fair and her eyes are blue. Do you think you can find a mantle that will both enhance her beauty and liven her spirits?"

"I will try, messire. How much would you like me to spend?"

He shook a bag of silver and placed it in her hands. Vespera could tell by the weight that it was a generous sum. She let her eyes widen accordingly so these two would think they had bought themselves a good servant. "The sum is less important than the piece. It must be rich and worthy of my sister's beauty. You may keep what is left for yourself. And if it would not be too much trouble for you, I have carefully written this short letter to my father's friend, the Coventry priest." He pressed a small scroll into her hand.

"The priest," she repeated.

"Monseigneur Trothmore," he advised. "And madam, this priest is not well liked in this burg. I would appreciate your silence on the matter of family friendship. Our welcome here is sorely strained as it is, and I would rend it no further by association with a man who has been cast from this town. Oh, yea, I have heard the fair Félise banished him. It was a contest I would like to have seen," he chuckled. "But, I only communicate with the priest out of honor to my father, God rest him."

"Your father is dead?" Vespera asked, a note of surprise in her voice.

"Aye, many years past. My stepfather lives and manages his lands now. I suppose they will be mine one day."

Vespera looked down, for she knew the shock would have registered on her face. Of course Boltof was too much older than Félise to be a son of Aswin's born after she had known him, but at the time the relationship was first mentioned to her, she had panicked at the thought. It had occurred to her when she first saw Boltof that there was some resemblance, but she wondered now if she had imagined that. Or perhaps Aswin sired the boy before she met him nearly twenty years ago.

All that had been clear to her at the time was that Aswin had a son, Boltof. And this son wished to marry her daughter. She had fled to Henry and thrown herself on his mercy. Henry's approval of Boltof would see brother and sister wed. It was the first time in twenty years she had named Félise's father.

And she had misunderstood it all.

"Madam?" Boltof questioned.

She looked down at the small, rolled parchment. It trembled in her hand. "Messire?"

"The missive. You will not mention it?"

"I will say nothing. But this priest, you do not know him?"

Boltof shrugged and smiled. "As I have said, I feel an obligation to my father to make contact with the man, since they were friends. I may visit him upon leaving here. But since I was a small child I have not seen him."

"I will take your letter to Monseigneur Trothmore and buy a cloak for Lady Celeste," she said, tucking the bag of coins and the note into her deep pockets. "Is there anything else you would have me buy?"

"Nay, that is all. You return on Sunday?" Vespera nodded. "Good, we will leave as soon as you deliver the cloak."

"Thank you, my lord. You are generous and kind."

"I will escort you to your mount," Boltof offered.

"There is no need, messire," she attempted.

"Ah, I insist, madam," he said, taking her arm.

Vespera had no alternative but to let him walk with her to where her horse and three escorts waited. An empty wagon would accompany them to give the impression that goods were being brought back to Segeland, although their purpose in going had nothing to do with making purchases, other than Celeste's cloak. But with Boltof's escort, Vespera lost the chance to read the message before leaving the keep.

Félise waited by the door below. She nodded briefly to Boltof, trying to remain expressionless. She concentrated on Vespera. "Do you remember every item?" she asked.

"Aye, my lady. Would you have me repeat them again?"

"Nay," Félise said. "Though 'twould be a simpler matter if I could give you a list to read to the merchants there." She noted Boltof's sly smile out of the corner of her eye. "You have never made a mistake in the past, and I will not worry now. I will walk with you to the gate."

"I will take her to the gate," Boltof said.

"You needn't bother, Sir Boltof, I — "

"But I consider it my obligation, since I have asked the good woman to make a purchase for my sister. A cloak of lighter weight to make the journey home more comfortable for her will liven her spirits. By your leave." He gave a short nod and took Vespera's arm again.

"Madam," Félise said, "have a care to be prompt with my goods. I have need of them by Sunday. Don't dally."

"Nay, madam."

"And do not wander from Royce's men. Take them with you on your errands."

"Aye, madam."

Vespera felt an urgency in Félise's manner, although the younger woman tried to remain poised. Before Boltof could become suspicious, Vespera quickly left the hall with him, for it was better to get on the road to Coventry than to delay. She knew well Félise's distress. They had all hoped to know the contents of Boltof's message forthwith. Now Royce would have to ride out on some excuse and try to intercept the travelers to know Boltof's plan.

Boltof walked with Vespera well away from the hall, leading her palfrey while the three escorts, two horsed and one managing the empty wagon, trailed along behind. Vespera paused as they entered the village and the gate was in sight. She turned to Boltof. "Will you give me aid in mounting, sir?" she asked.

He stopped, looked toward the gate, which Trumble was having pushed open, and must have reasoned he could watch her departure from where he stood. He placed his hands on her waist and gave her a lift into the saddle. "You needn't take guards on all your errands," he said softly.

"I know the Coventry streets quite well, monseigneur," she replied. "I need no escort."

He nodded, the look in his eyes conveying his belief that he had succeeded in getting his message to Wharton through Trothmore. Vespera gave her horse a gentle heel and proceeded ahead of the others toward the gate. She did not turn to see if Boltof watched, for she felt his eyes on her back. He would assure himself that his letter was safely out of Segeland.

As they moved down the village road, Vespera let her eyes travel to either side and gave a slight nod to those villagers she knew. The trains coming and going to Coventry had become a common enough sight to these people, for Félise's custom of making purchases for the hall and town was an accepted practice now. As she passed Ulna's cottage she looked there out of habit, for the widow usually came to the door when she heard the sound of creaking wagon wheels.

The top half of Ulna's door was open, and as Vespera looked, she saw a man standing in the frame. The darkness within the cottage made his features difficult to see clearly, but she knew the face far too well to be confused. Although he had accompanied Boltof and Celeste to Windsor, she had not seen him. But there was no mistaking him, it was Aswin Orrick.

Their eyes met over the brief space for but an instant. She looked away quickly before he had a chance to recognize her, although with her covered crown and high-collared mantle he would most likely not know her.

Her heart began to pound within her breast. She had not spoken to Royce that morning, but perhaps Aswin's presence in the village was the cause of Félise's agitation. They surely knew he was arrived; indeed, who but Royce or Félise would have placed him in Ulna's house? The widow was a trusted friend and it was unlikely she would hide a conspirator. Had Aswin come to aid his stepson in some plot, he would be in the hall, for he was nobly bred and in better graces with the couple than was Boltof. Royce must have hidden Aswin and enlisted his aid. That was all Vespera could imagine.

Before she was well out of the gate, she knew that her plans had been greatly changed. She would not return from Coventry, but leave from there to buy passage to Fontevrault. Some excuse could be delivered to Félise, and her meager possessions could be sent to her at a future time. She would not face Aswin. The pain had been too great, his betrayal of their love too deep. She would not allow that hurt to reach her ever again.

A thick tear gathered on her lashes and her breath caught. Perhaps it was better that there were no farewells. She would meet Wharton and convince him that he was betrayed, Boltof would be captured before he could do injury — her time with the young couple was done. She had been foolish to think it could go on much longer. She had given up Félise years before, knowing she could lay no further claim to the lass.

She gave her horse another spurring heel to hurry the pace. Once out of sight of the wall she would read Boltof's letter. Royce would surely reach them before midday to gather the information and, she hoped, reassure her that Aswin's presence in the town was to aid them. These chores, once accomplished, would be her last for Félise.

But although she knew she'd made the best decision for all concerned, her tears marked her cheeks just the same.

Royce had let the sun rise high above the keep before he set Hewe to the task of watching over Félise and rode out of the gate with a few men-at-arms, as was the landholder's rote. Vespera and her group had been gone for several hours, but he knew they would wait. Boltof was enjoying his favorite pastime of lounging in the main hall before the hearth and ordering the servants to fetch him ale or food.

The first time Royce left Segeland to survey his lands, Boltof had invited himself along.

"I ride the perimeters of the farmlands and hunting areas every day to be assured there are no trespassers on my property," Royce had rather brusquely replied. "I do not invite guests to ride with my men and me. Especially guests whose presence I do not understand."

Boltof had bristled at the rude remark. "I am at a loss as to why you are so determined to destroy our long friendship, Royce. I came here to pledge anew, in spite of the insult, and you have ignored us and asked us to leave."

"Perhaps you will wait upon an invitation in the future, Boltof," Royce had replied. And he went on to say, "It is on Sunday that you will leave, is it not? My hospitality will extend itself no further, that is certain."

"Someday, Royce, you may regret your lack of generosity."

"Perhaps," Royce had replied. "Then again, perhaps not."

From that time forward, Boltof must surely have been sorry for his presumptuous behavior, for he was allowed only the hall, the stables, and the hunting birds for his pleasures. They dined together in the hall, as all members of the household did. The conversations were strained and heavy. Celeste in the main stared at her plate, although Félise occasionally turned kind words her way. Boltof tried to turn the talk to old war stories, but in finding Royce sulky and uninterested, he let the subjects die. Boltof and Celeste were assured, upon Royce's arrival, that they were unwelcome and should not have come.

That Royce endured their presence beyond the first day after his return had only to do with Boltof's plan. Had Hewe not seen the two knights in Coventry and had Vespera not overheard the plotting, Royce would have provided an entourage to take the brother and sister away immediately. He often shook his head in wonder that Boltof assumed it was his cleverness that had gained him access and continued lodging in Segeland. He seemed not even suspicious that though Royce voiced his displeasure with their visit, he allowed them to stay another week.

When he returned from his afternoon ride, he found Félise seated in the main room, busily sewing an article of clothing. Hewe was faithfully near, rubbing a high shine onto his shield. And Boltof was there, swigging ale from a generous tankard and enjoying the company and the warmth of the hall.

"Do you find your lands in good order, Royce?" Boltof asked, unusually high in spirits.

"All is well," he replied.

Hewe's eyes were on him, and he considered calling a meeting, but thought better of it. He would make no excuse to speak alone with his wife and this young knight. Instead he pulled off his gauntlets and hauberk and made himself comfortable in the room. He asked for drink and aid in removing his boots, and proceeded to make small talk with Hewe about the hunting and planting that must proceed and what masons must be fetched from neighboring towns to begin the building of the church.

Boltof tossed in comments here and there, many of which were meant to be unkind. "It has been a long time since there was a church here, has it not?" he asked.

"Too long," Félise replied coolly. "That has all changed since Royce has returned to Segeland."

And later, Boltof interrupted their conversation with another comment. "I didn't know the villagers here had so many tools for their farming. On one of my brief visits with you, your people were hard put to farm, yet now it seems they could not want for more in the way of plows, hoes, shovels, and scythes."

"The generosity of Twyford," Royce snorted. "My wife's family saw fit to extend their purse to our needs."

"You seem to lack nothing now."

Royce looked at him closely. "Nay. We are well fixed."

"You have extended the farm plots," Boltof said. "You'll have need of more farmers, as well as masons and craftsmen."

Royce wondered at Boltof's attempts at pleasantry. "Already there are more villagers than upon our arrival. They are busy roofing their huts and enlarging their farm plots. Their number grows equal to our new prosperity."

Boltof looked into his cup. "You have been more fortunate than I realized." All eyes were on him, but Boltof looked at no one. "I have known you for a decade and a half, and your lot has changed greatly since our meeting. I remember when you battled the bad reputation of the Leighton name, for few trusted you. The Leightons paid no homage to church or king, and the place was poor. There were oft hostages here, and battles with neighboring barons. The people for miles around would bolt their doors when your shield was seen as we passed, for the Leighton family was to be distrusted and feared.

"I remember when you cared little about heirs and said, quite frankly, that you would be pleased enough to see my children inherit Segeland." Royce's head snapped in his direction. Had he been so bold as to confide even *that*? Looking back, he thought he might easily have done so, knowing that Boltof must have suspected he had lain with Celeste. Little had Royce known back then that Celeste must have proudly confirmed the fact. So, Boltof had had his eye on Segeland for some time. Perhaps the marriage to Celeste alone would not have been enough. Perhaps Boltof had long ago planned further treachery.

"Yet now," Boltof droned on, "the keep and town are rich, you have a beautiful wife to dote upon and the trust of the king and the mighty Scelfton family and lands in Aquitaine." He let his eyes rise to meet Royce's. "I know you must value the change. You must work hard to keep your reputation sound."

Royce gave him a leveling stare. "I never fought my family's reputation in the past and I do not struggle with mine now. Let people believe what they will. We will live on the same."

Boltof shrugged and smiled. "Perhaps you have finally buried the past, Royce, and it will not rise up against you again. I am happy for you." He tilted his cup and drained the contents.

Royce felt Félise's eyes on him and looked at her. The question was shining bright and torturous. She was eager to know if Boltof's message to Coventry further incriminated him.

Royce gave her a slight but firm nod. She let her eyes gently close and she gripped the shirt in her lap. The moments dragged like hours. They all waited, trying to keep suspicion from their eyes and all praying that their theories were right and Boltof would not surprise them with some move they did not anticipate. It would prove a very long two days.

Boltof, it seemed, was the only one at ease. When Celeste joined them for the evening meal, he was solicitous of her comfort, fawning over her in a most gallant, brotherly fashion. He helped her find a chair, propped up her feet, and called for a goblet of wine to soothe her. He apologized quietly for her sullenness and said she suffered from melancholia and must be dealt with gently. A side of pork sizzled over the hearth and Royce distractedly gave the meat a poke. Boltof moved to stand beside him. "You are right, Royce. I was foolish to bring my sister here and so strain our friendship. It has been difficult for all of us. I hope one day you will find it possible to forgive me." He shrugged his bulky shoulders. "I had thought myself well schooled in the finer manners of the nobly born, but I can see now that I presumed too much of you. I am sorry."

Royce looked at him closely. His words as well as his eyes held sincerity. He appeared at least as genuine as he had on that dim morning long ago when he had offered to support a story that he had been with Royce all through the night on which Aylworth was killed.

"Time may indeed lessen the strain, Boltof. But you must take Celeste home. It is clear she suffers here. You should have known better."

Boltof showed a childlike look of shame and fairly hung his head. He picked up a nearby poker and stirred the logs in the hearth. Royce felt the urge to grab him and shake him, for this kind of lying and plotting made his insides churn. This waiting while the snake slithered toward its victim gnawed at him. He'd rather meet an opponent in fair battle.

"I'll secure the stables before the sun sets," Royce said, no longer able to endure the hall. "See to your sister, should she need anything."

He turned from Boltof and went out into the late afternoon air, closing the huge doors behind him. He stood there, viewing his town before him, and made no move toward the stables. A long while passed as he stood watching the sun lower, deeply considering his situation. He thought he knew Boltof's strengths and weaknesses, but he couldn't imagine how he would tie the plot together.

He went over small details in his mind again and again: He will leave on a quick journey to a neighboring town on the pretence of meeting a friend, but he does not call for Wharton to meet him until early Sunday. How does he use Wharton? With arms or as a witness? He convinces Celeste that they can accuse me of adultery, but that fair dame cannot think such a ploy would prompt me to abandon Félise and marry her. Surely she is not so stupid. Yet she does his will. There is more to their plotting; there must be.

Royce shook his head for the hundredth time. He would have to lay in wait. There was no other way.

The door slowly opened and Félise came out onto the step, her shawl pulled tightly around her. He smiled and raised an arm to encircle her shoulders.

"I thought you were going to the stable," she said.

"I could bear no more of Boltof's good humor," he replied.

"His message?" she asked.

"He calls for Wharton to meet him at Hunter's Cross, well out of sight of the wall, on Sunday morning. I suppose he will extract an oath from Wharton that they were together in Coventry, and Boltof expects to be above suspicion." He sighed heavily. "To what purpose, I have no idea."

"Vespera is well on her way?"

"Aye, though I fear the good lady has lost ten years off her life. As she passed through the town, she sighted Aswin and was near sick with the fear that the old lord had arrived to help Boltof. I allayed her fears. When Boltof leaves, I will bring Aswin to the hall." He chuckled. "Surely Celeste will welcome her stepfather's protection."

"Royce," Félise gently asserted, "I know who Vespera is."

He looked down at her and saw the glistening of tears in her eyes.

"Lady Véronique de Raissa . . ." he began.

"Queen Eleanor's poetess," Félise added. "Oh, the many small mysteries finally formed one large one. You were the one to attest to the fact that the de Raissa lands were anything but modest and had been well managed for many years, and Vespera herself gave me clues, though I thought she spoke mostly from her close association with Eleanor."

Royce took her hand. "I urged her to tell you the truth, and by God she was fearful that you would not understand. All of her interference, her protective nature — it was all to do right by you. All these years she has been devoted to you. You must be honored to know this."

Félise gave a short, sentimental laugh. "There were times in the past few months when her eyes became so much like Lady Edrea's, her manner scolding like any mother's, and I did not understand. And other times when she sacrificed, although there was no need. She suffered no lack of money though she was never paid by me for her services, yet I did not see anything strange in this." She looked up at him, shaking her head, her chin trembling. "I am so spoiled, Royce, that I didn't even wonder at this added attention from a stranger. I am accustomed to having everything I desire."

"You deserve your every desire," he murmured.

"I wanted to tell her I knew before she left this morning, but Botolf would not allow us a word. I wanted to thank her and assure her I am pleased."

He gently caressed her cheek with his knuckles. "She was afraid to tell you," he whispered. "She feared you would be angry that she let you be taken from her so many years ago, yet I am certain the choice was not hers at the time. And you were well enough cared for."

"But she came back." Félise's voice was a mere trembling whisper. The emotional impact of the gesture had clearly shaken her.

"Aye, she came back, to see you wed to her satisfaction, to see that you inherited family lands that are rich and beautiful beyond your wildest dreams, and to assure herself that you were well and happy. All this for you, my love, for she asks nothing for herself. There is a great deal more to a parent's devotion than just spending years in common company."

"Do you know who my father is?"

"Nay. The lady will not name him, though she promised we need not fear for our children. She said he was a noble sire and the name would make me proud. Perhaps you can convince her of your right to know."

A tear traveled down Félise's cheek. Royce gently wiped it away and turned with her to look at the town.

"When she returns, you will tell her all you have come to know and ask her to stay," he said.

"May she? Oh, thank you, Royce."

"I think it only decent that you have her near through the birth of our son."

Félise smiled through her tears. "Aye, if we can just see the Sunday morn and be finished with Boltof."

Royce's smile turned instantly to a frown. "If I only knew *how* . . ."

They looked together toward the setting sun, outlining the rooftops of many huts. The gates to the town began to creak open. The evening was approaching and the spring night would be cold. The farmers with their carts, mules, oxen, and tools began to filter into the village from the fields outside the walls. Women opened village doors to welcome them and the hearth fires were stoked for the evening meal. The smoke drifted upward to make a pattern against the pinkened sky.

They stood silently watching the village settle for the night, neither quite ready to venture back into the hall to join Boltof and Celeste. Men below them took harnesses from their animals, left carts bearing tools and bags of seed against their huts, moved silently between gate, stable, houses, sheds, and outbuildings. One by one the doors along the main road began to close.

Félise sighed and gathered her shawl around her. "It's getting cold," she said. "Will you come inside now?"

"A moment," he said, staring toward the gate that was now closing to protect them against the darkness. She began to pull away from him to go inside. "Stay," he said, still watching the village.

She leaned against him until the gate was finally closed. The village lay quiet beneath them, the only signs of life being the dim lights from within the huts, a torch on each side of the gate showing Trumble's silhouette as he stood watch, and the smoke from the hearths. The tilling of soil, clearing of more trees to enlarge the farm plots, and some planting had begun with the first sign of spring. Until Félise had procured the additional seed and supplies and stock for the village, these simple folk had taken only their picks and hoes to the outer side of the wall to work the ground. But now there was a great deal to move from the inner bailey to the fields every morning and return every night.

"My God," he whispered, remembering Boltof's conversation in the hall.

"What is it?"

He pointed a hand toward a dark village road. "A man could

enter with a group of tired farmers and barely be noticed. There are a dozen ways: hiding on a cart brought into the village for the night, carrying a scythe and walking beside a mule in peasant garb, hefting a plow, or even leading an ox."

"But would they not recognize a stranger among them?" she whispered.

"Did you see them converse? Did they empty their carts? They enter the town separately to store their animals and carts, and move silently in and out of the stables and houses. They leave in much the same way at dawn, trying to get the best of the light. And again at midday the gate opens, when the women go to the fields to bring a meal to the men and boys. Our guard is stout and attentive, and no resident here hides his tools or seed, but leaves his cart full for morning." He took a breath. "A horse tethered in the wood, a change of clothing, and Trumble not even pausing to count the heads of unarmed, poor farmers."

"How very clever," she said.

"Now only one question remains," he said. "We know he has a way to enter and leave unnoticed, but to what end? Surely not to find me in his sister's bed. Forsooth, why am I needed in her room at all?"

Félise turned in his arms and looked up at him. "Royce, perhaps it is not very important where you are, but where you are *not*."

Royce thought for a moment and suddenly it all came to him. He thought perhaps he knew what Boltof intended. He smiled. "If he thinks to find you alone in your chamber, unprotected, he will be very surprised."

"What will we do?" she asked, the edge of fear in her voice.

"If he doesn't gather some good sense and abandon his plan, we have him, love. Aye, we have him now."

Chapter Nineteen

By the time Coventry was in sight, the sun was setting. The troop was delayed in wait for Royce, and the day had been a long one. Vespera was exhausted from the tension of the preceding days and the apprehension about her meeting with Wharton. That clever knight would be much distressed to see her, when it must have been planned that any messages delivered to him would come through Trothmore.

Although she was tired and hungry, Vespera would not eat and did not find sleep. She rose, finally, and ventured to the church in the dark. Although the priest there was evil, it was a church she needed first. She arrived before lauds, the prayer time designed to end at dawn. She had fasted for her confession, but could not trust Trothmore for this spiritual function. This confession was for God, and her prayers for guidance were so fervent she was weak.

She wondered how it was decided that her entire life would be spent for this, for that was how it seemed. Surely no other purpose for her had ever shown itself. She had grown up as a quiet and shy little girl to be used for the pleasure of the queen and her troubadours. As a woman, she had been lonely and had known only the briefest touch of love, of a man. As a mother, there had been just those few months of nurturing Félise. And now, if her part with Wharton was successful and she could convince him, it would bring to an end many years of treachery from Boltof. Was it the work of a tribunal of angels? A council of saints? Was it a divine plan, or simply the fate of one woman lacking the courage to make more of her life?

But, God willing, Royce and Félise would now be safe and well.

She would go to the sisters and now beg to become one of them. She saw her life as over, for her body was declining and good for little beyond prayer and humble chores at Fontevrault. She could no longer live among the nuns and pay a pittance for her board, for her demesne and its revenues no longer belonged to her. To live with the sisters, she would take the vows and work for them. And never leave Fontevrault again.

"Father, be merciful as you deal with Aswin, for though he used me poorly, his seed brought wondrous life and the child has grown strong and beautiful. Surely some magnificent plan kept us apart that she might grow within the Scelfton house, and for that my happiness is forfeit. Never could I have done so well by her as Edrea and Harlan have. And her gifts to You are great indeed, for she has love and compassion and can do more for those who have little than I ever could. Guard them all when I cannot, I pray."

Lauds passed as dawn broke the dark, and Vespera ventured out of the church. She walked away from it in the direction she had last seen Wharton take in leaving Boltof. She knocked on a merchant's door inquiring after him, but the sleepy man knew nothing. Another door, another disappointment. A score of doors opened to her early-morning inquiry before someone knew the man and told her where to find him. She didn't care that people looked at her strangely, or angrily. She felt one purpose only and moved with her typical quiet determination.

She rapped on the door where Wharton stayed and asked for him. The man who had given him rooms was reluctant to wake him at the early hour.

"Tell him, sir, that a message from Segeland has arrived. He will rise."

"Who will I say brings the message?" the man asked.

"A messenger," she said and smiled, refusing to give further answer.

The man opened the door wider that she might come within and wait, but she shook her head, preferring to wait in the street.

It was only a few moments before Wharton, obviously roused before his hour, came into the street. His hair was tousled, his clothes hastily donned, and sleep still clung to his lashes. His mouth was thick, his eyes were mere slits. She frowned, hoping he was alert enough to hear her.

"You have something for me?" he asked.

She nodded and stretched her hand out with the note. He took it from her, thanked her, and made for the house again. "Nay, Sir Wharton. I am to wait while you read it."

"Eh? Very well."

He leaned against the doorframe and read the few words. He looked at her in confusion. "There is no reply necessary for this."

"Nay, Sir Wharton. But if you fail to hear me, you will suffer. Boltof betrays you."

He sucked in his breath and glared at her suspiciously. "What say you?"

"He paid me to bring the message," she said, drawing out the bag of coin and giving it a shake to show its value. "But he tells you very little. He plans some crime in which you may be his accomplice or perhaps the one accused. Royce bade me seek you out and explain Boltof. It will be much as the night that Sir Aylworth died."

"What do you babble, wench? How do you know Aylworth?"

She shrugged. "I did not know Aylworth. But I have lately come to learn that Boltof killed him. And 'twas his plan to let you and Royce stand blamed for the crime."

"Does Boltof conspire with Royce?"

"Nay, Royce sent me to find you. Boltof does not know he is found out and meant this message to be delivered to you through Trothmore. His purpose in killing Aylworth was to secure a good purse on Royce and then help Celeste into marriage with him."

"How do you know this?" he demanded hotly.

"I heard him tell his sister. I have heard many things, and all show Boltof to be most intent on betraying all to get a fortune.

He will let you fall, Wharton. You must trust him no further."

"Royce sent you to trick me," he accused.

"Venture to this place . . . Hunter's Cross. Boltof will not be there. He will be caught and chained. If you abandon him now, you will not be injured. But if you conspire with him further, you may be killed. Remember, Sir Wharton, Boltof was the one to place you and Royce against each other. He would do so again, and emerge the winner — of the land in Aquitaine, the woman, Segeland."

Wharton's eyes were free of the film of sleep now. He stared at her for a moment and then leaned more heavily against the doorframe.

Vespera did not waste time waiting but, while she had him snared, gave him more. "Boltof sets you against the Twyford men as well as Royce, but he will not fight. Boltof lies to you, for the Scelfton family supports Royce with mighty arms that even now will journey to the ends of hell to lay low any man who threatens their daughter. And Lady Félise will take no other man. Even Boltof's father hides now in Segeland's village in support of Royce."

"Why do you tell me this?" he asked.

"There is time for you to save yourself, if you are wise. Even as we speak, Boltof rides away from Segeland on the excuse of meeting a friend in a neighboring town, but he will hide himself in the wood. It is his plan to creep into Segeland under cover of night. This I heard him confide to his sister. His purpose is yet unknown, but I beg you to understand, he has killed a sleeping man before. He calls you to meet him and ride on Segeland with him. Will he take you to the keep, seek out the guard, and ask them if some evil has been done? Will he claim to have found you sneaking out of the town in early dawn? Or is it Royce he wishes to see accused of some murder, with you as the witness? Or . . ." she began, pausing very convincingly, "does he plan to kill Royce and name you the murderer? In truth, I can't name his plan. But you need not be a part of it, for Boltof has been discovered and Royce lies in wait to catch him."

She paused and looked at Wharton closely. He seemed to struggle with this information.

"Why should I trust you over Boltof?"

She laughed lightly. "Sir Wharton, I see no reason you would ever trust Boltof, but if indeed you do, venture to Segeland on Sunday, as he requests, and see if he will lead you astray."

"Aylworth," he growled, the memory still hurting deeply. "The knave wished to divide our booty to his advantage. But when have knights not quarreled over their shares? Would I kill a man who sleeps?"

"Would Royce?" she countered.

He scratched his chin as if considering this for the first time, when indeed he had believed Royce the killer for years. "Even though I did not take his share, I stood accused."

"Neither did Royce take Aylworth's share, but gave it over to Henry, thinking all these years 'twas you who slew the knight. Royce was alone, as you were, while Aylworth was killed. The story that Boltof and Royce were together was part of Boltof's plan, as it left him covered and the only man not suspect. Royce sends me to you with the message that he knows your innocence in that crime.

"I pray you remember, Boltof has never secured strong arms, nor built a fortune, but sought wealth through his sister's marriage or his alliance with Royce and now, through you. But how, Sir Wharton? He has used Celeste and Royce. How does he use you? Do you trust him enough to find out?"

"Boltof spoke of murder . . ."

"Whose?" she asked coyly.

His eyes rose to meet hers, and though his were red-rimmed for want of more sleep, there was a glitter of understanding.

"Ah," she sighed. "He speaks of murder, yet we know he will remove himself from suspicion. Whatever his plan, Wharton, he does not think he will be accused." She shook her head. "He plans no portion of the prize for you. To divide any of this with you would put you both under the Scelfton eye, for you know that Maelwine found you together in Coventry."

Wharton stiffened suddenly. "I will ride to Segeland and . . ."

"And place yourself in his company again? Or warn him? Or stop him so that he is *never* caught? If he sees you venture near that keep, he will either use you to his advantage or cease in his plotting for now. Left alone he will hang himself, for though he does not know it, he is watched. And whether or not you agree, Royce is most determined that Boltof must pay for Aylworth's death.

"Nay, Wharton, do not be a fool. Royce will take Boltof. Ride out of Coventry today. Find witnesses to prove you were not near Boltof or Segeland. When Boltof has done his worst and is caught, you will be far away."

"Royce sends you to warn me? But he hates me . . ."

She slowly shook her head. "That was the way of it while you were set against each other for Aylworth. Perhaps there is no love, but his hate is directed at another now."

"How have you come to be the one to seek me out and warn me?"

"I am a trusted servant of that household. I have served Lady Félise since her birth. The lord and lady of Segeland trust my loyalty, for I was the one to warn them of Boltof's treachery; I listened at his chamber door. And Wharton, you must believe Lady Félise has chosen her mate and will take no other. Their union is sanctioned by Henry and the Scelfton family. The only one foolish enough to conspire against them is Boltof. Unless you will stand alone against them all, have done with this plot."

He was quiet for a moment as he considered this.

"You say the Twyford knights approve?"

"Lord Scelfton lately sent a score of wagons filled with goods for Segeland. The Scelfton sons returned to their father with the news that their sister is secure and content. King Henry has signed the documents that name the land in Aquitaine for Royce. Even Trothmore will find little success in putting them in bad reputation with the church, for an honest priest has been found and they build their own church in the burg now. It is done, sir knight. There is no way Boltof's schemes can unseat the lord of Segeland."

"The surly bastard led me to believe that no one supported Royce but Henry . . . and that Henry could be moved with enough evidence against Leighton. As to Scelfton, Boltof swore the old lord hated every cursed Leighton — "

"Did you witness Maelwine's hate for his sister's husband?"

"Nay," he admitted. "Woman, I vow Boltof plots to kill Royce and name me the murderer."

"No one will die, unless it is Boltof," she assured him.

"As I sit in this sty while he plots at Segeland, I promise you that if he doesn't die by Royce's hand, he need fear mine." He stood taller, giving her a short bow. "You make good sense with your warning, madam, and I will take myself from Coventry today, but only for a short time. Then I ride with my men to Segeland, and if I find you have lied to me, you have cause to fear for your life."

"I have not lied. My only hope is that you will be wiser than Boltof. Mayhap one day you will bury your differences with the Lord of Segeland, but if not, at least you will both be free of the murder of Aylworth. And my lady will be safe."

"They must reward you handsomely for your handiwork. I have known no woman servant in all my life willing to do the things you do."

She smiled faintly. "I am rewarded well, sir. Better than you can know."

There was a loud pounding on the lord's chamber door. The sun was barely up and the noise rudely awakened Félise, causing her to bolt upright. Royce was ahead of her in rising, his legs already out of bed, feet planted firmly on the floor. With a wave of his hand he cautioned her to stay in bed, while he extracted himself.

The pounding came again and he leisurely drew on his chausses, knowing this form of rousing would not come from any of his men. No one would dare distrub him at this hour, in this manner.

Félise drew the cover up to her neck and watched from the bed as Royce opened the door. Boltof stood without, peering past Royce to look into the room. He was fully dressed in a leather gamberson, his broadsword at his side, wearing mail and hauberk and carrying a bag and his shield. He was ready to ride out of Segeland.

"Good morning, my lord. I beg you excuse my early hour, but I must ask a favor. I would ride to Daventry on a quick visit. An old comrade, Sir Morton, waits there before joining the duke, Richard. I would secure a place with that troop. If I don't go today, I will miss them."

"Today? What of Celeste? Am I to gather an escort to send her home?" Royce asked.

"Nay, Royce, but if you will have some servant see to her needs through the day, I will return for her on the morrow and deliver her home. Then I will leave her with Lord Orrick and meet Morton and Richard later. But unless I secure a position with his troop today, I miss my chance."

"I see," Royce said knowingly. "Where does Morton go?"

"To France with Richard," Boltof said. "I cannot waste away my days soothing my sister's hurt or farming for Aswin. And your troop does not ride for Henry. If I am to make my way in this world, I must find a good fight somewhere."

Royce smiled. "You seem in high spirits, Boltof."

"I don't have all this to tie me, Royce. Would that I had lands and money like you, and could spend my days prodding the villagers to work or counting my rents." He laughed. "Neither can I lie abed with a beautiful wife. I must get on the road again and see what lands can be won." He peered at Félise as she sat in bed. "My lady, my humble apologies. I will give your husband back to you at once. Royce? By your leave?"

"Of course, Boltof. Don't fret for Celeste. She will be well cared for in your absence."

"My thanks. And I shall make the journey quick, to return for her tomorrow by midday."

"I wish you well in your venture, Boltof. A good troop always brings a decent return."

"Aye, and Morton has a sound reputation. Would you agree?"

Royce gave a sharp nod. "I can think of no better vassal to Richard. And in spite of their differences, I trust Richard will inherit a kingdom from Henry one day." He raised one eyebrow. "We may yet ride together again."

"I look forward to the day, Royce. Until tomorrow." He gave a brief salute and turned from the door.

Royce slowly closed it and walked leisurely toward the bed. Félise began to tremble, but Royce had a pleased expression on his face.

"Morton is a good knight of Richard," he said softly. "And when I last saw him, he was serving Richard in Aquitaine, where he planned to remain for another year."

"He lies," she whispered.

"Aye, and he has assured himself that you take your rest in my chamber. As he rides away, he must think himself very clever." He looked deeply into her eyes. "And so it begins."

The day was filled with tedious chores meant to occupy the hands and give the appearance of a usual day. No one seemed to notice that Royce's men lingered more about the town than on other days, nor that Trumble did not take rest from the wall. Daria was instructed to take him a basket of food and did so without question, though usually the surly old knight went to her kitchen for his meals.

Royce did not ride out that day to observe the lie of the land, but rather stayed within the wall and busied himself in the hall or the stable. Félise worked mainly in the hall, going to the village only once, to bring yarn to Ulna's cottage. And by late afternoon many watchful eyes reddened, as if they'd spent many days on this one.

Celeste stayed mostly in her rooms through the day, descending to break the fast and then returning to sulk behind closed doors. Boltof's conspiracy wreaked havoc on that poor frame, for she looked more pale and drawn every time she was seen. As the hall filled with men-at-arms and squires for the evening meal and the sun began its downward path, Celeste appeared again. She kept her gaze lowered and did not see the pitying glances cast her way.

Royce stood again on his stoop, watching the villagers come home from their day's labors. None looked up to count the numbers of knights at the wall, nor to judge their watchfulness.

There were only two more than usual: one to help Trumble count those who entered at day's end and one to go to the hall with the report. When the gate was closed again, Royce entered the hall and sat near the hearth until the platters of food were delivered to the tables.

He watched Félise as she moved around the tables and helped the servants ready the room for the meal. He smiled warmly as he judged the seductive swing of her skirts and the way her willing smile played on her lips. When his eyes roved to Celeste, he saw that she, too, watched Félise, but the look on her face was not one of pride. Celeste looked so forlorn that Royce found himself hoping she would not snap under the pressure of Boltof's schemes, failing to see her part through. They depended on her betrayal.

He had given her many opportunities throughout the day to catch him alone and lure him to her chamber, but she had been much out of sight. There was little more he could do to make her ploy easy for her.

Royce lounged lazily, one leg stretched out toward the fire to kick occasionally at the ash that spilled over. He appeared as any confident lord of plenty: unhurried, unhindered, and comfortable in the warm hall in late day. Félise approached him with a chalice of wine and knelt beside his chair. As he took the goblet he judged her worried frown.

"Royce," she whispered. "Look on Celeste. I fear for her. She is too frail for this madness. She will die of fright before the meal is out."

He hushed her and smiled into her eyes for any onlookers' benefit. "There's no help for it, love. Let it be."

"Surely there is some way we can save her from this. Tell her we know of Boltof and free her from this agony. Though woman true in form, she is a child. She cannot endure this."

Royce gently touched his wife's cheek, warmed by her sympathy. "Nay, Félise. Though the price be dear, she must pay it. No one forced her to trust her brother. 'Twas her own poor choice, like many others."

Félise's eyes welled with tears. "Royce," she pleaded softly.

He raised a hand and his brows drew together fiercely. "Nay, I will not weep," she whispered. "But I tell you true, while I would fight Celeste to have you, it is certain she thrived on your love and now . . . it is so sad." She shook her head. "When first I met her, she was not so thin and pale, but vibrant. She grew beautiful on your love."

Royce's voice was low and hoarse and he'd rather have had a better time than now, but there was something he had to tell his wife. "I never loved her, Félise. I loved no woman before you. There was simply no one else . . . Celeste was the only one near. You must find a way to understand that I did not seek her, seduce her, woo her. It is a mercy that Henry separated us, for although I did not know it, I would have destroyed Celeste one day." He shook his head sadly and his voice was low. "We cannot pity her; this is much of her own making."

"But I do pity her," she said. "I think I would die if I lost you."

He leaned toward her slightly and gave her lips a gentle kiss. "Then you shall never die, my love," he whispered. "My captured bride has chained my heart."

When the food was hot and ready, Royce went to his place at the table. Boltof was conspicuously absent, his chair empty. Rather than taking her brother's seat, Celeste took her usual place, leaving a gap between herself and Royce.

There was little conversation, and Félise seemed to fidget more than ever as she waited. Finally, touching her husband's hand, she asked, "Has she approached you, Royce?"

He shook his head and addressed himself to his plate again.

A young squire of Royce's troop entered the hall, and when Royce looked his way he nodded once, then walked past all those dining to the rear of the hall. One more man had entered the town than had left that mornng. Royce relaxed in his seat, confident that Trumble knew where the extra man hid.

But still they waited. Celeste played with the food on her plate, but little reached her mouth. Royce could bear the wait no longer.

"Lady, is there some trouble?" he asked her. "Are you ill?"

She shook her head and he noticed that her hand trembled.

"Is there something you need?" he pressed. Again she shook her head and the meal passed with no word from her. Frequently Félise turned her questioning eyes to Royce, but Royce simply touched her hand to warn her toward patience. Many of those who took their meal in the hall were leaving, and Félise rose to supervise the cleaning of the hall and storing of the extra food. Royce sat, which was never his custom, in wait.

Celeste finally rose, looked into Royce's eyes, and murmured her excuses. "By your leave, messire. I would find my bed."

"Celeste, I worry that you're unwell," he said.

She only shook her head dejectedly and moved to the stairs. Royce felt his stomach tighten. Damn, he thought furiously. She's lost her nerve and won't do Boltof's will. She'll sour the whole of it and we won't catch him.

But as Celeste put her hand on the rail, she swooned slightly and, upon catching herself, fell into shuddering sobs. Royce rose to her instantly, quite surprised at her clever ploy to have a word alone with him. When he reached her, she was nearly collapsed and sat on the stair, trembling all over. "Celeste," he entreated. "What is it?"

"Royce, oh Royce. You have such cause to hate me."

"Nay, Celeste, I don't hate you."

"Royce, beware. Boltof plans some trickery here."

"Oh?" he questioned, ready to leap into her trap. "How so, Celeste? He has gone to Daventry."

"I don't know what he'll do, but I know that somehow he means to have all that you lay claim to. He pretends that I will be rewarded, but I am not so foolish as he thinks. I know he uses me."

He grasped her by the upper arms, frowning. Something had failed in their carefully designed plan. "What do you say, Celeste?"

"He told me to lure you to my chamber late at night, when the moon was set and the manor sleeps. You must *not* come. He plans to do you harm."

"How are you to lure me, Celeste?"

The woman wept harder, collapsing into Royce's arms, clearly distraught and unable to speak. Her face was wet with tears and her frail limbs shook so dreadfully that Royce waited long for her to finish.

"How, Celeste? You must tell me."

"With some tale of Boltof's plan. If I promise to tell you how Boltof will steal your bride, you will come to my chamber for the news. He will kill you, I know it."

"Did he say he would kill me? Is that what he plans?"

"Oh, nay," she whimpered. "He said he would return to Segeland to find you in my chamber and report this to Félise. But that is not his plan. I know what he will do. As I know my brother, I know his plan. My dagger is gone. Gone!"

"Celeste, tell me all. Hurry now!"

Her eyes cleared slightly, as if she was finding some strength in her confession. "I was not going to tell you, and then only I would suffer . . . but I am too afraid to die. Forgive me, Royce, but I am a coward. Even though I have nothing to live for, I am too cowardly to die."

Royce shook her until wisps of her hair floated down around her face. "What does he mean to do?" he demanded.

She looked at him through half-crazed eyes. "When you venture to my chamber, he will be waiting for you. How he plans to enter I cannot say. But he will slay you with my dagger and then . . ." She nearly lost her nerve to go on, but swallowed hard and faced him. "He will pierce my heart with the same and form my fingers above the knife."

"He did not tell you this," Royce blustered. "How do you guess his crime?"

"I know him," she snarled, her lip curling away from her teeth. "He would let our bodies lie there until they're discovered, perhaps by Félise. She would scorn your memory and welcome a man who would be true. Was that not the way with Aylworth? Was he not close at hand to help the poor accused pick up their shattered lives? He tells you much of my melancholy — does he pretend to know the depth of my pain? Will he know it on the morrow, when he journeys here with Wharton? I read a message he had carried to Wharton, and Boltof did not write what he swore he would. Wharton does not bring arms to ward off your attack, but meets Boltof in yon wood.

"Your lady will be widowed and Boltof will be close at hand to help her bury you. He will gently explain my madness and my jealousy. Royce, you must beware."

Royce stared at her in wide-eyed astonishment. He looked over his shoulder to see Félise standing near, listening. She frowned darkly. Royce knelt before Celeste, still holding her upright by the arms.

"Celeste," Félise said, drawing her attention for the first time. "You betray your brother. Why?"

Celeste seemed startled to find she had been overheard, but only a moment elapsed before she spoke. Though she had begged mercy from Royce and confessed her cowardliness, there was hatred in her eyes and voice as she answered Félise. "Though you have him, I love him still. And I won't have his blood on my hands."

"So, you save my husband, lady. But you save yourself as well, if you are right about Boltof's plan."

"Nay," she laughed, shaking her head. The tears continued to course down her cheeks. "I am afraid to die, and afraid to live. There is nothing for me now but to be my brother's pawn. When Boltof caused me to lose Royce, that was the end of my life. Though I die a slower death, alone, still I die each day." She looked back at Royce and again there was pitiful devotion in her eyes. "But you will live."

Royce stood and drew Celeste up to her full height. "Come, Celeste. The night is young and we must wait for the moon to rise. Look," he said, turning her to indicate the top of the stairs. There she could see Aswin, who stood leaning against his staff with a stout hunter's knife in his belt. He was far from young and his body less than agile, but he was a ready warrior tonight. And his fierce scowl spoke louder than words could. He would not be slowed by his afflictions tonight.

Celeste looked back at Royce. "You knew," she breathed.

"Aye. And I waited for your betrayal. I did not think you wise enough to see through Boltof's treachery, but perhaps you have removed the last question. We knew he would do something terrible, but none of us knew what or how."

Her eyes grew cold and dry. "Would that I had the courage to hate you as I should."

Royce smiled coolly into her pale blue eyes. He felt the strangest combination of scorn and pity. She had found no virtue in honesty all these years and allowed herself to be the victim of Boltof's misuse, yet she showed on this night that she could discern truth from lies, if the lie came close enough to pierce her own breast.

"How long have you known that Boltof killed my brother?" he asked her.

She looked at him as if she would look through him. Her chin lifted only slightly and her mouth was fixed in a straight line. She did not have to answer further. Whether before or after the crime, she had known and pledged herself to Royce just the same, encouraging him to trust Boltof, though he was a cowardly murderer. All these years Royce had thought Celeste noble and compassionate, for she had never mentioned his suspicious past or the many accusations levied against him.

His voice was cold and hard when he spoke. "Come, Celeste. We have an appointment when the moon is set. To your chamber, my love."

Chapter Twenty

THE CREAKING OF THE GATE AS IT CLOSED GAVE BOL-
tof courage. He smiled to himself as he crouched behind
a stall in the stable. He heard the sounds of men hang-
ing bridles and brushing their animals. Feed was put out for the
horses, and the beasts snorted and slopped as they ate. The last
to leave closed the stable door, but it was not locked. In this fair
village of Royce's there was no need for bolts, for the guard was
hearty, and once the wall was secure around the hall and town,
no one could enter. Boltof laughed.

It had been more simple than he had predicted. His face
averted, he had simply walked in behind a wagon. His step
weary, a hoe in his hand, he had moved silently to the stable and
into a stall and crouched there. No one even looked at him.

He judged an hour had passed and allowed himself to stand
and stretch. It perked up his pulse and his energy seemed to soar,
for he rather liked the creeping darkness. When it was time to
brace his lance or draw his broadsword, fear prickled him. He
had never admitted this, that he was frightened of battle. But he
hated it. Yet here, knowing that he would meet no equal foe, he
felt excited.

The sun was gone and there was no sound but the shuffling of
animals as they settled for the night with full bellies. He had
watched the hall and village for many nights, though no one
knew. Guards were posted on the wall near the gate but did not

roam the streets in the dark. Trumble had a bell that he could ring clamorously if he saw trouble from his perch. But Boltof had walked through the keep and town when all slept and no one had stirred. He knew a way to the hall that would not cast a shadow for Trumble to see.

He used the window in the back of the stable for his exit and sat on the ground, leaning against a wagon wheel, to watch the hall. He could see the whole length of the street from the gate to the front of the hall, where the double doors were closed against the darkness. Another hour passed while he chewed a piece of straw and patiently waited.

He sat upright at the sound of an opening door. An old woman came out of a cottage and began to walk toward the hall. She used a stick to lean on and her other arm was heavy with folded cloth. Her passage was slow and painful, her back slightly bent. A heavy woolen cloak with a hood that covered her head gave her more than ample protection against the chill of the spring night. Boltof watched her move to the hall, enter, and close the door. Moments later she left empty-handed, taking agonizing steps back to her cottage. He relaxed against the wheel again.

One by one the cottages darkened as the hour grew late. Boltof couldn't see the windows on the hall's second level, but he did not bother much about that. Two bright torches lit the doors on either side, but he wouldn't use those huge oaken portals for his entrance. There was another way in through the back, where the knights deposited their freshly killed game for the cooks. If he found that residents were still astir in their chambers, he could easily lurk in the stairwells and galleries while he waited.

When he judged the time to be right, he walked swiftly toward the hall and around the side to the rear; he damned the creaking door when he entered, but no one stirred. Pausing briefly, he could hear a few snores from the main hall as a knight or two slept. He smiled at the sound. These hearties would let an entire band of brigands through. Royce would do better not to work them so hard by day . . . but he would not have the luxury to consider that after tonight.

Boltof worried that Celeste would fail him, but he could get around that. His sister was weakening. He was coming to realize that the depressed spirit he spoke of was fact and not just a ploy he used. She required much encouragement from him to do her part. She whined and fretted and wept, accusing him of causing her despair. A year ago she would have risen to the task of summoning Royce to her chamber, and though she was not clever, she had been capable of simple chores like this. But Royce's marriage had taken its toll.

Celeste would not defy him, for she feared him. And he had promised her a beating if she gave the slightest clue to their planned trap. But she might indeed fail to summon Royce. He was a bullheaded man; he might simply refuse her. It didn't matter. He would simply take another route to his plan. He would peer into the lord's chamber first to see who slept there, and then he would go to Celeste.

The hall that joined the sleeping rooms on the second level was dark and quiet. A torch lit the wide gallery at the far end and cast his form as a shadow, but there was no one about. He passed his sister's chamber, noting with a smile that there was light creeping from under her door. He walked on, his soft cloth shoes making no sound. The poor wool of the peasant garb he wore chafed him, but he was like a cat as he moved and he would not so much as scratch.

The lord's chamber was dark and he listened for several moments with his ear pressed against the door. He slowly pushed the door open, again silently cursing the squeak of the leather hinges that announced his entry, but there was no sound within the chamber. He looked toward the high bed and saw the single, small mound under the quilt. So, she slept alone. Celeste had somehow managed to serve him one more time.

He went back to his sister's door and paused there, listening to the small whisperings within. She had done well. He could tell that her best whimpering delayed the knight. He felt the handle of the knife in one hand, his other hand lightly touching the door. Two knives were carried in his belt: a thick and sharp hunting knife and his sister's dainty, silver-handled dagger. He couldn't trust the lighter weapon to finish Royce, but who would crouch over his body and be assured it was not Celeste's blade that rent his flesh? A wound was a wound, and as long as the point pierced his back, it could be considered a woman's crime. There was no way Celeste could take the knight face to face, and it must look the part of jealous rage.

He silently pushed at the door; there were no screaming hinges here. He had carefully determined that much before leaving Segeland. His first sight showed him a man's back in the dim room, and Celeste sitting on a stool before the hearth, weeping into her trembling hands. Royce's back to his blade was too good to waste. He had earlier thought to enter the room to find them, demand that Royce leave, and slay him as he departed, but this piece of work was handy.

Boltof rushed through the door, arm raised high. Celeste gave the merest gasp of surprise, for there was no more time. Yet from behind he was struck on the wrist and the knife clattered to the floor. He whirled to face the powerful wrath of the lord of Segeland.

"It is over, Boltof," Royce growled.

Boltof looked in panic at the man he would have slain and watched as he slowly rose, using his staff to help him turn. Orrick eyed him with nothing less than hatred.

"You," Boltof whispered.

Celeste rose from the stool and looked at her brother. She wept no more but faced him with a look of serenity.

"You're finished, Boltof. It is chains, or your life," Royce warned.

Boltof knew a sudden prickling fear that matched nothing he had ever felt in his life. He would have traded a thousand battles for the towering rage that showed in the dark eyes of Royce. In a moment he would be dead if that one but yielded to his certain desire to strike. He could think of but one chance to escape and threw himself against Royce, knocking him away from the door.

Boltof gained the passageway and ran toward the lord's chamber, the dagger now in his hand. He hit the door with his shoulder as Royce clamored somewhere behind him. Boltof's face was twisted in a fierce snarl as he flew into the chamber and made for the bed. The little bitch who called herself lady here would help him make his way out of the keep. If he could but get to his horse, he'd make for Coventry. He was guilty of nothing yet, unless they meant to hang him for wearing farmer's clothes or walking the hallways and galleries at night. He'd hold the knife at her throat and her life would open every door in Segeland hall and town.

He tore back the covers on the master's bed and gasped in stunned surprise. An old hag rested where the lady should lie. He felt a viselike grip take him from behind and at the same time saw Royce come through the chamber door.

"Hold, Boltof," Hewe said from behind him. "You are finished here."

He squirmed within the young knight's firm grasp and felt his arms pinned behind him. The knife was taken away and he was clasped and held as if by an army.

"Well done, Sir Hewe," Royce said. He walked toward the bed and held out his hand. "My lady?" he beckoned, reaching to help Ulna out of his bed. The old woman laboriously extracted herself and moved toward the door to leave, humpbacked and slow, just as she had walked from her cottage to the hall. Boltof groaned as he saw their trick.

"Who betrayed me?" he demanded hotly.

Aswin and Celeste, much slower than Royce, had found the room.

"You betrayed yourself, Boltof. You were heard as you plotted and you were seen in Coventry with Wharton. And Celeste can abide your plots no longer. You've used her too poorly." Royce glanced over his shoulder at Celeste. "You were foolish to consider her a pawn for your greed. She is wiser than you reckoned and knew you intended her death . . . and mine."

Boltof looked at the eyes that observed him. Aswin glared at him but held his mouth clamped shut, refusing to speak. Royce's face held an expression of victory, but his eyes were no less furious. And Celeste, who had always done his will without question, showed only cold contempt. Boltof suddenly began to laugh loudly.

"Hah! So you've caught me. Well and good. What will you do now? Murder me?"

"Nay, Boltof, but you'll die for your crimes. By the grace of God you were stopped here, but Aylworth was not so lucky. You'll pay for his death."

"Aylworth? What say you, Royce? You can't blame me for Aylworth. You said yourself we were together the night he died. No one would believe you. You're without proof."

Celeste moved closer to Royce. "You killed him, Boltof, just as you would have killed Royce and me. Not in a battle worthy of honorable foes, not in a contest between men who stand tall for their differences, but in the dark of night with great advantage." She shook her head sadly. "Had I known what you would do, I would have found a way to stop you. But I waited too long and let you poison my mind with your ranting and your greed."

Boltof gnashed his teeth in frustration, for Hewe held him fast. The manor came to life all around them, and the sound of doors and voices below and the light from the stairway gave proof to the fact that they had all feigned sleep while they waited for him to make his move.

"Celeste," he warned, "you will *not* betray me further!"

"I have little choice. If I save you, you will only kill me one day. You must pay for your sins, just as I must pay for mine." She softened her voice but her eyes were still cold. "God's mercy on your soul, Boltof. You have cost us all much." She turned her back on him and left the room.

"Celeste! Nay, you *will not*!"

Aswin turned as well. "I'll be certain she causes us no more trouble," he said, following his stepdaughter.

Only Royce faced Boltof. "I should have known," Royce said. "You trumpeted the madness all around you. The Leightons, you said. Yet I suspect now that perhaps Aylworth was wrongly accused of poor rule. His estate here did not flourish, but he had held it for only a short time and without the wealth of a dower purse, as I have enjoyed. Mayhap by brother would have proven a decent lord, given a chance. And my father? Yea, his madness came from the woman he stole. He struggled for better than a dozen years to hold the wall against neighbors who *believed* him cursed and would attack him because of his sin. And the woman, his hostage-lady? Aye, she was mad. And how much of the Leightons' curse came from you? Or Trothmore?

"And lately you used Celeste's melancholy as a tool in deaths you planned to feed your greed. And yet in all this time, for all these years, it was you, Boltof. Crazed with greed, a coward who would kill a sleeping man." He looked at Boltof with pity. "You could have had much: a good father in Aswin, a faithful sister in Celeste, and . . ." He paused. The words soured in his mouth. "You could have had a friend in me."

"Wharton will come for me," Boltof taunted.

"Nay, he knows you betrayed him. Word of Aylworth's murder was taken to him in Coventry. You bought yourself a good servant . . . of mine." Boltof moaned miserably. "Should you escape me, Boltof, I am certain that Wharton will find you. Take him to the inner bailey, Hewe, and tie him in the courtyard in full view of the gate and hall. The night is mostly lost, but we won't sleep easily until he has accounted for his crimes. I'll allow no error. I will take him to Henry myself."

Boltof was dragged out of the lord's chamber and down the stairs. Trumble was just entering, escorting Félise home from Ulna's cottage. The old knight gave Félise over to Royce and aided Hewe with the prisoner. Boltof had little time to snarl at Félise before a big, hamlike fist cuffed his ear and turned his anger into a yelp of pain. No patience or kindness was wasted on him as he was dragged away.

Félise rushed to Royce's side and he wrapped his arm securely around her. She hovered there in the security of his embrace, feeling a warmth of safety that would be hers forever. Together they watched from the hall as Boltof was tied to a stake in the center of the yard between the hall and the town. Around him stood four guards. The night could be no safer than that.

Morning came and eyes that opened to break the fast were mostly bleary from lack of sleep. There was no mood of celebration at having caught Boltof. Relief and better ease could be seen on the faces of all who had kept themselves alert for more than a week, but Boltof's crimes had created great loss. Not the least of those grieved was Aswin.

When he descended to take his meal with Royce and Félise, his mood was not light, but most of his rage had been bled dry.

"Celeste will prove cooperative," he reported. "She has accepted the fact that her word will cost Boltof his life and is prepared to give it. I don't know what will become of her after that." He paused and took a steadying breath. "Mayhap she will become stronger and take her mother's home when I die. Then again, her days may be fewer than mine. Her losses were many. First her father. Then her mother. Then you, albeit not through death. And now Boltof. And she is not strong."

"Have faith, Aswin. She proved stronger last night than any of us would have guessed."

"Neither of them would let me be their father, though for Dulcine I did my best by them." He sighed heavily. "The woman must have known her children, Royce. She must have sensed their greed, though they were not fully grown when she died. Why else would she have written a document giving me her property until my death? She was careful to state that I might not dispose of it on any future heirs, slighting her children, but she would not have me cast out by Boltof. Perhaps Dulcine could have saved us much heartache, by telling what she knew."

"My lord," Félise appealed. "Do not in any way blame yourself or your lady wife. The seeds that grew into Boltof's greed and hatred were sown long before you. And you say Dulcine was a good woman, and I trust you to know goodness. That you would be his father though you didn't sire him was kind of you. If Boltof would willingly cast aside your gesture, it is not your fault."

"You warm an old man's heart, fair Félise, but the truth might be tougher to chew. Boltof was only a child when his father, who was strong and true, died upon the field. And the little one, so adoring of his mother and trying to live faithful to his father's memory, encountered me when he was but twelve. And I, not a straight and mighty warrior, but one bent and crippled by an accident, took his mother's attentions away from him. Dulcine nursed me for a year before I could even rise. And all that time I was a poor wretch in need of her gentle ministrations. We were not man and wife."

"But neither is that your fault, my lord," Félise gently coaxed. "An accident — "

"What the boy saw must have made him hate me. Ah, damn, let it be out! It has burdened my soul long enough.

"There was another, before Dulcine. I worshiped her, adored her. She was my life and my reason for living. And when my head was smashed in my fall, I raved in an injured stupor, calling out for her all the while. Dulcine knew as she tended me that I loved a woman, yet the kind widow took care of me. Had she left me alone I might have died. Perhaps that would have been better, for I have never lived a day without mourning my love lost."

"My lord, don't tell us things that — "

"That would shame me? Nay, 'tis no shame to love. That is not my crime." He became wistful and his eyes clouded with tears. "She was the most beautiful woman a man had ever seen. She rivaled your beauty, Lady Félise, which is a hard thing to do. Indeed, she wore tresses of red and gold much the color of your own hair . . . and eyes the green of emeralds that glittered in the sun. She was the queen's handmaiden, a poetess who sang for the court of love. Many admired her; most men desired her. And I courted her very boldly . . . before I was crippled by my fall."

Félise sat a bit straighter in her chair. "The queen's poetess?" she questioned meekly.

Aswin barely noticed the attention his story was getting from the couple. He went on in blissful memory. "I counted myself a prince, at least, for having won her favor, and rode off with a token from her worn in my tunic. We went on a southern campaign, not dangerous by any man's measure. Hah! Hardly a battle, for our troop was all weary with lack of duties. We drank, staged mock tourneys, courted the local wenches. 'Twas in such a state that I took my fall. I could blame no one but myself for that.

"But she had given me as much as a kiss, indeed more! Yea, I was too bold with the woman, but I was young and used little restraint. And then the accident and a year taken from my life. When I returned to London to seek her out, perhaps I was even relieved that she had gone. I did not know how I would face her, with a hand that could not properly caress her soft skin and a leg that hangs like a useless log at my side."

He peered closely at Félise, nearly whispering his words. "All the while that Dulcine nursed me, I cried out for Véronique, my love, my heart. This was what her children heard. And when I was well, I stayed within her care, no longer crying out in madness for my lover, but stating boldly that when I could walk and ride, I would return to her. *This* her children heard, as they watched the woman tend me unfailingly. And when I could mount a gentle steed and stay astride, I bid Dulcine farewell with only thanks for her patient care. Though she begged me to stay, I *left*," he said, and his fist hit the table sharply. "And this, too, Boltof took as a token of my chivalry . . . to use the woman so and leave her for another. Aye, I taught the lad much of nobility."

"My lord," Félise attempted. "Dulcine's goodness demanded no more of you than that. You must not — "

"Nay, I know what I did. I left Dulcine to seek out Véronique, terrified of what I might find. What if there had been a child of our love? Scorned as a bastard, Véronique shamed? Perhaps she would look at my crooked body and laugh. Or would she have taken another lover?" He shrugged. "I never saw her again. I was told she had left and no one would tell me where she had gone. Those fellows who were with me when I fell did not report our foolery while we were on the king's business, but simply said I could be found with the rich widow in the south of England. I have asked after Véronique all these many years, but no one has word of her.

"Yea," he nodded, flushing slightly. "Even after I wed the widow Dulcine, I asked about my lover." He sat back in his chair and grew solemn. "I taught young Boltof much of honor as I longed for another while I wed his mother. I taught him much of trust as I took management of a rich demesne that was not mine, but his. I could not hope to make him see that I didn't think he was ready for the lands. He saw a selfish old cripple use his mother and her wealth. Perhaps it is my fault that he is wicked."

Félise's smile was warm and understanding. She touched his hand. "Though you lost your one true love, I cannot believe you were ever cruel to Lady Dulcine."

"Perhaps not cruel, but neither did she have all the love and devotion of spirit that she deserved. Yet she loved me fully, with all of herself. And she took from me what I had left, never asking more."

"And you never found the fair Véronique?" she asked, smiling, one finely arched eyebrow raised in question.

"If she is even alive now, I would not know where to look. But I never traveled in the last twenty years without casting my eyes about for the beautiful temptress who haunts my dreams. I would have traveled to the moon to find her, but not one clue to her whereabouts was laid my way. After several months of exhaustive travel, my body so bent, I gave up and returned to Dulcine."

"She is alive now, messire," Félise said softly. "This one you seek, Véronique de Raissa, will return to us today. She uses the name the sisters of Fontevrault gave her. Vespera." Her voice became a whisper. "There was a child. She is my mother."

Aswin's eyes grew wide in surprise. "But you are Harlan's . . ."

Félise slowly shook her head. "Eleanor took me from my mother to see me raised near her court. My mother retired to the sisters when I was a baby. But when Eleanor was confined at Old Sarum Castle by the king, I lost my noble home and was dependent on the mercy of anyone who would feed me and give me shelter. The Scelftons had lost their own daughter and took me in. I have never wanted but for one thing: to know my true parents and why they could not keep me."

She reached for her husband's hand and gave it a light squeeze, feeling him return the gesture.

"She will come home to us today, my lord, and neither of you will leave me again. Now that I've found you both, I will pray it is not too late for you to find each other."

By midday all but one traveler had returned to Segeland. In Vespera's place came a letter, excusing herself from further duty to Félise. Only the most essential information was contained in her message: she had convinced Wharton and expected he would ride to Segeland in due time to test the truth. She had enough money to take her back to the convent, and she sorely missed the sisters. And a line or two referred to the prayers she would continue to direct to the good fortune of Segeland and the lord and lady.

Less than an hour after the escorts had returned, Aswin was ready to mount his own steed.

"Let me go with you," Royce attempted.

"Nay, Royce, this is mine to do."

"I would go alone and bring her back here. You are not fit to ride."

"I'll show you how fit I am," he said, grabbing the saddle with his good hand and pulling himself up. "Youngsters," he snorted. "I've gotten through these many years without your services. I'll manage a few more."

"You could wait for the morning," Félise attempted.

"Nay again. She escaped me once, she won't again! By damn, she'll hear my excuses and I'll beg her forgiveness or follow her trail for the rest of her life. We both hid ourselves away and pitied our poor lot, when we might have found the truth years ago." He looked pointedly at Félise. "We might even have raised you ourselves, though that blasted Harlan did as well with you as I could have."

Félise laughed at the mere thought of the two fathers she could now claim. "As if it is not enough that I must endure my lord Harlan's sorry temper, I shall have two of you blustering about."

"God willing, lass," Aswin said hopefully. "That is, if I can find the woman and talk some sense into her. Royce, you say she has complained of a lost love? You are certain?"

He nodded. "My guess is that her longing has matched yours, but through many years of confusion. I think you have nothing to fear from the woman. But you have much to set to rights, Aswin. Godspeed."

Aswin gave a brief salute and clicked his tongue. "I'll accept your prayers. I once fancied myself a gallant troubadour who knew much of love . . . but I'm sore out of practice and could use some help in wooing her. We are old now, you see."

Félise looked at him with tear-filled eyes. "Just bring her home, my lord. There is time enough left for us to share."

The old lord smiled brightly. "Ah, but there lies the hope, child. We old lovers have not many years left. We are careful not to waste time as you young people are wont to do." He held the reins and leaned down toward her. "I hope she is as impatient as I. 'Tis time I made good my affections."

Félise rose on her toes and placed a kiss on his cheek. "Then hurry, lest you must follow her all the way to France."

He took the advice and turned his horse down the road. Looking back only once to wave, his urgency showed in the brisk trot of his steed, and he did not slow his pace as he passed Boltof. That one slumped in the hot sun, secure within his ropes.

"I envy him," Royce said. "Still eager for his proper mate after all these years."

Félise looked up at him with laughter in her eyes. "Oh? Do you mean to imply that you will not be eager for me . . . when we are old?"

"When my back aches and I cannot ride so swiftly? When the grandchildren pester me for stories and lessons? When you are round and your hair is gray and thin?" he teased. He bent and swept her into his arms, carrying her into the hall and up the stairs. He kicked open the door to his room and with his heel pushed it closed behind him. He dropped her on the bed and, in spite of her giggles, threw himself on top of her.

"You had better hope my back aches, wench. Otherwise we will spend little time out of bed."

She looped her arms around his neck and kissed him long and lovingly. "Oh, Royce, I do love you! Rid the house of pests, my noble husband, and let us find those old bolts and bars and make ourselves prisoners here for a month of new springs. Hasten hose two from our house quickly, that you can return to me with rouble finally gone." She smiled temptingly. "I have plans for ou."

His lips brushed hers. "With pleasure, lady. In just a little vhile. Boltof and Celeste can wait. I cannot."

SEGELAND CASTLE

Christmas, 1185

SIR TRUMBLE'S BELL SOUNDED TO ALERT THE RESI-
dents within Segeland's main hall. A large fire warmed
the room, ale and wine flowed freely, and all within enjoyed a festive mood for the Christmastide celebrations. At the
sound of the bell, Félise jumped to her feet and excitedly ran to
the large oaken doors, throwing them wide in spite of the wintry
cold.

"God's blood, she hasn't changed a bit," Lord Scelfton blustered. "Félise, be damned, close the door 'til they've come."

"Harlan, be still," Edrea scolded. "Neither have you
changed."

Félise ignored the lord's command, just as she ignored Edrea's
scolding. She stood in the frame of the door and waved. A man
and woman traveled toward them on horseback, while behind
them a heavily laden wagon was pulled.

Royce moved to stand behind his wife and when he did so,
pulled the door slightly closed to spare the inhabitants of the hall
any unnecessary cold. He rested a hand on Félise's shoulder and
waved with her. Within moments the riders were before the hall
and Félise could contain herself no longer. She ran to them, her
long, unbound hair flowing behind her, without giving the
slightest thought to a cloak.

The sky was a clear blue, a soft cover of snow lay on the earth, and the winds were gentle for the travelers. She could not wait for Royce to help her mother down, but reached her arms up to her before she had dismounted.

As Royce strode toward them, Aswin was already struggling down from his horse. Royce frowned at the man's stubbornness and moved to the lady. "Madam," he greeted, reaching for her. "You look as though the journey agreed with you."

He helped her to the firm ground and Félise embraced Véronique again, a laugh escaping from the mother at the sheer power of her daughter's affection. When she could breathe, Véronique faced Royce.

"Our travels did agree with us. Aquitaine prospers, as you might guess. Celeste is settled and I do think she'll be happy with the sisters. Fontevrault is a good shelter for abused and troubled dames, and since Boltof is gone — " she paused, crossing herself and muttering a brief blessing — "ah, since his life is forfeit for his crimes, Celeste has no interest in her mother's lands." Véronique shrugged and smiled. "We'll keep the property and if she changes her mind, well . . . and good. But I think perhaps Celeste has finally found her place with the sisters. They are kind. And," she said, looking sideways at Aswin, "we were wed in the de Raissa manse. It is finally done," she chuckled. "Our sins are laid away to rest." The twinkle in her eye gave the lie to her supposed guilty conscience.

Véronique took Félise's hands in both of hers and held herself away, looking her up and down. "You have changed, my dearest. Motherhood agrees with you."

"Come, madam," she said brightly. She pulled Véronique into the warm hall filled with members of the Segeland household, the Scelfton family, and now two more cold travelers come to join them in celebration. The cheer within the room was bright and joyful. A smile graced all lips but Harlan's, whose face, it must be said, would break into many pieces should he smile.

Edrea came quickly toward Véronique and gently kissed her cheek, all the while very mindful of the bundle she held. She pulled away and drew back the blanket that protected the baby from the blistering cold and showed Véronique a bright thatch of red on its crown. "Madam, our granddaughter," she said, holding the baby toward her.

"Ah, love," Véronique sighed, holding out arms to take the baby. "Your letter spoke true. She is beautiful."

"Humph," Harlan grumbled, moving toward Aswin with his hand stretched out in greeting. "Another head full of devil's red and another lifetime full of beating the lads off the stoop. Aswin, you wounded old stag, did I hear tell of a wedding? I thought you were too old for such nonsense."

Aswin took the hand gratefully, smiling broadly. "Too old? Nay, she adds wine to my cup and takes away a score of my years." To that Véronique cast him an unquestionably embarrassed glance over her shoulder. "Too old? Mayhap you are too old, but I am not."

Harlan's hand gently patted his Edrea's posterior, earning him a damning look. "My *lord*," she gasped.

"Be careful who you call old," Harlan blustered, the corners of his mouth tugging upward in a smile.

"Sit you down," Royce urged. "Get these people hot wine to warm them and stoke the fire before my daughter freezes. Félise, a goblet for Lady Véronique and somethng to slow the wit of those two old war-horses. By God," Royce cried, raising a handy cup high in the air, "we are in no short supply of grandparents." Cheers went up and around the room and those who had a cup drank.

He let his arm drop around Félise's shoulders and watched the scene before him. Véronique and Edrea cooed over the baby, but each found an extra hand to accept a drink. Maelwine and Evan rose to greet Aswin. Dalton and Hewe braced arms in a contest of strength at a nearby table. Cloaks were taken by pages and brew delivered to each guest found to be lacking a cup. Royce raised his cup again. "To family, large enough to please many noble households."

Many voices agreed, many hands tilted cups. Roasting meat spat at the fire and dry logs crackled with a friendly sound. The room began to quiet slightly as Royce and Félise stood closely watching the happy gathering. " 'Tis well," Royce confirmed.

"Since my wife is not shy of my affections, we have need of many grandparents for our children." He dropped a husbandly kiss on her brow. "And uncles," he added, lifting his cup in the direction of Félise's brothers.

An infant's squeal rose in defiance of the last toast and laughter shook the room. Félise giggled happily. "It is not that our fair daughter has no use for her uncles," she promised. "It is only that she can remember the day these noble Twyford knights were too much in the way of things."

"In the way?" Royce questioned. "Not quick enough. Our family was started without their permission. My pardon, sirs," he said, bowing toward the Scelfton brothers.

The child began to whimper anew and Félise left her husband's side to take her and nurse her. She excused herself to a quiet corner to settle the baby at her breast. Royce was soon beside her while all the others held their noisy reunion just paces away. Félise softly hummed to her child and Royce placed a possessive hand on her shoulder. She found his wandering days over, his reclusive nature gone. He was never very far away now.

She looked up at him with glowing eyes. "We can rest easy now, my lord. We are all home. At last."